W9-BTB-912

ONLY WITH A HIGHLANDER

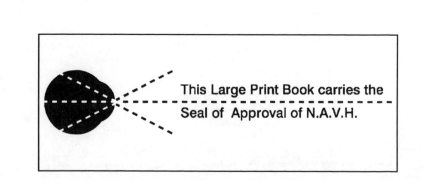

This Large Print Book carries the
Seal of Approval of N.A.V.H.

ONLY WITH A HIGHLANDER

JANET CHAPMAN

THORNDIKE PRESS

An imprint of Thomson Gale, a part of The Thomson Corporation

THOMSON

GALE

Detroit • New York • San Francisco • New Haven, Conn. • Waterville, Maine • London

THOMSON

GALE ™

LIBRARY OF CONGRESS CATALOGING-IN-PUBLICATION DATA

Chapman, Janet.
  Only with a Highlander / by Janet Chapman.
    p. cm.
  ISBN 0-7862-8905-8 (alk. paper)
    1. Scots — United States — Fiction. 2. Women artists — Fiction. 3. Wizards — Fiction. 4. Time travel — Fiction. 5. Maine — Fiction. 6. Large type books.
  I. Title.
PS3603.H372O55 2006
813'.6—dc22   2006024973

U.S. Hardcover:
ISBN 13: 978-0-7862-8905-9
ISBN 10: 0-7862-8905-8

Published in 2006 by arrangement with Pocket Books,
a division of Simon & Schuster, Inc.

Printed in the United States of America on permanent paper
10 9 8 7 6 5 4 3 2 1

For
Grace Morgan,
Whose friendship is the true
stuff of magic

WITH HEARTFELT THANKS

To *Liz Lima,* for helping to keep my life on track while I was so involved writing this book. Always know that I treasure your friendship. And I must say, you certainly throw a great party!

To *Liam Gavin,* for giving me the wonderful gift of awareness. Whenever you see a crow, think of me.

To the wonderful folks at *Acadia Zoo* in Trenton, Maine, for giving me an up-close look at your big cats, especially your magnificent leopards. Your knowledge of the animals in your charge is surpassed only by your obvious love of them. The few hours I spent in their presence was awe-inspiring and mystical.

To *Ping,* for braving the snowdrifts in the wee hours before dawn to follow me to work, and for somehow knowing when I need a purring cat hug. You have the heart of a mighty panther, my little friend, and the spirit of a most unusual muse.

And to *Lisa and Nick,* for giving Robbie and me a most precious and perfect grandson. Welcome to the world, Alex!

CHAPTER ONE

Winter MacKeage lost the thread of the conversation the moment the large male figure stepped into view. Rose continued talking, however, oblivious to the fact that the most gorgeous man ever to set foot in Pine Creek had just stopped to look at the painting hanging in the front window of Winter's art gallery.

"Tell her I'm right," Rose demanded, nudging Winter's arm. "Tell Megan that no one is whispering behind her back. Hey," Rose said more loudly, grabbing Winter's sleeve to draw her back into the conversation. "Your sister thinks everyone in town pities her."

Winter looked away from the divine apparition in the window and blinked at Rose and her sister, Megan, trying to remember what they had been talking about.

Rose sighed. "Darn it, Winter, help me out here. Tell Megan she's not the center of town gossip."

Winter finally looked into her sister's tear-washed eyes. "Oh, but everyone is talking about you, Meg," she said, nodding. "But only because you walk down the street looking like a rag doll that's been left out in the rain all summer."

"That's not helping," Rose snapped, using her grip on Winter's sleeve to nudge her.

Winter stepped away, crossed her arms under her breasts, and ignored Rose in favor of glaring at Megan. "You always have such a long face, it's a wonder you don't trip on your own chin. You scuffle along like a beaten puppy." Winter reached out and touched her sister's hunched shoulder. "Pregnancy is not a disease, Meg," she continued more gently. "Nor is it the end of the world. The only one pitying you around here is you. And if you don't soon quit, your bairn will be born with a permanent pout."

Megan MacKeage swiped at her flushed face and met Winter's tender smile with a fierce glare. "You can say that when *your* heart gets broken," Megan hissed, "and you come running home because the love of your life walked out when you told him you're having his baby."

Winter took hold of Megan's shoulders and leaned close. "I love you, Meg. Mama and Papa love you. Rose loves you. Everyone here in Pine Creek loves you. That one stupid jerk in a thousand loving people *doesn't* is not worth what you're putting yourself through. Wayne Ferris is a conniving weasel who's too stupid to appreciate what a wonderful woman you are. You have to let him go, Meg, and focus on your child. Being depressed and crying all the time will make your unborn bairn think you don't want it."

Megan moved her gaze past Winter's shoulder, looking at nothing, her lower lip quivering and her eyes misting again. "I thought he loved me," she whispered, looking back at Winter through eyes filled with despair. "He said he loved me."

"He loved what you could do for his career," Winter told her just as softly, gently squeezing her shoulders. "But camping out on the tundra for months at a time does not mix well with babies. That Wayne chose —"

The tiny bell on the gallery door tinkled, drawing everyone's attention. Just as Winter began to turn, she noticed that Rose was staring at the door in utter disbelief. Megan's eyes had gone equally as wide, her jaw slack. Winter spun fully around and actually took a step back. Who wouldn't feel a punch in the gut when finding herself in the presence of such incredibly virile . . . maleness? The man was just too stunning for words.

Which seemed to be an immediate problem for Winter, as she couldn't even respond when the tall, handsome stranger nodded at her — though she did hear Rose sigh, and she did feel Megan poke her in the back.

"Ah, may I help you?" Winter finally said.

Enigmatic, tiger gold eyes met hers, and it took all of Winter's willpower not to take another step back. The man was standing just inside her spacious gallery, yet he seemed to fill up the entire space.

"Is the painting in the window by a local artist?" he asked.

The deep, rich timbre of his voice sent a shudder coursing through Winter, and another sharp poke in her back started her breathing again. "Ah, yes," she said. "She lives right here in Pine Creek." Winter waved a hand at the east wall of her gallery. "Most of the paintings are hers. Everything we sell is by local artists," she finished in a near whisper, unable to stop staring at his beautifully rugged, tanned face.

He simply stared back, his eyes crinkled in amusement.

"Feel free to look around," she added with another halfhearted wave, thankful that her voice sounded normal this time. "I can answer any questions you have."

"Thank you," he said with a slight nod, before turning to the wall of paintings.

As soon as he looked away, Winter spun around to face Megan and Rose. Neither woman noticed her warning glare, however, as they were too busy gawking at the man. Worried that he'd turn around and catch them, Winter grabbed them both by an arm and hustled them ahead of her into the back room.

"Cut it out," she quietly hissed. "You're being rude."

"Did you see how broad his shoulders are?" Rose whispered, craning around to look back at the gallery.

Winter moved the three of them farther away from the door. "Rose Dolan Brewer, you're a happily married woman with two kids. You shouldn't be noticing other men's shoulders."

Rose smiled. "I can still look, as long as I don't touch."

"Did you see his hair?" Megan whispered, her eyes still wide, not a trace of a tear anywhere in sight. "He's wearing a suit that probably cost more than my entire wardrobe, but he's got a ponytail. What sort of businessman has long hair?"

"And those eyes," Rose interjected before Winter could respond. "They're as rich as gold bullion. My knees went weak when he looked at you, Winter."

"That does it. Out," Winter said, crowding them toward the door that connected the back office of her gallery with Dolan's Outfitter Store. "You're going to scare off my most promising customer today."

Rose snorted and stepped into her store, combing her fingers through her short brown hair. "I doubt anything could scare that man," she muttered, smoothing down her blouse as she turned to Winter. "Send him over to my store after," she said with a cheeky grin. "I'll, ah . . . fit him into more suitable clothes for around here."

"Do you suppose he came in on that plane that flew over?" Megan asked. "We saw it bank for a landing at the airport. It looked like a private jet." Megan sighed. "My God, he's handsome. Maybe I should stay and help you set out the figures Talking Tom brought in this afternoon."

Winter didn't have the heart to remind Megan that she had sworn off men — handsome or otherwise — when she'd come home from her fieldwork in Canada last month, abandoned and two months pregnant. It was rather nice to see her sister's face flushed from something other than tears.

"Thanks," Winter said with a tender smile, "but I think I'll wait and put out Tom's carvings tomorrow."

Megan took one last look toward the gallery door, sighed, then followed Rose down the aisle of camping equipment. Winter softly closed the connecting door, ran her fingers through her own mass of long red curls, straightened to her full five-foot-six height with a calming breath, and headed back into the gallery.

Mr. Tiger Eyes was still facing the wall. He had worked his way down the wall to a painting hanging toward the front of the store, his arms folded over his broad chest and his chin resting on one of his large, tanned fists. The pose pulled the material of his expensive suit tightly across a set of impressively wide shoulders. He glanced only casually at Winter when she stepped up to the counter, then went back to studying the painting.

He was looking at a large watercolor she had painted last spring, which she had titled *Moon Watchers*. It was a nighttime scene set deep in a mountain forest awash with moonlight. Three young bear cubs were gathered around a thick old tree stump, their harried mother catching a quick nap as they played in the shadows. One of the cubs was perched precariously on top of the stump, its tiny snout raised skyward as it brayed at the large silver disk in the star-studded sky, its siblings watching with enchanted expressions on their moon-bathed faces. And if one studied the painting long enough, he or she would eventually notice all of the other nocturnal creatures hidden in the shadows, curiously watching the young bears in the moonlight.

It was a painting that usually drew the attention of women more than men, with its endearingly familial subject and somewhat playful and mystical mood.

Winter slid her gaze to the man standing in front of it.

He was at least as tall as her cousin Robbie MacBain, and Robbie was six-foot-seven in his stocking feet. This man's shoulders were equally as broad, his legs as long and muscled beneath that perfectly tailored suit, his hands just as large and blunt and powerful looking. He had the body of an athlete, which said that whoever he was, he didn't spend all of his time sitting in boardrooms or shuffling papers.

Like Megan, Winter found herself questioning his choice of hairstyle if he truly was the successful businessman he appeared to be. His soft brown hair was thick and smooth, neatly brushed off his face and tied at the nape of his neck with a thin piece of leather. It wasn't overlong; Winter guessed that when loose, it would just brush his shoulders.

She suddenly realized she was staring just as rudely as Megan and Rose had been. With a silent sigh, Winter dropped her gaze to the small piece of paper that Tom had tossed down on the counter when he'd brought in his latest batch of wooden figures. It was a short list, Winter realized as she tried to focus on something other than her customer. Only five carvings this time, written in very neat, tiny black letters.

The first figure on the list was a chipmunk, and Tom had written one hundred and fifty dollars beside it. Next was a fox that he'd priced at two hundred. Then a swimming trout at four hundred dollars, and a snowy owl at two hundred.

Winter smiled at the last figure listed — crow tending young in nest — priced at twelve hundred dollars.

Tom, or Talking Tom as he was affectionately known to the locals, carved a lot of crows. And he always demanded a higher if not sometimes ridiculous price for them.

The amazing thing was, Winter had sold quite a few of Tom's crows in her gallery over the last year and a half. It seemed the more expensive something was, the more desperately the tourists wanted it.

Talking Tom. He was at least seventy years old, had simply appeared in Pine Creek one bright April morning two and a half years ago, and kept mostly to himself. Not much was known about him, other than the fact that he could be heard talking to himself when he walked the woods — thus the nickname Talking Tom. He was also quite good at tending sick animals, and the townsfolk had gotten in the habit of bringing Tom their ailing pets rather than traveling the forty miles to the nearest veterinarian.

As far as Winter knew, Tom had never mentioned his last name to anyone. He had appeared seemingly from nowhere and taken up residence in an old abandoned cabin just east of town, on Bear Mountain, which rose above the eastern shore of Pine Lake.

Winter had immediately taken to Tom, having recognized a kindred spirit. Like her, when creating his artwork Tom endowed the forest and its creatures with a sense of magic and mystery. His carefully carved wooden figures — like her paintings — were often more mystical than realistic.

It had taken Winter nearly a year to persuade Tom to let her sell his delicate figures in her gallery. His wants and needs seemed to be minimal, and a good deal of the money he earned from his carvings was often spent on others. When he was in town, Tom could usually be found in Dolan's Outfitter Store, and every female — from birth to ninety-nine years old, married or single — would leave the store with a box of chocolates. Rose had started ordering chocolate by the caseload, once she realized Tom's penchant for spoiling the ladies always kept her in short supply.

"Does she do commissions?"

Winter looked up on an indrawn breath. How could she have forgotten she had a customer in the store? Especially this customer. "Excuse me?" she asked.

"The artist," he said, nodding toward the wall of paintings, "does she take commissions?"

"Ah, yes. Yes, I'll take commissions."

One of his dark, masculine brows arched. "These are your paintings," he clarified softly, more to himself than her as he looked back at the wall. He studied the large watercolor for another moment in silence, then turned fully to face her, his deep golden gaze locking on hers. "I'll take *Moon Watchers,*" he said. "But I would like to leave it here until I have a wall to hang it on."

Winter drew her own brows together in confusion. "A wall to hang it on?" she repeated.

He took several steps toward her, then stopped, his mouth lifting in a crooked smile that slammed into Winter like another punch in the gut. It was the smile of a cajoling little boy, and it didn't belong on a face that . . . that . . . *masculine.*

"I'm building here in Pine Creek," he explained, "and I would like to leave the painting with you until my home is finished." He nodded toward the wall while keeping his gaze on her. "You can leave it on display if you wish. That way I can come in and look at it whenever I want. Just put a sold sign in place of the price. Would that be okay?"

She had to stop staring into his eyes! She couldn't think, much less keep up with the conversation. Well, curses. She was acting sillier than Megan and Rose. Winter tore her gaze from his and searched the counter until she found her sales book under Tom's list. Then she found a pen.

Next she found her wits, and then her voice again. "I don't have a problem with you leaving it here. Tell me, what is it that drew ye to *Moon Watchers,* Mr. . . . Mr. . . ." She trailed off, her pen poised to write his name at the top of the slip.

She looked up when he didn't immediately answer and found him standing just two feet away, his golden eyes once again locking on hers. "It's Gregor," he said softly, his deep voice sending another shiver down her spine. "Matt Gregor. And I've always had a fondness for bears."

Okay, this was bordering on the ridiculous. He was only a guy. Granted, he was a stunningly gorgeous guy, but she was acting like she'd never even spoken with a man, much less been attracted to one. Winter again forced her gaze from his and wrote his name on the slip. She wrote the title of the painting, and then started to write the price beside it.

A large, unbelievably warm hand covered hers, and Winter stopped breathing. She looked up to find Matt Gregor smiling that little boy smile again, and she could only helplessly smile back.

"Twenty percent discount if I take a second painting," he said, his beautiful eyes sparkling with challenge. "I also want to buy that small watercolor of the panther."

Winter slowly — trying very hard not to let him see how disconcerted his touch made her — slipped her hand from under his. "I'm sorry, but the panther's not for sale," she told him. "It's part of my personal collection. It's only on display because I had an empty space on the wall I wanted to fill."

Matt Gregor's expression instantly turned from that of a little boy to a fully engaged hunter. His eyes stopped smiling, their penetrating stare sending Winter's heart racing in alarm. "I'll pay as much for the panther as for *Moon Watchers,"* he said with quiet force. "No discount on either."

Double curses! When he looked at her like that, she wanted to *give* him every painting in the gallery — *especially* the panther. Winter just barely caught herself from snorting out loud. It was obvious Matt Gregor was used to getting what he wanted.

But then, so was she. *"Gesader* is not for sale," she told him, shaking her head to strengthen her words. "Choose something else that you like, and I'll give you a discount on it."

He crossed his arms over his chest and studied her much the same way he had studied her paintings. Winter felt a warmth creep into her cheeks, but she stubbornly held his stare, determined not to let him see her discomfort. She decided then that this would be a lesson to her: stunningly gorgeous didn't automatically mean nice. In fact, it could sometimes be downright rude.

Then again, it could also be exhilarating. Winter couldn't remember the last time she had felt this provoked by a man. Or felt this warm and fuzzy inside. Or this challenged.

She set down the pen and stepped from behind the counter, walking past Matt Gregor to the east wall of her gallery. She stopped in front of a tiny pastel drawing and crossed her arms under her breasts. "If you like cats, I have this drawing of a Maine lynx."

She sensed him moving to stand beside her, but she continued to look at the drawing of a confounded lynx that was searching for the hare it had been chasing. In the background, its head just slightly showing above a snowdrift, was a perfectly camouflaged snowshoe hare watching the lynx. "If you're building a house here, Mr. Gregor, you might consider works depicting local wildlife. We don't have panthers in Maine, but we do have lynx and bobcat and bear."

"Where did you come up with the name *Gesader?*" he asked, not addressing her suggestion.

Looking down the wall until her gaze fell on the small watercolor of the black leopard napping on a large tree limb, she smiled affectionately. "It's Gaelic for 'Enchanter.' "

"Gaelic," Matt Gregor repeated, stepping around to face her. "I thought I detected a slight accent. Are you Irish?"

"Nay, Scots," she said in an exaggerated brogue. She nodded toward the information card pinned next to the drawing and held out her hand. "Winter MacKeage."

His own hand swallowed hers up, his grip warm and firm but not overpowering. "My pleasure, Miss MacKeage." He lifted one brow again. "Or is it Mrs.?"

"Miss. But it's Winter to my patrons."

His grip tightened. "I'm not a patron yet, Miss MacKeage. We haven't concluded our negotiations."

Winter forced herself to leave her hand in his. "Full price for *Moon Watchers,* and you can have *By a Hare's Breadth* for half price," she offered, nodding toward the lynx drawing.

Matt Gregor, still holding her hand, let out a soft sigh. "Nothing I offer you will get me that panther, will it?"

Winter finally slipped her hand free, tucked it behind her back, and rubbed her fingers together as she slowly shook her

24

head. "I'm sorry, but he's not for sale. Do we have a deal?"

He moved his gaze from hers to the lynx drawing, studying it for several seconds before looking back at her. "Deal," he softly said with a nod. He pulled the tag from the wall, then moved over to *Moon Watchers* and pulled its tag. He walked back to the counter and set both tags down next to the sales slip she had started to fill out, while Winter walked behind the counter and picked up her pen.

"About that commission," he said as she started to write.

She stopped and looked up. "What is it you want? I must warn you, I don't do paintings of mechanical things."

He folded his arms back over his chest. "It's not a painting I want from you, Winter MacKeage, but your vision."

Winter set down her pen. "Excuse me?"

"Your artist's eye," he said just as cryptically. "I want to commission you to pick the spot where I should build my home."

Winter could only stare at him.

"And then I want you to do a watercolor of what that home should look like," he added.

She was thoroughly confused now. "What it should look like?" she repeated. "You mean, from the architectural plans? But they usually give you a model to look at."

He shook his head. "There are no plans as of yet. I intend to take your watercolor to the architects and have them design the house you envision, sitting on the spot you choose."

More than being confused, Winter was utterly speechless.

Matt Gregor let out another soft sigh, set both hands on the counter, and leaned toward her. "It's a simple request, Winter. I purchased Bear Mountain two years ago, and now I'm ready to build on it . . . just as soon as you pick the best spot and the best type of home for the land."

"But why me?"

He leaned even closer. "Because I've decided I like what you see and feel for the forest."

"But a home is a very personal thing."

"Yes," he readily agreed, straightening up and crossing his arms again. "But after spending a few days with me hiking my land, you'll get to know me well enough to come up with something I'll like."

Winter was no longer confused, she was back to being alarmed. A sudden thought struck her. "Shouldn't your wife have some say in what you build for a house?"

"I'm not married."

"Oh. Ah . . . well . . . I'll have to think about your request. I'm an artist, Mr. Gregor, not an architect."

"It's Matt," he said softly, reaching inside his suit jacket and pulling out a slim, black leather wallet. "And I've explained that I'm not asking you to design my home, but to simply envision it and choose where it should sit." He pulled out a credit card and set it down on the counter next to the still-incomplete sales slip. "I've taken a suite at the TarStone Ski Resort," he continued, pulling out a business card and setting it beside the credit card. "You can call my cell phone tomorrow morning at ten and give me your answer."

He then picked up the pen she'd been using, wrote SOLD in bold black letters on the back of the tag, and walked over and pinned it beside *Moon Watchers* on the wall. He came back, did the same to *By a Hare's Breadth,* walking over and pinning it beside the drawing.

Winter finally finished writing out the sales slip, ran his card through her authorization machine, tore off the credit slip printout, and handed it to him to sign.

He scrawled his signature in bold letters, then took the credit card and receipt and slipped them in his wallet. "You have no problem with my leaving my paintings here?" he asked.

"No problem," she agreed. "So you own Bear Mountain? Are ye moving to Pine Creek, or just building a vacation retreat?"

"I'm building a home, but I haven't decided yet when I'll be moving here," he told her, tucking his wallet back inside his suit jacket. "That depends on my brother."

"Your brother?"

Matt Gregor smiled benignly, nodded, and headed toward the door. He stopped and looked back. "I'll expect you to meet me in the lobby of TarStone at ten in the morning, to tell me you've accepted the commission. Don't disappoint me, Winter. I don't take rejection well." That said, he opened the door, walked out to the tinkle of the overhead bell, and disappeared down the street as quickly and mysteriously as he'd appeared.

Winter picked up the business card he'd set on the counter. Matheson Gregor, it read in solid green letters, with a New York City address but no mention of what type of business he was in. She looked over at *Moon Watchers*.

He had a fondness for bears, he'd told her.
And he owned Bear Mountain.

Another shiver ran down Winter's spine, but this time there was nothing warm and fuzzy about it. It hadn't been a tiger's eyes that had captured her attention this afternoon, but those of an equally impressive creature.

Matheson was Gaelic for "son of the bear."

CHAPTER TWO

"Curses on you, you stubborn old beast," Winter growled as she tugged on the saddle cinch for the tenth time in as many minutes.

A soft chuckle came from her left, and Winter looked over to see her papa striding along the row of stalls. "Cursing poor old Snowball hasn't worked once for ye in twenty years," Greylen MacKeage said as he crowded Winter out of the way, then patiently waited until the aging draft horse grew tired of his game and finally released his breath. Greylen quickly tightened the cinch, then lowered the stirrup into place. "And just where are ye sneaking off to so early this morning?" he asked, turning to face her. "It's still an hour to sunrise."

Winter shot him a sheepish grin. "What gave me away? Was it that floorboard you refuse to fix? I was sure I missed it this morning."

Her papa gave an affectionate tug on a

loose lock of hair that had escaped from the single thick braid hanging down her back. "I'm not needing a creaky floorboard to know when one of my daughters is sneaking around. My ears haven't slept since Heather was born." He turned serious. "You're heading to Bear Mountain, aren't you? I thought we decided at dinner last night that you won't be taking Gregor's commission."

"*I* didn't decide anything. It was you and Mama who decided, and you based that decision on Megan's say-so alone."

"Your sister told us Matt Gregor is a dangerous-looking man," he softly countered, his rich, spruce green eyes darkened with fatherly concern. "And she also mentioned that he's as big as Robbie. I don't care for the idea of you roaming the woods with him."

Winter rolled her eyes. "Megan thinks every man is big and dangerous looking. She's five-foot-three; *I'm* large to her."

"We know nothing about Gregor," Greylen countered, crossing his arms over his chest and planting his feet in his "I'm your father and you'll do as I say" stance. "Only that he checked into our hotel yesterday and told the clerk he'd be staying at least a month."

Her papa's posturing hadn't worked on

Winter once in the last twenty-four years, and it wasn't going to work this morning, either. Winter smiled and patted his arm. "I'm just going for a ride on Bear Mountain, Papa. And I'm going alone. I only want to have a look around before I give Mr. Gregor my answer."

"Ye're going to take his commission," Greylen muttered. Then his eyes narrowed in warning. "I will allow it, but only as long as ye promise to always take someone with ye when ye're hiking the woods with this man."

"Does Gesader count?" she asked, holding in her grin.

Greylen MacKeage thought in silence, rubbing his chin, then finally nodded. "That beast would kill anyone who tried to harm ye." He shook his head. "It still baffles me that ye survived yer childhood before that panther came along. Every gray hair on my head is from constantly having to hunt ye down or pull ye out of some scrape ye got yerself into."

Winter lifted up on her tiptoes and kissed his cheek. "I'm sorry for being such a trial to you, Papa. But I do love those gray hairs," she whispered, brushing her fingers through them. "They make you look so wise and noble."

Before she could step away, however, her papa pulled her into a hug that lifted her toes off the floor. "You're not a trial, baby girl, you're my eighth most precious blessing."

Winter smiled into his shoulder. Her mama was her papa's first blessing, and his seven daughters made him eight times blessed, he was always telling them. "I love you, Papa. Please don't worry about me. I have a whole forest full of protectors."

"Aye," he growled, with one last squeeze before he set her back on her feet. He unhooked Snowball from his tether and handed her the reins. "Wait for me outside. I'll ride partway across TarStone with you."

"And just where are you going so early this morning?"

His eyes sparked fiercely. "The old priest asked me to come up and have breakfast with him." He shook his head. "I'm thinking he's wanting something mighty important if he's daring to summons me rather than Robbie MacBain."

Winter gave a laugh and started leading Snowball out of the barn. "And your curiosity has gotten the best of you," she said over her shoulder. "So you're also sneaking off before sunrise."

Once outside, Winter led Snowball over to

33

a set of stairs built specifically for mounting. Her uncle, Ian MacKeage, had built the steps nearly thirty years ago, when Winter's oldest sister, Heather, had first started riding.

All seven MacKeage girls had learned to ride almost as soon as they'd learned to walk, much to their mama's dismay. But their very opinionated uncle Ian had taught them all to handle huge horses, at the same time trying to convince Grace MacKeage that her daughters were safer on docile, bomb-proof draft horses than they were on ponies. Snowball had been Ian's gift to Winter on her fifth birthday, and she could still remember her mama's scream when she had walked directly under her new pet's belly without her hair even touching.

Snowball and Winter had taken immediately to each other, and they'd spent twenty adventurous years exploring the forests surrounding TarStone Mountain.

"I know you still miss yer uncle Ian, lass, but understand that he's happy now," her papa said as he led his own horse over to her.

Winter realized she was staring at the steps her uncle had lovingly constructed for them so long ago. "I didn't even get to say good-bye," she reminded her father. "He left without saying good-bye to any of us."

Her papa lifted her chin so she could see his tender smile. "He left you a note, baby girl, telling you how much he loves you."

"Do you . . . do you think he's still alive, Papa?" Winter asked as she mounted Snowball.

"Aye. He's only been gone just over two years, and Ian had many good years in him still. He's with his wife and children, Winter. He's happy, and you need to be happy for him."

"I can be happy for Ian and still miss him," she said, standing up on the top step and turning to Snowball. She looked back. "You . . . ah, promise you won't suddenly disappear too, will you, Papa?"

He slowly shook his head. "I promise. I'm here until the angels wrestle me away from you."

Greylen also mounted up, then nudged his horse forward as he looked toward the summit of TarStone. "That damned old priest had better not be up to something," he said, looking back at Winter with a scowl fierce enough to burn toast. "I'm getting too old for his antics."

"Then I guess you're too old to win a horse race!" she called out, urging Snowball into a clomping gallop.

Within seconds, her father was beside her again, his own horse moving with an easy stride. Greylen MacKeage did not ride a draft horse like his daughters, but a semi-wild beast descended from the warhorse that had come through the maelstrom with him thirty-eight years ago.

The old priest, Daar, who was really an ancient *drùidh* named Pendaär, had cast a spell that had brought four MacKeage and six MacBain warriors — along with their warhorses — eight hundred years forward through time from medieval Scotland. Five of the MacBains had died within their first two years here. Winter's father, Greylen, and her uncles Ian and Callum and Morgan, as well as Robbie's father, Michael MacBain, were all that were left of the original ten.

Except that Ian had returned to his old time two and a half years ago. Robbie MacBain had taken him back through the powerful maelstrom, Robbie being the ordained guardian of the two clans, and possessing magical powers himself that allowed him to protect his loved ones while keeping Father Daar under his tenuous control.

Winter had heard their fantastical story almost from birth and had understood from a young age that it was a carefully guarded

something only ye can decide." He stopped his horse again and frowned at her. "I do intend to have Robbie use his old military connections to look into Gregor's background, though, but only for my own peace of mind. If Gregor is nothing more than the businessman he appears to be, I will simply stand aside and let ye two work things out for yerselves."

Winter frowned at her father. "Aren't you getting ahead of yourself? I only said that he bothered me. For all I know, I didn't have any effect on Mr. Gregor."

Her papa let out a soft chuckle. "Trust me, ye bothered him, lass. The man dropped over six thousand dollars on two of your paintings, and all but demanded you spend time with him hiking his land. Aye, Gregor was bothered all right; he took one look at yer beautiful face and found the surest way to see it again."

Winter's frown turned into a scowl, and she started Snowball walking down the tote road at a brisk pace. Her papa, still chuckling, trotted to catch up. They rode in silence until they finally came to a fork in the road and stopped again.

Greylen looked around in the strengthening light. "Call in yer pet," he told her. "That I might have a word with him."

"What makes you think he's near?" Winter asked.

"Because he's been stalking us since we left Gù Brath."

Winter put her fingers to her lips and gave a sharp, single-note whistle that cut through the crisp September air.

Gesader stepped out of the shadows not ten feet away.

Gesader showed his large white teeth in a snarling smile, and her papa dismounted, allowing his nervous warhorse to skitter away. Greylen walked up to the panther and got down on one knee to hold out his hand. Gesader moved straight into his palm and ducked his head to get his ears scratched. Winter slid down off Snowball and watched her papa continue his conversation with her pet.

"I'm wanting yer opinion on this Gregor fellow," he told the panther. "One good sniff should let you know if his intentions toward our baby girl are honorable or not."

"Do you truly believe he knows what you're saying?" Winter asked. "You talk to him as if he were human."

"So do ye," Greylen reminded her. "And if Gesader were human," he said, standing up and turning to face her, his smile reaching all the way to his evergreen eyes, "I certainly wouldn't have let him sleep in yer bed these last two years." He looked down at Gesader. "Though Megan could use his company at night right now."

"Gesader has spent a lot of time with Megan since she came home," Winter said while absently rubbing his ear. "He goes with her when she walks the woods, and I've caught him in her bed some nights. It's like he knows when she needs a good cuddle."

"Animals have a way of sensing our moods," Greylen agreed. He walked over to his horse and mounted back up, turning it to face her. "Keep yer wits about ye when ye deal with Gregor. Try not to turn into a 'blithering idiot' the next time ye see him. Enjoy the thrill, lass. If ye're blessed, it will only come along once in yer lifetime."

His instructions given to both of them, Laird Greylen MacKeage reined his horse up the path leading to Daar's cabin, giving a wave over his shoulder as he disappeared into the dense forest.

Winter looked down at Gesader and ruffled the fur on his powerful shoulder. "You may come with me, but remember to keep out of sight. There have been more rumors going around town of a large black cat in the forest, and your safety depends on your staying only a rumor. Hey," she said with a gasp, getting down on her knees and taking his neck in both hands. "What happened to you?"

She pulled her right hand away and rubbed her fingers together. "That's dried blood," she said, pushing his head to the side so she could see better. "It's *your* blood," she added, running a finger over a crusted cut on his neck just above his shoulder. "What have you done to yourself? Did your dinner last night fight back?"

Winter knew Gesader hunted his own food, even though she always kept plenty of meat available for him at Gù Brath. When Robbie had given him to her as a tiny cub, both he and her papa had repeatedly warned Winter that her new pet was a wild creature, and that once he grew up his instincts would likely take over.

"I'm taking you to see Tom," she told him, standing up and brushing her hands on her jacket. "We're not supposed to let anyone know you really do exist, but we can trust Tom. He can tell us if that cut needs stitching. Come on," she said, going over and gathering up Snowball's reins. "Let's get going."

Gesader let out a low rumble from his throat and padded off into the forest as

44

silently as he'd appeared. Winter used a nearby old stump to mount up and headed toward Bear Mountain.

CHAPTER THREE

"Tom. Are you home?" Winter called out as she rode into the small clearing on the east shore of Pine Lake. "Tom!"

She dismounted and led Snowball toward the one-story cabin nestled in the trees at the back of the clearing, where it sat safely out of reach of the powerful storms that sometimes blew in off the lake. The precariously leaning structure had to be over a century old, its vertical logs weathered to a shiny gray patina, its oversized roof eaves nearly touching the towering pines on either side.

Every time she came here, Winter couldn't help but smile. The cabin's crooked stovepipe wafting smoke, two tiny front windows, and narrow wood door gave it a magical air, and she always expected to see a gnome come strolling out to greet her instead of Tom. She'd said as much to him once, and Tom had simply smiled his endearing old smile and told her to be careful what she imagined, as she might be surprised one day when something even more unbelievable greeted her.

"Tom!" she shouted again, dropping Snowball's reins and walking around the side of the cabin toward an equally run-down shed out back. "I'm wanting some tea and toast!"

"I don't remember our having a breakfast date," Tom said, emerging from the shed as he brushed flecks of dust off his thick flannel shirt. He stopped and wrestled the rickety old door closed, then turned and smiled at her. "To what do I owe this pleasant surprise?"

Winter frowned at him. "You're a master woodworker, Tom. Why don't you just fix that old door?"

He shrugged and walked past her, taking her hand on the way by, and led her back to the front of his cabin. "I don't want to spoil the ambience of the place. So what's up?" he asked, stopping long enough to greet Snowball and take off his bridle. The horse immediately wandered off to graze on whatever grass he could find.

Tom opened his cabin door, then held his arm out to usher Winter inside. "If you're here for a peek at what I'm working on, the answer is still no. Nobody sees my work until it's done. Especially you."

Winter stopped in the doorway and brushed some of the remaining dust off his shirt. "Won't you at least give me a hint about what you're working on? I could see something big in there, covered with a sheet. Hey, this isn't sawdust, it's stone dust," she said, rubbing the powder between her fingers. Her eyes widened. "Are you working in stone, Tom?"

Tom took hold of her dusty hand and led her into the cabin, directing her to a table and chairs near an ancient potbellied stove. "I might be," he said as he opened the stove door and stirred the embers. "If it's any of your business, Miss Curious." He looked over his shoulder, his clear blue eyes bright with amusement. "Then again, I might have been sharpening tools on my whetstone."

As she sat down, Winter slipped off her jacket and let it fall on the back of the chair. "We're business partners, Tom. We're not supposed to have secrets from each other."

He straightened and faced her, his eyes dancing in the strengthening sunlight coming through the still-open door. "You tell me one of your secrets, and I'll tell you one of mine."

"Okay," she said, folding her hands on her

lap with a smile of anticipation. "There really is a panther living on TarStone. His name is Gesader, and he's my pet."

The amusement left Tom's face. He sat down across from her, his own hands clasped together on the table. "So he does exist," he whispered. "I knew I hadn't been seeing things. He's your pet, you say?" One of his bushy gray brows lifted into his equally thick gray hair. "As in you get to actually touch him, or that you've just adopted him the same way you've taken to all the woodland creatures?"

"As in he sleeps in my bed most nights," she said, her own eyes dancing with excitement. "I got him as a tiny cub."

Tom sat back in his chair and rubbed the sparse white stubble on his chin. "Gesader, you called him. I'm assuming that's Gaelic. What's it mean?"

"Enchanter."

"Is he a leopard or a jaguar?"

"A leopard. Ye can see the spots in his black coat when the sun hits him just right."

"How old is he?"

"Three next spring."

Tom's brow lifted again. "And you've been able to keep him a secret all this time? So why are you telling me?"

"Because I trust you. And because Gesader has a cut on his neck I want you to look at. I need to know if it requires stitching."

Tom straightened in his chair, his gaze shooting to the open door. "He's here?" he whispered. "He came with you this morning?"

"Yes. He's in the woods, waiting for me to call him."

Tom stood up and brushed his hands on his pants, still staring at the door. "You're just going to call out, and a panther is going to come walking in here?"

"Yes," Winter repeated, also standing up. "He won't hurt you, Tom. He's really just an overgrown baby."

Tom darted a look at her. "A baby with sharp fangs and claws as long as my fingers," he muttered. He took a deep breath. "Okay, then. Call your . . . ah . . . pet."

Winter didn't bother to put her fingers to her lips this time, but simply let out a sharp whistle toward the open door. Gesader silently appeared in the doorway, but instead of coming inside, the large black cat sat down and gave a fierce snarl that nicely showed off his fangs.

"Behave," Winter scolded, walking up and tapping the top of his head. "You needn't show off to Tom. He's going to help you."

Gesader turned his piercing, golden-eyed gaze on Tom.

Winter waved her friend forward. "I promise, he won't hurt you, Tom. He's only trying to impress you."

Tom still didn't move. "I am impressed," he whispered, his own wide-eyed gaze locked on the panther beside her. "Where is he hurt?"

"His neck, just above his shoulder." Winter knelt down and moved Gesader's head to the side. "It's already crusted over. It must have happened last night sometime. You . . . ah, could probably see better if you came closer."

"I can see the cut from here. It looks fine, Winter. Wild animals have amazing immune systems. He won't likely get an infection."

Gesader, apparently realizing he might have shown off a little too much, stood up, padded into the cabin right up to Tom, and lapped the old hermit's hand.

Tom didn't so much as twitch, and Winter wasn't sure, but she thought her friend stopped breathing. With a laugh she followed Gesader into the cabin and sat down at the table. "Ye just got a panther kiss, Tom. Gesader is usually quite stingy with his kisses."

Tom finally looked down at Gesader. "He

. . . ah, he seems amiable enough." He looked at Winter, and she noticed his shoulders finally relax as a soft smile lifted one side of his mouth. "Assuming he wasn't just seeing what I taste like."

"Go ahead," Winter urged, nodding at Gesader. "Pet him."

Slowly, Tom sat down in his chair and gently laid his hand on Gesader, moving the broad black head to the side so he could see the gash on the panther's neck. "It doesn't need stitching, Winter. It looks worse than it is because it's in a hard place for him to tend for himself." He gave Gesader's ear a gentle scratch.

Winter frowned. "There's another reason I came here this morning, Tom. A guy by the name of Matt Gregor came into my gallery yesterday and bought two of my paintings, and he said he owns Bear Mountain."

Her news seemed to puzzle Tom more than disturb him. "You rode out here just to tell me that? Why? I don't care who owns Bear Mountain."

"You might care, if he doesn't want you living on his land. He's going to build a house here."

Tom shrugged. "The mountain is big enough for both of us."

"Papa said that if you can't stay here, you

can have a place on TarStone. Or maybe my cousin Robbie will let you use his cabin on West Shoulder Ridge."

Tom leaned on the table, his hands clasped in front of him and his clear blue eyes leveled on hers. "I like this cabin. Tell your father thanks for the offer, but I prefer to stay right where I am."

"But Mr. Gregor might —"

"If Mr. Gregor owns Bear Mountain, he owns over two thousand acres," Tom said softly, cutting her off. "He can build his house on any one of the other nineteen hundred and ninety-nine acres. This acre is already occupied."

Winter gave up. She wasn't going to argue about something that might not even be a problem. Besides, she had accomplished her goal of warning him. "Okay," she said, sitting up straight and mimicking his posture by clasping her hands together on the table. "Your turn. Tell me a secret."

One side of his mouth lifted in a grin. "I can't dance."

"That's not a secret! You come to the grange socials and stand in the corner the whole evening, no matter how hard the ladies try to lure you onto the dance floor. Come on, tell me a good secret. Something equal to my panther."

He leaned closer, his hands reaching out and capturing hers on the table. "Okay, then. But you have to promise not to tell anyone."

"I promise," Winter said, leaning closer herself.

"I witnessed something strange on the mountain last night," he whispered. "I was walking home from town when I heard a terrible racket coming from up the mountain."

"This mountain?" Winter whispered. "Bear Mountain?"

"This one," he confirmed, his gaze moving to her left as he focused inward. "I thought it was two rutting bull moose fighting, the noise was so loud." He looked back at her. "So I snuck up toward them, until I came to that meadow on the north side of Bear Brook. You know the one I mean?"

"I know the meadow," Winter said softly, leaning closer in anticipation. "Did you see them? Were two big bulls fighting?"

He shook his head, his hands tightening on hers. "It was two men," he told her. "Dressed very strangely. They looked to be wearing kilts."

"Kilts!"

"And the noise I heard was the clashing of swords. They were having a sword fight."

Winter slipped her hands free and sat back in her chair, staring at Tom. "You're pulling my leg! You didn't see two men having a sword fight."

Tom also sat back, folding his arms over his chest. "I did," he said calmly, nodding. "The full moon lit up that meadow nearly as bright as day, and I saw two men dressed in kilts, having a sword fight." He leaned forward slightly, his eyes narrowing on hers. "And they weren't merely sparring, but really going at it. I thought they were going to kill each other."

Winter thought furiously. Could two of her cousins have been out playing warrior games last night? Robbie? And maybe her uncle Morgan's oldest son, Duncan? But she couldn't think why. The festival had been late last spring.

"Did you . . . ah, did you recognize either of them?" she asked. "Could they have been from town? You know my cousins love swords and stuff. They go to the Scottish games every spring down on the coast. Could it have been them, Tom?"

He slowly shook his head. "I didn't recognize either of the men. They were both big like your cousins, but one of them had really long hair, halfway down his back. And it wasn't MacKeage or MacBain plaids they were wearing. These plaids looked to be more gray, with maybe some green and red in them." He cocked his head in thought. "It's hard to tell colors in the moonlight," he said, looking back at her. "But I did get a good look at the long-haired guy's face, and I didn't recognize him."

"Did they say anything?"

"No," Tom said, shaking his head again. "They seemed to be too busy trying to slice each other in half."

Winter was back to gaping at him. Tom couldn't have seen what he was claiming he saw. Who would have been out on Bear Mountain in the middle of the night, fighting with swords?

"I don't want you to mention this to anyone, Winter. Not even your father. Greylen would worry I might really be crazy, and I prefer people around here to think I'm only a little odd," Tom said with a crooked smile. He gestured toward Gesader at his feet. "Like your pet here, I think our swordsmen should remain figments of our imaginations."

"But you really did see them," she whispered.

He nodded. "I saw them. They fought for over half an hour, and then they suddenly stopped, silently faced each other for several heartbeats, and then turned and walked into the woods side by side. One of the men slapped the other man on the back, and left his arm there. I heard them laughing as they disappeared into the forest," he finished, shaking his head. "One minute they were trying to kill each other, and the next minute they were laughing together."

He sat forward, stretching one hand toward her on the table. "I know you're in the habit of roaming the woods at night, Winter, and that's why I'm telling you what I saw. I think you should paint only daytime scenes for a while. I'd hate for these men to stumble upon you in the woods."

"But I have Gesader," she reminded him.

He looked down at the panther napping at his feet, then back at her, and shook his head again. "Your pet is no match for two men with swords." He gave her a stern look. "Promise me you'll stay out of the woods at night, or I'll go to your father myself and tell him what I saw."

"But you just said —"

"I said I prefer Greylen not to know what I witnessed," he said, cutting her off. "But your safety is more important than my reputation. So save us both a lot of trouble and stop being stubborn and give me your promise."

"Okay, Tom," she softly assured him. "I promise I won't go in the woods alone after dark." Winter stood up. "And I am not stubborn. I'm willful," she proclaimed.

"No, you're spoiled," Tom countered, as he stood and turned his smile on her. "And someday some man will come along and fix that."

"I am not spoiled. I've a good notion to tell Gesader to bite you," she threatened, glaring at Tom.

Tom gave a tiny snort and shook his head. "You're the youngest of seven daughters, Winter. By the time you came along, I suspect your parents had given up trying to control any of you girls." He walked around the table and took hold of her shoulders. "You're the dearest friend I have, and I love you." He smiled tenderly down at her. "There's a big difference between being spoiled and being a brat, you know. And it's with great affection that I point that out to you."

Winter frowned up at him in confusion. "So you're saying being spoiled is a good thing?"

Tom nodded. "You live life on your own terms. You chase your own future, and thumb your nose at what others might think of you." Tom laughed and walked to the open door.

Winter walked up to him and set her hand on his chest. "How did you get so wise, Tom? Who were you before you came here?"

He covered her hand on his chest. "I was you, Winter," he said softly. "Born to a father and mother who gave me the same solid foundation yours gave you. I defied convention and traveled my own path, which seems to have led me here to Bear Mountain . . . and to you," he finished, squeezing her hand.

"But who were you between being born and coming here?"

He reached up and tapped the end of her nose, his smile crinkling the corners of his shining blue eyes. "I'll tell you that on your twenty-fifth birthday. My life story will be my present to you." He cocked his head, his eyes dancing in the sunshine. "Along with what's under that sheet in my workshop."

Winter sucked in her breath. "It's for my birthday?" she squeaked. "You're carving something just for me?"

He stepped outside with a chuckle and called to Snowball before turning back to her. "I thought that might pique your interest, if not drive you nuts for the next three months."

"Can you give me a hint? Is it made of wood or stone?"

"Maybe it's made of both," he said cryptically, picking up Snowball's bridle and slipping it onto the old draft horse. "Then again, maybe it's made of nothing more than dreams spun from moonbeams."

He leaned down and cupped his two hands into a step, so she could climb onto Snowball. Winter let Tom vault her into the saddle, then took up the reins and smiled down at him. "I've never known anyone as secretive as you are," she told him.

He squinted up at her. "No? Maybe you should look in the mirror more often. You bring your Mr. Gregor over for a visit. I'm anxious to meet him."

"He is not *my* Mr. Gregor."

Tom patted her knee. "Don't lift your hackles at me," he said with a laugh, turning to Gesader, who was still standing in the cabin door. "Come along, Enchanter," he said. "Time to escort your lady safely home."

"Why is it all you men think I need a babysitter?"

Tom looked up at her. "When people care, we tend to get protective," he said as he turned and headed back to his workshop. "Remember your promise," he added over his shoulder. "And if you see a tall stranger in a kilt carrying a sword, Miss Curious, you run as fast as you can in the opposite direction."

Winter scowled at the closing door of Tom's workshop. Curses, the man was just as cryptic — and just as confounding — as Father Daar.

Winter finally urged Snowball toward town and spent the ride home trying to imagine what Tom was hiding under that sheet in his workshop.

And what he was hiding in his past.

She would have her answer in exactly three months from yesterday, Winter realized with a sudden smile — on the winter solstice, on her and her sisters' birthdays.

CHAPTER FOUR

While Winter was visiting with Talking Tom, Greylen MacKeage was standing in a cabin halfway up TarStone Mountain, trying very hard not to lose his temper and kill a priest. He knew damn well Grace would be mad at him if he did; but then again, if his wife could hear what Daar was telling him now, she just might offer to help.

"Ye promised I would be long dead before Winter came into her powers," Grey reminded Daar, his eyes sparking with anger as they bore into the old *drùidh*. "That she would have a normal life up until then, and be an old woman herself before ye started her schooling. She's not even twenty-five years old. Ye can't have her yet."

"But that was before," Daar said, moving to put the tenuous safety of the table between them. "I miscalculated, Greylen. I thought I would have more time. But as I've been trying to explain, there's terrible trouble brewing, and I need Winter to come into her powers now."

"Nay. I forbid it. Ye'll not have my baby girl as long as there's breath in me, priest." Greylen took a threatening step toward him. "And if ye so much as even hint to Winter about her destiny, I will dispatch ye to hell myself, old man, my own soul be damned."

Daar had been inching farther away throughout Grey's tirade and was now pressed up against the back wall of his cabin. The old priest took a calming breath and held out his hands in petition. "Laird Greylen —" He took another shaky breath and tried again. "Grey. Ye don't understand. Winter won't even reach old age if she doesn't step into her destiny now. None of us will be here. Hell," he muttered, shaking his head. "Life as we know it will cease to exist."

Grey crossed his arms over his chest. "Yer penchant for melodrama no longer affects me, priest. The sun will not stop shining if Winter has another forty or fifty years of peace and happiness. Ye cannot have her yet."

"But it's already happening," Daar whispered. "The energy has already begun to alter. Have ye not noticed the fierceness of the storms that have been coming with unusual regularity? They're the first sign of the trouble that's brewing, Greylen, and it's escalating at a rate even I didn't foresee."

"Weather is just weather, old man. Since the beginning of time, it has run in cycles. Grace can explain it to ye, if need be."

The old priest reached up and scrubbed his face with his hands, then scowled at Grey through narrowed, crystal blue eyes. "This is different, I tell ye. Something is disturbing the continuum, which in turn is causing my tree of life to die. And if it dies, the others will soon follow." He waved his hand wildly again. "And when they all die, the earth dies with them."

"What exactly is killing your tree?"

Daar shrugged and finally stepped away from the wall. He moved to the hearth and stretched his hands to the fire's warmth as he stared into it. "A transgression against the life force," he said without looking up.

"What sort of transgression?" Greylen impatiently growled.

Daar shot him a quick frown, then went back to watching the fire. "Well, I'm guessing it might be a *drùidh* or guardian . . . ah, misusing his powers," he said to the flames.

"Now what have ye done?"

"Not me!" Daar yelped, spinning to face him. "I'm not the one causing my tree to die. I'm trying to stop it!"

"Then who is?"

Daar shook his head with a calming sigh and dropped his gaze to the floor. "It could be any one of fifty or so souls. It matters not who, only that my tree is feeling the effects."

"Fifty?" Greylen whispered in horror. "There are fifty of you *drùidhs* running around?"

"Nay," Daar said, looking up. "There's only six to ten of us at any one time. The other souls are guardians."

"Then why isn't one of these guardians dealing with this problem? Ye told Robbie MacBain that it's his duty to protect us from you interfering bastards."

"That is precisely why I'm thinking it's a guardian causing the upset," Daar said, scratching his beard.

Grey let his arms fall to his sides and took a step back. "A guardian?" he whispered. "Are ye saying a rogue guardian is killing yer tree of life?"

"Nay, he's not doing it directly. He's just turned against his calling, I'm thinking, and that's upset the continuum. And that in turn is causing all the trees to weaken, until they die one by one. They cannot thrive when their energy is spent fighting to restore the balance."

The old *drùidh* stepped closer, his hands clasped tightly in front of him. "Winter is our only hope, Greylen. My powers have faded to the point that I can't keep my tree alive much longer. It will take a much younger, much more powerful wizard to save it. It will take yer daughter."

"Nay. Ye can't have her. She's still only a bairn."

Daar threw up his hands with a sound of disgust, then pointed at the hearth. "Do ye see that?" he growled. "Right there, that little knot of wood sitting on the mantel, do ye see it? That's all that's left of my once-powerful staff. I've spent almost all of my energy trying to save my tree, while at the same time trying to find out who in hell has upset the continuum. But without my staff, I can barely toast bread now," he ground out, still glaring at Grey.

"Then what do ye have to give Winter, old man? If yer powers are gone, what is there for her to inherit?"

Daar waved an impatient hand toward him. "Winter was *born* a *drùidh,* Greylen. She inherited the power from *you."*

Grey paled. "Me?" he whispered. "I don't have any powers, priest. I'm a warrior, not a wizard. Hell, I don't even have the power to control my own daughters most of the time."

Daar smiled. "Oh, Greylen. Ye have always carried our legacy in ye. Along with giving her yer warrior's heart, ye also gave Winter the knowledge of the universe. From birth, Winter has been a *drùidh.*"

"Then why hasn't she —" Grey suddenly stiffened. "Ye said *our* legacy. What do ye mean by *our?*"

"Just that," Daar said with a smug grin. He angled his head. "Have ye never wondered why I chose you to father my heir, MacKeage? It's because you and I are descended from the same ancestor. We're cousins, Greylen, with only five score of generations between us."

It was Grey's turn to scrub his face, as he tried to rub away the horrifying notion. He was related to Daar? Holy hell!

He still wanted to kill him.

"I couldn't father my own heir," Daar continued. "Because if a *drùidh* has a child, his powers are lost to a future generation. That's what happened with our mutual ancestor. He chose marriage over what Providence asked of him, and so his power was handed down to me, his grandson." Daar pointed at Grey. "But you also received the power of a *drùidh,* held dormant for all those generations, in case I gave up my own destiny or for when I finally needed an heir." Daar clasped his hands behind his back. "I chose to serve Providence, so I became a priest instead of a husband. Then I simply waited until I could match ye up with Grace Sutter, so ye could have seven daughters together. And yer last daughter, Winter, is my heir."

Grey thought about that. And he thought about his baby girl's destiny. He leveled his narrowed, evergreen eyes on Daar. "So you're saying that each *drùidh* has the choice of renouncing his destiny? All he has to do is have a child?"

"Aye," Daar confirmed with a nod. "Like everyone else on this earth, even *drùidhs* have free will."

"Then Winter still has the right to choose."

"Aye," Daar said, even while shaking his head in negation. "But if she chooses to renounce her calling, there will be at least a two-generation gap in our lineage. By the time a new *drùidh* is born in our line, it will be too late. My pine tree will surely die before then, and that would start a disas-trous reaction with all the other trees of life."

"Why can't another *drùidh* come here and

save yer tree?" Grey asked. "And ye can leave Winter out of it."

"Because they're all trying to protect their own trees," Daar rasped in frustration. "Each tree is dependent on its own lineage of *drùidhs* to nurture it."

"Then how were ye able to steal a root from Cùram de Gairn and grow it into yer white pine?"

Daar took a calming breath and dropped his gaze. "I . . . ah . . . Cùram's lineage dates all the way back to the beginning of the continuum. He's descended from master *drùidhs.*" Daar shrugged. "That was why Robbie had to get me a root from Cùram's tree. Its energy is — or was — the source from which every tree of life originated."

Greylen dropped his chin to his chest, absorbing all that Daar had said. He quietly asked, "But it is Winter's decision?"

"Aye. It's her decision," Daar said softly. "But knowing yer daughter, Greylen, do ye think she can turn her back on her destiny once she realizes the consequences? Is Winter capable of just letting the world come to an end?"

"Nay," Grey admitted, hanging his head again for another interminable silence. He finally looked back at Daar. "Why are ye so sure Winter can save yer tree? She's young and unschooled in the way of *drùidhs*." He shifted uneasily. "And this rogue guardian? Who's to protect her from him?"

"You will," Daar said. "And so will I, however I can. And don't forget Robbie. He is still a powerful guardian himself, Greylen. We'll all try our damnedest to protect Winter. Hell, even that beastly pet of hers, Gesader, would lay down his life for her."

"Ye sound more worried than confident," Grey said, taking a step toward him. "Can we really protect her?"

Daar held his ground this time, his eyes softening with understanding as he shook his head. "I honestly don't know, because I don't know exactly who or what we are up against."

"How do we find out, then?"

Daar continued to shake his head. "We'll find out when whoever he is lets us find out. If he's a rogue guardian, there must be a reason why he turned. But until his agenda is known, we might as well be wearing blindfolds on a moonless night."

"Why haven't ye gone to Robbie MacBain with this?"

"I have. He told me I must speak with you first."

"Ye will not tell Winter without my permission," Grey said, backing up his words with another threatening step.

Again, Daar stood firm and shook his head. "I have no intention of telling her anything. That's your duty, Greylen. Once Winter comes to terms with who she really is, she will seek me out on her own." Daar stepped closer himself. "I only ask that ye not take yer time about it, MacKeage. Once my pine tree falls, it might be too late to save the others." He shook his head. "And I worry my tree won't survive the coming winter."

Grey blew out a frustrated breath as he stared at Daar standing by the fire looking old and feeble and nearly defeated. Grey suddenly felt just as old and equally helpless. He silently turned, opened the cabin door, stepped out onto the porch, and simply stood staring at the lake below as it glimmered in the early-morning sunshine.

"You're still a powerful warrior, Greylen," Daar said softly as he stepped onto the porch beside him. "You're a highlander, MacKeage, with the strength and intelligence to help yer daughter through this. For as far as society has evolved since ye were born over eight hundred years ago, it still needs yer warrior's heart to save it. That, and Winter's powerful magic."

Grey silently continued to gaze at Pine

Lake, which was ringed by mountains draped in a mantle of colorful fall foliage.

"And ye have a small army at yer disposal," the old priest continued. "To help ye in the upcoming battle. Yer wife will stand by your side, Greylen. And me. And Robbie MacBain. And don't forget Grace's sister, Mary, is still with us. That Mary is a snowy owl is an advantage, I'm thinking."

Grey finally looked over at Daar. "I cannot fight what I can't see, old man." Folding his arms over his chest, he turned to fully face the priest. "If ye had to take a guess, who do ye believe is the threat? Who turned away from his calling?"

Daar squinted up at him. "Cùram, I'm thinking."

"But ye said it's likely a guardian, not a *drùidh.*"

"Ye know that *cùram* is Gaelic for *guardian,*" Daar reminded him. "He's both, Greylen."

"But how can that be? Guardians protect us from you *drùidhs,* ye told Robbie. So how can one man be both? It doesn't make sense."

"Aye," Daar said with a nod. "Ye would think not. But Cùram is a product of both a guardian and a *drùidh,* and they produced an heir who was unique and very powerful."

Grey paled. "If a *drùidh* mates with a guardian, their grandchild is even more powerful than them?"

"Aye. But it also balances out," Daar quickly explained. "Cùram might be a powerful *drùidh,* but he can't use that power against humanity. Ah . . . not directly, anyway."

"So ye think Cùram de Gairn has renounced his guardianship, and that he's the one killing yer tree?"

"Indirectly," Daar emphasized softly, turning to look out over the vista below. "Something has angered or hurt Cùram so badly that he's turned away from his calling. But in doing so, he's also negated a good deal of his powers." Daar looked over and squinted up at Grey again. "And that's why I'm thinking he's trying to find another way to get what he wants."

"And my daughter is about to step into the middle of the bastard's anger and try to stop him?"

Daar nodded. "Aye. Winter was born with the ability to save us."

"She was born a woman!"

Daar softly chuckled. "Aye. And that, MacKeage, is her greatest advantage. Being a woman gives Winter an inner strength no man can ever hope to match. Have ye not seen that same strength in yer own wife?"

Greylen found his first smile of the morning. "Aye. Grace has had me shaking in my boots more than once." He quickly sobered, turned away, and strode down the porch to his waiting horse. After mounting up, he reined around to face the priest. "I must think on what ye've told me this morning. Winter's not going to like this any more than I do. She's an artist, and all she wants to do is capture her beautiful animals and forest on canvas."

"I am well aware of Winter's wants," Daar said, lifting his neatly barbered, white-bearded chin. "Or are ye forgetting I'm the one who talked her into returning home from college?"

"I haven't forgotten, priest," Greylen growled. "Ye came close to getting your home burned down that day."

"She was miserable, MacKeage. She didn't belong in that world, and she knew it." Daar pointed an age-bent finger at him. "And so did you. That's why you and Grace drove all the way to Boston that very night, and packed up her belongings and moved her home."

Grey shook his head. "Aye. I've never been able to deny Winter anything. Or any of my daughters, for that matter. But then, neither have ye," he growled. "It was you who urged Megan to go to Canada with Wayne Ferris to study goose migration."

Daar hunched his shoulders and lowered his gaze, brushing down the front of his black wool cassock. "I'm not a soothsayer," he muttered. "I couldn't foresee that the man was a blackguard."

Grey urged his horse up to the porch rail, right up to the priest who had been interfering in his life for over thirty-eight years. "Then quit yer meddling," he ground out. "Ye've done enough damage already. Ye stay up here in yer cabin and away from my family."

Daar stepped back. "They're all grown up and following their own paths," he said, nodding furiously. "But I . . . I'm still invited to their birthday party, aren't I? I've made a gift for each of them."

"Ye may come to their birthday party," he conceded. "I'll let Robbie MacBain know when Grace and I decide to speak with Winter. Until then, ye tend yer tree and try to find out if it's truly Cùram de Gairn we're dealing with."

Daar nodded furiously, his hands clasped together in front of him. Greylen gave him one last warning glare, then turned his horse and headed back down the mountain.

Damn it to hell. He dreaded his upcoming conversation with Grace.

CHAPTER FIVE

Instead of stopping at the barn upon returning from her visit with Tom, Winter continued on through the thick stand of evergreens that separated her family home from the TarStone Ski Resort. As she guided Snowball across the nearly full parking lot and headed toward the hotel, she noticed that most of the license plates were from states south of New England.

"The leaf-peepers have arrived in full force," she told Snowball, reining him around a car of tourists backing out of a parking slot. "I hope Megan got the gallery opened early." As she rode under the stone and cedar canopy of the hotel entrance, she said, "Good morning, Paul. Only two more weeks of this craziness, then we'll have a short break before the snows come and the skiers arrive."

"I like it when it's busy," the porter said as he took hold of Snowball's bridle and smiled up at her. "The tourists can be entertaining at times."

Winter slid down off her horse and patted Paul's arm as she headed inside. "No need to park him in the valet lot this morning," she said with a laugh. "I'll only be a few minutes."

"There's a guy named Gregor waiting for you in the lobby," Paul told her just as she slipped through the huge glass door.

Winter immediately spotted her target and came to an abrupt stop. Matt Gregor stood with his back to her, studying the large mural of TarStone she'd painted six years ago, which covered the lobby wall all the way up to the balcony connecting the east and west wings of the hotel. He was wearing a pewter gray suit today, equally as expensive and as perfectly tailored as the one he'd been wearing yesterday, and his hair was again pulled back at the nape of his neck.

Saints and curses, the man was even more imposing than she remembered. She could fit ten of her galleries in the three-story lobby, and Matt Gregor still seemed to take up the entire space. Yet the several dozen people milling about were acting as though the most gorgeous man to set foot in Pine Creek didn't even exist. Were they all blind?

Or was she the one blinded by that confounding chemistry her papa had been rumbling about this morning?

Matt Gregor suddenly turned to face her, his sharp golden eyes immediately locking on hers. Winter stood rooted in place, the people having to step around her to exit, and tried to figure out how she was going to spend even one day with this man without making a complete fool of herself.

"You're late," he said from less than three paces away, his silent strides making short work of the large lobby. He stopped in front of her, also oblivious to the chaos around them as his deep, piercing gaze continued to hold her captive. "I've been waiting almost an hour."

"I had to tend a sick pet this morning," Winter said without apology, deciding that if she didn't quickly get the upper hand with this man — or at least get on equal footing — she might as well just throw herself at him right here in the lobby, right in front of God and the tourists. "And I had to visit a friend I've been neglecting. But I'm here now, Mr. Gregor," she continued when he started to say something. "To tell you that I'll take your commission, but with a few stipulations."

He folded his arms over his chest and

lifted one dark brow. "And those would be?" he asked ever so softly.

She already knew quite a lot about Matheson Gregor, Winter realized. Such as his body language, which said he got a bit impatient — if not downright irritated — when things didn't go his way or run on his schedule. Nor did he seem to care to have the conversation directed by someone else. Well, he was going to like her stipulations even less.

"We'll explore your mountain together," she told him, "but we'll always have a third person along with us."

Both of his brows dropped into a frown, his eyes narrowing at what she was implying.

"And," she continued before he could comment, "I'll pick three or maybe four sites for you to choose from, but my sister, Megan, can veto any or all sites if they're unacceptable."

His frown deepened. "Megan? Is she also an artist? I'm hiring you, Miss MacKeage, not a committee."

Winter merely smiled. "You might want to rethink that, Matt," she said, hoping that using his first name would help counter some of that imposing presence the man exuded like elixir. "Megan is a wildlife biologist, and it defeats the purpose of coming to the wilderness to build a beautiful home if you end up destroying that wilderness while you're at it. I've heard there's a deer yard someplace on Bear Mountain, and there are delicate habitats you need to work around. Megan can help you navigate the environmental regulations, and she can ensure that your house and the road to your house are both environmentally friendly and legal."

As she suspected, Matt Gregor might fancy the notion of an artist choosing the location of his home, but he didn't much care to have someone actually telling him what he could and could not do. "What's a deer yard?" he asked.

"It's where the deer gather together to survive the harsh winters. It's usually the same sheltered spot every year, with plenty of feed so they don't have to expend a lot of valuable energy trekking through deep snow. Some yards can hold over a hundred deer, and building a road through one, or even close to one, could be devastating to the herd."

"And your sister, Megan, can get around these regulations?"

"No. She can make sure you don't harm the wilderness just so you can have a pretty

81

view out your front window," Winter said calmly, not caring that she was further irritating him. Actually, she was finding the notion rather invigorating. "We'll head to Bear Mountain this afternoon," she told him.

That imposing brow rose again.

"So you have time to do some shopping at Dolan's Outfitter Store," she continued before he could comment. "Business suits are not exactly horseback riding attire." And again, before he could say anything, Winter spun on her heel to head back outside.

But the lobby door refused to open. Winter looked down and saw a large, familiar hand holding it closed at about the same time she felt the heat of his body all but surrounding hers.

"Is there a reason we're not taking my truck?" he asked softly, his breath moving wisps of her hair.

"You have a truck? I thought you flew in," she said, without moving an inch.

"I bought a truck and had it delivered yesterday."

She finally turned her head to look at him, refusing to step out of his loose embrace. "If you want a true feel for the land, you need to see it on horseback."

Someone pulled on the lobby door, trying

to get in. Matt Gregor let go, stepped back, and Winter slipped out past the people coming in. She took Snowball's reins from Paul and lifted her left foot for him to help her mount.

But instead of her foot being grabbed, two large hands spanned her waist instead, and Winter was effortlessly lifted onto Snowball's back before she could finish gasping. She set her feet in the stirrups and glared down at Matt Gregor, who was looking up at her with eyes glimmering with amusement.

"Megan and I will be here at two," she said before he could speak. "And dress warmly. We likely won't be home until after sunset."

One of those blasted brows rose again, along with one side of his mouth. Matt stepped back with a sudden, chest-rumbling laugh. "I'll see you and your chaperone at two o'clock then," he said.

Winter turned Snowball around with a muttered thank-you to Paul and headed for home without looking back. Not that she could have even if she'd wanted to, what with Matt Gregor's deeply resonating, utterly male laughter still pulsing through every nerve in her body.

■ ■ ■ ■

Winter walked in the back door of Gù Brath and took off her boots before stepping into the monstrous kitchen. "Oh good, you're here," she said to her mother as she walked over to the counter. "I was wondering if you could watch the gallery this afternoon."

"Sorry," Grace MacKeage said without turning away from the counter. "I'm packing a lunch. Your father and I are headed to the summit for a picnic."

Winter plucked a piece of chicken off the platter and popped it in her mouth. "Papa's taking you up the mountain?" she asked once she'd swallowed. "He never mentioned anything about a picnic to me this morning."

"Your father came in from his morning ride and told me to pack a lunch," Grace said, tossing her head to settle her long blonde hair back over her shoulders. "And I'm not pressing my luck by asking questions." She glanced at Winter. "Sorry. You'll have to find someone else to watch the gallery. Maybe Libby's mom can. You know how much Kate enjoys being needed these days."

Stealing one of the slices of tomato, Winter

bolted away from the counter. "That's a good idea," she said. "I'll ask Gram Katie. If she has any problems, Rose is right next door."

"Where are you and Megan off to this afternoon? Before she left this morning, your sister implied she'd be at the gallery until closing."

"She doesn't know it yet, but we're taking a ride to Bear Mountain," Winter explained, opening the fridge. "Megan can still ride a horse, can't she? She's only three months along."

Her mother's hands were clasped against her bosom and the smile on her face was wide enough to make Winter fully straighten in alarm. "What?" Winter asked. "You look like I just discovered the secret to ion propulsion. What are you smiling at?"

"You," Grace said softly. "You're taking Mr. Gregor's commission."

"Then you should be throwing a fit, not smiling. You didn't want me to take it last night."

"No," her mother contradicted with a shake of her head. "Your *father* didn't want you to take it. I just went along with Grey until I could get him alone and change his mind."

"You want me to take Matt Gregor's commission?" Winter whispered. She shook her head with a laugh. "Well, curses. This morning Papa was acting like it was *his* idea."

Grace snorted. "After I spent half the night explaining to that hardheaded man that he had to stop holding onto you with an iron grip." She smoothed down the front of her apron, clasped her hands at her waist, and cleared her throat. "I think you should stop hiding, Winter, and come out and join the living. And if Matt Gregor bothers you as much as I think he does, he just might be the man to make that happen."

"He might also be a serial killer."

Grace gave Winter the same motherly smile she used on her daughters whenever she was determined to get a point across without losing her patience. "The mathematical probability of finding a serial killer wearing an expensive suit, flying here in a private jet, and paying thousands of dollars for a whimsical painting of bear cubs is about the same as your papa asking Father Daar to come live with us at Gù Brath."

Winter closed the fridge door and held up her hands in petition. "Please, no more probabilities," she groaned. "I still haven't gotten over the last time you pointed out my chances of ending up an old hermit like Tom."

"You're a good part of the way there already," Grace said softly. She walked up, pulled Winter's long single braid over her shoulder. "What is it you think you're risking, Winter, by letting your heart lead you into the arms of a man?"

"Independence, maybe?"

Her mama gave her braid a tug. "I've been married for thirty-three years to possibly the bossiest man in the universe," she said, her motherly smile turning even more tender. "And have managed to raise seven well-adjusted daughters despite him. And contrary to popular belief, the day I married your father is the day I *gained* my independence. It's quite liberating, Winter, to follow your heart."

Winter leaned over, kissed her mama's cheek, and stepped away. She headed to the counter and snatched up a slice of tomato, popped it in her mouth, and studied her mother while she chewed and swallowed. "A man came into my gallery yesterday and offered me a commission to choose a building site for him," she finally said. "He did not ask me to marry him, contrary to how you're all acting." She waved a hand at the air. "He didn't even flirt, not even a little bit. Heck, he got irritated when I wouldn't sell him my painting of Gesader. And here you and Papa are acting as if I've turned down his marriage proposal."

"So you aren't attracted to Mr. Gregor?"

"Of course I am. The man is gorgeous."

"Then what's the problem?"

"*I* don't have a problem. You and Papa do. You're telling me to follow my heart when all I said last night was that a man had caught my attention." Winter sighed and shook her head at her frowning mother. "You don't have to worry about me, Mama. I promise I won't become a hermit. I'm taking Matt Gregor's commission, and I'm taking Megan along as chaperone to keep Papa from throwing a fit. And if Matt does ask me out on a date," she said, walking toward the door that led into the hall, "I just might accept. Have fun on your picnic." Winter stopped and pointed a finger at her mother. "Just remember there are hikers out there. I'd hate to see you caught in a compromising position."

"Better me than you," her mother called out as Winter headed down the hall with a laugh.

Pendaär sat in the sunshine on the porch of his cabin, absently running his fingers over the knotted cherrywood burl on his lap, and stared out at Pine Lake as he thought about his conversation with Greylen MacKeage that morning. No man wanted to hear that his daughter was about to enter a battle of such magnitude, much less that she was destined to live a very long life of solitude.

Pendaär remembered his own emotional struggle some eighteen hundred years ago, when he had come face-to-face with his own destiny. But the true pain would likely come with the realization that she was going to witness the deaths of her loved ones for generations to come, while she went on living without them, alone, for centuries.

Robbie MacBain had called Pendaär's destiny a curse once, and there were days Pendaär couldn't help but agree with him. Everyone he had ever loved had died, while he had been forced to carry on without them; his own mama and papa, his four brothers and two sisters, his nieces and nephews, and on and on it had endlessly gone for dozens of lifetimes.

He'd tried once, about fourteen hundred years ago, to simply keep his distance from people. But Providence was an undeniable master, and a dispassionate *drùidh* could not be an effective servant. So Pendaär had spent nearly two millennia caring for and then watching his loved ones die — just as he was going to watch Greylen and Grace die, and Morgan and Callum, and even Robbie MacBain. And then there were Grey's six oldest daughters . . . and their children . . . and their grandchildren . . .

Only Winter would be with him this time, until his own eventual death — and then the precious lass would be on her own.

Pendaär stood up, tucked the cherrywood burl in his pocket, and leaned against the porch rail as he stared out over the circle of mountains cradling Pine Lake. This trouble that was brewing, it was being carried in on a cold wind of utter hopelessness. Pendaär could all but see the colorless void of a soul who had simply given up. And of all the human frailties, hopelessness was the most insidious, feeding upon itself until it became all consuming.

Pendaär scratched his chin as he wondered what had happened to Cùram de Gairn to turn him so bitterly away from his calling. Aye, he was positive it was the young wizard stirring the storm clouds, as Cùram was the only *drùidh* who couldn't be accounted for right now.

As Grey had suggested in their conversation this morning, Pendaär had already gone to his fellow *drùidhs* and asked for their help. And all of them, along with their own army of guardians, had told him they were too busy trying to save their own trees to offer assistance. They had, however, agreed that the storm was brewing almost directly over Pendaär's head, and therefore it was his duty to stop it before it reached them.

Pendaär had grown frustrated with their political posturing and had left the council with every intention of saving their sorry souls despite themselves. With Winter's help, of course.

He took the cherrywood burl out of his pocket and gazed at it with a tired sigh. It wasn't much to show for his years of nurturing the energies of life. He'd been hoarding what was left of its knowledge, refusing to tap into the white pine he had hidden high up on TarStone Mountain. Winter would need whatever energy remained in the weakened tree, and this afternoon he must prune one of the branches to make Winter her own delicate staff.

Pendaär clasped the burl to his chest, letting its weak hum softly resonate through him as he slid his gaze toward Gù Brath. Aye, Greylen must explain her destiny to his youngest daughter soon, before the storm broke over them with the vengeance of a hopelessness that even Winter's powerful love of life might not be able to overcome.

CHAPTER SIX

"I still don't see why I have to ride Butterball instead of Goose Down. Yesterday you said being pregnant isn't a disease, but today you're treating me like an invalid."

Winter frowned at her grumbling sister riding beside her. "Matt needs to ride your horse," she explained yet again as they rode away from the barn, with Winter leading the riderless Goose Down behind her. "You haven't exercised Goose in weeks, and I don't want you getting thrown. And since we both know Butterball is too lazy to buck off a fly, he's perfect for you."

Megan actually smiled. "But it's okay if Goose bucks off your Mr. Gregor?"

"He's not *my* mister anything," Winter said through gritted teeth, glaring at Megan. "And you behave yourself today and not make any sly remarks. This is a business venture we're on."

Megan snorted and urged Butterball into

a trot, but the aging draft horse only managed an extended ambling walk, completely ruining Megan's offended act. Butterball really belonged to Camry, who now lives in Florida, working for NASA.

Winter followed in silence as she half anticipated, half dreaded seeing Matt again. Oh, how that man disturbed her in so many ways, on so many different levels. He was handsome as all get out, mysteriously compelling, and . . . well, dang it, he also seemed familiar to her. Yes, there was something about Matheson Gregor that made Winter think she knew him — or should know him. His eyes, maybe. When she looked into Matt's deep, golden eyes, she had the eerie feeling they had met before.

Matt's size certainly didn't bother her; she'd grown up in an extended family of large, physical, imposing Scots. Even Matt's arrogance wasn't a problem; she was used to male posturing that was more often bluster than menace.

So how come he disturbed her so much? Why did her heart race whenever she saw him?

Curses, this chemistry thing was confusing.

Winter sighed as she followed Megan

through the parking lot toward the hotel entrance. She was just going to have to play this out, she decided, and see where it led.

Paul stepped away from a group of tourists gathered at the entrance, greeted Megan and Winter with a nod as they walked under the tall canopy, and took hold of Butterball's bridle.

Matt Gregor stepped through the lobby door just then and abruptly stopped, his polite smile instantly disappearing at the sight of the two women and three horses. "What the hell?" he whispered, his glare settling on Winter. "I am not riding a plow horse."

As powerful and imposing as he looked in a suit, Matt Gregor in casual dress defied description. Faded, muscle-hugging jeans, scarred work boots, and a soft-looking, muted-gray flannel shirt had transformed the polished businessman into a rugged outdoorsman.

Remembering her need to keep the upper hand, Winter gave Matt a taste of his own medicine and lifted one brow. "Our horses have pulled a few pranks on us over the years, but I assure you, they have never pulled a plow."

"That," Matt said, pointing at Goose Down while keeping his glare locked on her, "is a workhorse."

Winter patted Goose as he lazily nuzzled Snowball's neck. "Goose is a Percheron, and he's perfect transportation for where we're going today. He's sure-footed and bomb-proof." She kicked up a slight grin. "Assuming he likes you well enough to let you ride him."

Matt's eyes narrowed at her challenge, and he walked over and took Goose's reins. He moved Goose away from her, carefully tied his jacket to the back of the saddle, then set his left foot in the stirrup and mounted up with the ease of a man who was obviously comfortable around horses.

He expertly reined the suddenly alert Goose over to Megan and held out his hand. "Matt Gregor," he said with an amiable smile. "I appreciate you giving up your afternoon to be our chaperone."

Megan dropped her gaze to the hand he was holding out. "Ah . . . Megan," she whispered, finally setting her tiny hand in his.

Matt gently shook it, then looked at Winter and gave an imperial wave of that same hand. "Shall we ride, then," he said. "I'm anxious to finally see my land."

"You bought Bear Mountain without even seeing it?" Winter asked in surprise.

Matt started his own horse toward the parking lot. "I saw a map of it, and aerial photos." He looked over when she caught up with him. "I could just make out a small cabin in one of the photos, on the shoreline. I thought it might be a good place to build a house, since someone else must have thought so, too."

"If you don't mind rebuilding four miles of old tote road," Winter said. "That cabin is out on a narrow point, and the only access is by way of a winding logging road that travels halfway up and down Bear Mountain." She gave him another challenging grin. "Or you could park on the main road and hike the mile of shoreline to get to your new home."

"Or I could just build a road along that shoreline."

"No, actually, you can't," Megan interjected, finally getting Butterball to catch up so that they were riding three abreast up the driveway that led through the woods to Gù Brath. "You'd have to cross a large bog and then build a bridge across Bear Brook where it runs into Pine Lake. The regulations regarding wetlands are strict, and I doubt you could even get a permit."

Matt frowned ahead of them, then looked at Megan. "So I can't build anywhere on the shoreline?"

"You can, as long as you keep a large setback from both the lake and any nearby bogs."

"Or you could build farther up on the mountain," Winter suggested, drawing his attention. "The trade-off to hearing the waves lap the shore would be to have a really spectacular view."

Matt nodded thoughtfully. "That might work." He turned to Megan. "Are the regulations as —" He suddenly brought Goose to an abrupt halt. "Is that a castle?" he asked, staring at the large structure in front of them.

"That's Gù Brath, our home," Winter explained, not surprised by his reaction. She let her gaze follow his, to travel up the towering walls of their stone and granite home. "And it's a keep, not a castle. A keep is only part of a castle, usually the central, most secure tower. Our papa and uncles didn't need a home as big as a castle, so they built a keep."

"Is that a moat?"

"Not really," Winter said with a chuckle. "It's the stream that runs off the mountain, and it's only on this side of the structure. The bridge you have to cross to get to the door does pull up, though, like a draw-bridge."

It seemed Matt couldn't stop staring at Gù Brath. "It hardly has any windows," he said. "And that black stone. What is it?"

Winter shrugged, but Matt didn't see the gesture. He was busy examining her home. "It's the rock TarStone gets its name from. It runs in fissures through the gray granite of the mountain, as wide as a football field in some places. The stone was brought down the mountain to build our home some thirty-five years ago."

Matt finally looked at her. "You called it Gù Brath. What does that mean, and how is it spelled?"

"It's spelled G-U B-R-A-T-H, and it's Gaelic for 'forever.' Our papa and uncles named their home *Forever* because they said they were never moving again."

Matt narrowed his eyes at her, apparently suspicious he was getting only the tourist's version. He went back to examining her home. "That section on the left side. That looks newer than the rest of the . . . house," he observed.

"That's our family wing, added twenty-six years ago. The wing has nine bedrooms, a swimming pool, a computer lab, and a really big kitchen."

Matt looked at her again. "Did I hear right yesterday? There are seven of you Mac-Keage girls? I mean women," he quickly amended with an apologetic grin.

"Yes. Though just Megan and I live at home now."

"Where do you fall in the birth order?"

Winter widened her smile. "I'm the baby girl." She nodded toward Megan. "We have a sister named Elizabeth between us, and then there's Megan's twin, Chelsea, our twin sisters Sarah and Camry, and Heather is the oldest."

"All are married but you?"

Despite thinking he was being impolitely curious, Winter decided to continue explaining her family to Matt, so he would know what he was getting himself into — just in case he *might* be thinking of asking her on a date. "Heather is married and living in California with her husband and three bairns. Sarah is married with one bairn, and lives in Scotland. Camry is single and a scientist for NASA in Florida, Chelsea has four boys and is a lawyer in Bangor, and Elizabeth teaches third grade here in Pine Creek. She has two kids," she finished with a laugh at his look of awe.

"And when are you and your husband

expecting your child?" Matt asked, looking at Megan.

Megan's face turned three shades of red. "I . . . I'm not married," she whispered.

"Forgive me," Matt murmured. "Seeing your condition, I just assumed —"

"How do you know she's pregnant?" Winter asked, drawing his attention away from her mortified sister. "She's not even showing yet."

Matt shook his head, his smile softening his features, then turned that smile on Megan. "Women have a certain look when they're expecting," he softly told Megan. "A beautiful glow." He reached out and laid a hand on Butterball's mane, just above where Megan was holding the reins. "I apologize if I've embarrassed you. But at the risk of being even more impolite, is the father around?"

Megan, looking down at his hand on Butterball's mane, merely shook her head.

"Does he know about the child?"

"He knows," Winter snapped, deciding Matt Gregor was getting much too personal about something that was none of his business. "And Megan is better off without the slimy coward," she added, using Snowball to crowd Matt's horse into moving up the trail. "We need to get going or we'll miss the sunset from Bear Mountain."

Matt settled Goose back down to a walk, continuing up the forest road just past Gù Brath, and turned to Winter, looking not the least bit apologetic. "I only asked because I have several connections in my business," he softly told her the moment they were out of Megan's hearing. "Which allow me to reach people in a multitude of ways. Give me his name, and I can make him show up here tomorrow, vowing his undying love for your sister."

Winter blinked at him. Was this guy for real? He couldn't be offering to strong-arm Wayne Ferris.

Matt sighed and shook his head. "Look, I know it's none of my business. But I hate —" He moved his gaze to the trail ahead. "I had a sister once in the same situation, only at the time there was nothing I could do to help her." He looked over his shoulder to check on Megan, then back at Winter. "But I can certainly help your sister, if you want me to."

"Why would Megan want a slimy coward declaring undying love to her? She's better off without him."

Matt grinned. "You have a point. Okay then, give me his name and I'll make him sorry he ever met Megan."

Winter found her own smile, thinking of Wayne Ferris getting his comeuppance. "Just like that," she said to Matt. "You would go after a man you don't even know, for a woman you just met?"

"It would be my pleasure," he said ever so softly, once more checking on Megan before looking back at Winter. "I couldn't do anything for my sister, but I can help Megan."

Winter thought about that, about this new facet of the man whose golden eyes she found so compelling. Apparently, he had a personal code of justice he lived by, albeit a tad skewed if he was willing to punish one man for another man's crime. How interesting. And disturbing.

"I thank you for your offer, but we Mac-Keages take care of our own." Winter suddenly spotted Gesader high up in a large oak tree, sprawled on a branch overhanging the tote road, his huge, unblinking yellow eyes locked on the procession making its way toward him. "So," she said brightly, turning to Matt with a broad smile, "why don't you tell me what it is you want in a home, so I can begin to picture it in my mind."

Matt looked at her sharply, and Winter realized she may have sounded a bit too enthused while changing the subject.

"I don't want a very large home," he said. "Something more comfortable than showy. I was thinking logs, maybe. A northern lodge, all wood inside and out, with a tall central room that has a large stone hearth."

Winter nodded. "That would certainly fit nicely on your mountain," she agreed, canting her head and looking upward, as if she were picturing Matt's home. "With plenty of windows facing west to catch the sunset," she added as they slowly rode under her silent, motionless pet. She looked behind her and waved to Megan. "Come on, Meg. Get Butterball moving," she called back, turning her glare up on Gesader, who had turned his head and was now watching her and Matt riding away.

Gesader gave Winter a panther smile that nicely showed off his fangs, then casually started cleaning one of his paws with his broad pink tongue.

"I was thinking of getting the timber for the house off my land," Matt continued. Winter turned back around and smiled at him. "I've read that a sawmill can be set up right on the site to make dimensional lumber."

"There are some portable mills around here," she told him. "But I think the logs have to season before you build with them. You'll have to ask a contractor."

Megan finally caught up, giving Winter an amused look while bobbing her eyebrows to say that she had seen Gesader. Megan then took over the conversation with Matt, helping him weigh the pros and cons of cutting his own timber.

Winter only half listened, thinking instead that she was going to kill that black imp for taking such a chance, when it suddenly dawned on her why Matt seemed so familiar.

Matheson Gregor's eyes were the mirror image of Gesader's.

Matt sat reclined on the high, flat boulder and slowly savored the last bite of his tart apple pie. Megan had pulled an entire picnic from her saddlebags about half an hour ago, when they'd stopped on a bluff high up on Bear Mountain. Matt had taken the generous portion of food Megan had handed him and climbed up on the huge boulder to eat while the two sisters opted to sit on a log about twenty feet away. But instead of enjoying the stunning view of Pine Lake over a thousand feet below, Matt found watching Megan and Winter a far more interesting diversion.

They were definitely sisters; they both had rich, strawberry blonde hair, trim figures, flawless complexions, and similar facial features and mannerisms. Winter's hair was woven into a single braid that reached clear to her waist, while Megan's hair fell loosely down to her shoulders. Winter was about three or four inches taller than Megan, and maybe a tad more curved in all the right places. Both wore snug jeans, scuffed boots, and heavy fleeces over turtleneck jerseys.

The only difference between the women was their eyes. Megan's eyes were a sharp, clear green, while Winter's were an even more vivid crystalline blue, as deep and as reflective as the late September sky overhead. Both women appeared comfortable in the forest, though Matt wasn't surprised, learning that Megan was a field biologist and having seen Winter's paintings.

Winter MacKeage didn't just paint animals, she painted . . . well, she painted their souls. She somehow managed to draw an observer deep into the world she created on nothing more than canvas, bringing the flat surface to life in an almost mystical way. Hell, even her carefully detailed trees and moss-covered boulders seemed to resonate with energy.

The moment he'd spotted the painting

hanging in her gallery window of a mother deer and two fawns grazing in a springtime meadow, Matt had realized he not only had to meet the artist — which he had innately known was female — but that he had to find a way to enter her mystical world.

Winter MacKeage's physical beauty was merely a bonus.

Matt thought back to their conversation at the resort. He'd almost blown it back at Gù Brath, when he'd let his anger at Megan's predicament get the best of him. He'd come damn close to scaring Winter off, and that was definitely the last thing he wanted to do.

Matt lazily brushed the crumbs off his chest, listening to the low hum of Megan and Winter talking as he gazed out over Pine Lake. The sun hung low in the sky, and he guessed they had about two hours before it dropped behind the chain of mountains on the western shore of the lake, which was nearly thirty-five miles long and seventeen miles across at its widest point. It was a massive body of water, set close to the Canadian border to the northwest, completely surrounded by rugged mountains and wilderness broken only by occasional small towns.

His research had also revealed the lake

was fast becoming a retirement community for corporate executives who were tired of urban congestion. Retirement wasn't what had brought him here, though. No, it was the land itself that had drawn him: the mountains, clear waters teeming with fish, and the hum of energy that seemed to pulse through the air like nuclear fission.

That, and his unfinished business with his brother.

"How come you have a slight accent and Megan doesn't?" Matt asked, brushing the last of the crumbs off his hands.

Both women looked up, Megan smiling and Winter frowning.

"I've spent most of the last nine years away from my family," Megan answered before Winter could. "College wiped out what was left of my brogue."

"College didn't wipe out your brogue?" he asked Winter.

Her frown turned into a scowl, and Matt held in his smile. Winter MacKeage was a prickly little thing, always trying to stand her ground against him.

"I didn't care for college," she said, getting to her feet and gathering up the leftover food rather than look at him.

"You didn't even attend art school?"

She finally looked up, her expression saying it was none of his business. But again it was Megan who answered for her, also standing up. "College isn't for everyone," she said. "Not if their path is leading them in another direction."

Matt jumped down from the boulder and held up his hands in supplication. "I have nothing against uneducated women," he said, watching with amusement as Winter bristled in outrage.

"I am well educated," she snapped.

Again Matt held up his hands, finally freeing his laughter. "I'm teasing, Winter. There's an intelligence in your paintings the rest of us can only hope to have. You see and feel and understand more about life than a whole university of scholars. I was just teasing," he repeated.

The poor woman didn't seem to know how to respond, all that bluster she'd worked up slowly deflating as she stared at him.

"We need to get down to Talking Tom's," Megan said, packing up what was left of the picnic. "It's going to get chilly as soon as that sun sets, and you need to get your jacket, Winter."

"Talking Tom?" Matt repeated, going over and helping Megan by handing her the wrappers to put in her saddlebags.

"He lives in the cabin on the point," Megan explained. "And Winter forgot her jacket there this morning."

"In my cabin?"

Megan straightened, her chin lifting defensively. "Tom's lived there for the last two and a half years, not bothering anyone. It's an old run-down cabin, and it's only accessible by boat or on foot. He's not bothering anyone," she repeated.

And again, Matt held up his hands. "I was just surprised to hear that anyone lives there. Why do you call him Talking Tom?"

"Everyone calls him that, because he talks to himself when he walks the woods," Winter told Matt, apparently having gotten over his teasing, though her scowl was still in place. "He talks to himself so the bears hear him coming. There's nothing nastier than walking up on a surprised bear. That's why we have bells on our horses."

"I wondered about those. They were driving me crazy."

"Better crazy than mauled."

"So this Talking Tom. Who is he?"

Winter shrugged. "He showed up here a little over two years ago," she told him. "Do you remember seeing the wood carvings in my gallery? Tom did them."

"And nobody knows anything about this

man, who just walked into town and took up residence in someone else's cabin?"

Winter waved at the forest around them. "There's dozens of old abandoned cabins in these woods. Most of the land belongs to the paper and lumber mills, and as long as they're not actively cutting an area, they don't bother people who aren't bothering them."

"You won't kick Tom out, will you?" Megan asked, looking at Matt with worried eyes. "He respects the land and the animals. He's not hurting anything by staying there. And . . . and we don't think he has any place else to go."

Matt couldn't help but smile at the pleading woman. "Is that why you don't think the point would be a good place for me to build?" he asked, looking at Winter to include her. "Because you don't want Talking Tom evicted?"

Both women shook their heads. "You'd have to clear all the trees to put a home on that narrow point," Winter said. "And that would expose your house to the strong winds that blow in off the lake."

"And building up here wouldn't?" he asked, waving at the open expanse in front of them. "This is just as exposed."

"The point is too narrow for the legal

setback from the lake required for new construction," Megan said. "You can't build there even if you wanted to."

Matt took the saddlebag from Megan, carried it over to her sleeping horse, and tied it on the back of her saddle.

"Well?" Winter asked, untying her own horse's reins. "Are you going to evict Tom?"

"I haven't even met the man," he said, untying his own horse and mounting up. He looked down at the two women glaring up at him and smiled. "But I'll take your resounding endorsements of his character into consideration."

"If you kick him out, I'm not taking your commission."

Matt nodded. "I will also factor that in."

Winter looked mad enough to spit. Matt turned his horse away before she could see his amusement and headed in the general direction of the point of land Talking Tom was calling home. But he stopped and looked back when he realized he was riding alone. Both women had led their horses over to what was left of an old stump, and Winter held her sister's horse while Megan tried to mount up.

"Wait," he called, trotting back to them and dismounting with a laugh. "I forgot you can't reach your stirrups." He leaned over and laced his fingers into a step for Megan. "You two ride such massive animals. Why not normal horses?"

Megan stepped into his hands and Matt lifted her into the saddle. She gathered up her reins and smiled down at him. "We had a rather opinionated uncle who thought draft horses were the only safe pet for us girls. He said ponies were spoiled brats and regular horses were unpredictable." She nodded toward Matt's horse. "Goose Down is my second pet. The first horse Uncle Ian gave me, Lancelot, had to be put to sleep ten years ago when he broke his leg."

"So Goose is really your horse?" he asked as he turned to help Winter mount, only to find her sitting in her saddle. Apparently, she was back to being mad at him.

"I'd like to meet your uncle Ian," Matt said, remounting and reining Goose into step behind Winter as she headed out of the clearing.

"He . . . ah, died three years ago," Megan said.

"I'm sorry," Matt murmured, falling silent as they carefully made their way down the side of the mountain. They eventually came upon a shallow gorge, the granite and tumbled boulders worn smooth by cascading water as it swirled down the mountain with seemingly endless energy. "Bear Brook, I take it?" Matt asked loudly, to be heard above the noise. He moved between Winter and Megan as they stood with their horses' hooves just touching the water so they could drink. He gave Goose his head, so he could also drink.

Winter looked over at Matt, her expression aloof. "There's a clearing downstream that might make a good building site."

"Is there a view of the lake?"

"You can see the lake from anywhere on this mountain, if you don't mind chopping down acres of trees."

Matt leaned over to Megan. "Is your sister always this pleasant with her patrons?"

"She's just worried about Tom," Megan told him, also leaning close so Winter wouldn't hear. "Otherwise, she usually has a great sense of humor. And she's still a little touchy about leaving college after only one semester."

Matt gave Megan a nod, backed Goose out from between them, and turned to start down the mountain along the stream. They rode for several minutes, winding their way through the thick forest, and Matt let Goose pick the easiest route. The stream eventually broke through to a natural meadow, and part of Pine Lake came into view again.

"We can cross here," Winter called out.

Matt turned Goose into the stream, and the horse stepped through the knee-deep, babbling water with sure-footed care. Once he was on the other side, Matt looked around the meadow as Winter and Megan moved up beside him.

"I like it here," he said. "Where would I place the house?" he asked, looking over at Winter.

She pointed toward the high side of the meadow. "Up there, maybe. That would be the best view."

Matt looked at Megan. "Can I build here without disturbing too much of the wildlife?"

Megan shrugged. "Probably. I know there's a deer yard up here somewhere. Tom might know where it is."

"What about building a road? We've come, what . . . three or four miles from the main road?"

"It can be done," Megan assured him. "If you have deep pockets. Roads and bridges aren't cheap."

"But the logging companies build hundreds of miles of forest roads all the time," Matt pointed out. "They must have a system that doesn't break the bank."

"You could hire men from their crews,"

Winter suggested. "To build it on week-ends."

"That would take forever to finish four miles of road." He shook his head. He looked at the lengthening shadows creeping across the meadow and urged Goose forward. "Let's go get your jacket," he said. "And you can introduce me to my tenant."

They rode three abreast through the meadow until Megan suddenly stopped. "Look," she said, pointing at the ground. "See the disturbed grass?" She looked around the clearing, then over at Matt, and smiled. "I bet there was a big battle up here last night. Have you ever seen two bull moose fighting, Matt?"

"No," he said, shaking his head as he visually examined the broken shrub and matted grass. "Is it rutting season?"

"It's just starting," Megan clarified, walking her horse in a circle as she studied the ground. She looked at Matt. "This is moose country. I hope you don't mind sharing your home with huge animals that think landscaping shrubs are candy. In the language of the Micmac Indians, moose means 'twig eater.' "

"What about bear?" Matt asked, scanning the edge of the clearing. "I'm assuming they named it Bear Mountain because bear live up here."

"The mountain was named for what it looks like rather than what lives on it," Winter interjected. "If you see this mountain from the lake, you can just make out the image of a sleeping bear." She pointed to an area just below the summit. "From a distance, that dropped ridge would be his head, stretched out over his front paws. The brook cuts a winding path that makes the outline of a rear leg tucked against his body, and the long, narrow peak," she said, pointing first to the south end of the knife-edge peak, then to the north, "is his back, finishing the illusion."

Matt just stared at Winter in silence, watching her hand stroke out a drawing only her mind's eyes could see. This was it; he was witnessing firsthand the magic he'd felt in her paintings. Winter's eyes sparked with passion, her whole body moving into each gesture as her hand gracefully stroked out the lines of her vision. She had forgotten he and Megan were even there, Matt suddenly realized. Winter was completely immersed in a painting only her imagination could see.

Dancing to a magic only she could feel.

If he had any doubts before, they were

vanished at the sight of Winter MacKeage the artist. And one way or another, Matt decided, he would find a way to capture some of that magic for himself.

CHAPTER SEVEN

Winter hadn't been bluffing up on the mountain: if Matt told Tom he had to move out of his cabin, she wasn't taking his commission. She'd be danged if she would work for a man who didn't have a heart.

Winter led the silent procession along the shoreline to the tiny clearing and stopped in front of Tom's cabin. She quickly slid down off Snowball and headed out back to the workshop.

"Tom," she called as she rounded the side of the cabin. "I forgot my jacket this morning."

Tom emerged from the workshop, once again taking the time to wrestle the rickety door shut before he turned and greeted her with a crooked grin. "I'm glad your head is attached to your shoulders, or you probably would have forgotten that, too."

"Tom," Winter said softly, rushing up to

him. "The guy who bought Bear Mountain is here."

"Good. I've been looking forward to meeting your Mr. Gregor ever since you told me about him this morning," Tom said calmly, using his finger under her chin to close her gaping mouth.

Winter spun around and followed Tom as he headed to the front of the cabin. Tom reached Megan just as Matt had finished helping her down off her horse. Turning Winter's sister around to face him, Tom folded her into a warm, grandfatherly embrace.

"It's good to see you out and about, Meg," he said, kissing her forehead, then leaning back with a tender smile. "I've been waiting for you to come visit me." He brushed Megan's hair back into place. "I have something for you."

Megan shook her head with a laugh. "No more chocolates, Tom. I'm getting fat."

"No chocolates," he said, stepping away. "It's something I made just for you." Tom turned to face Matt and held out his hand. "Name's Tom, Mr. Gregor. Welcome to Bear Mountain. You own a very special piece of land."

Winter held her breath as the two men faced each other.

"So I've been discovering," Matt said, reaching out and shaking Tom's hand. He looked around the tiny clearing, then brought his gaze back to Tom. "But you should know, having lived here for over two years."

Tom nodded. "I do," he agreed, heading for his cabin. "Megan, come see your surprise." He stopped and looked at Winter. "Don't take their bridles off," he told her. "The sun sets in another hour, and you have to be back in town by then."

"We were planning to watch the sunset from the high meadow," Matt said, still standing beside Megan's horse.

Tom looked at him. "I want the girls out of the woods by dark."

Matt narrowed his eyes. "Because of the panther?"

"What panther?" Winter asked, drawing Matt's attention. "The one in the painting in my gallery?" She shook her head. "I just felt like painting a jungle cat."

"That's not what I heard in town yesterday. Rumor has it a large black panther has been seen around TarStone Mountain." Matt looked over at Tom. "I have a gun rolled up in my jacket."

Winter grew alarmed. "You brought a gun? Why?"

Matt just lifted a brow at her.

"Because he's a smart man," Tom said, looking directly at Matt and nodding. "But it's not four-legged animals you're likely to tangle with after dark, but two-legged poachers trying to get a jump on hunting season." He studied Matt for several seconds and then said, "You want to see a sunset from the meadow, I'll take you up there tomorrow afternoon."

Matt contemplated his tenant in silence, glanced briefly at Winter, then nodded to Tom. "I'll be here at three."

Winter became even more alarmed. What was Tom doing? Didn't he realize Matt could kick him out of his home?

But then she relaxed. Maybe their spending time together would work in Tom's favor. Maybe once Matt realized how harmless Tom was, he wouldn't care that her friend was living out here on the point. Heck, Matt might even consider it a plus, to have someone overseeing his land when he was in New York.

Yeah, maybe Tom knew exactly what he was doing.

Tom turned and went into his cabin while Megan stood beside the door. He reemerged with a small object in his hands, bundled in a towel. Both Winter and Matt moved closer to see.

"I started it when you came home last month, finished it just last week," Tom told Megan, holding the bundle in one hand and slowly peeling away the towel. "But I was waiting until you came out here to visit me to give it to you."

Megan's eyes widened the moment her gift was revealed, her gaze shooting to Tom before looking back at the wooden figure.

"It's beautiful," Winter said on an indrawn breath, stepping even closer.

"Take it, Meg," Tom said softly. "It's not as delicate as it looks. I carved it from oak. You won't break it."

Megan finally reached out and carefully took the foot-tall carving of a bear. "Oh, she's got a cub tucked in her legs," Megan said, turning the figure to study it. She looked up at Tom again, and Winter saw the sheen of tears welling up in her eyes. "She . . . she's beautiful," Megan said, dropping her gaze back to the mother bear. "And her tiny cub. It's looking up with an expression of such . . . such . . ." Megan's voice trailed off as her throat closed with emotion.

"With trust," Tom finished for her. "And love." He reached out and tucked Megan's hair behind her ear. "That cub knows his mother loves him more than life itself. And he trusts her to protect him. It's a bond that began in the womb, Megan."

Megan clasped the mother and cub to her chest, brushed away an escaping tear, and rose up and gave Tom a kiss on his reddened cheek. "Th-thank you," she whispered. "I love it."

"You set it by your bedside," Tom softly told her. "So at night when you sleep, you'll dream of your own little cub growing inside you. Bears are fierce protectors, Megan, as well as symbols of healing. And you," he said, lifting her chin to make her look at him. "You, Megan MacKeage, have the heart of a bear."

Winter felt her own eyes misting as she stared at the figure clutched to her sister's chest. She had seen many of Tom's carvings over the last two years, but this one . . . this one outshone all the others. The expression on the mother bear's broad face was fierce and loving and proud as she looked down at her tiny defenseless cub.

Tom gave Megan's shoulder a pat, then suddenly turned to Winter with a crooked smile. "You don't get your gift for three more months, so don't even ask. Besides," he said, tucking her arm through his and leading her over to Snowball, "you need to practice your patience."

But just as Tom bent over to lace his fingers together to make her a step, another set of strong hands took hold of her waist and lifted her into the saddle. Winter managed only to give a small squeak this time, and turned and glared down at Matt. Tom chuckled and headed to the cabin, shaking his head.

Matt returned her glare with a triumphant smile, turned, and took the rewrapped bundle from Megan and carefully stowed it in her saddlebag. Then he leaned over, laced his fingers together and helped Winter's still-emotional sister mount up.

Tom came out of the cabin carrying Winter's jacket. "You head straight home on the shoreline path," he instructed, handing her the jacket. "I'll be at your gallery early in the morning to settle up. I noticed my large moose carving has sold."

"Some lady from Arizona wasn't leaving Maine without it," Winter told him. "I swear she made her husband buy that moose its own airline seat for the ride home. She wouldn't even trust it to be shipped, afraid an antler might get broken."

Tom stepped closer and lowered his voice. "Can you find a way to get my money from that moose to the Dalton family without them knowing where it came from? I want those kids to have some toys under their tree this Christmas."

"I can find a way," she whispered back.

"Good," Tom said with a nod. "Sam Dalton needs the help, but it can't look like charity."

"I'll use the same method I used with the Greeleys."

Tom suddenly turned to Matt, who had mounted up and was frowning at them. "You're going to need a road built, Gregor," Tom told him. "And I know just the man to build it."

Matt lifted one brow. "You?" he asked.

Tom shook his head. "A guy by the name of Sam Dalton. He busted his leg up pretty badly a couple of months ago, but his head still works fine. He used to be on the paper mill's road crew. Sam knows construction."

"Then I'll look Dalton up, once Winter decides where I'm going to build."

Tom nodded and stepped away from Snowball. "Get going then," he said to Winter. "The sun's setting."

But it was Megan who led the way out of the clearing with a final wave to Tom, taking the path that wove through the woods along Pine Lake. Winter fell into step behind Megan and Matt, looking back just as the forest started closing in on them. Tom was standing in his clearing, his arms folded across his chest and his feet planted wide, watching them leave. Winter turned back around and stared at Matt's broad shoulders as she contemplated the old hermit's expression with growing alarm.

Aye. Tom had been looking much too smug, she decided.

They reached the main street of Pine Creek just as the setting sun washed the sky in a glow of purple and red twilight. Winter stopped Snowball in front of her gallery and was just dismounting when her cell phone rang.

"Hello," she answered as Matt helped Megan dismount.

"Where are ye?" her papa said without preamble.

"I'm standing in front of my gallery. Megan, Matt, and I just rode into town. Where are you?"

"We're still on the mountain," her papa said. "I'm calling to tell ye we're spending the night up here."

Winter frowned. "You are? Why?"

Greylen chuckled. "Because yer mother wants to."

"But it's supposed to get below freezing

126

tonight. And you didn't take camping gear."

There was a heartbeat of hesitation on the other end of the phone before her papa softly drawled, "I believe I still remember how to keep my wife warm."

Despite his humor, Winter heard the strain in her papa's voice, and her frown deepened. "I'm sure you do. I'm just surprised, is all. Is everything okay?" she asked. "Can I talk to Mama?"

There was another, longer hesitation. "Nay," her papa said softly. "She's having a nap."

"But —"

"I'm just calling to let ye know we're staying the night," he said, cutting her off. "So ye won't worry. We'll be back tomorrow. Ye lock up tight tonight, and if ye girls need anything, call Robbie."

"But —"

"We'll see ye tomorrow, baby girl," he said gently, cutting her off again.

Winter could only stare at the tiny phone in her hand when the connection suddenly went dead.

"Was that Papa?" Megan asked. "What did he want?"

"They're staying up on the mountain tonight," Winter told her, still frowning. "He claims it was Mama's idea, yet he wouldn't let me talk to her because he said she was napping. But I was sure I could hear her in the background, and it sounded like she was . . . sobbing or something."

"Sobbing?" Megan repeated, stepping closer. "Are you sure it wasn't an animal you heard? A squirrel, maybe? Or the wind?"

Winter blinked at her sister, then shrugged. "It could have been, I suppose. But they hadn't planned on spending the night, and don't have any equipment. And when they left this afternoon, Papa was . . . well, he seemed preoccupied. Like something was bothering him."

"It's a little late in the season to be camping out, isn't it?" Matt asked.

"Not really," Megan said, turning to him. "Not for our family. We're used to camping out in all kinds of weather."

Matt nodded, though he still seemed concerned by Winter's and Megan's obvious worry. He suddenly smiled. "Then I guess you ladies are at loose ends tonight. Why don't I take you both to dinner at the resort?"

Megan immediately shook her head. "Thank you," she said, "but I'm babysitting tonight." She looked past Matt and broke into a wide smile. "And here's my ride now."

Winter turned just in time to be swept up

in a firm hug. "Hello, baby girl. Been out painting pretty pictures today?"

Winter could only mumble into the chest against her face. Her attacker laughed, kissed her on the forehead, then let her go and turned to Matt. "Robbie MacBain," he said, extending his hand. "Have these two outlaws been giving ye a private tour of Tar-Stone Mountain?"

Winter stilled in the act of brushing a strand of loose hair off her cheek, alarmed by the expression on Matt's face as he stared at Robbie. What the heck was going on? Matt Gregor looked angry enough to chew nails.

Still keeping his hand extended, Robbie reached out with his other hand and pulled Winter up against him in another possessive embrace. "Did I hear ye asking my girls out to dinner tonight?"

Winter reached under Robbie's jacket and pinched him quite hard in his side, just above his belt. He didn't even flinch, but he did squeeze most of the air from her lungs.

"I should warn ye, this one isn't a cheap date," Robbie continued, still holding out his hand, still waiting for Matt to shake it. "She might be tiny, but my cousin has the appetite of a moose."

Matt Gregor's shoulders suddenly relaxed

and his eyes went back to their warm harvest gold as he finally reached out and firmly shook Robbie's hand. "Matt Gregor," he said. "And I think I can afford to feed her."

Winter wiggled free and stepped away, trying to decide if what had just happened was a good thing or not. Had Matt really been jealous? And had Robbie really been goading him?

Curses, men were confounding.

"Megan and Winter have been giving me a tour of my land," Matt continued. "I own Bear Mountain, and I've commissioned Winter to help me choose a building site."

Robbie folded his arms over his chest and studied Matt. "Did ye meet Talking Tom?" he asked softly.

Matt studied him back. "Tom's taking me up Bear Mountain tomorrow afternoon, to watch the sunset from the meadow."

The door to Winter's gallery opened and Robbie's stepgrandmother, Kate, came out onto the sidewalk, drawing everyone's attention. The elderly woman leaned down to fit the key in the lock, and Winter rushed over to her. "Here, let me get that, Gram Katie," she said. "How were sales today?"

Kate straightened and handed Winter the key. "Booming," she said. "I sold the painting of the mother deer and her fawns you had hanging in the window. They're waiting until tomorrow to pick it up though, because they want to meet the artist. And one of Tom's carvings sold. It was the wolf standing on the bluff, howling at the moon." She leaned closer and lowered her voice. "I think it was underpriced, Winter. You could have gotten twice what you asked. It's a very intricate piece."

"Tom sets the prices," Winter explained, checking the doorknob to make sure it had locked as she smiled at Kate.

Kate shook her head. "Then you need to have a talk with Tom. He's practically giving his stuff away."

Winter linked her arm in Kate's and led her over to Robbie and Megan and Matt. "Gram Katie, I'd like you to meet Matt Gregor. He bought *Moon Watchers* and *By a Hare's Breadth.*"

Matt reached out to the feeble hand Kate extended and gently clasped it. "Miss Katie," he said with a crooked smile and gallant nod.

Kate's cheeks reddened as her eyes sparkled with amusement. "Call me Gram Katie. I seem to be everyone's grandmother around here," she said. "It's nice to meet you, Mr. Gregor. You know beauty when you see it. *Moon Watchers* is one of my favorites."

"I do appreciate beautiful things," Matt said, his eyes briefly locking on Winter's before looking back to Kate. "And please, call me Matt. I want to thank you for covering for Megan this afternoon, so she could accompany us to Bear Mountain."

Kate's blush deepened as she waved away his thanks. "It was my pleasure. At my age, a woman looks forward to being useful."

"Mum's waiting supper for ye, Gram," Robbie said, stepping up and lacing Kate's arm through his. He looked at Megan and asked, "Ye ready to practice being a mama, Meg? Baby Angus will likely sleep most of the evening, but Hamish is potty training and he still fights going to bed. And Nathan and Nora have a movie and they're expecting popcorn."

Winter couldn't help but smile at her eagerly grinning sister. Baby Angus was Robbie's and Catherine's ten-week-old son, and Hamish was their two-year-old hellion. Then there were Catherine's two older children, eleven-year-old Nathan and nine-year-old Nora. Robbie and Cat also had two foster boys living with them, but the teens had their own plans for the night. Either that or Catherine wasn't quite ready to turn

132

her newborn over to their care quite yet.

"I think I can handle your crew," Megan said. "It can't be any harder than babysitting a bunch of undergraduates counting Canada goose nests on the tundra."

Robbie nodded with an answering smile. "Gunter and Emily might stop in for a visit. Gunter said he has a snake skin he wants to show Nora, so she can identify it for him."

Gunter was one of Robbie's previous foster boys, who was now married and working in Robbie's logging business. Gunter and Emily were expecting their first child next spring.

"Robbie, have you spoken to Papa today?" Winter asked. "Or Father Daar?"

"No, why?"

Winter shrugged. "No reason. It's just that since Papa came back from visiting Daar this morning, he's been in a strange mood. He took Mama up the mountain for a picnic today, and he just called and said they're spending the night." She shrugged again, trying to dismiss her concern even as she voiced it. "He sounded . . . upset, I'm thinking. Maybe even angry. I just wondered if Daar said something to upset him."

Robbie gently tapped the tip of her nose. "Daar's always upsetting Greylen, baby girl. Your papa probably just wants your mama

133

to himself for a while." He took hold of Kate's arm again. "Come on, Gram, let's get ye home." He looked at Megan. "Ye might as well come with me now. Cat set a place for ye at our supper table. But as soon as ye sit down, Cat and I are off to our own dinner reservations at the Crooked Antler in Greenville." He stopped when he stepped past the patiently waiting horses and looked back at Winter. "Ye can lead old Butterball home okay?"

Winter waved him away. "Sure, assuming I can wake him up."

Robbie looked at Matt. "When I bring Megan home, I'll probably visit with Winter a bit. I expect that will be around eleven o'clock."

Matt, apparently receiving Robbie's message loud and clear, simply nodded.

Winter held in a groan. Robbie was acting like she was sixteen years old, warning Matt that he would be checking up on her! Oh, for the love of —

She was almost prepared this time, when Matt's hands came around her waist and lifted her onto Snowball's back. Winter gathered up her reins and turned Snowball toward Megan's sleeping horse, but Matt quickly mounted up himself and took Butterball's reins before she could.

She still didn't look at him; she was too darn embarrassed. Or maybe she was just plain mad enough to curse for real. The men in her life were starting to get on her nerves, not the least of which was Matheson Gregor himself, who had to trot to catch up with her.

"I noticed there's both a lounge and restaurant at the resort," Matt said. "You want formal dining or comfortable eats tonight?"

She had a good mind not to go at all.

Matt reached over and took hold of Snowball's reins. "Don't even think of refusing, Winter," he said softly. "It's going to take someone bigger than your cousin to scare me off."

Winter smiled at him even as a shiver of awareness tightened her stomach. "How about an entire family of large men?" she asked. "I have a whole army of uncles and male cousins, and not one of them is under six feet tall."

Matt let go of Snowball's reins and started Goose walking again, towing Butterball in his wake. "They wouldn't be the first army I've taken on, nor likely my last."

"What exactly is it you do for a living?" Winter asked, urging Snowball to catch up.

Matt looked over once she was beside him

again. "Have dinner with me tonight and I'll tell you," he said, his challenging gaze reflecting the colors of the deepening autumn twilight.

Winter turned off Main Street and took the forest shortcut to TarStone, which caused the world around them to darken to almost night. "Okay," she finally said. "I'll meet you at the lounge at eight."

"No," Matt countered with soft authority from behind her. "I'll come to your house at eight, and we'll walk over together."

Winter sighed and rode the rest of the way home in silence as she kept a close watch on the woods, knowing darn well that Gesader was lurking in the shadows, just like he'd been for their entire trip to Bear Mountain and back.

Just what she needed — one more overly protective male making sure she died a virgin.

Chapter Eight

Matt stood on the drawbridge of Gù Brath and listened to the rushing water below as he contemplated the large, solid oak, windowless door in front of him. Damn if his little artist didn't live in a castle. He felt like a knight trying to court a princess; he had the wealth and social standing, all he lacked was a suit of armor.

That, and a kingdom to carry her off to.

But then, Bear Mountain might fill that requirement, though he wished it wasn't located quite so close to Winter's army of tall uncles and male cousins. Robbie MacBain looked more like a warrior than a husband and father of four young children, and carried himself in a way that said he was prepared to back up his not-so-subtle warning this afternoon.

But then, Matt never could resist a challenge.

And Winter MacKeage was definitely a

challenge. When he'd first seen Winter in her gallery, he couldn't believe some starry-eyed young man hadn't already snatched her up. But having spent the afternoon with her, Matt was beginning to think that a suit of armor might really be necessary to get within kissing distance of the aloof little wood sprite.

Winter was an exciting paradox of beauty, intelligence, and prickly independence. And like her cousin MacBain, she also had a protective streak a mile wide. She was determined to protect the old hermit and was also quite protective of her sister. All in all, Matt suspected Winter could be just as formidable as her warrior cousin, albeit employing different means to back up her bluster.

With a smile of anticipation for the evening to come, Matt finally reached out and firmly pounded the iron knocker on the door. His smile went even broader when the door suddenly swung open before he could even pull his hand away.

He lifted one brow. "You're punctual as well," he drawled.

"You said eight."

"But it's been my experience that women like being late, so they don't appear too eager."

She simply stared at him, nonplussed. "I'm hungry," she finally said.

Matt gave a slight bow and held out his hand to her, just to see if she would take it. "Then I guess I better feed you." He patted his lapel with his other hand. "I brought my platinum card to pay the enormous bill you're going to run up."

Just as he suspected, his goading lifted her chin and she all but slapped her hand in his. Matt folded his fingers around her delicate hand, reached in and pulled the door closed, and led her across the drawbridge. And he didn't let go of her once they were on firm ground, despite her subtle attempts to wiggle free.

"You surprise me," he said the moment she settled down to walk beside him, apparently resigned to her hand-holding fate.

"Surprise you how?"

"You don't dress like the artist who painted those pictures." Matt kept his grin to himself as he became aware of her frowning at the moonlit path ahead of them. "Except for your hair," he clarified, lifting his hand holding hers just enough to touch the waterfall of loose curls draping down to her waist.

"As opposed to what?" she asked guilelessly. "How would the artist who painted my pictures dress?"

Matt waved his free hand at the air. "Like a drama queen trying to personify her paintings — colorful, mysterious, otherworldly. You look lovely tonight, Winter. I especially like that you're not wearing four-inch heels in an attempt to level the playing field. That tells me you're very comfortable not only with yourself, but with me. And you're wearing pants, not a skirt, which also says you're secure in your femininity."

Matt saw her look down at herself, and then she suddenly stopped walking and looked up at him, her moon-bathed expression once again nonplussed. "Do you always analyze your dates?"

"Only when I'm trying to distract them."

"You're trying to distract me? From what?"

He smiled. "From realizing that I have every intention of kissing you tonight. Want to get it over with now, or would you like to spend the evening savoring the prospect?"

Her mouth opened and closed, but not a sound emerged as she blinked up at him. Though Matt was quite pleased to see two flags of color darkening her cheeks.

He'd intended to wait, and he would have followed through with his plan, but the tiny wood sprite nervously licked her lips. Matt let go of her hand and carefully cupped her exquisitely fine face. "Now, I think," he whispered, bending down and gently pressing his lips to hers.

Small, strong hands immediately wrapped around his wrists, but they didn't push him away or pull back; Winter instead went utterly still, as if testing his — or her own — intentions.

She tasted of mint, her hair surrounding him with the smell of roses as he deepened the contact by tilting her head and parting his lips. Matt drank in her fresh and wonderful flavor, and was soon rewarded — and delighted — by her response.

She was hesitant at first, maybe even shy. But then he felt Winter's grip on his wrists relax and her neck muscles soften as she moved ever so slightly toward him and parted her own lips.

And that was when he got his first taste of that energy he'd seen in her paintings; it hummed through his body with the force of intoxicating passion.

Yes, he was definitely tasting the sweet promise of Winter's magic.

Winter thought she was going to explode. Talk about unpredictable chemistry. If she didn't faint from the currents of electricity coursing through her, she was going to burst into flames. Matheson Gregor kissed like a man who had no intention of stopping until he had her complete surrender. He wasn't being demanding or aggressive; he was being . . . overwhelmingly gentle.

And that, Winter quickly realized, was where the danger lay.

She could easily forget she needed to exercise caution when dealing with Matt; that blindly giving herself over to him could quickly lead somewhere she wasn't prepared to go.

Oh, but he tasted so fine. His heat simmered around her with a strength that beckoned Winter to lean in just a little bit closer, and open herself just a little bit more to the sensations churning inside her.

As if of their own accord, her hands left his wrists and slowly wrapped themselves inside his open jacket to around his waist, moving her deeper into his embrace. He answered her action by letting go of her head, carefully wrapping his arms around her shoulders, and pulling her more possessively against him as he moved his mouth over hers.

And even though she had initiated their further intimacy, Winter felt the first flush of panic. He was much too much for her.

She had kissed her share of boys, but they suddenly seemed like toads when compared to this prince of a man. Her body might be willing, and curses, even her heart was galloping in pleasure, but her mind . . . some still-functioning corner of her mind told Winter she'd better get herself out of this mess before it was too late.

She finally broke the kiss, but instead of pulling away she buried her face in his shirt, finding it impossible to look at him — at least until her cheeks cooled and her heart quit racing.

Matt's chest expanded on a deep breath, and he cupped her head to him with a gentle rumble of amusement. "I am definitely glad I didn't wait." His finger came under her chin and lifted her face to look at him. "You're lovely, Winter. Please don't go all shy on me. I'm attracted to you, and it's only reasonable to expect that attraction to lead to kissing."

She couldn't respond to save her soul. Matt gave another soft laugh and kissed her on the forehead, then let her go, took hold of her hand again, and started them walking down the moon-shadowed path toward the hotel.

"So," he said conversationally, "do you think the meadow would be a good place for me to build my house?"

Winter was thinking a meadow in China would be even better. "It certainly has everything you're looking for," she said, proud that she had found her voice and that it had sounded quite normal. She sensed him looking at her, but she continued staring at the path ahead. "Though I've always thought living within a stone's throw of the water would be as equally appealing as a magnificent view," she added, trying to ignore the heat of his hand surrounding hers.

Aye. This was nice, Winter decided. The man kissed like a prince, yet he felt so wonderfully comfortable to be with. Her poor scattered emotions were bouncing from wanting to kiss him again and wanting to simply cuddle into his warm embrace.

Cursed chemistry.

It seemed he needed to think about that, until he finally said, "Living on the water does have a certain appeal, but it's such a narrow perspective. Up in the meadow a person has a sense of . . . well, of the largeness of the world."

"Aye," Winter agreed, her nerves finally settling down the closer they got to the hotel. "It reminds you how insignificant we really are in the overall scheme of things."

Matt gave a laugh, his hand tightening on hers as he lifted it to his mouth and kissed her knuckles without breaking stride. "I prefer to think we have great significance," he said as they walked under the hotel canopy. "Otherwise, what's the point of our being here?"

Winter blinked up at him as he held the lobby door open for her. Matt's smile was warm and genuine — and rather breathtaking when he was amused. "The point is, we're supposed to be seeking the point," she said, finally stepping into the lobby ahead of him. "We're all on a collective journey," she continued as his long, easy gait brought him beside her again. "But individually, we're mere whispers in a very crowded universe."

She stopped and waved at the mural she'd painted of TarStone Mountain in wintertime. "That's why the skiers are nothing more than single dots of paint," she explained. "And why the resort itself took only a few brushstrokes. Compared to the timeless, massive energy sitting dormant in the granite, soil, and timber of the mountain, people are just like little animals taking advantage of TarStone's energy."

"You talk as if the mountain were alive," he said softly as he studied the mural. He looked over at her, his eyes dark and enigmatic as he lifted one brow in question. "Is it?"

"Aye, it's quite alive," she said just as softly. "You can lie prone on its granite with your eyes closed and feel the mountain gently breathing."

"Stone is inert, Winter," he argued. "It doesn't breathe, much less live or die. It's nothing but matter."

She tilted her head. "Did you not feel the powerful weight of Bear Mountain when you sat up on that boulder this afternoon and ate your lunch?" she asked. "Did a sense of peace not come over you? For those few moments of time, did you not feel you were part of something just as alive as you are?"

"Is that what happens when you sit in your forest and paint? You get this sense of being part of everything, of being one with the animals as well as the rocks and trees?"

"Yes," she said simply.

He took hold of her shoulders, moving closer when a group of people walked by, his darkly intense gaze remaining locked on hers. "Can you teach me that, Winter? Will you take me with you the next time you paint, and let me see if I can feel it, too?"

Without even thinking, Winter reached up

146

and laid a hand on his chest. "But you *can* feel it, Matt. There's nothing special about me; anyone can feel the energy if he only stops long enough to notice."

"Tomorrow, then. We'll head up to my meadow and we'll sit on a rock and listen together."

"Tomorrow I'm meeting Tom at my gallery in the morning," she told him. "And you're meeting him in the afternoon."

Matt stopped her from lowering her hand by covering it with his own. "Then when?"

"Tom can show you when you go see your sunset. He's just as aware of the energy as I am, Matt. You only need to look at the carving he did for Megan to see that."

Matt pressed her hand more firmly against his chest. "I don't want Tom; I want you."

There was a loud commotion at the front of the lobby, and Winter turned with a frown — and suddenly gasped. "Father Daar," she said, as the old priest used his cane to push his way through a group of people congregated by the door.

"Winter!" Daar called as he scurried past the desk clerk trying to head him off. "I'm needing to talk to ye!"

"It's okay, John. I've got him," Winter told the clerk as she met up with Daar. "Father," she said calmly, covering his arm holding the cane so he would stop waving it around. "What's wrong?"

"Where's Greylen?" he impatiently asked, his face flushed with worry as his gaze searched the lobby. "I'm needing to speak with your papa," he said, bringing his frantic eyes back to her.

"He's not here, Father," she said softly, edging them both away from the main-stream of guests. "He and Mama are camping on the mountain tonight."

Daar pulled away and thumped his cane on the floor. "I need him now!" he snapped. "I need Greylen. Or Robbie. Where in hell is MacBain? This is a crisis," he ground out, shaking his head. "I need them now."

"Can I be of help, Father?" Matt asked from behind Winter.

"Who the hell are ye?" Daar growled, glaring past Winter's shoulder. His eyes suddenly widened, and he pointed his cane at Matt as he looked at Winter. "Is he yer date?" he yelped. He furiously thumped his cane on the floor again. "Ye're not supposed to date anyone!"

Winter moved between them and took hold of Daar by both arms. "You need to calm down," she said softly. "Tell me what's happened and I'll try to help you."

Even as she held his upper arms, Daar

started wringing his hands together, causing his cane to bump her shin. "It's my tree," he whispered harshly. "Someone's killed my tree. I need to speak to Robbie and Greylen. They have to help me."

Winter sucked in her breath. She looked over her shoulder at Matt and said, "Will you excuse us a minute, please? Just long enough for me to calm him down?"

Though he was obviously concerned, Matt nodded and stepped back a few paces. Winter smiled her thanks and looked at Daar. "What do you mean, someone killed your tree? The pine tree?"

"Aye," Daar said, vigorously nodding. "It's been cut clean off about thirty feet up. The entire top is gone." He reversed their grip and clutched her arms tightly, this time causing his cane to smack her thigh. "And I can't find the top. It's been stolen. I need Robbie to find it!"

Winter wiggled free and stroked her hands soothingly along his arms. "Robbie will help you, Father. Just as soon as it's daylight, both Robbie and Papa will start looking for the top of your tree. Let me take you to Gù Brath, and when Robbie gets back from his dinner with Cat, we'll tell him what happened and he'll know what to do."

"Nay," Daar growled. "I must go home. I

need to be up on the mountain. Ye get Robbie from his dinner and tell him to come to me right now."

"You can't do anything about it tonight," Winter reasoned. "And I'm not letting you walk home alone," she added, thinking about the two swordsmen Tom had told her about. "Robbie will be back in a few hours. Until then, I'll call Papa on his cell phone and tell him what's happened."

"I tried that!" Daar snapped. "I stopped at Gù Brath and used yer phone, but all I got was some foolish woman wanting me to leave a message. She wouldn't tell me where Greylen is."

Winter couldn't help but smile. "That lady is a recording, Father. Papa likely shut off his phone," she explained, turning and linking her arm through his to lead him toward the lobby door. "Come on. I'll make you a nice cup of hot tea, and I'll give you some cookies while we wait for Robbie."

He pulled free. "I want to go home."

"Okay, then," Winter said quietly, still edging him toward the door. "I'll get my truck and drive you home."

"I'll drive," Matt said, stepping around them and opening the door so they could walk outside. "We can take my truck. It's in the parking lot."

Winter blinked at Matt. Good heavens, she'd forgotten him. She started to tell him he needn't bother, but the look in his eyes made her snap her mouth shut without uttering a word.

Matt smiled. "Wait here while I get the truck."

"I want ye to call Robbie," Daar interjected, first scowling at Matt, then Winter. "I want MacBain."

"This is Robbie and Catherine's first night out since Angus was born," Winter told him gently but firmly. "We are not ruining their evening when nothing can be done until daylight anyway. Robbie will come to see you as soon as he gets home."

Daar pointed at Matt. "We don't need him."

"You need me if you want to get home tonight," Matt said. "Because Winter is not traveling that mountain alone at night."

Daar lifted his chin, his crystal blue eyes filled with challenge. "Winter's been traveling that mountain at night since she was ten," he said. "She knows it better than anyone."

"Nevertheless, it's me and my truck, or you have dinner with us here while you wait for MacBain."

Daar turned his glare on Winter. "Since

when are ye letting a man tell ye what to do?"

"Since she agreed to have dinner with me tonight," Matt said before she could respond. The polite smile Matt had been using on Daar turned amused when he looked at Winter. "I'll be right back," he said as he started jogging toward the parking lot.

"Well, I never —" Daar muttered, shaking his head at Winter. "Ye shouldn't be dating that interfering man," he told her. "Ye shouldn't be dating anyone!"

"Maybe I should run away and join a convent instead."

"Aye," Daar said with a thoughtful nod. "That would work."

Winter scowled at him. "I was joking, Father." She patted his arm and softly urged, "Please calm down. Everything will be all right. Robbie will find out what happened to your tree."

Daar dropped his gaze. "I cannot believe someone cut my pine," he muttered. He looked up at her. "Not one of the other trees around it was touched. I had it hidden in a stand of several other pines, and it's the only one that was cut." His eyes suddenly widened and he took a step back. "Greylen," he said on an indrawn breath. "He chopped down my tree!"

"Papa?" Winter said in a whispered yelp. She immediately shook her head. "He wouldn't, Father. He knows the importance of that pine tree. He wouldn't dare harm it."

Daar scowled at her, obviously thinking furiously. "He would if he was trying to protect . . . ah, someone," he said. "Greylen would dare anything. That's why the black-guard can't be found tonight," he hissed, looking toward the summit and thumping his cane on the ground between them. "He's probably up there with yer mama right now, burning the top of it."

"Think, Father," Winter said. "Why would he cut the tree thirty feet up from the ground? If Papa wanted to kill it, he would have cut it off at the stump."

Daar eyed her as he rubbed his short white beard with the butt of his cane. "Aye," he said softly, his eyes narrowed in thought. "I did wonder about that."

A large, black, four-door pickup pulled under the canopy and came to a stop beside Winter and Daar. Matt got out, walked around the front, and opened the back passenger door. "Let's get you home, Father," he said, reaching to help Daar.

Daar thumped his cane again. "I'm riding in the front."

153

"There's only bucket seats in the front," Matt patiently explained. "And since Winter needs to show me the way, that leaves only the backseat or the cargo bay."

"It used to be people respected priests," Daar muttered as he finally climbed in the backseat with Matt's help.

Matt handed Daar the seat belt. "Used to be priests were pious servants," he countered with a chuckle. "Or so I've been told."

Daar squinted at Matt, clearly taking umbrage. "Ye're a godless man, Mr.—" He suddenly looked over at Winter. "Ye didn't even introduce us proper, girl."

"Father," Winter said with a smile, "this is Matt Gregor. He owns Bear Mountain and is building a house there. Matt, this is Father Daar . . . ah, an old friend of my family. He lives up on TarStone."

Matt gave a slight, formal bow. "Father Daar," he said.

"Gregor," Daar repeated softly as he studied Matt. "Ye seem familiar, now that I've calmed down enough to look at ye. Where are ye from?"

Matt shrugged. "Here and there. New York most recently."

The door Matt was holding moved as a strong gust of wind blew under the open canopy, buffeting them and the truck in a flurry of dried leaves. Winter looked toward the summit and saw the moon peaking out from a bank of dark, roiling clouds. She looked at Matt. "A storm must be moving in."

"Aye," Daar interjected. "One hell of a storm." He reached over and took hold of the door Matt was still holding. "I want to go home," he said just before he slammed it shut.

Matt turned to Winter with a crooked smile. "You have some very colorful friends," he said. "First Talking Tom and now Father Daar."

"Hey, I can't pick my neighbors."

Matt opened the front passenger door, and before Winter could put her foot on the running board to climb in, he lifted her into the front seat. She didn't even squeak this time, but only gave him a smug smile as he softly closed the door.

Matt walked around the front of the truck and climbed in behind the wheel.

"Which way?" Matt asked as he reached over and finished fastening Winter's seat belt. "Toward town or straight up the ski slope?"

"We head up past Gù Brath, on the same road we took this afternoon," she told him as he fastened his own seat belt. "Then we turn right on another old tote road two miles up. That's when it really gets rough and steep. I'm glad you thought to buy a four-wheel-drive truck."

He put the truck in gear, shot her a smile, and started them toward Gù Brath. "I own a mountain," he reminded her, then said over his shoulder, "So, Father, did I hear you say a pine tree was cut down? It must be special for you to be so upset. Were you growing it for Christmas?" He turned off the paved driveway and onto the tote road. "Isn't it a little early for someone to be stealing a Christmas tree?"

"It's not a Christmas tree," Daar said. "It's . . . I . . . ah, I'm studying the genetics of white pines, and I was going to collect the cones for their seeds. But somebody cut off the top last night."

Winter was impressed. She couldn't have come up with a better excuse, though she wasn't surprised by Daar's explanation, considering all the time the priest spent at Robbie's logging operation. Daar was always begging for rides and asking questions about clear-cutting and regrowth. This was obviously a fib Daar felt comfortable playing out.

"But why would someone want to steal its pine cones?" Matt asked. "Is the tree a hybrid you've developed?"

"It's . . . I was . . . It's . . . ."

Winter realized Daar might not know such a modern term, and quickly said, "It hasn't been genetically altered or anything. It's just a naturally occurring seed tree for lumber. Lumbermen are always looking for really straight trees with thick trunks, as they make perfect saw logs for dimensional lumber. Daar has been watching this particular tree for several years and hoped to give my cousin the seeds. Robbie owns several thousand acres of timberland, and he has to replant the areas he cuts."

Matt squeezed her hand and gave a nod. "So the real worry is that someone trespassed and cut down a tree he didn't own, is that it?"

"Yes, I suppose so," Winter said. "As well as how that person even knew about that particular tree. Turn here," she said, pointing at the narrow road on the right.

Matt turned, causing the truck's headlights to close into a narrow beam as the overgrown path gave the illusion they were traveling into a rising, twisting cave. Matt let go of her hand and pushed the button that engaged the four-wheel drive, but before Winter could pull away, he again covered her hand with his to rest on the console. And he didn't let go again until the trail really got rough and he needed both hands to control the sometimes halting, sometimes slipping truck.

"Is there a reason you don't rebuild this goat path?" he asked, after muttering a rather colorful curse when the truck side-slipped on a steep outcropping of ledge.

Winter was holding on to the handle just above her door, and was turned around checking on Daar. "We usually make the trip on horseback," she said. "Or by snow-cat in the winter." She smiled at the sight of Matt's scowling face illuminated by the dash lights. "And keeping it impassable discourages the tourists."

"And Father Daar lives up here . . . why?"

"Because I like my privacy," Daar interjected, also mouthing a curse when his cane smacked his own shin. "I don't like people."

"Really?" Matt drawled.

They rode in silence for another twenty minutes, the rutted path that had overgrown to nothing more than a trail taking all of Matt's concentration. Branches scraped along the side of his new truck, and Winter winced when she heard a loud thud hit the frame.

"For a fancy truck, this thing rides like a damn donkey cart," Daar said, giving a grunt as they came to an abrupt stop.

"Did you see that?" Matt asked, staring out the windshield.

"See what?" Winter asked, also scanning the trail ahead in the beam of the headlights.

"I swear I saw a cat. It darted into the bushes just beyond the beam of the lights. It was big and black, like that picture in your gallery. What did you call it? Gasser?"

"Gesader," Winter told him, shaking her head. "But he's not real. You must have seen a lynx."

"Are lynx black?"

"It could have been a bear."

"Do bears have tails as long as their bodies?"

"You didn't see a panther, Matt. They're jungle animals."

"I've seen a dark, long-tailed lynx," Daar interjected. "He's a big one, too. He lives over on West Shoulder Ridge, but he hunts over here sometimes. He must be one of them hybrids," Daar finished smugly.

Great, Winter thought. They were all going to hell for telling lies, and she would be responsible for taking a priest down with her. "The cabin is just a few hundred yards farther up the path," she said. "There's a clearing where you can turn around."

Matt moved his narrow-eyed stare from

Daar to her.

"I'm sure Father Daar will make us some tea and toast, since we missed dinner and he's so thankful we brought him home," she continued. "Won't you, Father?" she asked without looking away from Matt.

"Aye. I think I have an old loaf of dry bread and some tea left," Daar returned, sounding anything but hospitable.

Without saying a word, Matt put the truck back in gear and slowly started forward again. And other than the occasional scrape of a branch, a person could have heard a mouse sneeze in the cab of the truck. Daar's cabin came into view a few minutes later, and Matt turned in a wide circle that ended at the porch stairs. He shut off the engine but left the headlights on, and the silence became even more pronounced but for the occasional ping of dried leaves hitting the truck roof and windshield.

"If you don't mind, Father," Matt said quietly, "I'll take a rain check on the tea and toast. I need to have Winter back by eleven, or her cousin is going to stomp me into the ground."

Winter let out a relieved breath, grateful Matt was going to stop pursuing his panther sighting. She unfastened her seat belt and got out, then turned to help Daar from the backseat. Matt came around and took his arm as they climbed the porch stairs.

"I'm sorely tired," Daar said as he stood at his door and looked at Winter. "Ye promise ye'll tell Robbie what's happened the minute he gets back?"

"I promise."

Daar looked at Matt and lifted his chin. "My manners compel me to thank ye, Gregor, for bringing me home."

"You're welcome," Matt said, with a slight incline of his head. "Do you want us to come in and build up your fire?"

"Nay. I can tend my own fire."

Winter leaned over and gave Daar a kiss on his bearded cheek. "Good night, Father. I'll likely see you tomorrow. I'll come up to help Robbie and Papa in the afternoon."

"Nay," Daar said with a quick shake of his head. "I only want the men."

Winter wasn't insulted. In fact, she was assured Daar was back to his cantankerous old self. She patted his arm with a laugh, then turned and walked down the steps and over to the passenger door of the truck. Remembering Tom's swordsmen, she warned, "You stay inside tonight, Father. You can't help Robbie if you catch a chill. He'll be up as soon as he can."

"Aye," Daar agreed, the headlights illuminating his wave from the porch rail. "I'll be right here when Robbie arrives."

Winter opened her door and waited, only to frown when Matt didn't lift her in. She turned to find him standing behind her, his hands on his hips, smiling.

"It's no fun when you're expecting it," he said.

Winter rolled her eyes with a laugh, stepped on the running board, and climbed in the truck. Matt softly closed the door and walked around the front, stopping when Daar said something to him that she couldn't hear. They exchanged words, then Matt finally climbed in behind the wheel.

"What did he say to you?"

He shrugged and started the engine. "Just another friendly warning," he told her, putting the truck in gear and slowly easing out of the clearing and back onto the steep path. He darted a quick glance at her. "That if I value my life, I might want to find another lass to charm."

"Oh, no," Winter muttered, covering her face with her hands and shaking her head.

"He also kindly explained that your father is even more protective of you than your cousin, and that getting on the wrong side of Greylen MacKeage was tantamount to suicide." Matt brushed back her hair and

162

pulled one hand from her face, exposing one of her eyes so she could see his smile. "He also suggested I spend more time praying and less time pursuing a woman destined for the convent."

Winter did groan then, quite loudly, and covered her face again as they bumped their way down the mountain.

"I'm beginning to realize why you aren't already married. How many boyfriends have your army of protectors scared off?"

"Dozens," she muttered before lowering her hands to smile at him. "That I know of. That's not counting the guys who never even dared to ask me out."

Matt kept his attention on the path ahead. "Well, Miss MacKeage, your army has just come up against a man who doesn't scare easily." He braked to a stop and looked at her. "Do you?"

CHAPTER NINE

"The only thing that scares me," Winter said softly, watching his face in the dash lights, "is not being able to tell if what I'm feeling is real or just my imagination."

"You're not imagining me, Winter Mac-Keage. I assure you, I'm very real."

Winter clasped her hands on her lap and stared out the windshield. "Then that does scare me," she whispered.

He said nothing to that, but sat with his own hands loosely holding the steering wheel as he also stared out the windshield. Then, still without saying anything, he finally began easing the truck down the rutted trail again, the stark, pregnant silence inside the cab making Winter's heart pound with dread.

Had she just blown it? Had she finally managed to do what Robbie and Father Daar hadn't been able to? Had she just scared off Matt by letting him know she was attracted to him?

She knew better! She knew men didn't like being chased by infatuated, starry-eyed women; they wanted to be the pursuer. Men were like bears: run from them and they would go after their prey without questioning why, but stand firm and make a lot of noise and they'd just as likely turn tail and run.

Matt had been enjoying pursuing her, giving chase by buying her paintings, commissioning her time, even kissing her on his own terms. But she had just told him she liked him so much it scared her, and now he was suddenly rethinking his intentions toward her.

Aye, she'd blown it big time.

The sound of the bushes scraping the truck grated on Winter's nerves like nails on a chalkboard. She had met Matt only yesterday, yet in that short time she'd experienced a whole roller coaster of emotions. She'd gotten angry at both him and herself, been intrigued, infatuated, charmed, and quite wonderfully kissed. Maybe she really should join a convent; it had to be easier than maneuvering through this quagmire of feminine awareness.

But curses, running away wasn't the solution, either. Hadn't her parents always taught her to follow her heart? Well, despite what her mind was all but screaming, Winter's heart was telling her that Matheson Gregor was one man worth making a fool of herself over.

So what the heck, she suddenly decided with a determined lift of her chin, she might as well begin as she intended to go on. And if Matt Gregor couldn't handle her own intentions, it was his loss!

"If you want to really feel the mountain," she said into the silence, "the best time is when a storm is moving in."

He stopped the truck, put it in neutral, and looked at her.

"There's a sheltered bluff not a hundred yards away, where we could feel the mountain breathing."

He shut off the engine and then the headlights, plunging them into absolute darkness. Winter twined her fingers together, both dreading and hoping he'd say something — anything — to put her out of her misery.

She flinched when his large hand covered hers, stilling her action. "I finally understand your family," he said through the darkness. "You really do need looking after, don't you? You've put yourself on a mountain in the middle of nowhere, with someone you've just met, and now you're offering to take a walk in the woods with a complete stranger who outweighs you by at least a hundred pounds."

She pulled her hands from his and crossed her arms under her breasts. Okay, so maybe this hadn't been a good idea. Whether Matt was angry or amused by her not-so-subtle offer, he was definitely surprised. She sensed him leaning back on his side of the truck, and could just make out his own arms folded over his chest as her eyes slowly adjusted to the darkness.

"What about that cat I saw?" he asked after a long silence.

"He'll smell us before we see him and will keep his distance," she said in a near whisper, profoundly thankful the darkness was hiding her scorching red cheeks. "Lynx are curious, but they're not aggressive."

Matt suddenly moved, causing Winter to flinch again when he opened his door and flooded the interior of the truck with light. He climbed out, then turned and started rummaging under his seat, his hand finally emerging with a flashlight and tiny case.

"W-what's that?" Winter asked, beginning to worry she was about to get more than she'd wished for.

He set the flashlight on the seat and

unzipped the case. "A pistol," he said, taking the automatic out and tucking it in his jacket pocket.

"No," Winter said harshly. "You don't need a gun."

About to pick up the flashlight, he looked at her. "It's just a precaution," he assured her. "We're in the woods, it's nighttime, and I don't care for surprises."

She shook her head. "I'm not leaving this truck if you bring that gun," she said, thinking about Gesader's penchant for lurking in the bushes. "There's nothing in the woods that isn't more afraid of us than we are of it."

He frowned at her, studying her face. "You're serious," he finally said. "Do guns bother you, Winter? You seemed concerned this afternoon when I told Tom I had one rolled in my jacket."

"Guns don't bother me when they're necessary," she said, shaking her head again. "But you don't need one now." She unfastened her seat belt and turned to face him, leaning on the console and pointing at the flashlight. "We don't need a gun or a light," she told him. "Our eyes will adjust to the darkness, and we won't be more than a hundred yards away from the safety of the truck."

He hesitated, then finally reached in his pocket, pulled out the pistol, and slipped it back in its case. He put the case under the seat and softly closed his door without picking up the flashlight, then walked around the truck to open her door, and reached inside for her hand.

It took Winter a full minute to set her hand in his and slip out of the truck.

"Stand there a minute," he said, opening the back door and reaching under the seat, once more bringing on the cab lights. At this rate, Winter feared their eyes were going to be so confused they'd never adjust.

He straightened, tucking a blanket under his arm. "A picnic kit came with the truck," he said in explanation as he closed the door and felt around in the darkness for her hand again. He gave her fingers a squeeze and chuckled aloud. "I don't know which of us is more trusting — your trusting that I'm not a serial killer, or my trusting that nothing out here is going to eat us."

"I've been told the probability is slight that you're a serial killer," Winter said, finally starting to relax as her eyes adjusted to the darkness. She started leading Matt farther down the path, deciding everything would be okay, that the woods were the safest place she could be. "And besides, I could easily slip away in the darkness, leaving you as bewildered as that lynx in my painting you bought."

He laughed again, his hand tightening on hers as she stepped off the path and into the forest. "That's reassuring. Are you warm enough?"

"I like the cold. Watch that log," she said, guiding him around a fallen tree, slowly relaxing the farther they went into the woods. "It's hard to believe in another couple of months the snow up here will be deeper than I am tall."

"I need to buy a plow for my truck," he said as they finally broke into a tiny clearing.

"I don't think your pickup will keep your road open all winter," she said, stopping at the foot of a large outcropping of ledge. "You need a heavy truck to wing back the snowbanks each time." She grinned at him through the darkness, just barely able to make out his face. "You may not have enough money left to buy heaven when you're done building your home, Matt."

A chuckle rumbled from his chest as he took hold of her shoulders and gently pulled her against him. "Then I guess I'll have to make Bear Mountain my heaven," he said, holding her close in his strong, warm embrace. He ran his fingers into her hair and used his grip to gently tilt her head back to look at him. "How are we going to hear the mountain with the wind blowing?"

"You feel it more than hear it," she said, laying her hand over his heart. "In here."

His heartbeat felt wonderfully strong as he stood silently staring down at her, and Winter's own heart started to race with anticipation. He was going to kiss her again, and she decided that this time she was kissing him back.

But he suddenly let her go and disappeared, and it took Winter a moment to realize he'd bent over and was picking up the blanket he'd dropped. "Where should I spread this out?" he asked, stepping over to the wall of granite rising above them and shaking open the blanket. "Here?"

"That's good," she muttered, rubbing her suddenly chilled arms, missing his warmth.

"I wish the clouds wouldn't keep covering the moon," he continued, kneeling on the blanket and feeling the ground for hidden rocks. "I bet we could see the lake from here." He sat down on one half of the blanket and held his hand out to her.

It was the sight of that blanket that finally made Winter realize exactly how outrageous her idea had been. What in hell had made her suggest they lie up here in the darkness together? She simply couldn't get on that blanket with a man who turned her mind to mush. It was an intimate if not brazen situation she'd created, and Winter wondered how she was going to get out of this mess without truly making a fool of herself.

"Come on," he said, dropping his hand and patting the blanket beside him. "I promise I'll keep my fingers laced behind my head," he told her, his voice coaxingly gentle. "You have my word, Winter, nothing will happen between us that you don't want to happen."

And therein lay the very heart of her problem.

Another thick flurry of leaves blew off the ledge above them, scattering like snowflakes over the blanket and catching in her hair. Matt stretched out on his back with a sigh and folded his hands behind his head like a pillow. "The ground is warm," he said into the darkness. "I expected it to be bone-chilling cold."

He looked so strange, lying in the forest in his expensive suit and dress shoes. Not that he seemed any more worried about ruining his wardrobe than about scratching his truck. In fact, Matt was a contradiction of refined sophistication and rugged strength. Winter could picture him in a boardroom commanding an army of suits just as easily as she could see him commanding an army of warriors on a battlefield. Matt Gregor was an intriguing mix of brawn and brain, she decided.

"The ground doesn't feel cold because it's still warmer than the air," she explained, stepping closer when he squirmed into a more comfortable position. "The mist you see rising from the forest in the morning comes from the temperature difference."

"I wish the moon would stay out. It's full."

Winter took another step closer. "Actually, it was full last night," she said, finally sitting on the ground beside the blanket — but not on it. She gathered up her blowing hair and twisted it into a tail that she pulled over her right shoulder. "It was also the autumnal equinox yesterday. It's rare that both occur on the same day."

"A full moon and an equinox," he said, just as the clouds thinned enough that Winter could see his eyes were closed and a soft smile lifted the corners of his mouth. "That must have brought the fairies out to dance last night."

Winter found her own smile as she gazed off toward Pine Lake, just barely able to make out the large body of water. "Wouldn't it be nice if fairies really did exist?" she mused.

"They must," Matt said. "If you put one in *Moon Watchers.*"

She turned in surprise. "You saw her? You saw my fairy?"

He opened his eyes to look at her. "Just barely. You tucked her in a high branch and made her nearly translucent." He resettled himself, closed his eyes again, and frowned. "I can't feel anything. No hum. No breathing."

"That's because you're not being quiet," she told him, finally lying back — but only so her head was on the blanket.

"Then stop talking," he muttered. "And let me concentrate."

Winter smiled at nothing, closed her own eyes, and listened to the wind filtering through the treetops around them. She could hear the squeak of a tree trunk rubbing against another trunk; dried leaves crackling as they rolled over each other across the ground; an acorn ricocheting off several branches with sharp pings, finally landing on the forest floor with a muted thud. More rustling came with the scurrying of tiny feet, then the alarmed chatter of a nocturnal flying squirrel scolding them for invading his favorite acorn patch.

If only two days ago someone had told Winter she'd be lying on a mountain at night with a handsome, undeniably appealing man, she'd have told them to pull her other leg. But for reasons she couldn't quite understand, Winter felt this was about as right, and as real, as it got.

"If you would quit humming, I might be able to hear your mountain," Matt said softly.

Winter rolled toward him with a laugh. "I'm not humming. That's the mountain. It's sharing its energy with you, Matt."

He opened his eyes and looked down at her, the slash of his smile bright enough to rival the moon. "So you weren't telling tales. It really is alive."

She wiggled closer, until she was completely on the blanket and her head was even with his. "Yes. The mountain is brimming with energy."

"Kiss me," he whispered.

She blinked into his dark, unfathomable eyes.

"I want to feel *your* energy, Winter Mac-Keage. Kiss me."

Still she didn't move, caught in his mesmerizing gaze.

Matt lifted his head only slightly and wiggled his laced fingers. "I keep my promises, Winter," he said, his voice deep with coaxing sincerity. "You're safe with me tonight. My hands are staying behind my head. Kiss me."

Heaven help her, she wiggled closer, until she was actually leaning over him.

"Ah, Winter," he said on a sigh. "You're as beautiful as the pictures you paint. Give me a taste of your magic, and let me feel what you feel."

If wishes were horses and beggars could ride, then Winter decided she was about to gallop straight into her wildest fantasy. With her heart racing faster than her mind could keep up, she slowly leaned down and softly touched her mouth to his.

He let out another sigh that parted his lips, and Winter pulled in his familiar taste, easing higher until she was fully draped across his broad chest. His chest rose on an indrawn breath that he held, and she could feel the pounding strength of his heart thumping against hers. The knowledge that she was affecting him as much as he was her gave Winter the confidence to lift her hand and touch the side of his face as she deepened her kiss.

He tasted so good, felt so fine beneath her, so solid and warm and substantial; the charged energy of the mountain hummed through him into her. Prickles of electricity tightened her skin even while embers of awareness flared deep in the pit of her stomach. Winter parted her own lips and touched her tongue to his, shyly exploring the heady sensations that boldly urged her to move her fingers over the taut lines of his rugged face.

He'd asked to feel her magic, but it was *his* magic that caught Winter up in its spell; two hearts beating against each other, lips touching and tasting and savoring, the energies of the timeless universe dancing in mystical harmony.

This journey of separate souls seeking each other, that's what was happening. The magic of being here — with this man, on this mountain, on this storm-energized night — was what Winter had been waiting her whole life to experience.

Matt suddenly turned his head from hers, ending their kiss, his chest expanding on a deep, shuddering breath. "Ye're one second away from making me break ma promise to ye," he softly growled.

Winter blinked at him through the darkness, crashing back to reality with a jarring thud that made her rear up in surprise. "You have a brogue."

There was just enough moonlight to see

Matt's eyes flare and his hands — still behind his head — tighten into fists. He took another calming breath. "A throwback to my youth," he said, his enigmatic gaze locked on hers. "I was born in Scotland." He lifted his elbows in a sort of shrug, still keeping his hands behind his head. "When I get . . . er . . ." He suddenly grinned. "When I get completely focused on something, I tend to regress. And hanging out with you today seems to have brought my accent closer to the surface."

Winter rolled away and lay on her back beside him, clasping her hands on her stomach as she stared up at the churning clouds dancing around the moonlight. "Did you drop the Mac from your name? Is it really MacGregor?"

"No. Just Gregor."

"Do you know what *Matheson* means?"

"I know the *son* part means *son of*."

"Aye. And *Mathe* is Gaelic for "bear." Your name means *son of the bear*."

He rolled toward her, propping his head on one hand and laying his other hand on his thigh. "Then I guess I own the right mountain, don't I?"

"What do you do for a living?"

"I build jets. Military as well as private."

Winter digested that. It fit, she decided —
a powerful man making powerful aircraft.
"We saw a small jet fly in yesterday. Was
that you? Do you pilot your own plane?"

He nodded, reaching over to lift her blowing hair off her face and tucking it behind
her ear. "Did you feel the energy, Winter?"
he asked softly, his hand returning to his
thigh, but not before she saw it ball into a
fist. "That wasn't the mountain humming,
was it? That was you."

Winter felt a blush scorch her cheeks, and
she went back to studying the sky. "We're
all part of the same energy," she told him.
"You, me, the mountain, the animals, the
storm moving in, we're all connected."

"I like the idea of that," he said, his voice
deep with an emotion she couldn't quite
define. "I like the idea of being connected
to you, Winter MacKeage." He suddenly sat
up. "But in the interest of keeping my
promise that you're safe tonight," he said,
turning to smile at her, "and my interest in
not getting stomped by your cousin, I better
take you home now."

Winter also sat up, capturing her blowing
hair and pulling it over her shoulder again.
"I think you better."

He stood, then reached out to help her
up. Winter let him pull her to her feet, but

Matt kept her momentum going until she was pressed against his chest with his arms wrapped firmly around her. "One more taste, I think," he whispered, just as he lowered his lips to hers.

He was definitely doing the kissing this time, completely in charge, once again taking up the chase. Winter's heart rejoiced as his mouth moved over hers with a gentle aggression that sent another charge of electricity coursing through her. She hadn't scared him away, she realized, as she parted her lips on a relieved sigh and kissed him back.

She melted into the hard, solid heat of his body, and Matt slid one hand down the base of her spine and pulled her fully against him. Winter immediately discovered just how aroused he was, but instead of being alarmed, she boldly moved her hips into his.

Matt lifted his head with a snarl that sounded a lot like Gesader when her pet was disgruntled, and Winter buried her face in Matt's shirt with a smile of delight. His chest rumbled with a lingering growl as he held her so tightly that his expanding torso squeezed the air from her own lungs.

"Dammit, lady, ye best not be amused," he growled in her hair, his lips sending another shiver through her. "Ye should be slapping my face. No," he said, gripping her shoulders and setting her away, "I should be slapping my own face." He took hold of her hand and started leading her out of the clearing toward the truck.

"Your blanket," she said, attempting to get it.

He didn't let her go, but kept dragging her through the thick woods. "Leave it," he growled. "I'm taking ye home. Now."

Winter let him lead her away in silence, unable to keep her smile contained. Bears didn't have much of a tail, but she'd just managed to give this one's tail a good tug.

And his reaction looked very promising.

CHAPTER TEN

The storm hit just after midnight, and Winter lay in bed listening to the rain beating on the windows, her scattered thoughts and still-humming emotions making sleep impossible. She reached down to where Gesader usually slept, felt only the quilt, and smiled. Her panther, obviously annoyed at her, had given Winter a throaty snarl when she'd let him in the house, then had padded off to bed with Megan.

It never did take much to put Gesader's nose out of joint, and apparently Winter's being on the mountain with Matt had angered her pet. She knew Gesader had been up there. Heck, he'd probably been crouched in the bushes not twenty feet away.

When Matt had all but dragged her back to his truck — in utter silence except for her heart screaming with joy — Winter had noticed several strands of black hair on the windshield when the interior lights had come on. Gesader had been letting her know that he'd been near them the whole time, and that he hadn't liked being forced to stay hidden.

The night usually belonged to just the two of them, when Winter would paint her nighttime scenes and Gesader would doze beside her. He was a possessive pet, and Winter had never considered how her having a boyfriend might affect him.

Boyfriend, Winter thought with a grin, testing the word in her mind. Did kissing her senseless make Matt her boyfriend? "No," she whispered to the dark ceiling, shaking her head. That was too corny a label for Matheson Gregor. When she thought of a boyfriend, Winter pictured Patrick Rooney, a nervous teenager holding a wrist corsage, shaking in his polished shoes as he stood at the front door with her papa, waiting to take her to their senior prom.

Patrick had been a boyfriend. Matt Gregor was . . . curses, he was far more confounding than Patrick Rooney had ever been. She'd never gotten all mush-minded and shivery when Pat had kissed her. Nor had she ever wanted to rip off Pat's clothes and run her hands over every inch of his body. But that was exactly what she'd wanted to do to Matt up on the mountain

— what she would like to do to him right now.

Good heavens, Winter thought with a start, kicking off the suddenly stifling blankets. She was lusting after Matheson Gregor. She frowned at the ceiling. Well, go figure. This chemistry thing was pretty powerful stuff.

Winter felt like one of those itty-bitty wood ticks that would lay dormant on a leaf for over eighteen months at a time, just waiting for a warm body to come brushing by. Well, hadn't she been lying in wait for nearly twenty-five years? But when Matt Gregor had stepped into her gallery, she'd taken a good look at him and jumped off her leaf with every intention of going for a wonderful ride.

Winter smiled again as she remembered how Matt had stopped his truck at Gù Brath, walked her to her door, and with only a softly spoken good-bye and no goodnight kiss, left without looking back. He'd been restraining himself, Winter decided, her smile turning smug; nice guys did not take advantage of women they cared about after knowing them only one day.

Aye, Matt was a truly noble gentleman.

In a way, he reminded Winter of how her papa treated her mama. No matter how frustrated her father got with his wife, he never took advantage of his strength or size. Not that Grace didn't push his buttons occasionally, sometimes just for the fun of it, Winter suspected.

Just like she was tempted to do with Matt.

Winter's smile disappeared as her thoughts bounced to her parents, picturing them holed up in some cave on TarStone. Or more likely they'd sought shelter in the summit house and were cuddled up in front of the giant stone hearth.

But she still didn't know why they'd suddenly decided to spend the night; she was only sure that something was wrong. It couldn't have anything to do with Daar's pine tree, she decided. Her papa wouldn't mess with the magic, not when it was all that was keeping him from returning to his old time.

Winter had told Robbie about Father Daar's latest crisis when he'd brought Megan home. Robbie had scrubbed his face in frustration, let out a tired sigh, and promised to go see the old priest that night. He'd also told Winter not to worry about Greylen, that he'd find him tomorrow and let him know what was going on, and for her to simply go about her business as usual.

Robbie hadn't liked the part of her story

where she'd told him Matt had gone with her to take Daar home. He'd given Winter a ten-minute lecture about trusting men she knew nothing about, and she'd listened and smiled and nodded in all the appropriate places. Finally realizing his lecture was falling on deaf ears, Robbie had stopped talking with a resigned snort and headed home to mount up and go see Father Daar.

Winter finally closed her eyes with a tired sigh, deciding it was time to let this enchanted day come to an end. It had begun before sunrise, and if she didn't get some sleep, she was going to greet the next sunrise with a scowl.

And she didn't want anything to ruin her wonderful mood. She had kissed the man of her dreams tonight, and she couldn't wait to get another taste of Matheson Gregor's own special magic.

Matt lay in the king-sized bed in his suite, completely naked and the covers thrown off him, listening to the wind-driven rain hitting the windows. His body still hadn't cooled down, and little Miss Prickly MacKeage was responsible for his foul mood.

She'd come damn close to losing her virginity tonight, and it was the very fact that she was a virgin that had brought Matt to a screaming halt. Yes, he had realized the moment he'd kissed her in her driveway that Winter had never been with a man, not intimately, anyway. If she were experienced, they wouldn't be lying in separate beds right now; he would have been all over her up on that bluff, and he wouldn't have stopped until morning — storm or no storm.

That she had held out for so long, yet had come so damned close to giving him her most precious possession tonight, made Matt break out in a cold sweat all over again. He dismissed the notion that he had stopped out of concern for her feelings, knowing how horrified she'd be in the morning. He even dismissed his long-lost conscience in some rusted region of his mind, that taking her on the ground in the middle of the woods made him no better than a rutting bull moose.

Or bear, he thought with a self-debasing laugh.

A heartless son of a bear.

Well, hell. He had to get over this damnable notion that Winter MacKeage was anything more than a means to an end, because she wasn't. He was here for one reason only, and once Winter helped him kill his brother, he didn't give a rat's ass if her mountain of magic blew itself to hell or not.

Nor did he care if he blew to hell with it.

Grace MacKeage sat a short distance away on a fallen log, watching the three men examine what was left of Daar's precious pine tree. She moved her gaze up the thirty-some-odd feet of remaining trunk and branches and stopped at the bluntly cut top, which was bleeding thick fingers of pine pitch. Robbie had climbed the trunk when they'd first arrived, calling down that it didn't appear to have been cut with a chain saw, but with an old-fashioned crosscut saw.

His observation had only served to deepen the mystery. Why had someone bothered to climb thirty feet into the air to cut the tree? And where the hell was the top?

Grace looked down and studied her chewed fingernails, blocking out the hushed conversation between Grey and Daar and Robbie as they searched the woods for signs of what had happened while speculating on *why* it had happened. Her eyes felt too big for her head, swollen and itchy from a sleepless night of crying. What had started out as a pleasant picnic with Grey yesterday had quickly turned into a nightmare for Grace when her husband had told her about his visit with the old priest that morning.

Their beautiful, innocent, unsuspecting daughter, Grey had explained, was being asked not only to step into her destiny now, but to face an adversary the likes of which none of them could even imagine. Cùram de Gairn, Grey had said, was likely here — in this time and on their mountain — seeking revenge for the death of his own tree of life. That, or he had some other agenda they couldn't figure out. All Grey had emphasized was that Winter was their only hope of stopping the bastard.

The fate of the world, it seemed, rested on the delicate shoulders of a twenty-four-year-old child.

Oh, how Grace wished for her predictable science to be all that there was again. At one time her world had been filled with only numbers, equations, and dreams of traveling into space. But when she had met Greylen MacKeage, Grace had discovered that the true wonders weren't *out there,* but right here on earth, as close as the mountain she'd grown up on. That was when her science had run headlong into the magic, and thirty-three years and seven daughters later, that magic was threatening not only her innocent baby, but the future of all of mankind.

A shadow fell over her, but Grace didn't look up. Her husband lowered down on his haunches, lifting her chin so that she was staring into his deeply worried eyes. "Any idea, wife," he asked softly, "why the tree was cut so high up?"

She let out a shuddering breath and shook her head in his hand, tears stinging the backs of her eyes again.

"I need ye, Grace. I need ye to be strong right now for Winter. None of us can fight what we don't understand. Please stop being a mama and be a scientist just long enough to help us figure out what's happening." His eyes softened with a tender smile. "Then ye can go back to protecting yer daughter."

"But I don't know why it was cut so high."

"Robbie said he thinks he can save the pine, at least for a little while," Grey said softly, turning to sit on the log beside her. He wrapped his arm around her shoulders and held her to him, just as he had been doing since yesterday afternoon. "He's going to cap the wound so it will stop oozing pitch, and we'll mulch the roots with leaves and pine needles to keep the frost away for as long as possible."

"What's the point?" Grace whispered, leaning into him, just as she had been doing since yesterday afternoon.

"It's not dead yet," Grey told her. "And it's all that's left of Winter's power. Robbie will cut one of the remaining branches so Daar can make her a staff."

Grace looked up without lifting her head off his shoulder. "You're sending our baby after this monster with nothing but a branch from a dying tree?" she asked. She sat up and clutched his arm. "Why can't Robbie give her some of his power? Or Mary? She's still around. I saw the snowy this morning, when Robbie came to the summit house to get us. Why can't the guardians lend Winter some of their powers?"

Grey held her face in his hands and used his thumbs to brush away her tears. "The white pine is their energy source as well as Daar's," he softly explained.

Grace pulled away and stood up, hugging her arms as she stared at the old priest studying his wounded tree. "Then he's won," she said. "Cùram de Gairn stole back his power, and he's won the fight without us even realizing we were at war." She turned and faced her husband. "It's over. Winter doesn't ever have to know about her destiny. Telling her would only make her think she's failed us somehow, when it's really our fault for wanting her childhood to be normal." Grace lifted her hands, then let them fall back to her sides. "We'll *all* just die together."

Grey stood up to his towering height and ran his palms soothingly over her arms and shoulders. "Daar doesn't believe it was Cùram who did this," he said, nodding toward the tree behind her. "He thinks Cùram would have taken a piece of the tap root, and then likely burned what was left of the pine."

"And you believe that senile old goat?" Grace snapped, stepping away and angrily waving at the air. "Most days he can't even remember what year he's living in!"

Her husband brought her into his arms again and held her head to his chest. "Shhh," he crooned. "Calm down, wife. Ye can get angry when this is over." He tilted her head back so she could see his smile. "We'll get angry together, I promise. But for now ye need to think about Winter and how we can help her."

"Grace," Daar said from behind her.

Grace tried to turn, but her husband shifted them both toward Daar while keeping her in his embrace.

"Grace," Daar said again, wringing his hands, his eyes fraught with worry. "Ye have to tell Winter today."

Grace pulled free and glared at Daar. "I am not telling my daughter a damn thing," she hissed. "And neither is Grey and neither are you."

"But —"

She pointed an angry finger at him. "You say one word to Winter, and you're going to discover I can be just as dangerous as my husband. I will cut out your heart, you interfering old goat," she growled, taking another threatening step closer.

Daar took several steps back, his eyes widened in shock. He'd never heard her speak to him like that, and truth told, Grace was a bit surprised herself. But dammit, she was angry enough to kill something.

Grace spun around at the sound of her husband's laughter, only to have Grey pull her back against him in a tight hug. "And that, old man," Grey said over her head, "is what happens when ye threaten a mama's bairn. I agree with my wife. We find out who cut yer tree, and why, before we tell Winter anything."

"But —"

"Ye make my daughter her staff, priest, and worry about saving what's left of yer precious pine. When we feel the time is right, Grace and I will have our talk with Winter. But until then, ye'll just have to wait for yer heir. If," he tightly whispered, "Winter even *wants* to follow her calling. The choice is ultimately hers."

Grace smiled into her husband's chest. Now she remembered why she'd married this wonderful man. She'd fallen in love with a highland warrior formidable enough to scare the whiskers off a charging lion.

CHAPTER ELEVEN

Despite only getting about six hours of sleep, and waking up still worried about her parents, Winter did spend the morning doing as Robbie had suggested by going about her business as usual. The storm had quickly spent itself out overnight, giving way to a late September sun that was shining brightly through the sparkling clean, floor-to-ceiling windows of her art gallery.

Megan, having survived her evening of practicing motherhood, seemed to be in a domestic mood this morning. By nine o'clock, she had already feather-dusted every painting and display in the gallery, and had gone outside to remove the street grime from the windows with a long-poled mop and squeegee. Having finished a good half hour ago, Megan had next turned her mop on the windows at Dolan's Outfitter Store, and then shared tea with Rose by the potbelly stove in Rose's store.

Winter had spent her first hour at the gallery setting Tom's newest figures out and getting caught up on her paperwork. She was now sitting on a stool behind the counter with a sketch pad and pencil, so engrossed in her vision of Matt's home nestled in the highland meadow that she never heard the overhead doorbell tinkle. She gasped in surprise when a large shadow suddenly appeared over her drawing and would have fallen off her stool but for the strong hands that caught her.

"What are you working on?" Matt asked with a chuckle, letting her go and tucking his hands behind his back as he looked over her shoulder.

Winter slapped the sketch pad to her chest and turned on her stool to scowl at him. "I'm just doodling."

He stepped around to face her and folded his arms over his chest. "That looked like a house you were 'doodling.' " He lifted one brow. "Is it my house?"

Winter stood up and closed the pad. "Maybe," was all she said as she slid the pad under the counter.

"Can I see?"

"No. I don't show my work until I'm done."

His brow lifted again. "Why not?"

"Because my work never makes sense to people until it's completed. What I start out with is usually a lot different than the final product."

"So your doodling is really your thought process?"

"Yes," she said, frowning when she noticed what he was wearing. "You have to start dressing more appropriately, Matt. You're going to ruin all your nice clothes."

"I am dressed appropriately," he said, glancing down at his crisp gray suit, then back at her, "for the office. I have to fly to New York this morning, but I'll be back early this evening. Have dinner with me again tonight?" He grinned crookedly. "I mean, *try* to have dinner with me tonight?"

"You expect to fly to New York and be back before dinner?"

"Better yet," he said, taking hold of her shoulders. "Come with me. We'll eat at Lutèce, and I'll have you back by bedtime."

Winter just got her second surprise of the morning. "Come with you to New York City?" she squeaked. "In your jet?"

His grin broadened. "I'll even let you try your hand at flying," he offered, his face lit with that same cajoling expression he'd used on her the first day they'd met, when he'd been trying to get a discount. "Ever fly at mach one?"

She eyed him suspiciously. "Private jets don't go that fast."

"Mine does. It's a modified fighter."

Her suspicion grew. "You couldn't have landed a jet that powerful at our tiny airport. The runway's too short."

It was his turn to look suspicious. "You seem to know an awful lot about planes."

"My mother's a scientist. She freelances for private space exploration companies." Winter shrugged her shoulders under his hands. "I inherited some of her knowledge by osmosis. All us girls spent a lot of time in Mama's computer lab while we were growing up. So you can't tempt me with promises of flying at mach one in your little jet, Mr. Gregor, because I know it's impossible."

"Nevertheless, it's true."

"How?" Winter asked, lifting her brow just to bug him.

He gave her shoulders a squeeze and let go with a laugh. "That's a company secret. Let's just call it magic. Come with me today."

Winter wondered what Matt would think if he knew what *real* magic could *really* do. "Thank you, but I can't," she said, shaking her head despite wanting to go with him. It would certainly be one way to learn more about the man behind the suit. She returned Matt's smile with a sad grin of apology. "Not unless you can fit my army of chaperones in your jet."

He instantly turned serious, his eyes narrowed to golden slits as he studied her in silence. "You're using your family as an excuse," he finally said. "What's the real reason you won't come with me?"

She lifted her chin. "I'm not flying to New York City with a man I barely know."

"You came damn close to knowing me quite well last night," he whispered, taking a step closer.

Winter looked down and brushed a speck of lint off her sleeve. "That was different," she whispered back, feeling the heat of a blush spread across her cheeks. "Last night I could have disappeared into the woods anytime I wanted." She looked up at him. "But in New York City, I'd be completely helpless."

He folded his arms over his chest, his enigmatic golden eyes studying her for what seemed like forever. "Okay," he softly conceded. "Point taken." He stepped forward, took hold of her shoulders again, and kissed her on the forehead. "I'll be back by seven, and I'll pick you up at your door at eight."

"What about your sunset with Tom this afternoon?"

Matt stepped away and walked around the counter to the wall of paintings. "I was going to ask you to explain to Tom when he came in this morning that I had to leave unexpectedly," he said, studying *Moon Watchers.* "We'll reschedule." He stepped closer to the painting, then suddenly turned to her with a grin. "A fairy isn't all you've hidden in here," he said, turning back to the large canvas and pointing at the top left corner. "I almost missed the wolf hidden in the shadows."

Winter walked over and stood beside him to also look at *Moon Watchers.* "That's my grandfather, old Duncan MacKeage."

"Your grandfather was a wolf?"

She smiled. "My papa told me Duncan MacKeage had the heart of a wolf, so that's how I portrayed him."

Matt pivoted to face her. "You put dead people in your paintings?"

"Sometimes," she said, nodding. "As a reminder that their spirits still walk with us," she explained. "And to acknowledge that each generation stands on the shoulders of the previous generation, forming the foundation that helps us face the future." She took hold of Matt's hand and led him to the back wall of the gallery. "See that snowy owl?" she asked, pointing to the upper right-hand corner of another wintertime scene. "That's my mama's sister, Mary Sutter. She's Robbie's mother, but she died when he was born." Winter glanced at the silent, contemplative man beside her as he looked at the drawing. "There really is a snowy that lives on TarStone. I like to think she's my aunt Mary, watching over all of us."

Matt looked at her. "So the painting you do for me, of my house . . . you could put a member of my family in it?"

"Yes, if you tell me about the person. I need to get a feel for who it is. Do you have someone in particular in mind? Male or female?"

"Female," he said, folding his arms over his chest and resting his chin on one hand as he gazed at the snowy owl. "Her name's Fiona, and she'd also be a bird, I think. A beautiful hawk, maybe."

"Fiona," Winter repeated, testing the name. "Is she your mother? Grandmother?"

"My sister."

"Ah, my spirits are usually . . . they're usually deceased, Matt," Winter said softly.

"Fiona died in childbirth."

"Okay," Winter said even more softly, putting two and two together between Matt's reaction to Megan yesterday and this revelation about his own sister. "Do you have a photograph of Fiona I could see?"

Matt glanced at her, and Winter nearly stepped back at the look of anguish in his eyes. "I don't have anything of hers," he said tightly. "Not even her locket."

"Locket?"

"Fiona had a gold locket our mother had given her on her sixteenth birthday, which had belonged to our grandmother." He looked back at the painting, though Winter doubted he was seeing anything other than his sister in his mind's eye. "But I could never find out what became of it."

"You mentioned having a brother the first day you were here. He doesn't know where the locket is?" Winter asked gently.

Winter saw Matt stiffen. "No," was all he said, that one word completely devoid of emotion.

"Then you'll just have to tell me about Fiona," Winter continued brightly, attempting to wash away the chill that had suddenly descended over her gallery. She took hold of Matt's hand again, ignoring the fact that it was balled into a fist, and led him back down the side wall. "Over dinner tonight, if you want, you can tell me why you think

Fiona's spirit is a beautiful hawk. Here," she said, stopping in front of a large watercolor of a moose. She pointed at the bushes, where she had hidden the nearly translucent image of a red fox. "This is my uncle Ian. He's the one Megan told you about yesterday, who insisted we ride draft horses."

Again, Matt studied the painting in silence.

Winter didn't know what to think, much less what to say to him. She did decide that getting to know Matt Gregor was a lot like painting her pictures; the process was proving painstakingly complex, with only vague snippets being revealed the deeper she delved. He had a brother, apparently alive but obviously estranged, and a sister he'd loved who had died in childbirth. He built jets, seemed to go after what he wanted with the efficiency of a successful businessman, and he kissed like a prince.

Well, he had certainly awakened this sleeping princess, and she was just as determined to get to know her prince a whole lot better. "I'll be ready at eight," she said, turning to walk back to the counter.

He stopped her by reaching out and capturing her face between his broad hands, his fingers splaying through her hair at the back of her head, his palms lifting her chin to look at him. "I'm sorry," he said gutturally. "The subject of my brother is a sore one." He took a deep breath that ended with a smile. "I'm going to kiss you, Winter MacKeage, right here in front of your ancestors, so they'll see exactly what my intentions are."

Winter's heart skipped several beats, then started thumping with the force of a sledge hammer. "W-what are your intentions?" she whispered, unable to look away from his intense, mesmerizing, so deeply golden eyes.

His smile went from warm to heart-stopping handsome. "You'll have to ask *them,*" he said, nodding toward her paintings, "or trust me enough to discover that for yourself."

"I — I tru—"

He lowered his head and covered her mouth with his before her declaration could even reach her ancestors. Winter rose on her toes and parted her lips, welcoming whatever his intentions might be as his tongue sought hers. The onslaught of energy that hummed through her body was as immediate and just as powerful as last night. Matt smelled of fine wool, the forest, and crisp autumn air. Winter could taste just a hint of coffee, and she reveled in the feel of his fingers curled into her hair as he carefully moved his mouth over hers. She wrapped her arms around his waist inside his jacket, snuggling closer as he lowered one hand between her shoulders and pulled her tightly against him.

Tiny bells started tinkling in her head.

Matt suddenly broke the kiss, held her shoulders to steady her, and turned with a harsh glare aimed at the door. Winter quickly stepped back at the realization they were no longer alone, spun on her heel, and ran behind the counter.

"Good morning," Tom said. "That was quite a wild storm we had last night, wasn't it?"

Not nearly as wild as the one raging inside her right now, Winter decided. "Ah, good morning, Tom. You're out early."

Tom didn't answer her, his attention focused on Matt. The old hermit tucked a package under his left arm and extended his right hand. "Morning, Gregor," he said, shaking the hand Matt extended in return. "You don't look like you're ready to hike the woods this afternoon."

"I'm afraid I have to take a rain check on our sunset," Matt said. "I need to go to my office and take care of a small matter. I'll be back this evening, though. Maybe tomorrow?"

Tom nodded. "I believe I might be free tomorrow. That your jet I was looking at this morning up at the airport?"

"It's mine."

"Will she really do mach one?"

Winter could only gape at Tom. How could he possibly know Matt's jet went that fast?

Matt apparently wondered the same thing. He folded his arms over his chest and lifted one brow. "What makes you think she goes mach one?"

Tom shrugged. "I'm a bit of an aviation junkie," he said in way of explanation. "Seems I remember reading an article about a company in Utah trying to adapt military jet engines to corporate jets a couple of years back." He grinned. "I also remember, now that I think about it, that the owner of the company was someone named Gregor."

Matt inclined his head, a slight smile lifting one side of his mouth. "She goes mach one," he confirmed. He nodded toward Winter. "Though our little friend here doesn't believe me."

Tom laughed. "Winter's more likely to believe fairies fly at mach one," he said, lifting the package from under his arm and unwrapping it. "I have something for you, Gregor, for your new house."

Curiosity propelled Winter around the counter to see what Tom had brought.

"It's just one part of a prototype, as they say in your business," Tom said, finally revealing his surprise. "The scale is eight to one, and the final piece should probably be made of granite rather than wood."

Winter leaned closer and frowned.

Tom held the foot-tall statue toward her, angling it to show her the front. "Have I got the wording right?" he asked. "The book I looked it up in wasn't that clear."

Winter read the words to herself: *Saobhaidh a' Mhathain.* She nudged Tom to give the statue to Matt. "It's right," she said. "You pronounce it Seu-vee uh Va-han."

"And it means?" Matt asked, taking the wooden piece and holding it up to examine, even turning it upside down before he looked at Winter for his answer.

"The bear's den," she told him. "It's Gaelic, and that's the perfect name for your new home."

Matt looked sharply at Tom. "What made you choose a bear's den for me?"

Tom shrugged. "You own Bear Mountain, so I thought that if you're building your home there, it was only appropriate."

Matt's eyes narrowed. "Why Gaelic?"

"Why not?" Tom returned. "Gregor is

Scots, isn't it?"

"But where's the bear, Tom?" Winter asked before Matt could respond, taking the wooden figure from Matt to examine.

Tom had carved a miniature bear's den in a wooden likeness of a granite cliff surrounded by trees and boulders. The bottom of the cliff had been hollowed into a cave, the interior floor lined with straw and fir branches. Over the top of the den was a board with the Gaelic name carved into it. But the den was empty.

"I haven't carved the bear yet," Tom said.

Winter narrowed her eyes at him. "You couldn't have done this in one day," she said. She shook her head, looking at the delicately carved trees, granite, and boulders. Even the fur bows and cut grass inside the cave were perfectly detailed from the single piece of wood. "This would have taken you weeks."

Tom shrugged. "It took me nearly a month. I started it quite a while ago, then shelved it." He looked at Matt. "But when I learned you were building a house on Bear Mountain, I dug around until I found it again, and thought you might like to have a full-scale statue for your new home."

Matt took the statue from Winter, gave it another careful inspection, then turned a calculating look on Tom. "How much?"

Tom grinned. "About two and a half years of rent for a run-down cabin out on a point of land you own. Oh, and a ride in that jet of yours," he tacked on.

Matt gave a bark of laughter and handed the statue back to Tom. "Then you should probably hold on to this, if it's your working model. Can you have the full-scale project finished by the time my house is done?"

Winter wanted to shout with joy, but instead she reached over, grabbed Matt by the sleeve, and pulled him down to give him a big kiss on the cheek. "You have an artist in residence, Mr. Gregor," she said, smiling broadly at his stunned look. She turned to Tom, her smile turning smug. "And you, Mr. Tom, are brilliant."

She spun back to Matt. "You need to get out of here if you want to be back by dinner, mach one or not." She stepped closer and lowered her voice. "I might even wear a dress this evening."

Matt's eyes locked on hers. "What color?" he asked softly.

"Green."

He nodded, his heated gaze holding her captive. Curses, he wasn't even touching her and Winter felt herself melting into a puddle of mush! She was just starting to buckle at the knees when Matt broke the spell by looking over her head at Tom and nodding. "I'll be at your cabin tomorrow afternoon about an hour before sunset," he said before suddenly walking out the door. The tiny bell made Winter's nerve tingle with awareness as she watched Matt head toward the black truck parked just down the street.

"It's about time a man came along and put some color in your cheeks," Tom said.

Winter turned to find Tom wrapping up his model. She reached over to stop him, giving him a good glare. "Not one word about his straightening out my being spoiled," she said, taking the carving and walking behind the counter. She set it down on the counter and smiled. "You're more sneaky than Gesader, Tom. I couldn't have come up with a better idea myself. Now Matt can't kick you out."

Tom walked over and stood opposite her. "This man you thought so poorly of because you feared he might evict me — I'm surprised to find you kissing him."

Feeling her cheeks flaming red again, Winter wanted to crawl inside the little bear's den sitting on her counter and pull one of its bushes closed behind her.

Tom laughed and picked up the model, handling it as if it were no more precious than an old rock he'd found on the shore of Pine Lake. "I better start earning my rent," he said, wrapping it back up in the towel. "So, Goldie Locks," he added, tucking the carving under his arm and grinning at her. "I mean, so Miss Strawberry Goldie Locks," he amended with a grin, "do I put a mama, papa, and baby bear in my den?"

Winter blinked at him, her jaw momentarily slackened in shock. "What is it with everyone around here?" she snapped. "You all have me practically married to a man I met two days ago."

Tom's eyes danced with amusement. "Seems to me you've gotten rather well acquainted in only two days," he said, turning and starting toward the door. He stopped with his hand on the knob and grinned at her. "And from the look in Gregor's eyes just before he left, I'm guessing I'll only have to wait a few weeks to know how many bears to put in my sculpture," he said with a laugh as he stepped through the door.

Winter just stared after him, stunned to the roots of her strawberry hair. She couldn't decide if she'd just been insulted or challenged. Was Tom telling her she was going after Matt too quickly, or that he thought she should move even faster?

Curses, would she ever understand men?

Winter reached under the counter and grabbed her sketch pad. She sat down on the stool, opened the pad, and stared at the two-story log and stone lodge she'd been sketching. But all she saw was a mama, papa, and baby bear snuggled up together inside the cozy little den Tom had carved.

No, she thought with a quick shake of her head, erasing the image from her mind. She was just learning to deal with her strong attraction to Matheson Gregor; she wasn't anywhere near ready to start dreaming about having his babies — no matter how warm and fuzzy that made her feel.

CHAPTER TWELVE

Sitting opposite Grey beside the brightly burning hearth in the main living room of Gù Brath, Grace lifted her eyes from the book she'd been pretending to read to the clock on the mantel. It was twenty minutes to eight, and Grace knew her husband was also pretending to be so engrossed in his newspaper, one might think he'd forgotten all about his youngest daughter's impending date.

"Ye still haven't addressed the fact that Winter is going to live for centuries and her husband will not," Grey softly said into the silence.

Grace looked over at him, not at all surprised he knew her thoughts, not after thirty-three years of marriage. "Would fifty years of happiness not be worth it, though?" she asked just as softly. "Or twenty years? Or even ten? Would you have Winter close her heart off completely?" Grace shut the book on her lap and leaned forward. "If I had died ten years ago, and you were sitting in this room right now with only your memories of me, would you be wishing instead that we'd never met? That we hadn't had at least twenty-three wonderful years together?"

"Nay."

"Then why would Winter be any different? Do you really believe she's going to live hundreds of years without forming strong attachments? She can't, Grey, because she feels things too deeply. Her heart will still get broken over and over again. Why do you think Daar keeps himself isolated up on the mountain? Is that what you want Winter to become? Another Father Daar?"

"Nay."

Grace set her book on the floor and scooted down to settle between Grey's knees. She cuddled against him and leaned her head on his pounding heart, sighing when he wrapped his strong arms around her. "And who knows," she continued. "If Winter got rid of this Cùram jerk and saved Daar's tree of life, there's nothing to say she couldn't live happily ever after." She tilted her head back to look at Grey. "Even super-heroes eventually retire. Women today are having their careers first and then their families. Winter can save the world and *then* have her babies." Grace squeezed his rock-solid torso. "The important thing is, *she* chooses her path. Not us, and not Father Daar."

"It's a path we haven't even told her about yet," Grey reminded her. "She needs to know before she gets too involved with Gregor."

"No," Grace said, straightening to look Grey level in the eyes. "We agreed to wait until we solve the mystery of the mutilated pine tree."

He gently pulled her back against him and held her head to his chest. "Then remind me to get Robbie to look into Gregor's background. I forgot to ask him today because I got involved in that damn tree."

Grace bolted upright again. "No," she said, giving him a fierce glare. "You and Robbie will not interfere. And tonight, when we meet Matt Gregor, you will be the epitome of politeness. You will not scowl or in any way try to intimidate him."

Grey scowled now. "Gregor's not much of a man if a little fatherly posturing is all it takes to scare him off." Grey pulled her back against him, holding her head down with his chin and hugging her fiercely on a deep sigh. "Ye'd think I'd be better at this, having gone through it five times already."

Grace was just snuggling closer when Grey suddenly stiffened and sucked in his breath. "Jesus, Joseph, and Mary," he whispered. He removed himself from his wife's arms and stood up. "Ye go right back upstairs and change," he growled, pointing toward the living room door.

Grace scrambled to her feet and turned to see Winter and Megan standing in the doorway, Megan grinning like a Cheshire cat and Winter gaping at her papa. "Oh, you look beautiful," Grace said, going to Winter. "I knew when I bought that dress it was perfect for you." She took hold of Winter's shoulders and turned her around. "Just perfect."

"She's not leaving here looking like that," Grey snapped.

Grace ignored him, turning Winter back to face her. "The heels aren't too high, are they?" she asked, checking out the shoes she had bought to match the calf-length dress. "They're only an inch high."

"They're fine, Mama," Winter said, running her hands down the dark green velvet material. She looked past Grace's shoulder at her papa and scowled right back at him.

"There is nothing immodest about this dress."

"Aye, and that's the problem," Grey returned from right behind Grace. "Ye look *too* modest. And that is more enticing than if ye were wearing a bathing suit." He waved a hand at his again-gaping daughter. "At least braid yer hair, so it doesn't fall over yer shoulders so . . . so provocatively."

Grace rolled her eyes at her daughters and burst into laughter as she spun to face her husband. She was just giving him another poke in the chest, about ready to scold him, when the door knocker sounded. "Be good," she said instead. She turned to capture Winter's hand to keep her from answering the door. "Let your sister get it," she commanded, pulling her into the living room while pushing Grey ahead of them. "My God, you're acting like Winter's sixteen," she muttered, shoving her laughing daughter in the chair beside the hearth and Grey into the opposite chair. Grace then turned while smoothing down the front of her blouse, folded her hands at her waist, and plastered a welcoming smile on her face just as Megan stepped into the living room doorway with Matt Gregor.

Grace immediately went weak in the knees.

The man was utterly gorgeous. Definitely imposing. His eyes . . . they were . . . she couldn't tear herself away from his fantastically golden eyes. Holy hell, she thought with a shiver, no wonder Winter was a mess of churning emotions. Grace was getting a bit emotional herself.

"Mama," Megan said, leading Matt all the way into the room. "This is Matt Gregor. Matt, these are my parents, Grace and Greylen MacKeage."

Grace was just getting her racing heart under control when Matt Gregor gave her a smile that stopped it completely. He inclined his head and held his hand out to her, and Grace found she couldn't breathe. In thirty-three years of marriage she had never once reacted to another man this way, most likely because she'd never met a man who could even come close to rivaling Greylen Mac-Keage.

Until now. Grace placed her hand in Matt's, immediately noticing how solid he felt. "Mr. Gregor," she said, praying she sounded normal, "it's a pleasure to meet you."

"The pleasure is mine, Mrs. MacKeage," he returned, his deep voice resonating with warmth. "I can see where Winter and Megan get their beauty. And please, call me Matt."

"Gregor," Grey said, extending his right hand while gently pulling Grace away from their guest. "I understand ye own Bear Mountain. Are ye planning on developing it?"

"Mr. MacKeage," Matt said, shaking Grey's hand. "I bought the land for my own use. I plan to build my home there."

"It's a rather long commute to New York City."

Matt shrugged. "But worth it, I think," was all he said as he leaned to the side to better see Winter standing behind Grace.

Grace was impressed with Winter's restraint so far, and not at all surprised by Grey's lack thereof. Her husband was looking at Matt as if he were a bug he was wanting to crush.

To Matt's credit, he didn't seem worried, but his polite smile did disappear the moment Grace stepped to the side. His eyes locked on Winter with such intense male appreciation, Grace went weak in the knees again.

"Where are ye going tonight?" Grey asked, moving between Winter and Matt.

"To the resort restaurant," Matt said somewhat absently, completely focused on their daughter. He took a step around the mountain of fatherly concern and held out his hand. "You look lovely, Winter. I take back what I said last night. I think I do prefer you in a dress."

Winter placed her hand in his, gave Grace a "will you please control Papa" look, and moved to stand beside Matt, linking her arm through his. "In the interest of not turning into a pumpkin, I'll be home by midnight," she said. She looked at her father and smiled smugly. "You needn't wait up," she finished as she quickly led Matt out of the living room.

But her escort brought her to a halt in the doorway, turned back to the room, and inclined his head. "I'll have her home by eleven," Matt said. He looked directly at Grey. "Let me know where and when you want to meet for coffee, and I'll answer any questions you have about me."

Grey said nothing, merely nodded.

Matt nodded in return, lifted Winter's gaping jaw closed with his finger, and finally led her out the front door.

The moment the door shut, Megan burst into laughter. "Oh, Papa, I wish you could see your expression right now," she said, walking up and rising on her tiptoes to give him a kiss on the cheek. "I can't remember the last time anyone, male or female — other than Mama," she whispered, "caught you off guard." She turned to Grace. "And you. You should be ashamed of yourself for getting all flustered by Matt's good looks."

"I'm old, not dead," Grace said with a laugh.

"Go to yer room," Grey told Megan. "Ye're no better than either yer mama or yer sister."

Not the least bit bothered to be treated like she was only sixteen, Megan turned on her heels and all but bounced across the foyer to the stairs. She stopped on the bottom step. "I like Matt," she said. "And so does Winter."

"Ye don't even know him," Grey snapped.

"I know Gesader didn't eat him when Matt kissed Winter up on the mountain last night," Megan returned, again laughing at her father's stunned expression. "Winter told me Gesader was there, but that he didn't so much as growl. So Matt must be a nice guy. Animals are good judges of character."

It took both of Grace's hands over her mouth to stifle her laughter.

The first rumbles of a growl started deep in her husband's chest, only to finally erupt in a full-blown curse when he turned to Grace. "Ye're laughing while our innocent daughter just left with a man who's interested in only one thing." Grey waved an angry hand at the door. "Dammit, did ye not see how Gregor was looking at our baby girl!"

Grace reached up and traced a finger down the side of his scowling face. "I most certainly did," she said, patting his cheek. "And I remember seeing that same look in your eyes thirty-three years ago, husband." She rose on her toes while pulling down on his shirt collar to gently kiss his taut cheek. "And I can't tell you how much that pleases me."

"Pleases ye?" he repeated, stepping back to better glare at her. "What about a predator dating our daughter pleases ye?"

Grace mimicked his stance by folding her own arms under her breasts. "I'm pleased because I've just realized something you and Robbie and Father Daar never considered, which changes the entire equation of Winter's destiny," she said. "None of you factored in the possibility of someone like Matt Gregor coming along. The man I just met has no intention of letting something as insignificant as our daughter's destiny stand in his way. Yes, I could see that he wants her, and I say let him go for it."

Grace unfolded her husband's arms and held both his hands. "I love you, Greylen

MacKeage. You've been my rock and my wings and my fiercest protector. Let Winter have what we've had. Let Matt Gregor be her superman."

"So ye've decided he's superman after meeting him for all of two minutes?" Grey asked softly. "How can ye know that?"

Grace looked down at her fingers twined in her husband's strong hands. "I just know." She smiled up at him. "You might call it magic, but I prefer to call it motherly intuition."

He studied her for several heartbeats, then suddenly turned away. "I have to go to the office," he said, grabbing his jacket from the row of pegs on the foyer wall.

"Oh, no you don't," Grace muttered, grabbing the jacket away from him and hanging it back on the peg. "You are not going anywhere near that resort tonight."

"I have paperwork to do. Morgan and Callum and I are meeting with our accountant in the morning."

Grace captured his hand reaching for the jacket again and pulled it around her waist. She took hold of his other hand, settled it around her, then wrapped her own hands around his neck. "*Our* meeting tonight is more important," she whispered, leaning into him.

Her husband always had been a quick study. His hands around her waist tightened at the realization of exactly what their meeting tonight was about. His cheeks darkened, his eyes focused completely on her, and his mouth swooped down and captured her pleased smile.

Thirty-three years, and the magic still managed to catch her by surprise. Grace parted her lips to her superman, which instantly caused flashes of brilliant, sizzling white light to charge the air around them. Just that quickly, and just that intensely, she was caught in passion's spell as Grey lifted her off her toes and deepened the kiss.

"Take me to bed," she whispered into his mouth. "Make love to me, husband."

She didn't have to ask twice. Grey bent to capture her knees and swept her up in his arms. "I know what ye're doing, woman," he growled as he carried her up the stairs, his fiercely intense eyes locked on hers. He suddenly smiled, rather ferally. "Remind me to give ye hell in the morning."

Grace rested her head on his shoulder so he wouldn't see her own smug smile. With any luck, they'd both be too tired in the morning to do anything more than sleep in.

CHAPTER THIRTEEN

Winter finished brushing Snowball and started saddling him up as she thought about how she had known Matt Gregor for over two weeks now, and how the entire time she'd been in a state of giddy happiness. She had spent the last two weeks exploring Bear Mountain with Matt by day and going out to dinner with him almost every evening. Sometimes Megan would join them on their daytime rides, and sometimes they rode to Tom's cabin and he hiked the mountain with them.

And although they had found several suitable building sites, Matt always seemed to come back to the high meadow as his first choice. But after two weeks and four sketch pads full of ideas, Winter suspected Matt's unwillingness to simply declare the meadow his favorite site had more to do with wanting to spend time with her than an inability to make a decision.

Five days ago Matt had bought camping equipment from Dolan's Outfitter Store, and even though he had kept his hotel suite, he was now living on Bear Mountain and only coming back to the resort to shower before picking her up for dinner each evening.

Matt had set his campsite at the top of the high meadow in a cave hallowed into an outcropping of rock that overlooked both the meadow and Pine Lake. He'd made a cozy little camp that was still within earshot of Bear Brook and seemed surprisingly comfortable roughing it despite October's increasingly cold weather. The second night sleeping out, Matt had awakened to a two-inch blanket of snow, though it had completely melted by noon. But instead of scaring him off, the snow only seemed to further endear Matt to his mountain.

When Matt had first mentioned his plan to camp in the cave so he could get a better feel for the mountain, Winter had become alarmed. She'd talked to Tom about the two swordsmen he'd seen in the meadow, worried that Matt might run into them.

Tom had reminded her Matt had a pistol and that a bullet beat a sword any day of the week. Her boyfriend appeared more than capable of looking out for himself, Tom had assured Winter. And telling Matt there had been two men dressed in kilts, fighting with swords in his meadow in the light of a full moon, would only make him think his artist in residence might be crazy.

So Winter had taken her petition to Gesader, explaining her worry and asking her pet to please keep an eye on Matt for her. She wasn't sure if the panther had understood her request, much less cared what happened to Matt, but Gesader hadn't been home for the last five nights. Winter could only hope it was because he was lurking around Bear Mountain, watching for Tom's elusive swordsmen.

Matt had flown back to New York City several times in the last two weeks, and each time before he left he would stop at Winter's gallery and ask her to go with him. Each time she would tell him no, and each time Matt took her refusal with the graciousness of a gentleman.

Not that he kissed like a gentleman. Nay, Matt's kisses had grown increasingly more . . . well, more heated as Winter had grown more comfortable with him — which is exactly why she refused to go to New York City. The night on the mountain when they'd taken Daar home, when she'd all but thrown herself at Matt, had made Winter realize how close she'd come to nearly blowing it.

She liked Matt. He was everything she could want in a man: intelligent, successful, attentive, charming, utterly gorgeous, and sexy as all get out. The only flaw that she could find was that he was *too* honorable.

Winter could no longer deny that she wanted Matt Gregor so badly her heart actually ached. That first night they'd kissed had definitely been too soon for anything more, but dang it, how much longer was he going to drive her crazy with only kisses? The chemistry was right — she *knew* it was right. And she knew Matt also felt what she felt. So what in curses was he waiting for? For her to finally go to New York with him? Was he seeing her refusal as a sign she wasn't ready to take the next step?

Surely he realized she needed that monumental step to be right here in Pine Creek where she felt safe, didn't he?

Winter led Snowball out of the barn as she thought about the predicament she was in. How was she supposed to let Matt know she wanted him, but that their first time had to be on *her* turf? And then how was she going to explain being twenty-four years old and still a virgin without looking like a silly child?

She wasn't a prude; she was just fussy, was all. She simply had never met a man who made her insides hum with desire — not until Matheson Gregor had walked into her gallery. So how could she take the next step without coming across as a sex-starved hussy, and without having to go to New York City?

She couldn't ask her mama, Winter decided with a frown as she stepped onto the mounting block and swung into the saddle. She couldn't quite see herself explaining how badly she wanted to make love to Matt, much less asking Grace to please give her some pointers on how to go about it. Aye, she thought with a snort, that would be quite a conversation between mother and daughter.

Her mama seemed to have bigger worries right now, other than her daughter's sex life. Winter's last two weeks of happiness were marred only by the fact that she still couldn't discover what was bugging her parents. Their moods seemed to be getting worse as time passed, not better. Her papa rode daily with Robbie up TarStone Mountain to Father Daar's, and Winter knew the three men were still trying to find out what had happened to the pine tree.

And her mama was up there with them

today, which was why Winter was heading up TarStone herself. Matt had flown to his factory in Utah last night after dinner, and had said he probably wouldn't be back for a couple of days, which left Winter plenty of time to spy on her parents. One way or another, once and for all, she was going to find out what the big secret was.

Instead of taking the tote road, Winter urged Snowball into a canter straight up the ski slope. She would go almost to the summit and approach Daar's cabin from an unlikely direction. She'd leave Snowball a good distance away, sneak up on the cabin, and listen to what was going on inside.

She had Megan's wholehearted approval, both girls deciding they were being caring daughters, not spies. Winter preferred to think she was helping Megan, since constant fretting on top of a broken heart was slowly turning Megan into a basket case. That was why Winter had talked her sister into watching the gallery this morning while she followed their parents.

Winter pulled up the collar on her jacket to ward off the chill October breeze as she eyed the bank of clouds moving in from the southeast. A storm was moving up the New England coast, and it was predicted to dump Atlantic moisture ahead of it across the entire state of Maine. For the coast that meant rain; for the mountains, six-to-ten inches of wet snow. It was still early yet for accumulating snow, despite the unusually cold and stormy fall, but even if a foot of snow fell, it wouldn't likely stick around more than a week.

Winter pulled Snowball back to a walk as she guided him off the ski slope and onto a narrow trail that wove through the woods. They hadn't gone twenty yards when Gesader stepped into view and sat down right in the middle of the path. Snowball stopped, tugged on his bit to loosen his reins, and nuzzled the panther's head. Gesader returned Snowball's greeting with a throaty growl and a rough lick to the horse's nose.

"Well, good morning," Winter said, leaning forward in the saddle to look down at her pet. "How come you didn't come home last night? Matt's gone."

Gesader snarled in greeting, turned, and padded up the path ahead of them. Snowball automatically started following him, and Winter chuckled to herself.

Either Gesader could read her mind or he knew this path ended at Father Daar's cabin, because her pet continued to take up the lead for the next twenty minutes. He suddenly stopped in a thick stand of trees about two hundred yards above the cabin's clearing, sat down, and simply stared up at her.

"Yes," she whispered, dismounting and tying Snowball's reins to a bush. "You can help me spy."

As if he understood exactly what she wanted, Gesader led the way to the clearing on the south side of Daar's cabin. Winter saw only two horses tied up out front, her papa's warhorse and old Butterball, which meant Robbie wasn't there. She nudged Gesader with her knee, signaling him to work his way around the perimeter of the clearing toward the front. "Ye keep a watch out for Robbie," she whispered as she started working her way around the clearing, using the trees for cover.

She watched and listened for a good five minutes, then finally tiptoed across the open space and up to the back wall of the cabin. Keeping her back against the weathered logs, she inched her way toward the window and slowly straightened to peer inside.

Daar was sitting at the table opposite her papa, Daar softly talking and her papa listening. Her mama was standing at the wood-fired cookstove, poking bacon in the large iron skillet with a wooden spoon. Grace suddenly stopped, turned to the men with a frown, and waved her spoon at them.

"I don't know what makes you think Winter can find him if none of us have been able to," Grace said angrily. "Even Mary hasn't been able to discover anything. And that puny staff you made for Winter can't even light a candle."

Winter scowled. What in hell were they talking about? Have her find who? And what staff? Had Daar made her a staff like his? Come to think of it, Winter realized she hadn't seen Daar's thick old staff for months now; he'd been using a wooden cane made from a maple sapling to get around. So why would he have made *her* a staff instead of one for himself?

Curses, what was going on?

"It will have plenty of energy in Winter's hands," Daar countered, glaring at Grace. "Once she gets her mind off that Gregor fellow and onto the business at hand." He turned his glare on Grey. "Ye need to tell her now. We need Winter's magic. The pine is *dying.*"

They needed her magic?

She didn't have any magic. That was Robbie and Daar's calling. Winter stepped away from the window and pressed her back to the cabin, frowning at the trees across the clearing.

Her magic? *Her* staff? Tell her *what* now?

She turned to the window again when she heard a chair slide back. Her papa had stood up. He walked over to Grace, took hold of her shoulders, and said, "He's right, wife. We can't wait any longer. We have to tell Winter today." He leaned down and kissed the top of Grace's head. "Putting it off is only compounding the problem," he continued. Winter saw his hands tighten on her mama's shoulders, and Grace looked up at him, tears welling in her eyes. "If ye want Winter to get on with her life," Grey said, "then we have to tell her now, so she can help us find and destroy Cùram."

Winter sucked in her breath. Cùram? The wizard Robbie had stolen the tap root from? She was supposed to find him?

And destroy him?

Winter never did hear her mama's response, what with her screaming when a pair of large hands suddenly caught her at the waist, spun her around, and tossed her over a broad, solid shoulder.

"Oh-ho, didn't yer mama tell ye it's not nice to spy?" Robbie said with a laugh as he strode along the side of the cabin with her over his shoulder.

Winter squirmed furiously, but when that only got her a smack on her bottom, she pinched Robbie's back just above his belt. "Let me go," she hissed, rearing up and smacking his shoulder. "I wasn't spying. I was getting Daar some firewood."

All she got for an answer was a laugh, but she did have the satisfaction of hearing Robbie grunt when her flailing feet connected with his thigh. The final indignity came as Robbie was mounting the steps, when Winter caught sight of Gesader lying in the bushes at the edge of the clearing, lazily licking his paws.

Robbie entered the cabin and set Winter down on her feet, grabbing her wrist as if expecting her to bolt. "Ye have varmints lurking in yer bushes," he said to the startled occupants of the one-room cabin. "I warned ye, old man, not to toss yer scrap food out so close by."

"Winter!" Grace said with a gasp, rushing up to her. "What are you doing here?"

Winter lifted her chin. "I'm trying to find out what's been bugging you and Papa for the last two weeks." She tugged her wrist free and turned her furious glare on her papa. "What is it you've finally decided to tell me? What's going on? And what did you mean by *my* magic?"

Winter became truly alarmed when her papa broke eye contact and looked at the floor, his face paling to ashen white. Never, ever, had Winter seen the powerful Laird Greylen MacKeage back down — certainly not from one of his daughters, and certainly not from a direct question.

"Winter," Grace whispered, taking her hand and leading her over to the table, urging her down in a chair. She pulled another chair up beside Winter, took hold of her hand again, and squeezed it as she darted a worried glance at her husband. "Th-there's something your father and I need to tell you," she said softly, looking at Winter and leaning closer. "Something we've been keeping from you all this time."

"W-what?" Winter whispered, feeling the blood drain from her own face as she looked into her mother's turbulent eyes.

The silence became absolute, until her papa suddenly pulled up a chair to sit beside her and took hold of her other hand. "Ye're . . . the reason we . . . ye —" he began, only to pale again and look at Grace. Winter followed his gaze, looking at her mother in question.

"Have you never wondered why Daar brought your father forward in time thirty-seven years ago?" Grace asked softly.

"No," Winter said. "Yes," she quickly contradicted with a shake of her head. "Of

236

course I've wondered. All us girls have." She nodded toward the silent priest standing by the hearth. "But the only logical reason we could think of was that Daar had messed up another one of his spells."

Grace shook her head. "No, he didn't make a mistake. Daar brought Greylen here on purpose." She smiled crookedly. "The others, the MacBains and your MacKeage uncles, they were a mistake. It was only supposed to be Greylen who came forward."

"But why?"

"To meet me," Grace said softly, squeezing Winter's hand again. "So we could have seven daughters together."

Winter blinked at her mama. Daar had brought a highland warrior eight hundred years through time just to make babies?

Grey snorted. "Aye, it seems so," he said, and Winter realized she'd spoken out loud.

"I was supposed to be the seventh son of a seventh son," Grace continued, drawing Winter's attention again. Her crooked smile broadened. "But I was born a female, and it appears that it was my seventh daughter who was destined to be gifted."

"G-gifted?" Winter whispered.

"Aye," her papa said, scooting closer and lacing his fingers through hers. He took a deep breath and reached up and brushed a strand of hair off her face. "Ye have a very special gift, baby girl," he said. "Ye were born with the knowledge of the universe in ye."

"I — I don't have any knowledge," she whispered, darting a worried look at her mother before locking her gaze back on her father. "If I did, I . . . wouldn't I *know* it?"

"Nay," he said with a slight shake of his head. "It seems ye need to be made aware of yer gift first. Ye need to be taught the skills of a *drùidh.*"

"*Drùidh!*" Winter yelped, untangling herself from her parents and standing up, sending her chair skittering across the floor. She pointed at the still-silent priest. "Like him? Are you saying I'm like Daar!"

Both Grey and Grace immediately stood, but when Grey stepped toward her with his hand outstretched, Winter took a step back and gave a curt shake of her head. "No." She took another step back. "I'm not a wizard. I can't be a wizard! I would know if I was," she cried, slapping her hand to her chest. "I would know!"

"Ye don't know because the magic is dormant until ye're made aware of it," Daar interjected, stepping away from the hearth.

"Stay out of this, old man," her papa growled.

"Nay," Daar countered. "She needs to know the truth." He looked at Winter. "Ye wouldn't realize ye have the magic in ye, lass, unless ye knew to look for it. Ye've always carried the energy, but ye must look deep inside yourself to find it. It doesn't just come to ye, ye have to go in search of it."

"It was exactly the same for me, Winter," Robbie said, stepping away from the closed door he'd been leaning against. He smiled warmly at her. "I was twenty-six years old before my papa explained my calling to me."

"But you were only eight when you saved Rose Dolan in the snowstorm when she was just a few months old," Winter pointed out. "You were a guardian even then. You nearly died saving her."

"Aye," Robbie agreed. "But I was only acting from instinct to save an infant. I had no idea what I was doing."

"But I don't even have instinct!" Winter cried, backing away from everyone. "I have nothing!"

"Ye have it all, Winter," her papa said softly. "It's been right there in yer paintings since ye first started drawing with crayons. The spirits ye hide in yer work, do ye not find it strange that ye see their energy as plain as ye see the real animals, yet others do not?"

"But they're only figments of my imagination," she argued, looking from her papa to her mama, then to Robbie, her hands lifted beseechingly. "I drew them for whimsy."

"They're not your imagination, Winter," Daar said. "They're as real as the flesh-and-blood animals ye draw. Ye paint what ye see, and ye see the full spectrum of energy."

"I don't want to be a wizard," she whispered, looking down at the floor, no longer able to face any of them. "I only want to paint."

"Then that's all ye have to do," her papa said gently. "Ye have the right to deny yer calling."

She looked up at her papa in surprise, her gaze then darting to her mother. Grace nodded. Winter looked at Robbie, and he also nodded and smiled. "Aye," Robbie said. "Ye have the choice of accepting or denying yer gift."

"Did you have a choice?"

"Aye. I could have renounced my calling when I learned about it."

"But you didn't."

"I chose to honor my destiny, Winter, because despite the enormous responsibility that comes with being a guardian, there's also the satisfaction of protecting my loved ones." He crossed his arms again and gazed deeply into her eyes. "But being a guardian and being a *drùidh* are not the same. My decision to follow my calling should not influence yours. You must walk yer own path, Winter."

"I don't want to turn out like Daar," she whispered to no one in particular.

"I beg yer pardon," Daar said, straightening his shoulders and smoothing down the front of his cassock. "I served my calling well for nearly two millennia, and I'm damn proud of that fact."

Winter gave him an apologetic frown. "No offense, Father, but you bungle your spells more often than you succeed."

He picked a piece of lint off his sleeve. "Only in this last century," he muttered, looking up with a scowl. "Before that, I was a powerful force to be reckoned with." He stepped closer, holding his hands cupped together in front of him. "Ye can have that same power, lass. All ye have to do is decide ye want it, and ye can hold the knowledge of the universe in yer hands."

"To what end?" she asked. "So I can interfere in everyone's lives? Uproot people from their natural time and send them hurtling into another century?" She suddenly gasped, shooting her gaze to her parents. "I'm going to live for centuries," she whispered in horror. "I'm going to outlive everyone!"

"Aye, there is that," Daar said with a sigh, drawing her attention. "But ye get used to it," he added with a negligent shrug. "Ye learn to adjust, because ye know ye're serving the greater good."

"I'm going to turn into a cranky old goat just like you."

He grinned broadly. "Aye, that is one benefit. I can be just as cranky as I want, and no one can do much about it."

Winter stood frowning at Daar when another thought suddenly struck her. She looked at her papa. "What were you talking about earlier? Something about Cùram, and that I'm supposed to find him." Winter felt the blood drain from her face as the realization set in. "I heard you saying you expect me to destroy Cùram. But Robbie told us he's a powerful wizard. I can't fight a wizard."

"It's up to you, Winter," her papa said. "You don't have to do anything you don't feel up to. And if you did choose to accept your gift, you wouldn't be alone, baby girl. You'd have us guarding your back."

Winter blinked at him, then slowly looked

at everyone else. "No offense, people, but a bumbling old *drùidh,* a warrior, a rocket scientist, and a guardian are not exactly a match for this Cùram guy, if he truly is that powerful. And I can't even light a candle without using three or four matches."

Robbie chuckled. "We also have Mary," he reminded her. "And Daar has made ye a staff of your own."

Daar rushed to the hearth and took down a thin, smooth, five-foot-long stick from the mantel. Winter decided her mama was right, it did look puny.

The old priest walked over and held it out to her. "It's made from a branch of my white pine," he said, his voice laced with quiet reverence. "It's weak yet, but it will grow strong as ye develop yer energy."

Winter tucked her hands behind her back. "I don't want it," she said, shaking her head. "I don't want your magic."

Daar gave her a fierce scowl that should have fried her on the spot, then turned his scowl on her papa. "Make her take it, MacKeage. Tell her what happens if she doesn't."

Winter looked at her papa in alarm. "What happens? What's the big secret you've all been keeping for the last two weeks?"

Her papa looked at the stick the old priest was still holding toward her and shook his head, his gaze locked on Daar. "It's not really free will then, is it, old man, if I tell her the fate of mankind rests on her shoulders," Grey said, his voice sounding so defeated that Winter's insides knotted in fear.

"The fate of mankind?" she whispered, looking at her mother. "Mama, tell me what he's talking about."

Grace walked up and put her arms around Winter, giving her a fierce hug. "Daar's pine tree is dying," she said into Winter's hair. "And its death is going to cause a chain reaction that will eventually kill all the trees of life. And when they die, the world dies with them."

Winter pulled back only enough to look into her mother's deeply troubled eyes. "Just because someone cut off the top of the pine?" she asked. "Killing just one of the trees of life will make the others die?" She looked past her mama's shoulder to Robbie and frowned. "But that doesn't make sense. Surely a tree of life isn't that vulnerable. That means even an innocent logger cutting timber could destroy mankind."

"Nay, the trees aren't that vulnerable," Robbie said with a shake of his head. "A saw would dull at the first slide of its blade into the trunk of one. But Daar's pine was dying *before* the top was cut. It had grown weak trying to balance the energies. Something has disturbed the continuum, Winter, and having its energy drained is what made the pine vulnerable."

"It was already dying before someone cut it?" she whispered, stepping out of her mama's embrace and turning to Daar. "So the problem isn't that someone cut your pine, but that . . . this Cùram wizard you've been talking about has upset the continuum."

"Aye," her papa said before Daar could respond. "We believe Cùram is here, and that he's come to destroy mankind."

"But why?"

"We don't know why," Grace said. "That's what we've been trying to figure out for the last two weeks."

"So did Cùram cut the top off the pine?" Winter asked.

"I don't know for sure, but I don't think so," Daar said with a sigh, finally lowering his hands holding the tiny staff. "That's another mystery we've been trying to solve. We don't know who cut it, or what that someone did with the top. The storm that night wiped out any signs we might have been able to follow."

Winter stared in silence at the staff Daar was now leaning on like a cane, then looked at her papa. "S-so you want me to take up my calling to be a *drùidh* so I can find Cùram and stop him? And if I don't, mankind will die?"

Her papa said nothing, merely nodded. Winter looked at her mama, only to find tears welling in Grace's eyes as she neither nodded nor shook her head. Winter then looked at Robbie, but finding his expression completely unreadable, she turned her attention to Daar.

"If I do this . . . if I choose to honor the destiny you claim is mine, and destroy Cùram and save the pine, can I . . . can I then go back to being just me? Can I renounce my calling after?"

"Nay," Daar said, breaking eye contact to look at the floor. "Ye have the free will to choose, but once ye do, there's no turning back." He looked at her. "If ye choose to take up yer power, ye can't suddenly decide ye don't want it anymore. Once knowledge is gained, ye can't simply forget what ye've learned."

"So if I take that staff," Winter whispered, looking at the frail piece of wood he was holding, "then I become a *drùidh* just like you?"

Daar frowned. "It's not that simple, girl. Ye can take this now," he said, holding it out to her again, "and nothing much will happen, other than ye'll get a feel for its energy. It's not until ye make the commitment in yer heart that yer come into yer full power."

Very slowly, more scared than she'd ever been in her life, Winter reached out and took the small, pale white staff from him — as everyone in the room it seemed, including her, held their breath.

The moment her fingertips touched the wood, a gentle, almost imperceptible trickle of energy moved through her, causing the fine hairs on her body to stir. The muted hum began as a whisper when her hand closed over the staff, then rose to a pulsing vibration that echoed each pounding beat of her heart. Colorful tendrils of light appeared, dancing through the one-room cabin, engulfing everyone in a strobe of sizzling, blinding energy.

"Hold tight," Daar called from a great distance. "Don't be afraid, lass. 'Tis only the magic welcoming ye. Embrace the knowledge, Winter, and feel its joy."

She *could* feel it: the energy filled her, charging even her hair with static, making her reel with weightless freedom. Time stopped. All five of her senses sharpened. She could even *taste* the powerful colors, individually distinct, swirling around the room in pulsing waves that seemed to begin and end with her.

And then Winter felt something even more acute as she clutched the thin staff to her chest, something indescribable; a sort of sixth sense settled over her in a blanket of knowledge, so powerful that Winter thought she might explode with awareness.

She suddenly cried out as the force of the turbulent maelstrom became too much, and ran for the door. She grappled with the knob, finally got the door open and stumbled onto the porch, mindless to the frantic shouts behind her. She had to get out. She had to leave before she was consumed!

She ran down the steps and into the clearing, nearly tripping over Gesader when he suddenly appeared in front of her. "Help me," she cried, groping for the fur of his back. "Please, help me."

Blinded by tears and the swirling energy pulling at her, Winter clutched her pet's fur as he led her stumbling up the overgrown trail. She had no idea how she did it without benefit of a stump, but the next thing Winter knew she was mounted on Snowball, leaning forward with her face buried in his mane, crying uncontrollably as her trusted friends took her away from the horror of Daar's cabin.

Chapter Fourteen

"Get out of my way," Greylen growled, preparing to move Robbie from the door if need be.

"Nay, Greylen," Robbie said, leaning against the door with his arms crossed over his chest. "Winter doesn't need any of us right now. We'd only be filling her head with more questions. Trust me, Grey," Robbie petitioned. "I had the same reaction she's having when I came home from the army and my papa tried to explain my calling to me." He smiled sadly. "I spent nearly a week alone in the forest before I was able to face anyone again, much less the man who had given me that calling."

Grey gave Robbie a good glare, then spun to face Daar. "Ye lied, priest. Ye told Winter it was safe to hold the staff, but it nearly killed her!"

Daar held up his hands, backing away. "Nay, MacKeage, I didn't lie. I just underestimated the strength of Winter's gift. I didn't know the staff would react so strongly."

Grey felt Robbie's hand return to his shoulder in a calming gesture, yet he didn't turn to his nephew but continued to glare at the priest.

"She'll be okay, Greylen," Robbie said, moving around to his side. "She has Gesader to look out for her, and Mary will likely tag along in the shadows. Winter has a good head on her shoulders. She'll eventually reason things out, and then she'll come back as mad as hell, demanding answers."

"But there's a storm coming," Grace said, lifting fretful, tear-filled eyes to Robbie as she hugged herself. "They're predicting snow. She can't stay away for days in a snowstorm."

Grey reached out and drew his wife to him, holding her head to his chest and absorbing her shivers. "Winter knows every nook and cranny on this mountain," he assured her. "And how to survive with nothing more than a knife no matter the weather. She has an emergency kit in her saddlebag, remember? Robbie's right, wife. Our daughter doesn't want anything to do with us right now."

"But ye *must* go after her," Daar interjected. "Ye forgot about Gregor. Ye didn't tell Winter she has to stop seeing him. Ye have to go after her and tell her now."

It was Grace who spun around and took a step toward the priest, her fists balled at her sides. "We are not telling her to stop seeing Matt," she hissed. "She's had enough bad news without realizing she has to spend the next two thousand years alone!"

"Gregor's away on business," Grey said, unable to stifle his smile as the old priest backed away from Winter's formidable mama. "I believe he's gone for a few days."

It was Grey's news and not Grace's threatening stance that seemed to make Daar back off. The priest sighed, walked over to the woodstove, and peered into the pan of soggy bacon. "My breakfast is ruined," he muttered.

"So's my daughter's life!" Grace shot back, going to the pegs on the wall and taking down her jacket. "I want to leave now," she said. "I have to go to the gallery and explain this to Megan." Grey helped her slip into the jacket, then turned her to face him. "Megan will worry herself sick if she doesn't hear from her sister," Grace continued as she buttoned up her jacket. "She was likely in on Winter's spying this morning."

Grey moved her hands out of the way and

buttoned the last two buttons, holding her collar in his fists as he pulled her forward to kiss her frowning forehead. "I'll go with ye to see Megan," he said before looking at Robbie and nodding. "Thank ye, MacBain, for being the voice of reason this morning. We'll try our damnedest to give Winter the time she needs."

Robbie nodded. "If she's not back in a few days, I'll help ye go get her."

Grey took his own jacket down from the peg, shrugged into it, and pointed at Daar. "Ye leave her alone, priest. She'll come to ye when she's done cursing ye out. Then she'll probably plague ye with questions." He grinned. "She'll likely come back with a plan to make her destiny fit her desires." Grey suddenly frowned. "Now what in hell are ye grinning at?" he snapped at Daar. "Ye look as pleased as a cat in a milk jug."

Daar had his hands clasped to his chest, standing in front of the woodstove, smiling quite smugly. "I just realized something," he said, his bright blue eyes sparkling. "For as distraught as Winter was when she left here, I notice she took her staff."

Unable to do more than simply hold on to her horse's mane as violent sobs wracked her body, Winter didn't know and didn't care where Gesader was leading Snowball. A raw northeast wind blew down from the summit, ripping what few leaves remained from the trees as it raked through the denuded branches with an eerie, ominous moan. Winter was oblivious to the building storm as she fought the emotional maelstrom howling inside her.

How could this be happening? How could her parents have kept such a terrible secret from her for twenty-four years? And Robbie. How could her cousin have betrayed her so wretchedly?

But even more horrifying, why her? Why had she been cursed with such an unimaginable destiny? She was nothing more than a dot of paint on a three-story-tall mural, not even significant enough to warrant a complete brushstroke. One human being in billions, and her parents dared to tell her the fate of the world lay in her hands?

And the power of knowledge? Most days she wasn't bright enough to come in from the cold when her passion for her work kept her focused only on her canvas. She certainly wasn't smart enough to find, much less defeat Cùram de Gairn.

Winter recalled the stories Robbie had told her about the young powerful wizard, when Robbie had given her the tiny black panther cub he'd brought back from medieval Scotland two and a half years ago. He'd returned from his eight-hundred-year journey not only with the tap root he'd stolen from Cùram's tree of life, but with the hissing, squirming bundle of fluff she'd named Gesader.

Cùram was a tricky bastard, Robbie had told her, his description conveying a perverse sense of admiration as much as distrust. Diabolical, he'd called Cùram, powerful enough to move mountains and cunning enough to hide his precious tree in a cave in the center of a lake he'd created.

One day when Robbie had come across Winter sketching in the woods and shared her lunch, he had told her he'd actually seen Cùram. And despite there being hundreds of yards separating the two men eight hundred years ago, Robbie told Winter how he'd still been able to feel the young *drùidh*'s anger. But he'd also sensed that the centuries-old war between Cùram and Pendaär was not over, but truly just beginning.

Untangling herself from Snowball's mane to close her collar against the chill settling in her bones, Winter suddenly realized she was still clutching the pinewood staff in her hand. She immediately tossed it to the ground.

Gesader stopped, which caused Snowball to stop. The panther padded back beside her, picked up the staff in his mouth, looked up to give her a deep rumbling snarl, and once again headed up the trail.

"I don't want it!" she shouted to his back, quickly grabbing the reins when Snowball started after Gesader. "Spit it out!"

Her pet ignored her, her words uselessly carried away on the wind. Winter hunched low in her saddle, burying her face in Snowball's neck as tears overwhelmed her in another wrenching fit of self-pity.

She didn't want to be a wizard. She didn't want to live for centuries, to become old and cranky and barely tolerated by people who provided for her from a sense of obligation. She would watch her parents die, and her sisters and cousins and nieces and nephews, until she was left alone with only Daar. She might love the old priest despite himself, but she didn't want to emulate him. She sure as heck didn't want to become him.

She wouldn't do it, she decided. Providence had no right to saddle her with such an impossible duty. She was only a young, untried woman against a powerful *drùidh,* no matter that her parents and Robbie had promised to help her. She didn't even know what she was supposed to do, much less how to do it.

Darn it, she had just started to get her life on track. She'd just found Matheson Gregor and fallen so deeply in love with the man, the mere thought of knowing he'd die a timely death while she went on living without him made her heart wrench in despair. There had to be a way around this mess, a way she could help Daar and Robbie defeat Cùram without completely binding herself to Providence.

Winter bolted upright in the saddle. That was it. She would find a way to lure Cùram into the open so her cousin could finish him off. Aye, Robbie was a guardian, and guardians had the power to protect mankind from *drùidhs*. He could defeat Cùram. He'd done so once before, he could do it again.

But *cùram* was Gaelic for *guardian*. Was it possible to be both a guardian and a wizard? Was that why even Robbie needed her help?

So many questions with only more questions for answers.

Snowball suddenly stopped, and Winter blinked at her surroundings. How long had she been riding? She was still on TarStone, but she couldn't recognize where exactly.

And then she saw it, just off to her right, the broad trunk of a majestic white pine. She moved her gaze up the perfectly straight trunk, from the fluffy pile of leaves and pine needles at the bottom, up past several jutting branches as thick as her waist, all the way up to the piece of tin covering the bluntly cut top. Broad fingers of dried pitch oozed down several feet from under the cap, mingling with shiny wet slivers of fresh sap.

This was it. Gesader had brought her to Daar's tree of life. He must have followed the priest or her papa or Robbie here at some time. But why had he brought her here now?

Gesader sat down in front of the pile of leaves at the base of the pine, the thin, puny staff still held in his mouth. It stuck out over two feet on each side of his head, a pale contrast to his solid-black fur.

"What?" she snapped, scrubbing tears off her face. "Leave it with the pine," she told him. "I want nothing to do with the magic."

Gesader emitted a rattling growl from deep in his chest as his long thick tail whipped angrily back and forth, stirring a flurry of leaves behind him.

"I don't care. I want to go —" She snapped her mouth shut. Where *did* she want to go? Not home. Nor to her gallery;

she couldn't face Megan right now. She couldn't face anyone, not even Robbie. Whenever she had been beside herself with grief or worry or excitement or joy, she had always gone to Robbie. But she couldn't even seek comfort in her dearest cousin. Not yet. Not until she could sort out the mess she was in.

Tom, then. She would go stay with her good friend.

And say what? *I'm sorry for crying all over ye, but I'm a wizard and I don't want to be one.* Nay, she couldn't go to Tom; he saw too much with his sharp blue eyes, read her too well.

Matt's camp. She could go to Bear Mountain and stay in the cozy little den Matt had made. He was in Utah for several more days, and surely she'd have her emotions under control by the time he got back. Aye, she just needed to be alone for a while, just long enough to figure out what she was going to do.

"Come, Gesader," Winter said, taking up Snowball's reins to head toward Bear Mountain. But the old horse didn't budge, even when she clicked her tongue and dug her heels into his sides. "Get going, you accursed beast," she growled.

She was answered by another growl coming from the direction of the pine. She looked over to see Gesader, standing now, the hackles on his back raised in anger. "What is it you want?" she shouted. "Why have ye brought me here?"

Gesader turned with the puny staff still in his mouth, leapt over the pile of leaves, and dropped the stick against the trunk of the pine. A deep, resonating sound — like that of a tuning fork — started the tree humming in shuddering puffs, sounding as if it were gasping for breath.

Winter blinked in amazement. She slid off Snowball and walked toward the pine, unable to look away from the pulsing trunk. Stepping through the thick pile of leaves, she slowly reached out and touched it.

She gasped, pulling her hand away at the realization that it was alive, that she had felt its weak spark of life struggling to surface. Without questioning why, driven by some unfathomable yet urgent need, Winter stepped up to the tree, wrapped her arms around it, and lay her cheek against the cold, rough bark.

A rainbow of colors immediately swirled through the air. Her arms and fingers tingled and her ears roared at the sound of pitch moving along the trunk's veins. With her chest pressed into the rough bark,

Winter felt the pine's energy slowly shifting . . . . until it finally matched the steady rhythm of her own pounding heart.

A calmness settled over Winter, both the internal and external storms receding, the swirling colors slowly fading away until only the purity of white remained. A loud *caw* came from above, and Winter looked up to see a plump black crow perched on one of the pine's remaining branches over her head.

Winter's knees buckled and she slid to the ground. She sat curled at the base of the tree, hugging the trunk as tightly as she could, feeling TarStone's vast store of energy moving through her. In her mind's eye she saw roots stretching deep into fissures that spidered through the mountain's granite. The trunk she was hugging expanded and receded with billowing breaths as the vital energy flowed up from the mountain and into the tree.

The crow gave another high-pitched *caw*, and Winter looked up to see it lift off the branch and flap skyward. It caught the wind and soared over the swaying treetops of the forest, disappearing into the dark, churning storm clouds.

Winter slowly straightened away from the pine, blinking in confusion. What had just happened? Had she actually become one with Daar's pine? Could she really have felt its pulse as strongly as she felt her own?

Yes, that's exactly what had happened, and Winter finally understood the true scope of her gift, as well as the very real threat Cùram de Gairn posed. For even though she knew the pine would live for months yet, she had also seen its eventual death — arriving on the chill wind of utter hopelessness.

CHAPTER FIFTEEN

The clouds had thickened and lowered by the time Winter crossed Bear Brook and entered the high meadow, the wind blowing at gale force and a wet snow falling with blinding intensity. Though she was wet to the skin and miserably cold, the closer Winter got to Matt's cozy little cave the calmer she became. Despite all her questions and confusion, she was confident she could figure out a way to lure Cùram into the open for Robbie.

But what was she going to do about Matt while she dealt with the magic? How could she keep such a powerful secret from him? She couldn't say when it had happened exactly, but Winter now accepted the fact that she loved Matheson Gregor with every fiber of her being. Until she had pictured herself having to live without him, she hadn't realized just how deeply he had become entrenched in her heart. As she rode across the meadow through the driving snow, Winter vowed that she would not allow Providence or the magic or some angry *drùidh* to mess with that love.

Gesader disappeared into the woods that separated the meadow from the cliff, having to twist his head to fit the long pinewood stick through the trees. Winter had deliberately left the staff at Daar's tree, but as soon as she'd found a stump and mounted Snowball, Gesader had taken up the lead again, once again carrying the blasted thing in his mouth.

Winter had no idea how the big cat knew its importance, but he did seem determined the staff remain with them. She'd often wondered if the tiny cub Robbie had brought her from eight hundred years ago was something more than he seemed. Even though panthers were not indigenous to Scotland, he had been living in the cave Robbie said had held Cùram's tree of life. But other than being unusually well-adapted to living with humans, Gesader had shown no signs of being anything other than a typical, semiwild leopard.

He'd never spoken to Winter the way Robbie's snowy owl spoke to him, nor did Gesader appear to possess any magic, much less act the part of a familiar. He was simply

Winter's cherished pet and steadfast companion. Yet he'd brought her to the dying pine, somehow knowing she needed to feel its waning energy in order to realize the seriousness of the situation.

And the crow she'd seen sitting on the branch above her. What had that been about? Tom certainly loved crows; he'd told Winter they were the harbinger of renewal and transformation, to be revered as spirits who helped restore order to the heavens.

Had the crow she'd seen today symbolized some sort of transformation? Had he been there to encourage her to fight for humanity's future?

Following Gesader, Winter guided Snowball through the narrow band of trees as she contemplated the meaning of the crow. They stopped at the granite cliff that rose thirty feet above the meadow. She slid from the saddle, nearly falling to the ground when her numbed legs buckled under her weight.

"I have to get us dried off," she said to her wet, snow-covered pets. "Or Matt is going to find three frozen blocks of ice when he gets home."

Gesader disappeared into the narrow opening of the cave, then quickly returned empty-mouthed. Winter undid Snowball's cinch and pulled the heavy saddle off, groaning when its weight nearly buckled her knees again. She let it fall to the ground and dragged it to the cave, dropping it just inside the entrance. She rummaged around in her saddlebag until she found a flashlight, then trailed its beam around the interior of the cave, stopping when she spotted the pile of blankets.

"Bless you, Rose, for being such a good saleslady," she said, taking one of the blankets.

Winter had helped Matt shop for his camping equipment, but Rose was the one who had insisted he needed extra blankets, a lantern, and a jug for carrying water from the nearby spring Tom had shown them. Rose had also sold Matt ten pairs of wool socks, several pairs of long johns, and a tarp to hang over the entrance of the cave in bad weather.

Winter noticed Matt hadn't bothered to hang the tarp, likely because the twisted entrance didn't allow rain or snow to reach very far inside. That way he could build his fire close to the entrance so the smoke wouldn't fill the cave.

It wasn't a very big cave, maybe twenty feet deep and about fifteen feet wide, but it was more than tall enough for Matt to stand upright. All in all, Winter had thought it an appropriate den for the son of a bear, which is exactly what she'd told Matt when she'd helped him settle in last week. She smiled as she carried the blanket outside, remembering how her comment had gotten her a very passionate kiss.

"I'm sorry you won't fit inside with us," Winter told Snowball, who had ducked his head into the cave and turned his rump to the wind. She tossed the blanket over his back, smoothing it out and frowning when it came only halfway down his sides. "I'll get a rope and tie it on you," she said, giving him a pat before rushing back to her saddle.

She pulled a small coil of rope from one of her bags, then ran back, looped the rope around Snowball's girth, and tied it securely. "There, that'll keep most of your heat in," she said, swiping a large snowflake off her eyelash so she could see to undo Snowball's bridle strap. She carefully let the bit slip from his mouth, then affectionately rubbed one of his ears. "Go find yourself a sheltered place to sit out the storm," she said, looking him square in his large brown eye. "I won't tie you up, so you can graze in the meadow and drink from the brook, but don't you go wandering off to Tom's," she instructed. "I don't want him knowing I'm up here, and I don't want him worrying about me, under-stand?"

Snowball let out a deep-bellied sigh that puffed a cloud of warm moist air toward her. He then closed his eyes without so much as taking a step toward shelter, ap-parently deciding this was as good a place as any for a nap. Winter turned to Gesader to see to his needs when she suddenly real-ized what she'd just said to Snowball.

She didn't want Tom worrying about her, but what about her parents? And Robbie? Come to think of it, she thought with a frown, how come they hadn't chased after her?

She was going through a terrible crisis here, and her mama and papa had just let her run away. And Robbie. What in curses kind of guardian was he, to let her shoot past him without even trying to stop her? Didn't they realize how traumatized she was? Didn't they care?

Winter's frown turned into a scowl aimed at herself. Of course they *cared;* they cared enough to give her time and space to think over their news. They realized coddling her wouldn't make the problem go away, but only make *them* feel better.

"Oh, Gesader," she whispered, falling to her knees to hug him. "They must be worried sick about me being out here alone in this storm. I'm the one who hasn't cared enough to let them know I'm okay."

She reached in her jacket pocket, pulled out her cell phone, and checked to see what kind of signal she had. Only one bar, but hopefully enough to get through. She pushed the speed-dial for Gù Brath, praying her parents weren't home as she listened to the phone ring on the other end.

She sighed with relief when the answering machine picked up. "I-I'm just calling to tell you that I'm safe and warm and that I probably won't be home for a few days. Gesader is with me, and we've found shelter, so I don't want you to worry," she said before reaching for the END button. She suddenly put the phone back to her mouth. "Oh, and I'm shutting off my cell phone to save the battery, so don't worry if I don't answer. Leave a message if you want, and I'll check my voice mail. I . . . I love you," she finished in a whisper, pressing END and then the power button before tucking the phone back in her pocket.

She buried her face in Gesader's wet fur as unbidden tears suddenly filled her eyes again. "Curses," she muttered, "I thought I was cried out."

A warm, rough tongue lapped the side of

her face, amplifying how very cold she was. But Winter didn't care, as this crying business was harder on a body than the weather. Darn it, she had to get herself under control. Wallowing in self-pity never solved anything.

Winter sat up and wiped her face with the back of her hand. "Come on, brat," she said with herculean determination, getting to her feet. "I've got to build a fire and get out of these wet clothes."

Gesader also stood and shook a gallon of water off his hide, along with a good pound of snow. He padded over to Snowball, startled the dozing horse with a quick lick on his nose, then padded into the cave ahead of Winter.

The first thing Winter did was find the lantern Matt had bought from Rose, then she rummaged around in her saddlebags for the watertight pack of matches she always carried. It took her three matches to light the kerosene lantern, which she then held up to visibly scan the cave, looking for firewood.

For an executive, Matt Gregor was proving to be an excellent mountain man, she decided with a smile, finding a three- to four- day supply of wood stacked against the side wall. Winter set the lantern on the ground in the center of the cave and gathered up an armful of dry logs, promising herself that as soon as the storm was over she would replace what she used. She crouched in front of the cold fire pit by the entrance of the cave and started fashioning a tepee of smaller twigs, slowly building it up with increasingly larger pieces of wood. Finishing just as a cold shiver wracked her body, Winter quickly searched the cave for paper or birch bark to use for starter. She couldn't find anything, other than a binder of printouts she couldn't decipher that had Matt's handwriting all over the pages. She definitely didn't dare burn that. Her search continued, eventually ending at Matt's sleeping bag when she spotted the pinewood staff Gesader had dropped there.

She stared at that staff, remembering the surge of energy she'd felt in Daar's cabin when she'd touched it. "Hmmm." She looked toward Gesader lying next to the unlit fire pit. "What do you think? Can I light a fire without starter or matches, brat? Robbie and Daar do it all the time."

Gesader didn't offer an opinion, but started licking his paws. Winter looked back at the staff. How hard could it be? Surely all she had to do was point the thing at the fire and command the wood to ignite.

She picked up the staff somewhat hesitantly, expecting the maelstrom to attack her again. But there was no light, no flashing rainbow of colors, no roaring in her ears. In fact, nothing more than a gentle tingle traveled through her, but it did warm her up a bit. Somewhat disappointed by the lack of fireworks, Winter scooted back to the pit. She stayed at least three feet away, pointed the staff at the tepee she'd made, and said, "Light my fire!"

A percussion strong enough to shake the entire cliff blasted inside the cave, along with an explosion of energy so powerful it knocked Winter flat to the ground. Gesader jumped to his feet with a startled roar and ran outside with a yelp.

Winter lay on the floor of the suddenly dark cave, blinking in dazed awe. But it wasn't until she smelled something burning, looked at the fire pit and saw nothing, that she truly became alarmed. "Curses!" she shouted, catching sight of the smoldering pile of blankets. She jumped to her feet, grabbed the blankets, ran to the entrance of the cave, and threw the pile outside. Then she started stomping on them, using her feet to spread them out and kick snow over the smoldering patches.

"Don't you dare laugh," she snapped at Gesader, who was sitting ten feet away in the swirling snowstorm, his lips curled up in his snarling panther smile. He sneezed three times in rapid succession and trotted past her back into the cave.

Winter looked down at the wet and dirty blankets. Was that blasted staff directional? Did it have a holding end and a lethal end, or what? Holy hell, Gesader had been running around with the accursed thing in his mouth all day. He could have caught the entire forest on fire!

The wind blew snow down the front of her open collar, and Winter shuddered. Darn it, she had to get warm and dry before she caught a cold. She picked up the blankets with a tired sigh, shaking them out one at a time to make sure the fire was extinguished, then folded them back into a pile. She carried the pile in the cave, but not before taking one last peek at Snowball. He had fallen asleep again, though now he was standing a good twenty feet away behind a large spruce tree.

The first thing Winter did after tossing the blankets back in the corner was hunt up the lantern, which she discovered on its side against the back wall. She thanked her lucky stars it was a safety lantern, and that the flame had blown out rather than exploding kerosene over everything and igniting a real fire. Gesader was again curled into a tight ball by the still-unlit pit, and Winter was back to not having anything to use for starter. She didn't dare pour kerosene on the wood, knowing how quickly that could get out of control — especially the way her luck was going.

Winter gave another sigh of self-pity and went back outside and started looking for a birch tree she could steal bark from. It took her another ten shivering minutes to return with a fistful of white paperlike bark.

"You could have at least come with me," she grumbled to Gesader, who growled back at her without even bothering to open his eyes. "And you leave that stick alone before you blow us all to hell," she said, scowling at the pinewood staff laying near the back wall of the cave where it had landed.

She carefully tucked the birch bark inside the tepee, found her matches, and used up five of them before she was able to get the cold bark to even start smoking. She hunched down and softly blew on the faint embers, sitting up when it finally warmed enough to burst into flames.

She sat on the ground and watched the tiny flames grow, carefully feeding more bark into the slowly expanding fire until she heard the first crackle of solid wood ignite. Gesader immediately stood up, moved closer to the fire, then laid back down again with a deep sigh. Winter got up, and while keeping a guarded eye on the fire, she stripped out of her wet clothes down to her wet long johns. Then she went over to Matt's duffel bag and pawed through it until she found a set of his long johns. She quickly finished undressing, shedding everything including her bra and panties, and slipped into Matt's cold but dry long johns. She had to roll the sleeves up about five times, and the legs even more before she could walk without tripping. She found a pair of his thick wool socks and put them on, then slipped into one of his bulky chamois shirts, rolling up its sleeves as she looked down with a laugh at the shirttails hanging below her knees.

"What do you think of my northwoods fashion?" she asked Gesader. "Will I turn many heads?"

Gesader opened one golden eye, then promptly dropped it shut again, apparently more tired than impressed. Winter went over to Matt's sleeping bag and dragged it and its pad closer to the fire. She unzipped the bag, crawled inside, and zipped it closed all the way up to her nose. Gesader immediately got up, walked around the now brightly burning fire, and plopped down on top of the sleeping bag so that he was tucked against her back.

"Thank you," she whispered, staring at the fire as she breathed in the odor of wet cat fur . . . and another smell she'd grown quite fond of lately. It was a smell that made her think of beautiful golden eyes, tasty warm lips, and strong arms holding her secure. Winter's last sigh of the day ended with a smile as she closed her eyes on a yawn.

Yes, she was quite in love with Matheson Gregor, and neither the magic nor Cùram de Gairn could alter that truth.

CHAPTER SIXTEEN

Matt muttered yet another curse as he fought to keep his truck from sliding off the bumpy, snow-covered tote road that wound up the side of his mountain. One more mile, he estimated, before he reached the end of this trip from hell. Not six hours ago he'd been sitting in an office in his Utah factory, about to fire his quality control manager, when an overwhelming need to return to Maine had suddenly stopped him in mid-sentence. Unable to explain the urgency tightening his gut — to himself much less to his confused but very lucky manager — Matt had simply walked out, gotten into his jet, and headed east at one and a quarter times the speed of sound.

He'd been forced to land at Bangor International Airport instead of Pine Creek because of the weather, since the small mountain airport didn't have instruments to land a jet in a blinding snowstorm. Then he'd had to rent a car and drive to Pine Creek to pick up his truck. What should have been only a ninety minute ride from Bangor had taken him over two hours, again because of the storm. From Pine Creek he'd been driving over half an hour just to get this far up his mountain, and he still had to leave the truck half a mile from the meadow and hike the rest of the way in the dark through the snowstorm — in his suit and dress shoes, no less!

Dammit to hell. He was almost home and his gut still hadn't settled down. And though he didn't understand the exact nature of the urgency pulling at him, he sure as hell knew who was causing it. Winter MacKeage wouldn't get out of his head. Back in Utah Matt had only known something was terribly wrong: he had felt Winter struggling in confusion, seen her face swollen from tears, sensed her wandering blindly through an emotional void that had thrown her safe little world into a tailspin.

But what Matt still couldn't wrap his mind around was how quickly and how deeply Winter had gotten under his skin in the first place. He'd known her only two weeks, and she was already driving him mad with worry. How else could he explain walking out of an important meeting, flying recklessly into a snowstorm, or his breaking into a cold sweat at just the thought of her crying? The woman had gotten under his skin without him even noticing, while he had been busy planning and plotting instead of guarding his back.

At least his heart was safely out of her reach, that one vital organ having hardened imperviously a long, long time ago. But dammit, how in hell was he supposed to deal with a fairy princess whose prickly antics made him laugh, who had him determined to shelter her from the harsh realities of life, and who made him want her so badly he'd sell his soul to possess her?

Matt instinctively knew Winter was at his campsite; he could feel she was nearby and physically okay. But instead of growing calmer the closer he got to the cave, the urgency in his gut only increased. He wanted her, no matter how many lectures he'd given himself to leave her alone, no matter that he knew the path she was innocently leading him down ended at damnation's door.

He had tried. Hell, he'd run off to New York four times in the last two weeks trying to get away from her. But every time he would come racing back as his need for Winter had grown stronger instead of lessening. Yesterday he'd made it all the way to Utah, but he'd barely sat down in his chair this morning before he'd finally realized how futile it was to fight her siren's call. Hell, just knowing she was upset was luring him home like a moth drawn to a flame — single-mindedly heading him straight toward destruction.

Matt finally brought his truck to a sliding halt in the middle of the road and shut off the engine and the lights. He let his eyes adjust to the darkness, reaching on the seat beside him for the package he'd picked up before leaving Bangor and tucking it in his pocket. He turned up the collar of his suit jacket, opened the door, and finally stepped into the howling storm. The road ran half a mile above the meadow, so with his head lowered and his shoulders hunched against the driving snow, Matt plunged into the woods, ignoring the seven inches of accumulated snow soaking through his dress shoes.

He actually lost his way twice, either from inattention or from unconsciously stalling. But finally, thirty minutes later, Matt stood at the base of the cliff that towered above the meadow, his mind warring with his body as he listened for sounds coming from inside the cave.

Snowball walked up and gently nudged his shoulder, and Matt absently gave him a pat while continuing to watch the narrow entrance. The dark shadow of a large black cat finally appeared, its hackles raised as it emitted a warning growl.

Matt reached in his pocket, pulled out the paper-wrapped packet, and tossed it just a few feet in front of Winter's pet. With an even more ominous growl, the cat stepped forward, standing with the packet on the ground between them, his lips curled back in a snarl. The cat sneezed and stepped to the side, as if trying to go around the packet, his tail whipping back and forth in agitation.

But in the end, the lure of the catnip was too much for the panther, just as Matt had known it would be. The cat circled the fist-sized packet several times, then lowered his head and rubbed the side of his face over it, pushing it through the snow with a snorted growl that ended with another sneeze.

"I'm as sorry as you are," Matt whispered when the great beast suddenly pounced on the package, scooping it up in his powerful jaws with a final snarl before bolting into the forest. "Forgive me," Matt softly petitioned to the retreating cat as it disappeared into the storm.

He turned and faced the cave again, once again torn between going inside or simply disappearing into the forest behind the leopard. It could be that simple; he could just turn and walk away and never be seen again. Winter might miss him; hell, she might even mourn him, but in the end she would be better off. At least her soul would be intact, which was more than he could say for his own if he entered that cave.

But his decision finally came down to one simple promise, given long before his heart had atrophied, when love had led Matt to an act of desperation, when hope hadn't been a curse. So he stepped forward as he unbuttoned his snow-covered suit jacket, slipping it off his shoulders and letting it fall to the ground as he quietly walked through the entrance.

The moment he stepped inside, the walls of the cave started pulsing in a warm golden glow that softly lit the interior. He unbuttoned his shirt next, pulled its tails from his pants, and shrugged it off as he stared at the woman sleeping at his feet. He slipped off his shoes, then straightened and unfastened his belt. Her hair was still damp, he noticed, and her cheeks were pink with warmth. She had one hand tucked under her head, the other hand clutching the sleeping bag up to her nose.

Matt dropped his pants and stepped out of them, kicking them out of the way as he continued staring at Winter. He noticed the indentation where the panther had been curled against her back, and felt a perverse anger at seeing evidence that the leopard had likely been sleeping with her for the last two and a half years.

But never again, Matt vowed. The only beast in Winter MacKeage's bed after tonight would be him.

Finally naked, Matt looked around the interior of the cave, his gaze stopping on the thin wooden stick laying against the softly glowing back wall. He walked over and picked it up, balancing its insubstantial weight on the palm of his hand. He smiled, rolling the smooth wood in his fingers before setting it on a narrow ledge near the ceiling, well out of reach of his fairy princess.

He turned back to Winter, absently scratching the hair on his chest, figuring he'd warmed up enough not to turn her into a block of ice when he crawled in beside her. He walked over and knelt down, slowly unzipped the zipper, worked the material out of her hand, and peeled away the top of the sleeping bag.

Matt sucked in his breath at the sight of her wearing his clothes, his long johns and shirt only amplifying how tiny she was. Beads of sweat broke out on his forehead as something stirred deep in his chest, someplace in the vicinity of his hardened heart.

She was so delicate. So beautiful. So damn innocent.

And his. After tonight, little Miss Prickly MacKeage would belong to him; her heart, her soul, her vivacious spirit would be his completely.

Matt lay open the sleeping bag to make them a double bed, then carefully laid down and gathered her into his arms. He smiled when she murmured something unintelligible and snuggled against him to bury her face in his chest. The moment she awakened, he tilted her head back to bring his mouth down on hers, capturing her gasp of surprise.

He kissed her deeply, holding nothing back, his gut relaxing for the first time in hours. She finally realized whose mouth was ravishing hers and responded with an eagerness that hit Matt square in the chest.

He pulled back to stare down at her, watching her lazy blue eyes gaze back as her warm, welcoming smile reached clear to her flushed cheeks. "You came home," she whispered. "Or am I dreaming?"

"You're not dreaming, princess. I'm really here."

She reached up and touched his untethered hair hanging down to his shoulders. "It's wavy," she said, her sleepy smile widening. "You look even more handsome with it down."

He kissed her again for her compliment, which she seemed to think was an appropriate response for him to make as she slid her fingers through his loose hair and kissed him back.

Once he'd gotten a good taste of her, Matt again lifted his head to look down. "What are ye doing here, Winter?" he asked. "Do yer parents know where you are?"

"No." She smiled, reaching up and locking her fingers together at the back of his neck. "I've run away from home, Mr. Gregor, and this was the only place I wanted to run to." Her forehead wrinkled with worry. "I hope you don't think I was being too . . . ah, too forward."

"I'm glad," he whispered, smoothing her wild red curls back from her forehead. "I like finding a fairy princess in my bed."

She smiled hugely. "A fairy princess?" she repeated. "Is that how you think of me?"

"Aye," he said, giving her a kiss on her

nose. "My beautiful fairy princess."

"Your brogue is back."

"I'm regressing again. It seems to be an affliction that appears whenever I hold ye in my arms."

She moved her hands from behind his head to hold the sides of his face. "I want to make love to you, Matheson Gregor," she whispered. "I want to feel you inside me, deep where I ache."

Her words hit like a tidal wave, washing over Matt with a shuddering force that tightened his gut in a knot of desire. He lowered his mouth to kiss her, but she wouldn't let him, holding him firmly to keep him looking at her.

"I — I haven't ever been with anyone," she softly confessed, her forehead again wrinkling with worry. "So I don't know what to do."

He turned his head to kiss her palm, then smiled down at her. "I'm thinking ye might start by taking off my clothes."

She moved her hands from his face to his shoulders with a relieved sigh, obviously pleased he was willing to guide her through their lovemaking. Her eyes widened. "You're naked," she said in surprise.

He nodded. "I was referring to my clothes

on yer body," he told her, plucking at her shirt.

"Oh," she said, wiggling out from under him so she could sit up and unbutton her shirt. She frowned, looking around. "How come it's so light in here?"

Matt pushed her hands away and finished undoing the buttons, slipping the shirt off her shoulders and down her arms, then quickly reaching for the hem of her long johns top. "Did ye leave the lantern going?" he asked just as he pulled the top up over her head, her answer getting muffled in the material as she raised her arms to help him.

Matt sucked in his breath, quickly capturing her now freed hands and holding them away from her body to fully appreciate her very beautiful, very plump breasts. "My God, you're lovely," he whispered, looking up to find her blushing even more beautifully.

He quickly leaned forward, using his body to press her down to the sleeping bag, covering her chest with his own as he captured her gasp in a searing kiss. Matt gathered both her hands in one of his, pinning them over her head so he was free to explore what his eyes had already told him were two wonderful pieces of heaven.

She nearly bit his tongue when his hand

closed over her breast, her hips surging up so sharply, Matt groaned and had to quickly pull his hips out of the way. Holy hell, his fairy princess was turning into a package of sensual energy.

But hadn't he known what she'd be like? Hadn't he felt Winter's explosive energy lurking just below the surface for two weeks now, every time he'd kissed her?

Isn't that exactly why he'd kept running away?

Aye. He had known within seconds of stepping into her gallery that Winter Mac-Keage was not some shy, delicate flower. The moment he'd locked eyes with her, Matt had seen a passionate woman just waiting for a brave man to cut through her thorny defense. And hadn't he heard the death knell tinkling when he'd opened her gallery door, of his destiny meeting his fate? If Winter's paintings had captured his interest, her obvious passion for life had caught him in an even more deadly spell. Just like a damned moth, he could no longer only dance near her flame.

Aye, she was beckoning him, and Matt was done running.

Still pinning her hands over her head for fear he might lose control if he allowed her to touch him, Matt slid his fingers inside the waist of her bottom long johns and slowly moved them down her legs. She made the task simple, what with her wiggling and writhing and kicking her feet to help him. But once she realized he wasn't freeing her hands, the little fairy went on the attack by using her mouth.

She kissed whatever part of him she could reach, starting at his jaw and working her way to his neck, then nuzzling his chest when he straightened over her again. Matt immediately retreated back down her body, leaving a trail of kisses from her throat to between her breasts. She arched against him with a sound of frustration, and Matt smiled to himself as he changed course, sliding his lips over one of her firm, plump breasts.

She gasped in pleasure when his mouth closed over her nipple and he gently suckled it to arousal. He became rather entranced with her taste, her heady and sweet aroma surrounding him to the point where she was able to free her hands. Aye, he didn't discover his mistake until her fingers raked up his back in an action that sent lightning surging through every nerve in his body. And while he was still trying to recover, she somehow managed to wiggle her way directly beneath him and wrap her legs around his hips, the intimate contact startling him back to reality.

When in hell had he lost control, and had the student begun teaching the teacher? Matt reared up to capture her very busy hands again as they headed for his waist, wrestling them back on either side of her head as he let loose a growl that made her go suddenly and completely still. Matt sucked in a calming breath as he stared down at her flushed face and wide-eyed, somewhat dazed expression.

"Am I doing something wrong?" she asked in utter sincerity.

Matt could only close his eyes and drop his chin to his chest, fighting the urge to laugh, knowing damn well she'd take it the wrong way. "Nay," he said, gaining back just enough control to look at her again. He moved her hands closer to her head, letting his thumbs trace the sides of her face. "But we have reached the point where I need to know if ye understand what's about to happen, lass. Do ye realize exactly what you're doing, Winter? That you're not dreaming, that I really am here, and that I'm about to make ye mine?"

"I — I love you, Matt Gregor," she said ever so softly. "I want to belong to you."

He smiled tightly. "I know ye love me, lass, or ye wouldn't be giving me yer most precious possession. But I'm asking if ye understand all that goes with it? Once you're mine, Winter, it will be completely and forever. Ye'll give me not only yer love, but yer trust and loyalty, with my being nothing less than yer husband. If ye can't give me all that, then say so now. It might very well kill me, but I will walk away and leave ye intact."

Her dazed expression turned somewhat confused, her flushed face growing pale. "What century are you living in?" she asked in a squeak. "I'm not expecting you to marry me just because we've made love."

"Aye, I realize that," he said with a solemn nod. "I'm the one expecting nothing less than marriage. But if ye give me your virginity, ye give me all that goes with it." He leaned down and softly kissed her, then pulled away to look at her again. "Do ye love me that much, Winter? Enough to give me everything?"

Matt was surprised, if not alarmed, when she answered so quickly. "Yes," she said, her body relaxing in feminine softness as her face glowed with the warmth of her smile. "I love you enough, Matheson Gregor, to give you all I have."

"You'll be my wife?" he clarified gutturally. "I'll have yer trust and loyalty?"

"Yes," she rasped, her smile disappearing as her legs tightened around him with obvious impatience.

Deep down in his chest, again near the region of his cold, dead heart, Matt felt the tiniest stirring. With a quiet curse aimed at the foibles of fate, he let go of her hands and swept Winter against him, kissing her deeply as he surrendered control.

She met his passion with blossoming desire, her body moving restlessly beneath him as he positioned himself to claim her. With his forearms under her shoulders, Matt gathered her beautiful hair in his fists, holding her mouth still for his tongue's invasion as he slowly eased his hips forward.

She wouldn't let him be gentle, wouldn't let him go slow, untangling her legs to brace herself and lifting her hips to meet his. With his mouth locked firmly on hers, Matt swallowed her sudden cry as he slowly pressed past her maidenhead and seated himself fully inside her. He stilled, intending to allow her to adjust, but Winter mocked his noble intentions by digging her fingers into his shoulders and throwing her head back with a moan of pleasure as she arched upward, taking him even deeper.

"Yes," she cried when he slowly retreated, surged forward, then did it again. She tightened around him as tiny droplets of dew broke on her forehead and her body dampened with passion.

Matt could do nothing more than marvel at Winter's response as she swept him closer toward her beautiful flame of promising bliss. The air around them charged with the energy of a thousand torches, the golden walls of his den pulsing to the rhythm of his pounding heart. She finally moved beyond the timeless void and into the abyss, and Matt shouted his wonder as the explosion of her passion wracked his body in surging waves, pulling him with her into the powerful storm of swirling colors.

That quickly, that irrevocably, it was over but for the lingering sensation of her body clenching around him. Matt lowered his weight to lie beside her, pulling her with him so that he remained inside and wouldn't miss even one of her waning spasms. He brushed her hair off her flushed face and kissed her closed eyes and the side of her smiling mouth as she sucked in calming, billowing breaths.

"Mmmm," she hummed, lifting her lazy blue eyes to him. "That was . . . wonderful," she said on a winded whisper. She patted his sweaty shoulder, leaving her hand there and closing her eyes again. "Everything I imagined it would be."

Matt propped his head up on one hand, keeping his other hand stroking her hair. "So ye've imagined making love, have ye? In general, or with me?"

She cracked one eye at him, her satisfied smile widening as she patted his shoulder again. "If I'd imagined it with men in general, my curiosity would have gotten the better of me long before now."

He kissed her sweet mouth for giving the right answer, then untangled his hand from her hair and trailed it down her body, closing it over her lovely backside and carefully withdrawing from her before tucking her up beside him. "So are ye going to tell me why you've run away from home?"

"No," she said, pulling on his shoulder to give him a kiss, then continuing to tug until he was sprawled on top of her again. "Later. Right now I want to feel you inside me again."

Matt immediately hardened to stone and reared up in surprise. "You can't," he growled. "It's too soon."

"For you or for me?" she asked with a laugh, the musical sound echoing off the walls of the cave.

He felt heat creeping up the back of his neck. "For you," he growled more than whispered, grabbing her wandering hands and holding them beside her head. "You're too tender."

Her brows lifted above wide blue eyes. "What century are you really living in? You're more old-fashioned than a Victorian spinster. I am a healthy, athletic, twenty-first-century woman," she said with another laugh as she slid her legs up the length of his, curling them around his thighs so that her heels pulled him toward her. She stuck out her lower lip. "But if *you're* too tender, then I guess we'll just have to cuddle until you . . . ah, recover a bit," she offered, all the while trying to wiggle herself into a more promising position, obviously well aware that he was not only *not* tender but quite recovered.

Matt slid back inside her with maddening slowness, watching her face flush with returning passion as his own desire soared into the stratosphere at mach two.

Winter MacKeage then proceeded to not only back up her boast of athletic health, she proved herself to be surprisingly free of inhibitions and provokingly curious for a woman so new to the sport. They made love several more times that night, sometimes with wild abandon and sometimes with lazy tenderness, sometimes dozing between sessions and sometimes just lying in each other's arms as they listened to the angry wind howling outside their cozy golden den.

And through it all, deep in the back of Matt's mind, was the realization that morning would arrive with either Winter's vow of loyalty passing the test, or the harsh reality of an even more deadly storm damning them both.

CHAPTER SEVENTEEN

Winter woke up with a smile, thinking she might have dreamt her night of passion but for the wonderful aches in every muscle she had and the very real taste of Matt Gregor still on her lips. She could tell she was alone without even opening her eyes, the cave's stillness so absolute after being filled with an energy so volatile that her insides still quivered with remembered sensations.

When her stomach rumbled, Winter remembered she hadn't eaten anything yesterday and decided she should cook Matt a nice breakfast to impress him with her one and only domestic skill. She opened her eyes and sat up to discover she'd thrown off the sleeping bag sometime in her sleep. Good heavens, had she been lying here stark naked while Matt had dressed and gone outside? She snatched up the sleeping bag and belatedly held it over her body, a blush scorching her cheeks as she blinked at her surroundings. She suddenly gasped.

The walls were glowing. Glowing! The granite was no longer a dark gray but a soft rich gold, and she could actually *feel* waves of heat radiating from them. No wonder she'd thrown off the sleeping bag; it had to be eighty degrees in the cave.

"Curses," she muttered, scrambling to her feet, her nakedness forgotten as she crept to the wall and gently touched the golden glow. It was hot!

Had her little incident with her staff yesterday charged the granite with ions or something? Could they be radioactive? She snatched her hand back just as another thought struck her. How in hell was she going to explain glowing walls to Matt?

Winter spun around, gathered up the clothes she'd been wearing yesterday, and quickly dressed, ignoring her protesting muscles as she contorted her arms to fasten her bra. She then hopped from one foot to the other to slip into her pants as she frantically searched the cave for her staff. Where in heck was it? She knew she had left the stick where it had blown against the back wall last night, but it wasn't there!

She stopped in midhop with another gasp. Gesader. Where in heck was her pet?

Winter sat down and put on her socks. He

must have heard someone coming through the woods last night and left before Matt had gotten to the cave. And the brat had taken that blasted stick with him, Winter decided as she crammed her feet into her boots and quickly laced them. But staff or not, she still had to find a way to explain the glowing walls.

Wait. A fire. She could build a huge fire in the pit, and Matt would think the flames were reflecting off the walls and making them glow. Yeah, and that would also account for it being as hot as Hades in here. Winter scooted over to the fire pit, threw several pieces of wood into a haphazard tepee, and started looking around for a starter.

Curses, she was right back to her original problem — no starter. She got to her feet, tiptoed to the entrance of the cave, and peeked outside to look for Matt. The wind had died down considerably, and only light snow was falling now, but all Winter saw were Matt's footprints heading toward the meadow. She sighed in relief, ran to the birch tree she'd mutilated yesterday, and ripped off several more strips of bark. She ran back, stuffed the bark inside the tepee, then started hunting for her packet of matches.

She lifted the sleeping bag and then the pad, tossing them away to see underneath, and found nothing but empty ground. She ran to the pile of blankets, pawing through them but still finding nothing. She did find the lantern sitting next to the side wall, but no matches beside it. Beginning to panic, she tore all the clothes out of Matt's bag looking for a lighter, something, anything to start a fire!

Winter walked back to the pit, circling it as she stared at the fireless tepee. Crouching down with her back to the entrance, she frowned. Robbie didn't use a staff to start fires when they ate lunch in the forest; he only had to touch the wood to get it to burst into flame. He never spoke any words, but just seemed to *want* it to light and it did.

Well, she was supposed to be a wizard, wasn't she? Winter reached out and touched the wood with her finger, willed it to burst into flame, and got . . . She got nothing, not even a fizzle.

She frowned, concentrating harder, this time *demanding* it to light . . . and still got nothing.

A large hand suddenly covered hers, holding her finger on the wood. "You need to calmly ask for what you want," Matt whispered just as the tepee gently burst into flame.

Winter scurried away with a startled yelp, standing up and backing against the wall of the cave, her eyes wide with shock. Matt fed a few more sticks to the growing fire, then stood and brushed flakes of snow off his shoulders as he faced her.

Winter opened her mouth but nothing, not even a squeak, came out. How could he . . . how had he done . . . she couldn't even comprehend what had just happened, much less articulate it.

He stepped toward her, and Winter scrambled sideways along the glowing wall. He stopped, tucked his hands behind his back, and smiled. "Good morning, wife," he said softly.

She opened her mouth again, and this time managed only an unintelligible squeak.

"Are you hungry?" he asked. "I know I'm starved."

"Wh-who are you?" she was finally able to whisper.

"Matheson Gregor," he answered calmly. "Guardian of Gairn."

"Cùram!" she gasped, clutching her hand around her neck, trying to stop the blood from draining from her face.

He bowed slightly. "Aye, but I prefer you

call me Matt. Or husband," he offered with a crooked smile.

Winter inched farther along the wall, its heat causing a trickle of sweat to run down her back. Daar and her papa and Robbie had been hunting for Cùram de Gairn for over two weeks, and he'd been right under their noses the whole time. She eyed the entrance of the cave, gauging her chances of getting past Matt — or Cùram or whoever the heck he was! — before he could get around the fire.

"Don't even try," he said softly. "I'll catch you before you can leave the meadow. And besides, there is no place for you to run, wife."

"Stop calling me that! I'm not your wife!"

He pulled his hands from behind his back and folded his arms over his chest, looking down at the balled-up sleeping bag at his feet, then back at her, one eyebrow raised. "We became man and wife last night, Winter," he whispered in calm contradiction to her shout.

"We are not married! Having sex isn't the same as having a wedding," she continued a bit more forcefully, anger rising to her defense. She folded her own arms under her breasts, not to mimic him, but to hug herself against the chill growing inside her despite the wall scorching her back. "There has to be an actual ceremony and a priest in attendance for it to be binding."

"Oh, it's binding, princess, if the two people exchanging vows do so willingly." He shrugged. "A priest is only a formality for society's sake." He lifted one brow again. "Did you not pledge me your love and loyalty last night, Winter? Did you not agree to my own declaration of marriage?"

She vehemently shook her head. "I didn't pledge anything to you!" She inched closer to the entrance. "I said those things to somebody else last night. I thought you were Matt Gregor, a simple businessman."

He inclined his head. "But I am a simple businessman. I've lived and worked in this time for two and a half years now, accumulating enough wealth to buy this mountain and build a home for us to live in."

Winter pressed more deeply against the wall. "You didn't come here to marry me. You're here to destroy mankind!"

He didn't so much as flinch at her shouted accusation, but merely lifted one blasted brow again. "Who told you that? Pendaär?" He snorted and shook his head. "That old bastard is more prone to melodrama than to reason. Destroying mankind is not my intent, though it will likely be one of the consequences."

"T-then why are you here?"

"For you, Winter. I've come here for you."

His softly spoken declaration finally sent Winter over the edge of reason and into a dark, swirling void of horror. She pushed off the wall and bolted for the entrance, kicking the sleeping bag into the fire as she ran past, tearing out of the cave as if the hounds of hell were nipping her heels.

She ignored Matt's calmly given shout as she wove through the trees toward the meadow. Where in curses was Snowball? And Gesader? The panther was supposed to be her protector, and now was not the time for him to worry about being seen.

Winter broke into the meadow at a flat-out run, praying the snow wasn't hiding anything to trip her, and shouted Gesader's name. She was answered by Matt's shout from behind her, only this time he sounded a bit frantic. And then she heard him roar *Nay!* at the same time something heavy slammed into her back, knocking her to the ground.

Winter tumbled through the snow in a tangle of flailing arms and feet and black fur. There was another violent impact that knocked a scream from her lungs as she rolled free to land facedown in the snow, the sound of a snarl and an even more angry growl rolling down the meadow away from her.

She looked up to find Matt and Gesader, only ten feet away, wrestling. Not wanting to leave her pet, but also not wanting to waste the opportunity he was so valiantly giving her, Winter scrambled to her feet and started running across the meadow again, this time in the direction of Tom's cabin. Gesader could take care of himself, she decided. A man was no match for a leopard.

She skidded to a halt and looked back. But a *drùidh?* Could Gesader hold his own against the powerful Cùram de Gairn?

Winter saw the two of them were facing each other now, both crouched in a striking position. "Don't run, Winter," Matt shouted without taking his eyes off his adversary. "He's drunk. He's wanting to chase anything that runs, and he might hurt you."

Winter gaped at Gesader. Drunk? Her pet was drunk?

It was a trick, she decided. Matt was only trying to trick her. Winter turned and started running again toward the bottom end of the meadow.

"Nay!" Matt shouted.

Winter looked over her shoulder and saw

Gesader pursuing her, moving at an alarming speed that was quickly closing the distance between them. She changed direction with her own shout of surprise, making Gesader lose his footing as he tried to take a passing swipe at her.

Winter was cleaned off her feet by Matt this time, but her landing was a lot less bruising as Matt wrapped her up in his arms and took the brunt of their fall. Before her head was even done spinning, Matt was on his feet and shoving her behind his back, putting himself between her and her snarling pet.

"Back off, Kenzie," he snapped. "Before you hurt her."

Gesader let out a roar that echoed through the meadow in bone-chilling waves, his tail whipping the air in anger.

"Go sleep it off, Kenzie," Matt said softly. "And don't come back until you're sober and ready to apologize to my *wife*," he finished, emphasizing the last word.

For Gesader's sake, Winter suddenly realized, not hers.

The leopard gave another angry roar, then turned and started walking down the sloping meadow, his tail switching in agitation as he growled under his breath. Matt turned to Winter, and she stepped back from his own angry expression.

"Your choice," he said roughly. "You walk back to the cave on your own, or I carry you back."

Winter lifted her chin. "You called him Kenzie."

"Aye, because that's his name. Kenzie Gregor."

Her gasp caused her to take another step back. "He's your brother," she whispered. "The first day we met, you mentioned you had business with your brother." She looked down the meadow just as the panther disappeared into the woods, then back at Matt. "You didn't come here for me. You came because of him."

Matt slowly shook his head. "Oh, I came here for you," he said, folding his arms over his chest. "I sent Kenzie ahead with your cousin, MacBain, then followed as soon as I could."

"But why?" Winter cried, holding her arms out in petition. "Why have you come here for me?"

He stepped forward, and before she realized what he was going to do, Matt captured her face in his broad hands and made her look directly into his eyes. "Because you're the only one who can help me," he said softly.

"H-help you what?"

He leaned closer, his dark, turbulent eyes only inches from hers. "Kill my brother," he whispered. He suddenly straightened, took one of her hands, and turned and led her back up the meadow toward the cave.

Winter could do nothing more than walk beside him in silence. He hadn't just said that. He couldn't want to kill his own brother. And he surely couldn't expect her to help him!

He'd gone mad, she decided. Cùram de Gairn was upsetting the continuum with his madness, and now he was trying to drag her down into that dark, hopeless void with him. She had to find a way to destroy him before he destroyed mankind.

Or . . . or she had to find a way to help him.

Neither option, however, was going to fix her broken heart.

Aye, though not very significant when compared to the fate of mankind, Winter couldn't get past the fact that Matheson Gregor had broken her heart so badly she didn't care if he and his drunken, traitorous brother rotted in Hades for all of eternity.

They continued back up the meadow, both in silence; Matt seemingly still angry at the panther, and Winter simply sad. But just as Matt led her into the cave, she had a sneezing fit so violent, she had to pull free and cover her face. Her head swam dizzily, her eyes watered with congestion, and her empty stomach clenched as if it were trying to climb up her throat.

"You're catching a cold," Matt said, leading her past his smoldering sleeping bag to the pile of blankets. He was about to help her sit down when he stopped, picked up one of the blankets, and held it up to let it unfurl in his hand. "What in hell happened to this?" he asked, staring at the scorched hole in the center of the blanket, then looking at her.

Winter's already hot, congested face heated even more as she remained mute, refusing to explain yesterday's debacle. She wasn't about to tell a fellow *drùidh* that she was so inept she couldn't even light a fire.

He smiled, tossed the blanket down, and sat her down on top of it. "I'll heat up some soup," he said, going over to one of the boxes near the far wall. "And see if we can't roust that cold before it settles in. Flying isn't much fun when your head feels like it's about to explode."

Winter stopped from wiping her nose on her sleeve and gaped at him. "I'm not flying anywhere."

Matt opened a can of soup and poured it in a pot, then put the pot on a heated rock beside the nicely burning fire. "I still have a quality control problem at my Utah plant, and now a little matter of a wedding ceremony to deal with. I figure I can take care of both with one quick trip west." He looked over at her and smiled. "It'll be a corny little chapel on the Las Vegas Strip, but it will be legal."

"I am not marrying you," she said, carefully enunciating each word. "I didn't marry you last night, and I sure as heck am not marrying you in a corny little chapel in Las Vegas."

He shrugged. "It's for your benefit, not mine," he said, pouring the steaming soup into a bowl and bringing it over to her. He found two spoons, came back and sat down on the ground beside her, and ate what was left in the pot while she wolfed down her own soup in silence.

"I — I have to go to the bathroom," she whispered the moment she was done, lifting her chin to counter the blush she knew was coloring her cheeks.

He set down the pot, stood up, and held his hand out to her. Winter ignored it and scrambled to her feet, sneezed twice, then strode out of the cave while wiping her nose on her sleeve again. He followed two steps behind her. She had just reached the edge of the woods when he stopped her by turning her around to face him. "Your word you won't run, or I stay right beside you."

She lifted her brow at him. "You'll take my word?"

He smiled. "I took it last night." He folded his arms over his chest. "I was under the impression you were a woman of honor. Was I wrong?"

"No," she snapped. "And you don't need to hide your brogue from me. Not anymore."

He chuckled, shaking his head. "I'm not hiding anything from you, Winter. I told you it only surfaces when I'm . . . er, under stress."

She spun toward the woods, but his hand on her shoulder stopped her again. "Promise me you won't run."

"I won't run," she said with her back to him. "I promise."

He released her shoulder and Winter rushed into the thick bushes, going until she thought she was safely out of sight. She quickly took care of business, then moved even deeper into the woods, pulling out her cell phone as she looked over her shoulder to make sure he wasn't growing impatient.

She stopped, opened the tiny phone, and turned on the power button to find two towers of signal. She put her thumb over the speed-dial for Gù Brath . . . but didn't push it. What could she possibly tell her parents? *Hi, I'm here with Cùram de Gairn on Bear Mountain. Why don't you rush up here and kill him for being an unholy bastard and breaking my heart?*

Winter hit the power button instead of the speed-dial, closed the phone, and tucked it back in her pocket with a sigh. As much as she hated him, as much as she wanted to find her stick and beat Matt Gregor to a bloody pulp, she certainly didn't want his death on her hands, even though she wasn't the one who would actually be doing the killing.

As perverse as it seemed, Winter realized she couldn't be in love with Matt one minute and then hate him the next, no matter who he was or what he was planning on doing. She hadn't given her love lightly, and it was going to take her some time to fall out of love with him.

Which gave Winter a whole new respect for Megan.

She turned and walked back through the bushes, stepped into the clearing beside the ledge, and saw Matt leaning against the cave entrance, his arms crossed over his chest, smiling at her.

"What about Snowball?" she asked as she walked up to him. "I need to check on him."

"He's fine. I took off his blanket this morning and sent him home."

"No, you didn't. That will only worry my parents."

He lifted a brow, still leaning against the cliff. "Didn't you just call them on the phone you always carry and let them know where you are?"

She shoved her fists in her jacket pockets and looked at his feet. "I didn't call them."

He said nothing, only held out his hand beneath her lowered gaze. Winter kept her own hands in her pockets and brushed past him into the cave. She immediately started straightening up by folding and replacing his clothes that she'd pulled from his duffel bag while she'd been looking for matches. "Where's my pinewood stick?" she asked as she worked.

"Up there, out of your reach."

She turned to see him nodding toward a high ledge on the still-glowing granite and saw the tip of her staff peeking out over the edge. She zipped up his duffel bag, scooted over, and started folding the blankets.

Large, warm hands settled on her shoulders. "Leave that and come over here," he said, helping her stand by pulling on her jacket, then leading her over to sit near the far wall next to the fire.

"W-what are you doing?" she whispered when he sat down directly behind her with his back to the wall.

"I'm going to brush out your hair."

She shot her hand to her hair, gathered the knotted tangles together in her fist, and pulled them over her shoulder away from him. "I can brush out my own hair," she said, raking her fingers through the tangles.

He reached around her, pulled her hands down to her lap, then slid her hair back over her shoulder. "But I want to," he said softly. "You just sit quietly while I tell you a little story. Then when I'm done, we can discuss our wedding plans."

Winter closed her eyes, going utterly still as a shiver raced along her spine when Matt's hands slid under her hair. Up the back of her scalp, then gently down through her curls his fingers moved, until they got caught in the tangles. Then she felt the gentle tug of a fine-bristled brush as Matt slowly started working free the knots near the ends of her curls.

CHAPTER EIGHTEEN

"Once upon a very long time ago," Matt began softly, "in a land far away, lived a young boy with dreams of becoming a mighty warrior. He lived with his mama and papa, and a younger brother and baby sister in a cottage high on a mountain."

Matt separated a thick lock of Winter's hair and started brushing it out, working his way up from the end. "As a bairn, the boy didn't think it strange that they lived so far from the village, or that he never got to play with other lads. Nay," Matt said, his voice lowering, "he was quite content to run through the forest with his brother as they fought mock battles with their wooden swords. The boy was too young and carefree at first to even wonder why he'd been told to avoid people and never form bonds with anyone other than his brother and sister."

Winter wanted to speak, to ask why, but a lump had started to grow in her throat.

"It wasn't until the boy began to feel the first stirring of manhood that he questioned his papa's refusal to let him train to be a warrior with the other lads in the nearby village." Matt stopped brushing. "Each day he grew more determined to be a warrior, getting into shouting matches with his papa that made his mama cry, his sister cower in the corner, and his younger brother hide in the woods."

Winter felt Matt pick up another knot of hair, and he again started gently brushing out the tangles. "By his sixteenth birthday he'd had enough. He ran away from home to the shouts of his angry papa and the desperate sobs of his mama. He ran as hard and as far as he could, traveling on foot for days, until he reached the sea and couldn't go any farther. There, wandering up the coastline, he found a village of hardworking but poor sheep farmers. One of the families took him in despite their poverty, and by day he worked tending their sheep and by night he trained with a group of old warriors who were desperate to protect what little their village had from reaving neighbors."

Matt stopped brushing again, and Winter felt him ball his hands into fists in her hair. "The boy couldn't understand why his parents had been so against him having anything to do with people. The village that had taken him in was populated by good folks. Generous and kind people." He started brushing again. "He lived with them for ten years, quite content with the new life he'd made, until one moonless night an army of thieving marauders sailed up the coast and landed on the village beach."

Winter stiffened, her fingers laced tightly together on her lap as she stared at the glowing wall in front of her.

"The villagers didn't stand a chance. Some were slaughtered in their beds, some burned alive trying to escape their homes. Women were raped and killed, the men mutilated before they were executed. Children were chased down and run through with swords, except for bairns under the age of three, who were stolen. Even the sheep were slaughtered, only their hides taken. Wheat fields were burned, wells salted. By daybreak the destruction was complete."

"A-and the boy?" Winter whispered in frozen horror, not even able to wipe the tears running down her cheeks.

Matt's hands tightened on her hair. "The boy was a twenty-six-year-old man then, lass, who had grown into a mighty warrior.

He killed over thirty of the murdering bastards with his sword, and at least ten with his bare hands when his weapon snapped, before he was finally brought down by a blow that sliced him nearly in half."

"H-he died?"

The hands on her hair, trembling now, slowly began brushing again. "He should have," Matt whispered. "The wound was mortal. But he lay with his blood seeping into the ashes of the wheat field and watched the burning village below while waiting for death to take him. But it never came. The sun rose and he still lived. It set again that night, and he still lay in a pool of his own blood, still waiting for death as he breathed the stench of slaughtered animals and people mingled with burnt flesh.

"Shh," Matt whispered, reaching around Winter and enveloping her into a tender embrace as he pressed the side of his face to hers. "Don't cry, lass," he said, his arms tightening. "The young warrior lives. By the next morning he's able to stand, and he binds his wound and sets out on the long and arduous journey back to his parents' home."

He used his thumbs to wipe her tears away, then started brushing her hair again.

Most of the tangles were gone, and Matt brushed in long strokes as he ran his free hand under her hair. "He nearly didn't recognize his old cottage," he continued, his voice as soothing as his gentle strokes. "It was in a state of disrepair and didn't seem to have anyone living in it. But he did find two graves out back, with the names of his mama and sister carved on two crooked crosses. His mama had died four years earlier, the cross read, his sister just three months before he'd returned. There was another board propped against his sister's cross, with the name Kyle carved into it, along with the age of three weeks and two days."

Matt stopped brushing, circled Winter's neck with his hand, and soothingly rubbed his thumb over her pulse when she tried to stifle a sob. Winter didn't know how much more she could take, yet she held herself perfectly still, afraid he would stop telling his story.

"The warrior searched the cottage for any signs that would tell him what had happened to his papa and brother," he continued as he started brushing again. "The place was a mess. Dishes were broken and grain spilled on the floor, but he could tell it had been from neglect, not thieves.

Cobwebs covered everything, so he knew no one had been home for months. Possibly not since his sister's death.

"Then he remembered the cave farther up the mountain, about a mile away. It was where he had often found his papa when the old man would go missing for days at a time. The warrior went to the cave, and there was his papa — drunk, half blind, dirty and smelly, and raving mad. The warrior tried to get him to come home, but his papa — not even recognizing his own son at first — refused. So they lived in the cave for nearly a month together while the warrior healed and the old man continued to tell his crazy, fantastical stories."

"W-what kind of fantastical stories?" Winter whispered.

Matt gave her hair a soft tug. "Be patient, lass." Instead of the brush, he started running his fingers through her curls. "The warrior did learn what had happened to his brother," he continued. "Not a year after he had left home, his younger brother had also left in a fit of anger. He'd gone in search of another clan to live with, since everyone in the nearby village considered the whole family odd and shunned them."

"He could do that?" Winter asked, trying to turn to look at Matt. "He could just go join another clan?"

Matt held her hair to keep her facing forward. "It wasn't uncommon to move between clans back then. Remember, this was very long ago, Winter. Long before even your papa's time. So," Matt continued. "Our young warrior stayed with his father until the old man simply didn't wake up one morning. He buried his papa next to his mother and sister and nephew, then burned their old cottage and raked the ground clean until no evidence remained that it had ever existed. He even disguised the graves before he set off to find the only remaining member of his family."

"But why burn the house and disguise the graves? What was he hiding?"

"His heritage," Matt said simply. He pulled her back into his embrace, leaning against the wall and folding his arms over hers just under her breasts as he stretched his legs along either side of hers. He used his chin to urge her to lay her head back against him, then continued.

"You see, the old man's ravings finally made sense to the warrior after hearing them over and over for weeks. It seems his papa was the son of a *drùidh* who had married a guardian."

Winter gasped, and Matt held her tightly

when she tried to sit up. "Aye," he said before she could speak. "My grandparents had been destined to serve Providence, but they chose love instead. So they married and lived in the same cave my papa had died in," he continued, relaxing his grip when he realized she was staying still. "My *drùidh* grandfather's powers were lost with my papa's birth, and wouldn't appear again until the next generation, in me."

"But Robbie had a baby and didn't lose his powers," Winter quietly pointed out.

"It's not the same for guardians. Guardians live a normal human's lifetime, then move on to become mere helpers. MacBain's pet owl, Mary, is an example of this. She was Robbie's mother, and can help him in his guardian duties, but she can't actually affect the physical world."

"You know about Mary?" Winter whispered.

"Aye. We've met, mostly eight hundred years ago, when she was trying to help MacBain steal my tree."

Winter stiffened, and Matt tightened his embrace and kissed the top of her head. "He brought back the tap root only because I wanted him to, Winter," Matt told her. "Because I needed my energy to be brought forward. Along with Kenzie," he added.

Winter stiffened again. "You said you wanted me to help you kill him," she whispered, tilting her head back to look up. "I won't. I can't."

Matt used one hand to gently ease her to face forward again. "Do you want to hear the rest of the story, or argue about something you know nothing about?"

She let out a deep sigh. "Continue," she softly growled.

Matt chuckled and dropped his mouth beside her ear. "So once I had wiped out any trace of my family," he softly continued, "I pointed myself north and started walking to where my papa believed Kenzie had gone. It took me over three years to reach him," he said, looking across the cave, seemingly amazed by that fact himself. "I kept getting waylaid by wars," he explained, his attention coming back to her. "Oh, I forgot to tell you that before my papa died, he told me where my grandfather's staff was. It was buried deep in the back of the cave he had been living in since he'd buried Fiona's babe beside her."

"W-what did her baby die of?"

Matt shrugged, shrugging Winter with him. "Neglect, most likely. My old man didn't know anything about bairns. And he certainly wouldn't know he couldn't feed raw cow's milk to a newborn."

"Before he died, did your papa explain why you had to live away from people?" she asked.

"Aye. He kept our whole family isolated in the hopes of protecting me from my destiny. He knew that if I took up my calling to become a *drùidh,* bonding with people would cause me to grow bitter as everyone I cared for died but I kept on living. It's what his own parents had told him would happen, and that he should discourage me from taking that path."

Winter frowned at the opposite wall. "But you did take it. You became a *drùidh.*"

His arms tightened again. "Aye. I didn't have a choice."

"Daar told me we all have a choice. That we have free will to follow either Providence or our own path. Your grandparents chose their own path, so why didn't you have the same choice?"

"Are you going to let me finish my story?" he growled.

Winter snapped her mouth shut.

"I finally found Kenzie after three years of hunting for him, but I was nearly too late. He was in the midst of a raging battle between two powerful clans, and his clan was being slaughtered. I almost didn't recognize him, since Kenzie had only been thirteen when I'd run away from home. And when I did finally fight my way through the battle to reach him, he was covered in blood. My first hope was that the blood belonged to his enemy and he was only stunned by the blow I'd seen him take." Matt's arms squeezed her tightly. "But Kenzie was mortally wounded, his guts spilling from a gaping hole in his belly."

"But you saved him," Winter whispered.

"Nay, not me. Providence saved Kenzie's life."

"P-Providence?"

"Aye. My calling as both a *drùidh* and a guardian became quite clear to me in that one horrific moment. As a warrior I could take revenge for Kenzie's death, but I couldn't keep him from dying. As a mere mortal, I could do nothing. But as a *drùidh,* I could summon the energies of the entire universe and command them to save the only person left in the world that I cared about."

"So you accepted your calling in order to save Kenzie."

"Aye. But *drùidhs* may not play God, and as a guardian I could not impose my will — no matter how powerful — on another soul without there being consequences. So I made a pact that day, not with the devil but with Providence, that I would accept my calling if Kenzie was allowed to live." He pulled her deeper into his embrace. "Do you realize what my decision meant, lass? I didn't save Kenzie; I damned him instead. And myself."

She frowned at the far wall. "By making him a panther?"

"That's the consequence that proves we should be careful what we ask for. I was so desperate not to lose him, I didn't care that Kenzie couldn't live as a human. All I cared was that his soul would remain on earth with me, even as an animal."

"But Gesader — Kenzie was only a cub when I got him."

"Animals have very short life spans compared to humans. In trying to save my brother, I ended up forcing him to live many lifetimes as different animals. No soul is allowed to repeat its same life; Kenzie had to die a man on the battlefield that day and return as something else."

"But why an animal?" Winter asked, again trying to turn to see Matt, and again Matt not letting her. So she settled back down and continued staring forward. "Why not let him come back as another person?"

"Then he wouldn't be Kenzie. He'd be

someone I wouldn't recognize, and who wouldn't know me. Our bodies die, Winter, but not our souls. So he couldn't come back as himself — he had already been Kenzie Gregor."

Winter pulled in a heavy breath and let out a frustrated sigh. "So Kenzie has been a different animal, living and dying over and over, since you found him?"

"Aye."

Before Matt realized what she was about, Winter turned in his arms and looked up to find his face paled to ashen gray and his eyes dark with pain. "You said you want me to help you kill him," she whispered. "Why?"

"Because he's asked me to," he told her just as softly, smoothing her hair off her face. He held her head in his hands. "In the beginning, Kenzie was happy to be alive and reunited with me. Even though he first returned as a young colt, he was still himself, and we shared many wonderful years together getting to know each other all over again. But the colt grew into a horse, then an old horse, and he eventually died. Next, Kenzie returned to me as a puppy. It's a cycle that's repeated itself for a thousand years, and my brother is tired of it. He wishes to die only once more, and he wishes to be a man when he does."

"So — so how do I fit in this story?"

Matt ran his fingers through her hair, gripping the bulk of it in his fists at the back of her head. "I'm needing your magic to make that happen, Winter. I've used up most of my own trying to reach this point. Now you must help me let him die."

"But will he . . . will he be Kenzie? You said he wants to die a man, but that a soul can't repeat its life."

"I don't know," Matt whispered, pulling her head down to his chest so she couldn't look at him anymore. "I have hopes he'll still be Kenzie. My gut says that your magic is powerful enough to let him finish his original life from where he'd left off on the battlefield; that he'll grow old until he dies a natural death here in this century, with me."

Winter closed her eyes, listening to Matt's pounding heart as she mulled over what he'd told her. She suddenly sat up. "You're going to die in this century?" she repeated. "But you're younger than Daar."

He shook his head, his eyes darkening to unreadable depths. "I've manipulated the energies so badly trying to grant Kenzie his final wish, that I'm afraid I've damned us all." He captured her hair in his fists again and held her looking at him. "Including you,

Winter. I committed the same sin against you as I did against Kenzie a thousand years ago, when I got you pregnant last night."

"Pregnant!" she gasped, rearing back.

But Matt's grip on her hair kept her from moving very far. "Aye. And in doing so, I've done the unforgivable. Just like I did with my brother, I've taken away your right to choose your own destiny. Having our child means you can't stay a *drùidh,* Winter, and that I will also lose my powers." He pulled her forward, kissed her forehead, then held his lips against her skin as he spoke. "But it's my sin, and I'll be the one to pay for it. We'll find a chapel in Las Vegas to make you feel married, we'll build our home here, and raise our child together while we wait for the end to come."

Well, saints and curses. Just what she wanted. A divested *drùidh* who was marrying her out of duty, willing to live with her while they patiently waited for the world to end.

"Hey," she said, pulling away enough to glare at him. "If you took away my powers by making me pregnant, how can I help Kenzie?"

Matt shook his head. "We won't lose our powers until our babe takes its first breath. In olden days, more bairns died in the womb than were born, so our power is not lost until the child has a chance of living. Providence is very practical; it won't close a door without opening a window first, and it won't chance losing a *drùidh* unless another one is certain to replace it." He sighed and rubbed his forehead. "Remember, there's also the possibility a *drùidh* will turn away from his calling, so Providence keeps its options open. You still have time to help me help Kenzie."

"You make it sound as if Providence is only in the business of making wizards!" she snapped, smacking him in the chest and scrambling to her feet before he could catch her. She pointed at the cave entrance. "Go away," she whispered. "Go see if your brother fell in the lake in a drunken stupor and drowned." She took a step closer. "What is he drunk on?"

Matt sat on the floor, looking up at her. "Catnip."

She spun around to face the opposite wall. "Go away," she whispered again, hugging herself.

He said nothing for the longest time before Winter finally heard him stand up, and when he next spoke his voice came from the entrance. "We need to leave for Utah tomorrow morning. You can tell your parents you'll be back the morning after tomorrow, if you wish to let them know."

She said nothing, and Matt — or Cùram de Gairn or whoever the heck he was — quietly walked out of the cave.

CHAPTER NINETEEN

Winter sat on the singed sleeping bag in front of a fire she didn't really need because of the warmly glowing walls. While staring up at her pinewood staff, she chewed the last bite of a candy bar she'd found in her saddlebag. She'd had a moment's guilt that Matt was probably hungry; the soup he'd eaten hours ago couldn't have sustained him very long. But her guilt had lasted only as long as it had taken Winter to remember how mad she was at him.

And she hoped Gesader — Kenzie — had a terrible hangover.

She couldn't believe she was pregnant. Didn't believe it. She would know something that important, wouldn't she? She'd always been able to sense the energy of spirits. Wouldn't she know if a little one was growing inside her?

They hadn't used any protection last night. Winter hadn't even considered the risk of pregnancy, much less been able to think about anything other than loving Matt so much her heart had near burst with wanting him. What was she going to tell her parents? How could she put them through this right now, while they were still trying to deal with Megan's pregnancy?

Winter's heart went out to her sister. She finally understood why Megan couldn't quit crying, as her own eyes hadn't stopped leaking since Matt had left over four hours ago — though some of those tears might be from her cold. Maybe.

But probably not. The Matt Gregor she'd fallen in love with over the last two weeks was still entrenched in her heart, though that was the only thing Winter was sure of. The rest — the story of the young warrior having lost everyone dear to him, and her pet panther actually being a man — she still couldn't decide how she felt about that.

It did explain a few things though, filling in most of the puzzle of what had been happening lately. Except . . . except she hadn't asked Matt why he'd cut the top off Daar's tree. If he truly did need her magic, why would he have risked weakening the white pine?

And this wedding he kept insisting they were having in Las Vegas tomorrow — how was she supposed to feel about that? Angry? Appalled? Grateful he wasn't abandoning her like Wayne Ferris had abandoned Megan?

Winter realized she had to remember what time Matt was from. Conceiving an illegitimate child centuries ago guaranteed a life of misery for both mother and baby. And his sister, Fiona. She also had to remember how Fiona's tragedy had affected Matt; how he hadn't been there to protect his sister when she'd gotten pregnant and had died in childbirth, her bairn dying soon after.

Poor Matt. He was riddled with guilt. He was supposed to be a guardian and powerful *drùidh,* but he hadn't been able to protect those he loved, not the villagers who had been kind to him, not his family, and ultimately not even Kenzie.

Which was why, despite deceiving her and despite messing up the magic so badly he'd doomed mankind, Winter couldn't bring herself to expose Matt's true identity to Robbie and Daar and her papa. Oh, she understood perfectly well why Matt had demanded those vows from her last night, why he'd hope to gain her loyalty at least long enough to keep his promise to his brother. He was counting on Winter to honor her word, even though she'd innocently given it to her enemy.

What a mess. It seemed she was damned if she did and damned if she didn't. She could betray her own family and pretend Matt was nothing more than the man she loved, or she could betray the man she loved and protect her family. Oh yeah, she could also betray all of mankind while she was at it!

There had to be a way to bring the continuum back into balance without creating even more of a mess. All she needed to do was figure out how to stop the pine from dying, grant Kenzie his wish, and redeem Matt's soul without losing her own. She was powerful, Matt had said. So powerful, in fact, that he'd chosen her to help him.

Winter stopped rubbing her nose on her sleeve in midswipe. But why *her?* Of all the wizards from all times, why had Cùram de Gairn come to this century to involve *her* in his damnation?

Curses, would the questions never cease? The more she learned, the more she didn't know.

Winter yawned, then sneezed so hard her head started to throb. She looked toward the entrance, realized it was already dark outside, and yawned again. Crying was definitely hard on a body, she decided for the second time in two days as she fluffed up the remains of the sleeping bag and laid down.

And tomorrow didn't look to be any more promising.

Winter woke up surprisingly calm, considering how disturbing the first half of her night had been. Within minutes of falling asleep, she'd experienced horrific nightmares of murdering thieves slaughtering defenseless villagers, of her frantically searching an unfamiliar mountain for unmarked graves, and of her chasing Matt through a dark void of hopelessness as she shouted his name and cried uncontrollably. But sometime in the wee hours before dawn her nightmares had changed, transforming into a colorful, pleasant dream filled with such promising hope that she was still reluctant to open her eyes and have it end.

She was pretty sure she knew why the nightmares had suddenly vanished, as well as exactly when. Matt had returned in the wee hours, wrapped himself around Winter until only her nose was exposed, and held her in his protective embrace for the rest of the night. In fact, he was still holding her, spooned against her back with his arm and leg thrown across her body, clinging in a way that told Winter just how desperately he needed her.

Because more than needing her help to keep his promise to Kenzie, Winter understood just how desperately Matt needed her to wrestle Cùram de Gairn's soul away from Providence and give Matheson Gregor back the gift of hope. The chill wind of hopelessness she'd felt when she'd hugged the pine tree — that's what was really upsetting the continuum, not Matt's manipulating the magic for his own benefit. Oh, she didn't deny it had been a selfish act when he had made his pact with Providence to keep his brother alive, but wasn't Providence just as culpable?

Winter had come to that blasphemous conclusion during her beautiful dream, in which she'd been walking through the woods on Bear Mountain and had come upon a large crow sitting on a stump. She'd had quite an interesting conversation with the crow; Winter asking questions about her calling and the wise black bird providing her with answers beyond anything she could have imagined. In her dream, the crow had taken on the voice of Tom, but Winter dismissed that assimilation because Tom was always carving crows, so of course the one in her dream reminded her of him. Nevertheless, their conversation had eventually led the crow to tell Winter about a shift in the continuum that had occurred nearly a thousand years ago.

Still keeping her eyes closed, Winter frowned at nothing, wondering if it truly was possible for a person to learn stuff in dreams. Because if she could believe what the crow had told her, then she may have figured out how to solve all of her and Matt's problems — and save mankind while she was at it.

The crow had told Winter that the moment Cùram de Gairn had made his pact with Providence, the continuum had immediately realized its mistake and started to alter its ways. Winter had also been surprised to learn that up until her birth, every *drùidh* to have ever lived had been male. And guardians, oddly enough, were usually female, although that was not a strict policy. Feminine energy was nurturing by nature, the crow had explained, as well as quite practical when compared to male energy, which had a penchant for getting a bit forceful when dealing with problems.

And hadn't Daar proven that theory more than once!

So had Cùram, the bird had told Winter.

Matheson Gregor had trained to be a warrior and brought those skills to his calling as Cùram de Gairn. In order to get himself to this century and into her bed, and still hold onto his power, Cùram had used cunning, trickery, and often brute force — all tools of a successful warrior. Hell, her dream crow had said Matt had gone so far as to blow up Snow Mountain eight hundred years ago, getting his tree of life destroyed in the process, to come to this century.

That was why the continuum had begun shifting long before then. The day Matheson Gregor had saved his brother by becoming Cùram de Gairn a thousand years ago was the day Winter's birth had been foretold.

She was pregnant, the crow had also informed her, but that didn't mean she had lost her precious right of free will. The bairn she carried was the product of two powerful *drùidhs,* and both she and Matt were still able to choose their own paths from this point forward — assuming of course, she could indeed rebalance the energy with the help of her mighty pine. The crow had said *her* mighty white pine, as its energy was attuned to Winter now, and no longer to Daar.

"You're awake," Matt said, his lips touching her hair.

"Yes," she acknowledged without opening her eyes.

"What are you thinking about?"

"Dreams. Do you ever dream, Matt?"

"I used to."

"And when you used to dream, did you learn stuff in them, or did you wonder if they were only wishful thinking?"

He finally moved, sliding his leg off her thigh and his arm from around her, and propped his head on his hand just behind her shoulder. "You were having nightmares when I came in. You cried and even called out in your sleep."

"Yes," Winter said, rolling onto her back to look at him. "But the nightmares left the moment your arms came around me."

He really did have a handsome smile, she decided. Winter wondered how much smiling Matt would be doing over the next three months, as she implemented her plan. Because if she dared to believe her dream, Cùram de Gairn wasn't the only cunning wizard in this cave.

"So," Matt said, brushing her hair off her face with his finger. "Are you flying out with me this morning?"

"Yes."

He lifted one brow, obviously surprised by

her simple and quickly given answer. "And we're stopping in Las Vegas?" he thought to clarify.

Winter kept her own smile hidden and shrugged. "If you don't want to let Father Daar marry us, then yes, I guess we should stop in Las Vegas."

Both his brows slammed into a frown. "I'm not letting that crazy old bastard marry us."

"Do you love me, Matt?" Winter asked calmly.

Two flags of red appeared on the sharp planes of his cheeks, peeking through his two-day growth of beard. "No," he whispered, rolling onto his back and lacing his fingers behind his head. "I can't ever love you," he told the cave's ceiling. He turned just his head to look at her. "I'm incapable of loving anyone, lass. I lost the ability to love centuries ago."

"No," she said, rolling toward him and laying her hand on his shirt-covered chest. "It's not the ability to love that you've lost, Matt, but your ability to hope."

His cheeks darkened, the color even more pronounced on the throbbing pulse of his neck. "You need to have a heart to have hope," he said gutturally. "And mine hardened and died a long time ago. Hope has nothing to do with anything."

"No," Winter disagreed again, kneading her fingers into his shirt. "You have your emotions mixed up. It's hopelessness that's made you mess with the magic to grant Kenzie's wish. Your heart is still very much alive."

He lifted one brow.

"Hopelessness is not the affliction of a soul incapable of loving," Winter said. "It's the exact opposite. Hopelessness can only affect someone who cares too much, loves too deeply, and who's been hurt so badly that utter despair is all that's left. But as long as there is life there is hope, and your heart is quite alive, Matheson Gregor," she repeated as she leaned over, kissed his cheek, and lifted her head to smile at him. "I'm going to marry you today, and have your bairn. And it will be *my* act of free will and not *you* making my choice," she said, giving his chest a poke — right over his very alive heart.

He suddenly sat up, and Winter let her hand fall to her lap as she also sat up. "If I can't have your love, do I at least have the other vows you mentioned?" she asked when he rose to his feet and turned to face her. "As your wife, will I have *your* trust and loyalty?"

He had to think about that, and what he was thinking didn't seem to be pleasant. He scowled down at her, two flags of color returning to his cheeks.

"Never mind," she said with a laugh as she leaned back on her hands and looked up at him. "We'll work on them together, one vow at a time."

His scowling eyes turned suspicious.

"How come Father Daar didn't recognize you as Cùram?" she asked before he could say anything. "Or Robbie? Robbie shook your hand, even."

It took him a moment to respond, as he was obviously still worried by her remark about their vows. He finally shrugged, then turned and walked to the boxes of supplies by the wall. "It's not difficult to cloak myself from others," was all he said as he rummaged through the boxes.

"Do you have a crooked old cane like Daar?"

He turned with a can of soup in his hand and started searching for the pot. "No. A staff is Pendaär's choice for carrying his power," Matt told her, popping the top off the soup and pouring it into the pot he'd found next to the boxes, where she'd put it last night after washing it.

"So how do you carry your magic

around?" Winter asked, deciding she liked watching him work.

He set the pot near the dead fire, threw some wood in the pit, touched it with his finger until it lit, then moved the pot closer to the flame. Moving to his jacket he'd tossed down by the entrance, he pulled something from the pocket.

He turned to her, holding up a beautiful gold and black pen. "I discovered that the real power of this century," he said, his smile almost reaching his eyes, "is not in the sword, but in the pen. So I carry my power in this fancy little fountain pen and use it to sign my name on contracts and very large checks. In the past I carried the sword I found in the cave."

Matt held the pen even with his chest, then suddenly rotated his hand. Before Winter could blink, the pen turned into a long, beautiful sword. Matt lifted the lethal weapon as he bowed, touching his forehead in salute. "Voilà," he said, setting its tip on the ground and resting his hands over the hilt. "Are you impressed?" he asked.

Winter saw just a hint of the man she'd fallen in love with smiling down at her. The same smile, she vowed, that she'd see many more times in their lifetime together. "I'm very impressed," she said with a laugh, getting to her feet. She visually examined the sword, then lifted her own smile to Matt. "Can I touch it?"

He swung the tip in an upward arc, caught the blade in his other hand, and held it toward her in his open palms.

Winter reached over and lightly touched the blade. She'd played with her father's sword many times, but this sword was shorter by about a foot, shinier, and had colorful jewels encircling the hilt behind the intricately carved hand guard. The blade was a bit thicker and appeared to be forged from a different kind of metal. "It's not at all like my papa's sword," she said, running her finger over the colorful stones. "What are these jewels?"

"They're diamonds, sapphires, emeralds, and tourmaline. And it's not like Greylen's sword because it's at least four thousand years older than his. I've since learned that it was my great-great-grandfather's."

Winter looked up at Matt and frowned. "They didn't have weapons this fancy that far back."

"Not for warring, no," he agreed. "But this sword wasn't designed for battle."

"But you said it's all you carried when you kept running into wars while searching for Kenzie."

Matt set the sword's tip back on the ground and folded his hands over the hilt. "It serves many purposes," was all he said.

Winter tucked her hands behind her back, rubbing her fingers that had touched the blade, and looked up at him again. "Will you teach me to use my pinewood staff, and show me how to summon the energy?" She thought of the singed blankets and quickly added, "And control it?"

Matt stared at her in silence, his eyes unreadable.

She laughed. "Why is it men always seem threatened by women with power?" She tilted her head. "How many women executives do you have in your company?"

Matt stepped around her and walked over to where her staff was, reached up and set his sword on the high ledge, and took down her pinewood stick. "None," he said, his face turning red again. "But only because I don't have any women working for me who are qualified to be engineering executives."

"You don't *have* any," she repeated, "or you haven't noticed any of them working in your plant, quietly doing their jobs and not causing waves for fear of losing the position they do have?"

He just stared at her nonplussed, her stick forgotten.

Winter smiled. "You're wasting a good portion of your intellectual resources, Matt." She shook her head. "At least you have an excuse, coming from a time when women were considered good for only cooking and cleaning and birthing babies. The sad part is, yours isn't the only business out there today that's wasting half its potential."

He lifted one brow. "So now you want to involve yourself in my company? Do you consider that part of your 'wifely' duties?"

Winter balled her hands into fists behind her back and widened her smile. Oh, she could see she had a long way to go before she got this ancient warrior to shift his thinking. "I want nothing to do with your company. I was just pointing something out, is all." She shrugged. "If you don't have any qualified women in your company, maybe you should take a look at your recruiting policies," she said as she bent down and gathered up the sleeping bag, giving it a good shake before she folded it.

A feather suddenly floated into the air and landed on her socked feet. Winter picked up the black feather, straightening up with a frown. It was about eight or nine inches long, sleek and healthy looking. A tail feather.

It was from a crow, she realized. She

hadn't been dreaming! She was holding the proof that her dream had been as real as the feather in her hand — and that must mean the information the crow had given her was just as real. Winter clutched the precious gift to her chest.

She was pregnant.

She was in love with Matheson Gregor.

And she knew exactly how to save mankind!

"What's that?" Matt asked, still standing by the far wall, still holding her staff.

She held it out for him to see. "It's a crow's feather. I dreamt about being in the woods last night, and there was a crow who talked to me."

Matt frowned at the feather, then lifted his gaze to her. "Seeing spirits again?" he asked.

She waggled the feather. "If he wasn't real, then explain this."

Matt walked up beside her, again frowning at the feather in her hand. "I must have carried it in on my clothing last night. Toss it in the fire. It's likely loaded with mites."

Winter carefully tucked the feather in her back pocket.

Matt held the pinewood stick toward her with a scowl. "Don't put your faith in dreams, Winter. They're nothing more than wishful thinking," he said, finally answering her earlier question as he reached down, lifted her hand, and wrapped her fingers around one end of the staff. "And getting what we wish for is not all it's cracked up to be, believe me."

The next three months were certainly going to be interesting if not maddening, Winter decided. It would definitely take all the magic she could summon to turn this stubborn man's thinking around.

CHAPTER TWENTY

From the copilot's seat of Matt's powerful jet, Winter looked out the side window, noting but not really seeing the weather observatory on top of Mount Washington as they flew northeast over the New Hampshire White Mountains. She lowered her gaze from the bright morning sun to her lap, replaying the last twenty-four hours in her mind as she studied the thick gold band on her left hand.

She had no idea where Matt had gotten the beautiful ring, only that he had pulled a pair of matching gold bands from his pocket when the minister (she was using that term lightly if not skeptically) asked them to exchange rings during their simple wedding in Las Vegas yesterday. Winter remembered how her hand had warmed the moment Matt had slipped the ring onto her finger, and how when she'd slipped Matt's ring onto his finger and he'd clasped their hands together, she had thought they might both burst into flames from the charge of electricity that had suddenly shot between them.

It was a beautiful ring, she decided, despite looking old and obviously used. Winter suspected it was a family heirloom that had belonged to his grandmother, the guardian. She also suspected Matt's ring had belonged to his grandfather, a man who had chosen love over his calling to be a *drùidh.* The rings were a good omen for her and Matt's own future, Winter decided. She loved Matt so much that she was giving up her calling for him, and she had faith that in time, Matt would love her just as much.

Winter suddenly wrinkled her nose. Even though she'd taken a shower yesterday in the suite Matt had booked them in Las Vegas — that they'd used only long enough to get cleaned up — and was wearing a completely new wardrobe purchased in the hotel shop, she kept catching the occasional hint of burnt cloth. The odor was still lingering in the jet, from their quick trip west yesterday morning, when they'd both smelled like smoke.

Before they'd left the cave, Matt had tried to show her how to use her pinewood staff to light a simple fire. But instead of directing the energy to the logs he'd set on the floor, she had caught the pile of blankets on fire again. Then she'd toasted his box of supplies, then singed her saddle. And bless his very alive heart, Matt's patience hadn't run out until his duffel bag had exploded. As soon as he'd finished stomping the smoldering clothes, he'd walked up and silently taken her staff away. He'd then made some fancy motion that turned her puny pinewood stick into an artist's sketch pencil, and tucked it into his jacket pocket. Then he'd turned his sword back into a fountain pen and led her out of the smoky cave and up to his truck, parked on the road above the meadow.

They'd driven to Bangor, climbed into his jet, flown west at the speed of sound, and landed in Las Vegas not two hours later. They'd checked into a hotel after buying a change of clothes and taken turns showering. Then, holding her hand in a death grip as they walked the Las Vegas Strip — apparently worried she might come to her senses and turn tail and run — Matt had found a rather surreal chapel not very far from the hotel.

Winter still couldn't decide if she'd spoken her vows to Matt in front of Elvis Presley or the Mad Hatter from *Alice's Adventures in Wonderland,* but she was pretty sure the quick ceremony had been witnessed by three members of the Hell's Angels. In fact, the fierce-looking trio of a woman and two men sitting in the back row had signed her and Matt's marriage certificate, which Matt had quickly tucked in his suit pocket the moment Winter had finished signing her own name with his powerful fountain pen.

Winter did give her husband credit for remembering to feed her before they boarded the plane again and continued on to Utah. By four o'clock Utah time, Winter had found herself standing on the floor of a massive plant, surrounded by planes and powerful engines in various stages of completion. When Matt had gotten involved in a serious discussion with several of his managers, Winter had quietly wandered off to give herself a tour of the factory.

Shyness not being part of her makeup, she'd soon found several women gathered in the lunchroom and had easily started up a conversation with them. Winter emerged less than half an hour later with one of the women in tow. Her name was Wanda Farley and she had a doctorate in mathematical engineering. Winter went in search of her husband to introduce Matt to his new quality control manager, Wanda.

Winter sighed and scanned the jet's many

instruments until she found a clock. It was 8:30 A.M., Eastern Standard Time she presumed, and they were only minutes away from landing in Pine Creek, which meant she was only an hour away from facing her parents as a married woman.

She couldn't wait for that happy scene to unfold.

"I think you should go to your resort suite while I go see my parents," she said into the mouthpiece of her headphones. "And I'll come to you after I've told them we're married."

Matt looked over at her, seemingly startled by her sudden intrusion on his own thoughts, and frowned. "I'm going with you to tell your parents."

"That's very noble of you, but I don't think it's wise. My mother will be shocked, and maybe hurt that she didn't attend my wedding, but she'll be happy, I think. But my papa," Winter said with a crooked smile behind her mouthpiece, "he's likely to take his sword and run you through." She reached over and patted Matt's arm. "I think it would be best if we let them get used to the idea for . . . oh, for a week or two maybe, before we plan our first family dinner."

"This isn't open to discussion, Winter. I

intend to be standing beside you when you face your parents."

"And just how do I introduce you? As my husband Matheson Gregor, or as Cùram de Gairn?"

Matt took his hand off the yoke and covered hers, making Winter realize she'd been wringing them together. "You can introduce me however you want, as long as I'm standing beside you at the time," he said softly. "Don't keep my real identity a secret, Winter, or you'll only hurt them further. I have nothing to hide from anyone. Not anymore. And neither do you. And you don't need to protect me, lass. I'm quite capable of taking care of myself."

"And Father Daar?" she asked. "And Robbie? You don't think they're going to be hopping mad when they find out I've married the man responsible for dooming mankind?"

Matt's smile turned tender as he ran his thumb over her knuckles. "MacBain is an intelligent and insightful guardian. He won't try to make you a widow without asking your permission first. And as for Pendaär, he's no longer a worry for either of us. His power is gone."

Winter's eyes widened in surprise. "Are you saying Father Daar is powerless now?"

Matt nodded. "When you hugged your

pine, you transferred all the energy Pendaär's been using all these centuries from him to yourself."

Winter narrowed her eyes. She'd finally remembered to ask Matt if he had cut the top off the pine, but he swore it hadn't been him, and that he'd also been trying to find out who had stolen a good deal of the tree's remaining energy. And though she ultimately believed him, she couldn't help being suspicious now. "How do you know I hugged the white pine?"

"I felt it," Matt said. "Even though I was in Utah at the time, I felt the energy shift. It's what drew me home to you."

Winter blinked in surprise. He'd felt her hugging the pine? That's why he'd come back? And Father Daar truly was powerless now? Just like the crow had told her in her dream?

"Does that mean Daar's not a *drùidh* anymore?" she whispered into the mouthpiece. "That he's going to . . . is he going to die?"

Matt squeezed her hand. "Aye," he softly confirmed. "But not because of you, but because that's simply the way Providence works. Pendaär knew this was going to happen, Winter, as he understands two *drùidhs* can't control the same energy." Matt squeezed her hand again. "He's not going to die tomorrow, lass. He'll merely live out the rest of his days as a mortal man."

Winter turned to look out the window, forcing back her threatening tears. She didn't want Father Daar to die defeated and powerless, no matter what a pest he'd been all these years. She certainly didn't want him to die because of her. She looked back at Matt. "What happens to Daar if I renounce my calling? Would he get to keep his power then?"

"No," Matt said with a shake of his head. "The energy has already shifted. If you renounce your calling now, it will simply lay dormant until your grandchild takes it up. That's why Pendaär kept trying to stop you from seeing me. Even though he thought I was only a mortal man, he knew that if you chose me over your calling, all was lost for both you and for him. He was worried only about keeping the continuum balanced and not about your love life."

"So he's known all along he would lose his power the moment I came into mine," she clarified, and Matt simply nodded. "But he said he would help me destroy you," she whispered.

"By teaching you how to summon the magic," Matt explained. He patted her hand, then took hold of the yoke again. "But I'll teach you now."

"Yes," she said with a frown, "but only enough to help you keep your promise to Kenzie."

"No," Matt said, staring out the windshield of the jet. "I'll teach you anything you want to know." He looked over at her. "Including how to destroy me."

Winter looked down at her hands and started toying with her wedding band again. She couldn't decide if she wanted to smack Matt or throw herself into his arms. He truly had given up — completely and irrevocably and utterly hopelessly.

"Do you talk to Kenzie?" she asked without looking up. "And can he talk to you?"

"Most of the time, no," Matt said. "Only when he walks the earth as a man."

Winter looked over in surprise. "Kenzie becomes a man sometimes? When?"

"Four times each year, on the solstices and the equinoxes. For twenty-four hours beginning at the moment of each seasonal transition, he turns into his old self."

"Two weeks ago!" Winter said, twisting in her seat to face Matt. "On the autumnal equinox, you and Kenzie were in the meadow on Bear Mountain, fighting with swords."

Matt looked at her sharply. "How do you know that?"

"Tom saw you. He told me he saw two men in kilts fighting in the meadow, trying to kill each other. But then you walked off into the woods together, laughing." She gasped. "The cut on Gesader's neck. He got hurt in your sword fight, when he was Kenzie."

Matt laughed and shook his head, looking out the windshield again. "We weren't trying to kill each other, lass; we were only working up a good sweat. My brother got distracted by a comment I made and let down his guard long enough to give me an opening." He looked at her, completely serious. "There's less than three months before the winter solstice, when Kenzie becomes himself again, and that's our best chance to make sure he stays himself."

Winter could only blink at Matt. She had less than three months to master the magic? Saints and curses, if she didn't get her staff under control by then, she'd likely blow Kenzie to kingdom come rather than save him.

Winter looked out her side window and quietly placed her hand on her blouse over the black feather she'd tucked inside her bra. Just three more months and she'd be able to stop worrying about saving mankind and start thinking about names for her baby instead. And by the winter solstice she would be designing a nursery for the house Matt was going to build them on Bear Mountain — even if she had to make her own pact with Providence to save her husband's soul.

Matt stood in the living room of the Mac-Keage home, unable to decide who was more stunned, Robbie MacBain and Winter's parents, or his gaping bride. He probably shouldn't have turned his pen back into his sword as they had crossed the keep's bridge, nor changed into his eight-hundred-year-old plaid just as he'd stepped through the door behind Winter, presenting himself as Cùram de Gairn.

But dammit, he knew she intended to keep his real identity a secret for as long as she could, out of some misplaced notion she needed to protect him. Now, though, she just looked like she wanted to kill him.

"They know we're married?" she said through gritted teeth, balling her hands into fists, probably to keep from slapping him.

Keeping a guarded eye on Greylen and Robbie standing across the room in front of the hearth, Matt simply nodded.

"Matt called us yesterday afternoon," a wide-eyed Grace said from beside Greylen. Matt didn't think Grace was as horrified by his appearance as her daughter, but only disconcerted. "And he told us not to worry about you," she continued. "That you were with him in Utah, and that you had gotten married in Las Vegas that morning."

"But why?" Winter asked, looking from her mother to Matt. "Why would you have called and told them we were married?"

"To give them a chance to get used to the idea," Matt said, finally giving Winter his full attention. "I don't know your parents or MacBain well enough to even guess what their reaction would be when you walked in here today and sprang this on them."

"You were trying to protect me?" she whispered, looking at the sword in his hand, then back up at him. "From my own family?"

Matt finally slid his weapon into the sheath on his belt and nodded. "Finish introducing me," he softly commanded.

Winter ran her gaze over his plaid, momentarily stopping on his half-naked chest before continuing up to meet his determined eyes. She stepped closer. "I think they've figured that out already," she whispered tightly. "But what I can't figure out is why tell them this way?" she asked, waving at his plaid.

Matt reached up and ran his knuckles over her angry red cheek. "Keeping secrets from your family will only make you sick with worry," he told her. "They need to know, lass, so they can decide how they should react."

"How *they* should react?" she hissed, grabbing his plaid and balling it in her fist. But whatever she intended to say next was lost when Greylen MacKeage spoke.

"Come here, Winter," the aging but still-imposing laird softly growled.

Other than letting go of his plaid so she could turn to face her father, Winter didn't move. "I can't, Papa," she said, holding a beseeching hand out to Greylen even as she lifted her chin. "He's my husband, and I must stand beside him now."

Matt felt some of the tension ease between his shoulders.

"He tricked ye," Greylen ground out. "Ye thought ye were marrying Matt Gregor. We'll have the marriage annulled. Now come here."

Winter dropped her hand. "D-don't make me choose between you," she softly petitioned, looking at her mother, then back at Greylen. "I don't want an annulment. I knew exactly who I was marrying yesterday."

"But ye don't understand what you've done," Grey whispered, his anger turning to desperation. "You've thrown away yer calling without fully knowing the consequences."

"No," she said. "I've embraced my calling."

"Ye can't have it both ways, Winter," MacBain interjected, frowning at her. "If ye have a bairn, your calling is lost. And even marrying another *drùidh* won't change that."

The knot of tension in Matt's shoulders returned, this time with alarm, when his wife folded her arms under her breasts and smiled at her cousin. "Are you positive about that?" she asked. "Surely two powerful *drùidhs* can give good old stuffy Providence a much-needed shake-up."

MacBain paled, Greylen swore rather crudely, and Matt could only gape at his wife.

"Winter!" Grey snapped. "Three days ago ye didn't even know ye had a calling, and now you're daring to challenge Providence? That's damn near blasphemous."

"This is serious, Winter," MacBain said, stepping away from the hearth toward her. "The continuum is dying."

"Dying?" Winter echoed. "Or merely shifting?" She also stepped closer. "What if I told you there's a way to bring the energy back into balance and save mankind without any of us risking our souls?"

"That's not possible," MacBain argued, shaking his head. He waved toward Matt. "Your *husband* here has messed with the energy so badly it may never recover. Ye need to renounce your marriage and get on with the business of saving the pine."

Unable to dispute nor defend his naively optimistic wife, since her boast was news to him as well, Matt could only watch in silence as Winter looked at her mother. "Tell them, Mama," she said softly. "As a scientist, explain to these stubborn men that nothing in nature is ever completely predictable. Tell them how everything must continue to evolve in order to survive, including the very energy of life."

Grace MacKeage frowned at her daughter, then finally nodded. "Actually, she's right," she said as she looked at her husband. "Just because something has worked for centuries, or even for millennia, doesn't mean it will continue to work indefinitely. Sometimes it's subtle and sometimes it's catastrophic, but change is constantly occurring." She looked at Winter, her face relaxing in a smile. "Ultimately, even the energy must change right along with us."

"Yes," Winter agreed as she turned to Matt. "As my husband, you have to trust me." She turned to her papa and cousin. "And I expect no less from either of you. I've accepted my calling, and now you must trust me to get us out of this mess." She pointed a threatening finger at the two men. "Without holding Matt to blame," she added in warning. She turned just enough to include him. "While I'm learning how to control the magic, I want the three of you to figure out who cut the top off my pine tree. There's an unknown player in this maddening game, and that's where the danger truly lies."

Matt folded his arms over his chest as he stared at Winter, finding his first smile since she'd demanded he make Wanda Farley his new quality control manager. It seemed his bride was a bossy little thing, if not downright fond of giving orders.

He'd have to do something about that, he decided . . . say in another ten or twenty years, just as soon as he figured out how to make himself immune to her magic.

The front door suddenly opened and closed with a window-rattling bang. "Did I get here in time!" Megan called out, rushing into the living room. She came to a halt by running into Matt's half-naked chest, jumping back with a gasp. "Who the hell are you?" she said, only to gasp again. "Matt?" Her expression turned from surprise to horror as she realized what he was wearing, her wide eyes stopping on the sword hanging from his belt. "Cùram," she whispered, taking another step back.

"It's okay, Meg," Winter said, rushing to her sister at the same time Grace did, both women reaching out to support the pale young woman. "He's not a monster like everyone thinks. He's just my husband." Winter shot Matt a look. "Say something," she demanded.

Matt bowed and gave Megan a warm smile. "Hello, sister."

Apparently not quite ready to have Cùram de Gairn call her sister, Megan tried to take another step back but seemed to go weak in the knees. Winter gave Matt one last scolding glare before she all but carried her stunned sister toward the stairs with her mother. "Come on, Meg," she said. "You can help me pack a few of my things."

"Y-you married Cùram?" Megan whispered as they mounted the stairs. "But why?"

Matt didn't hear Winter's answer as the three women rose out of sight, but he certainly heard the silence left in their wake, its center emanating from directly behind him. Matt turned to face Greylen and Robbie, holding his hands behind his back as he waited for the storm to arrive, which it certainly did, and with predictable impact.

"Ye have more balls than brains, ye bastard," Grey snapped, taking a step toward him. "I'm going to kill ye for what ye've done to my daughter."

Matt held his hands out from his sides. "You may try," he said softly. "Though making Winter raise your grandchild without a father might not be your wisest decision."

That stopped his father-in-law's advance much more abruptly than his sword could have. "She's pregnant?" Greylen said, his face paling.

"If you believe in miracles, then yes, Winter's with child," Matt told him. He tucked his hands behind his back again. "It's done, Laird MacKeage. I'm sorry I didn't ask you for Winter's hand in marriage, but I think you understand my position." Matt inclined his head. "You have my word as a warrior and guardian that I will do all in my power to keep her safe and happy."

"She was already safe and happy, Gregor! Why in hell are ye here?"

Matt glanced at Robbie, then settled his gaze back on Greylen. "I'm here to right a thousand-year-old wrong," he said softly, "and then simply live out what time is left with my wife and child."

"According to Daar, there is no time left because of yer arrogance and treachery."

"I'm well aware what I've put into motion," Matt agreed. "But Winter is capable of even more than Pendaär can know. She can certainly buy us enough time for you to build a relationship with your brother."

"Ye leave Morgan out of this!"

"I'm referring to your other brother, Michael MacBain," Matt said, deciding he needed to shift the laird's anger.

Grey took a step back, paling again.

"Ye know about my father?" Robbie asked, stepping forward.

Matt nodded, still keeping his hands behind his back. "I've known since the day Michael was conceived." He looked at Greylen to explain. "Your mother, Judy MacKinnon, had an identical twin sister named Blair. When your mother died, Blair came to help Duncan MacKeage raise you, even though she was promised by contract to wed Angus MacBain. But when she went to Angus a year and a half later, she was already carrying Michael. Which means you and

Michael are true brothers, both of you having the same father and identical twin mothers."

Greylen turned his appalled gaze on Robbie. "You've known about this? For how long?"

"For two and a half years," Robbie admitted. "From when I went back to your old village to get the tree root. But I kept it a secret because of Cùram," he said, nodding toward Matt. "I didn't know what he was up to, and I didn't want him to find out there was another lineage that shared Winter's calling. Protecting my brother and sisters was more important than telling ye, Grey. Ye made peace with my father over thirty years ago and have had a good friendship since then." Robbie looked at Matt. "If ye knew about Blair, why did ye fight Pendaär so hard back then for Judy MacKinnon?"

Matt shrugged. "I only fought hard enough to let the old fool think he'd won, so he wouldn't suspect that it was Winter I wanted all along."

"But why?" Greylen whispered. "What in hell do ye want from my daughter?"

"Her compassion," Matt said. "It's Winter's only weakness."

"Ye think that's a weakness?" Grey asked

in surprise.

Instead of answering him, Matt decided it was again time to redirect the conversation. "She's right, you know. There's another entity here who's messing with the magic. I didn't cut the top off Winter's pine, and like you, I haven't been able to discover who did."

Both men frowned. Greylen suddenly ran a hand over his face with a weary sigh, turned and sat down in the chair beside the hearth. But MacBain, it seemed, wasn't yet ready to drop either his anger or his guard, and continued to stand facing Matt.

"If you didn't cut it, and we certainly didn't cut it, then it likely was only a logger wanting the seeds," Robbie said.

Matt mimicked Winter's cousin by folding his arms over his chest, and shook his head. "Would a thief have wasted the time it took to climb the tree? And through your guardianship, have you not sensed a strange energy humming through the air? Even with my own power, I haven't been able to pinpoint where it's coming from, nor could I recognize its vibration."

"Aye," Robbie admitted, also giving a weary sigh as he sat down in the chair opposite Greylen. "I've felt it, but I thought it was you I was sensing."

Matt nearly burst into laughter when he suddenly realized what MacKeage and MacBain were just realizing themselves, that the three of them were going to have to be allies instead of enemies if they hoped to help Winter fight this unknown threat. Talk about irony. His compassionate little wife, he suspected, had known for two days that this moment would come, and had laughed her pretty little head off all the way to Utah and back. Hell, she was probably upstairs right now, bragging to her mother and sister how she'd managed to bring three lethal warriors to their collective knees.

CHAPTER
TWENTY-ONE

"You knew he was Cùram de Gairn, and you married him anyway?" Megan whispered, hugging Winter's old rag doll as she leaned against the headboard of her sister's bed, looking small and lost amid the pile of pillows. "But why? Why would you knowingly marry an evil *drùidh?*"

Winter turned from her closet with a sweater in her hand and frowned at her pale and sincerely confused sister. "There's not an evil bone in Matt's body," she softly scolded. "He's just . . . he's merely lost his way, is all."

"And you intend to help him find it again?" Grace asked, coming back into the room with a small cloth package in her hand. "Winter, since humans have lived in caves, women have been trying to help men find their way, and in all this time we still haven't come close to civilizing them."

Grace set the small bundle on the end of

the bed, walked up to Winter and took hold of her shoulders. "If you've entered this marriage with the notion you can change Matt, I'm afraid you're in for a big disappointment. The best you can hope for is to smooth out his rough edges, but you can't ever change a man's true nature."

"But his true nature is *good*, Mama. Matt is noble and honorable and compassionate, and he's only trying to fix the mess he's made." Winter dropped the sweater and took hold of her mother's hands. "And I will fight even Providence if I have to, to prove to Matt that his soul is not lost. He's given up, Mama," she whispered, tightening her grip. "And I don't care what it takes, I'm going to give him back the gift of hope."

"You love him that much? So much that you'd risk your own soul to save his?"

"Yes," she whispered. "I love him more than life itself."

"You've known him two weeks," Megan said from right beside them. "You can't fall in love in only two weeks."

Grace MacKeage pulled free with a laugh and turned to face Megan. "I fell in love with your father in less than nine days," she said as she led them both back to the bed. "If Winter says she loves Matt, that's all I need to know to give her my full support."

"But does Matt love her?" Megan asked, climbing back on the bed and grabbing up the doll again to clutch to her chest. She looked at Winter with turbulent, worried green eyes. "What if he's only using you?"

It was Grace who responded before Winter could. "Of course Matt doesn't love her, Meg. Men don't think in terms of love at first. They only think of possessing."

Both girls frowned at their mama, and Grace smiled warmly and patted Winter's arm. "Matt Gregor won't be able to help himself from falling in love with you, baby girl, but you'll need to be patient with him." She turned to include Megan. "It seemed like forever for your father to figure out that he loved me." She looked at Winter and lifted one pretty arched brow. "What did Matt say when you asked him if he loved you?"

Winter felt a blush rise to her cheeks at the realization that her mama knew her so well, and darted a look at Megan before she looked back at her mother. "He . . . ah, he said he couldn't ever love me because his heart had died a long time ago," she softly admitted.

Grace gave a quiet laugh as she turned to the bed with a shrug. "He'll eventually come around. You just keep loving him unconditionally, and one day Matt will finally realize that he also loves you more than life itself." She picked up the package she'd gone to her bedroom to get and turned to Winter. "You don't change a lifetime of suppressed emotions in two weeks, especially when that lifetime has spanned centuries."

Winter smiled. "Will I ever be as wise as you, Mama?"

Grace snorted. "You'll get wise real quick, baby girl, because you've fallen in love with a stubborn warrior," she said, unfolding the velvet corners of the tiny package she was holding. "This is your wedding present from your father and me." She held out the open cloth to reveal a beautiful locket. "We had planned to give it to you to wear at your wedding, but since we . . . ah, missed the ceremony, I'll just tell you what we told the other girls when we gave them theirs." Grace lifted the gold locket from the velvet. "This is to remind you that even though you have married and are now a Gregor, you will always carry our hearts with you, no matter where life leads you."

Feeling the sudden sting of threatening tears, Winter reached out and took the delicate locket made of spun gold threads loosely woven in the shape of a plump heart. Inside the heart were two loose little beads also shaped like hearts, made of shiny black stone that Winter instantly recognized as the rock that ran in fissures throughout Tar-Stone Mountain. No matter where she went, she would always carry a piece of home with her, as well as her parents' unconditional love.

Grace leaned forward and gently kissed a tear running down Winter's cheek, and Winter threw herself into her mama's arms. "I'm sorry you and Papa weren't at my wedding," she sobbed into her mama's shoulder as she held the locket in her fist.

"Shhh," Grace crooned, tenderly stroking her back. "I can see it was more important you prove your love to Matt by giving up a fancy wedding to marry him on his terms."

"But I want Papa to be okay with it, too," Winter said with a lingering sniffle, leaning back to look at her mother. "I want him to understand why I ran off without telling any of you."

Grace squeezed her shoulders. "You just leave your father to me. I'll make sure he understands why you did what you did." She reached down and took the locket from Winter and stepped around behind her. "Now we need to talk about birth control," she continued as Winter lifted her hair so her mama could clasp the locket around her neck. "You have enough to deal with right now without adding a baby to the mix."

"Too late," Winter squeaked, grinning at Megan when she gasped. "I'm already pregnant."

Winter felt her mama's hands still momentarily before she finished locking the chain around Winter's neck. Frowning, Grace silently walked back around to stand in front of Winter. "You can't possibly know that yet," she said. "You just met Matt two weeks ago."

Winter fingered the locket at her throat. "I — I don't understand how I know, I just know that I'm pregnant," she said. "It happened the first time, just three nights ago."

"Okay then," Grace said with a slow nod. "Then I suggest we keep this from your father for a while. Grey's going to need some time to adjust to having a *drùidh* for a son-in-law without adding a magical grand-baby into the mix. Does Matt know?"

Winter dropped her gaze to her locket. "Yes."

"And has he told you that having a baby will cause you to lose your powers?"

"Yes."

Her mama lifted Winter's chin to look at her. "Is that why he came here, to seduce you into giving up your calling?" she asked softly.

"No," Winter told her. "He came here so I can help him right an old wrong," was all she said, not yet willing to tell anyone about Kenzie. "He seduced me to gain my loyalty, so that I will be honor-bound to help him."

"So he *is* using you," Megan interjected, once again standing beside them. "And you're just letting him. But why?"

"Because she loves him," Grace said before Winter could, reaching out and brushing Megan's hair from her face.

Megan finished tucking her hair behind her ears and glared at Winter. "You said Wayne Ferris was only using me to further his career, and that I should want him to burn in Hades, but you've gone and married a man just like him."

"Wayne was merely selfish," Winter argued. "But Matt's motives are . . . they're . . ." She sighed and shook her head. Despite not liking the idea of Matt's brother hanging around her sister, Winter couldn't bring herself to explain that the panther Meg slept with most nights was really a man. At this time in Megan's life, Gesader was her only comfort. "Matt doesn't want my help for himself, but for a greater good."

"And that would be?" her mama asked.

Winter shook her head again. "I can't tell you what it is without breaking Matt's trust," she whispered, turning and walking to her closet and picking up the sweater she'd dropped.

"Then we'll just have to trust you," Grace said, taking the sweater from Winter. "And you'll trust *me* when I tell you that you and Matt are staying at Gù Brath tonight. You can decide tomorrow where you're going to live, once things have settled down."

Winter gaped at her mother. "Here?" she squeaked. "You expect us to stay here, in my bedroom?" She shook her head. "We'll go to Matt's hotel suite."

"Family does not stay at the hotel."

"But I can't, Mama," Winter whispered, fingering her locket again as she looked around her childhood room. "This is my . . . this is my *bedroom.*"

Grace set the sweater back on the shelf in the closet. "Your sisters stay in their old rooms when they visit with their husbands." She turned and lifted a brow. "Why should it be any different for you?"

"But Papa will throw a fit having a *drùidh* sleeping in his house. And Matt will . . . he'll . . . he won't agree to stay here."

"We've had a *drùidh* sleeping in this bedroom for twenty-four years," Grace said, laughing at Winter's startled look. "And Matt is part of this family now, so he might as well get used to it. And so must your father." Grace took hold of Megan's hand and led her out of the room, but stopped at the door and looked back. "Begin as you intend to go on, Winter, and establish your authority in this marriage. If you don't set the tone right from the start with these ancient men, you may never catch up."

"You make marriage sound like an ongoing battle."

"No, baby girl, not a battle, but a wonderful and exciting dance," Grace said with an utterly feminine smile. "And you'll find it quite pleasant if you're the one leading."

With her mother's final bit of wisdom still echoing in her mind as she lay in her childhood bed beside Matt that night, Winter decided it was definitely time she took over the lead in this marriage. Matt hadn't made love to her since their first night in the cave, nor touched her in an intimate way, not even a kiss. For newlyweds, there hadn't been much honeymooning going on, and Winter was feeling insulted. She didn't care if Matt thought he was being noble by not bothering her that way, or if he was feeling guilty for railroading her into this marriage, or even if he felt uncomfortable making love in her childhood bed with her father sleeping just down the hall. Curses, if she could get over that last fact, so could he!

But the problem with her leading the dance, Winter realized, was that she didn't exactly know all the steps. How did a woman go about seducing her husband when her entire sum of experience was one single night of salacious bliss?

Winter frowned up at the dark ceiling. Wearing her old flannel pajamas to bed probably hadn't been her brightest idea, considering they made her look about as enticing as a bag lady. And she probably should have left her hair loose instead of braiding it like she always did. Matt seemed to like playing with her hair, and she could have subtly draped it over his naked chest.

He'd undressed in the dark once she'd climbed into bed, but there had been enough moonlight coming through the windows for Winter to watch him strip down to his pants. He'd started to take them off, too, but had stopped suddenly, then climbed into bed with them on.

Matt had changed from his ancient clothing sometime while she'd been upstairs with her mama and Megan, apparently thinking it wouldn't be wise to sit down to dinner in his plaid. Dinner had been interesting, with her mama asking Matt questions about his company and her papa alternating between listening, glaring at Matt when he wasn't looking, and trying to disguise his discomfort by smiling at Winter. Megan had been unusually quiet, but Winter had caught her eyeing Matt more than once, apparently trying to reconcile Matt Gregor and Cùram de Gairn as one and the same.

The dishes had barely been stacked in the dishwasher before Matt had come into the kitchen and told Winter it was time they went to the hotel. Her mama had hustled Megan out of the room, leaving Winter alone to inform Matt they were spending the night at Gù Brath — in her room, in her childhood bed, not three doors down from her papa.

Winter had then patiently explained to Matt that her sisters didn't stay in the hotel when they came home with their husbands. She'd explained that he was part of her family now, whether he liked it or not. And then she'd grown impatient and told him she was staying in her own bed tonight, and he could sleep in the barn for all she cared if he wasn't up to claiming his rightful place as her husband in her papa's eyes.

Pride was a surprisingly effective tool when dealing with stubborn men, Winter had quickly discovered. Matt hadn't cared to discover he was married to an equally stubborn woman, but he had gone to his suite, showered and gotten a change of clothes, and returned to her bedroom *after* everyone else had retired for the night.

And now he was lying beside her, pretending to be asleep.

Winter reached down and slowly slid her pajama bottoms off, then used her feet to cram them down between the sheets. Then she unbuttoned her pajama top, sat up, shrugged it off, and dropped it on the floor.

"Why are you tossing about?" Matt asked, turning just his head over his shoulder toward her.

"I'm hot. You're like a blast furnace."

He rolled onto his back, took one look at her, and quickly looked up at the ceiling. "Put your clothes back on," he growled. "If you're hot, throw off the covers."

Still sitting up, completely naked, Winter pulled her braid over her shoulder, took off the elastic, and slowly ran her fingers through her hair to unbraid it.

"Now what are ye doing?" he hissed, his brogue growing pronounced. "Winter," he whispered tightly, "get dressed."

She lay back on the pillow, fanning her hair toward him, and folded her hands over her bare stomach with a sigh. "If I'd known sleeping naked against flannel sheets felt this wonderful, I'd have done this years ago." She wiggled deeper into the sheets, accidentally letting her leg brush Matt's thigh. "I understand if you can't . . . ah, if you can't be husbandly tonight," she said to the ceiling. "Or if you don't really want me, now that I married you. Good night, then."

"Dammit, ye don't understand," he snapped in a whisper. "I want ye, just not here."

She reached over and patted his arm. "I understand. Mama explained how men's . . . ah, plumbing works to all us girls growing up."

Heavens, she was going to fry in Hades, she knew, stifling a laugh when she heard a warning growl beside her. Winter ran her hand down Matt's tautly muscled forearm and tried to lace her fingers through his. But finding only a fist, she simply patted his hand. "We'll go to sleep then. Mama also explained how sometimes stress can be . . . how it can be debilitating."

He was on her before she could gasp, his hands gripping her hair to hold her face only inches from his. "That is not the problem," he softly ground out.

"I can feel it's not the problem," she breathed as Matt's anything but debilitated anatomy poked her thigh through his pants. She reached up and ran her own fingers through his hair until she freed it from its tether. "I want to make love to my husband," she whispered. "But I don't know how."

He closed his eyes on a groan and dropped his forehead to hers. "You're going to drive me mad, lass."

"That's my plan, just as soon as you teach me how," she whispered, tilting her head back until her lips brushed his. "I'm guessing we should start by taking off your pants?"

"Does your door have a lock?"

"N-no," she said on a shiver when Matt moved his lips down her chin toward her throat. "W-why?" she breathed, digging her fingers into his shoulders.

He leaned away to look at her, and Winter could just make out the slash of his grin. "Do you really want your papa running in here when I make you scream?"

"I won't scream. I'll be as quiet as a mouse."

"Just like last time?"

Winter frowned up at him. "I did not scream."

"Aye, ye did," he whispered, leaning down and kissing her nose. "Loud enough to wake the entire forest."

Winter felt herself blush. "I — I screamed?"

He kissed her mortified cheeks. "With abandoned pleasure, wife." He kissed her chin. "Several times. 'Twas a wonderful sound."

"Screaming is good, then?" she asked on an indrawn breath when his lips found the pulse on her throat and lingered and suckled gently, causing every nerve in her body to tighten with desire.

She was just sliding her toes up his legs when he was suddenly gone, leaving only the cool air of the room to rush over her heated skin. She scowled, hearing what sounded like Matt hopping from one foot to the other as he moved away. Her bathroom light snapped on, and Winter pulled the blankets to her chin as she watched her husband — utterly, beautifully naked now — walk over to the hall door and shove a chair under the knob. He walked back to her, his form in silhouette but lit just enough for her to see there wasn't one debilitated inch of skin anywhere on his body. Saints and curses, she needed to be careful what she asked for.

"You forgot to turn out the light," she whispered as she stared at the beckoning hand he held out to her.

"I didn't forget." He wiggled his fingers. "Have you changed your mind, then?"

"No," she whispered.

Apparently tired of waiting for her to take his hand, he wrestled the blanket from her fists, grabbed her wrist, and pulled her out of bed.

"Where are we going?" she squeaked, scrambling to catch up.

"You said you wanted to learn how to drive me mad, and I've promised to teach you anything you want to know," he said, dragging her into the bright bathroom even as she tried to dig in her heels. He pulled her up in front of him, standing them both facing the wall-to-wall mirror over the sink.

Winter stared into her own wide eyes, her gaze moving to Matt's broad, tanned shoulders behind her, then up to the taut planes of his face broken only by his tight smile. She sucked in her breath and looked down when his hands slid around her waist and slowly rose to cup her breasts.

"All ye have to do, wife, is whisper that ye want me," he said gutturally, his own gaze watching his thumbs trace circles around her aroused nipples. "A woman's desire is a man's greatest weakness. All she has to do is say she wants him, and he'll move mountains to please her."

Winter couldn't speak, couldn't respond other than to stare in wonder as his hands continued to caress her, lifting the weight of her breasts, covering them with his sensuous heat, rolling her puckered nipples until Winter thought she'd melt with pleasure.

She tore her eyes away and looked up, going weak in the knees when she saw the raw fire of passion burning his own cheeks as he watched not what his hands were doing, but her face. Then, with his eyes locked on hers, he wrapped an arm under her breasts and turned her to face him, lifting her up until she was sitting on the counter.

"Touch me," he whispered, settling his hips between her thighs. He took hold of her hands and lifted them to his chest, then reached down and took hold of her hips. "Just touch me."

Winter was amazed, and rather intrigued, to feel his muscles quivering beneath her hands. But even more amazing was the discovery that watching her fingers run over his downy-furred chest made her own body tremble with an energy that seemed to gather deep in the pit of her stomach.

"Aye," he whispered, his hands on her hips tightening. "Never underestimate the power of sight, lass, when coupled with touch. Ye want to bring a man to his knees, just let him see the desire in yer eyes."

She leaned in and kissed his chest, just above one nipple, then let her lips trail down until she covered it completely and gently suckled.

He pulled her hips against the solid evidence of her effect on him, then wrapped his arms around her, pulling her breasts against his chest with a groan as he tugged on her hair to lift her face for his kiss. His mouth stole her breath as the heat of his body assaulted her senses. She wiggled closer, feeling the tip of his arousal intimately pushing against the moist heat of her desire.

His arms tightened, lifting her off the counter just enough so she could wrap her legs around his waist as he carefully and so maddeningly lowered her over him. Winter felt herself stretching, molding around him, the sensation so intense she moaned in pleasure.

He quickly captured the sound with his mouth and his own responding growl. He turned then, pressing her shoulders against the opposite wall. He moved his hips upward, then back slightly, then upward again, his hands on her hips holding her secure for each erotic thrust. Winter gripped his hair, her elbows on his shoulders steadying her as sensation after sensation rocketed through her.

He tore his mouth free and buried his face in her neck. "Look in the mirror," he growled. "Watch us."

Winter opened her eyes and looked, only to gasp at the sight of her tiny white legs wrapped around his tanned body as his firm buttocks moved against her, the muscles of his back rippling with controlled strength.

She lost all sense of herself then, transported into a world of surreal sensations as she continued to watch their intimate dance. Charges of energy swirled around them as spectrums of vivid colors gathered in a tightening vortex that suddenly exploded into pure white light.

Winter closed her eyes on a scream that was quickly captured by her husband's mouth as his own shout of pleasure resonated through her with the force of an earthquake. He suddenly stopped moving, the pulse of his pleasure exploding against her own clenching spasms.

She had to tear her mouth free to gulp for

air, but before she caught her breath she felt herself moving and could only cling to Matt's shoulders. She moaned at the feel of him still inside her, still hard, as his strides drove him even deeper. He stepped into the shower with her wrapped around him, spun the faucet, and quickly turned to protect her from the first burst of cold spray.

She couldn't imagine where he got the strength to function, much less continue to hold her. But in the next second all manner of thought eluded Winter, as Matt pressed her against the shower's back wall and began moving inside her again.

Their erotic dance was slightly less urgent this time, as he pulled nearly out and slowly eased deeply inside her again. She clung to his shoulders as he leaned away, and stared into his eyes as she felt the sensitive tips of her breasts move against the soft hairs on his chest. And then Matt reached down between them, and with his eyes locked firmly on hers, touched her most intimately.

Winter tried to keep looking at him, to watch his expressive golden eyes watching her, but her lids dropped with her moan of surrender as he skillfully worked his magic. She felt herself tightening around him again, felt the returning vortex contract with building energy — which suddenly released with another burst of sizzling white light.

Winter captured her own scream this time by pressing her mouth into Matt's shoulder as pulse after pleasurable pulse wracked her body. She went limp as a noodle, not even caring if Matt had the strength to carry her full weight. Heck, if he did drop her, she'd just slither like melted butter down the shower drain.

"And that, wife," he whispered raggedly against her mist-dampened hair, "is the quickest way to drive me mad."

"You didn't warn me that I'd be doing myself in at the same time," she muttered into his shoulder. She didn't know where she found the strength, but she leaned back to look at him, and even managed to smile. "That was decadent," she said with a shake of her head. "In my wildest dreams, I never once thought about doing it in front of a mirror and actually *watching.* You're a —"

He stepped back into the spray of the shower, forcing Winter to snap her mouth shut before she drowned. "No name-calling," he said, slowly lowering her feet to the floor and holding her until she was steady. "Gather your hair and hold it up to stay dry."

She did as he said, turning her back on the spray, only to yelp when she felt Matt's soapy hands slide up her ribs. "Shhh," he said, lathering her up — quite thoroughly — his fingers gliding over every inch of her body. Winter closed her eyes and fought down the blush heating her face, but then suddenly smiled, realizing that surely she was expected to return the favor.

CHAPTER
TWENTY-TWO

It didn't happen very often, but every once in a while the universe somehow managed to surprise him. This time, however, Matt felt as if he'd been totally blindsided.

Pendaär's heir wasn't anything like he'd expected when he'd made his plans to seduce Winter MacKeage. To begin with, she was more beautiful than he was prepared to deal with, and vivacious and vexing and vibrantly sexy. She was also more stubborn than he cared for, and far more intelligent than he needed her to be. She was willful and spoiled and self-confident, and simply too damned optimistic for his liking.

And then there was the fact that she had come up with her own way to help Kenzie, which Matt feared was headed on a collision course with his own carefully devised plans. She seemed far too confident that she could not only grant his brother's wish, but somehow save mankind while she was at it. Oh yes, she was definitely more optimistic than Matt liked, and he was afraid that when she failed she would be devastated.

And for some reason, the thought of Winter being devastated was more than even his cold, dead heart could handle.

Matt kept his eyes closed to mere slits as he watched his once-again scheming wife come sneaking out of the bathroom while leaving the light on and the door cracked so she could see well enough to rummage through his clothes. It wasn't quite four in the morning, a good two hours before sunrise, but Winter was fully dressed in outdoor attire, her hair neatly braided and carrying her boots in her hand. While she'd been quietly dressing in the bathroom, Matt had gotten up and thrown on the spare set of clothes he'd brought from the hotel, and was himself fully dressed under the covers.

He watched with curious patience, trying not to notice how cute her backside was when she bent over, as she finally had to set down her boots to find what she was looking for. Matt knew he'd guessed right when she straightened holding his fountain pen and her sketch pencil. She turned just enough for the light to shine on her prizes, and Matt stifled a smile as he watched her examine his pen. She finally held it up next to her pencil, seemingly comparing the two, and frowned as she suddenly gave them both a violent shake. When nothing happened other than ink spurting all over her hand, she tucked the pencil in her jacket pocket, replaced his messy pen back in his own jacket, and straightened back up holding her boots. She tiptoed to the bedroom door, carefully pulled the chair free that he'd propped under the knob, and opened the door and peeked into the hall.

Matt had a pretty good idea where she was going, and why, and he had no intention of letting her go alone. He waited for several seconds, giving Winter time to get downstairs, then threw back the covers, grabbed his own boots and jacket, and stepped into the hall. He was just sneaking past the last door by the stairs when he stepped on a squeaky board and went utterly still.

The door opened and Greylen MacKeage appeared in the doorway, also fully dressed and his arms crossed over his chest. "I've a good notion where she's going," Grey said in a soft growl. "And I'll follow her to make sure she's okay."

"With all respect, MacKeage, she's my

responsibility now," Matt said just as softly, "and I'll tag along behind her without interfering."

"Ye may have to interfere," Grey said. "It won't be a pretty scene when she explains who she married."

"She survived yesterday well enough," Matt returned softly. "In fact, I'm thinking she came away completely unscathed, which is more than I can say for the rest of us."

Grey's grin slashed white in the dimly lit hall. "That's because she's a MacKeage, and we do like our victories."

"*Was* a MacKeage," Matt said. "She's a Gregor now."

"And here I thought her Sutter genes were keeping her one step ahead of you men," Grace said, moving up beside her husband and smiling at Matt. "Be patient with her, and learn to trust her," she suggested. "She loves Daar and needs to talk to him. And he would cut off his arm before he'd harm her."

Greylen snorted, and Grace laced her fingers through his. "Don't say it," she warned, giving his hand a tug. "He's been like a grandfather to all the girls, but he and Winter are especially close."

Matt darted a look toward the stairs, wanting to catch up with his wife, then turned back to his in-laws and inclined his head. "If you don't mind, I don't want her traveling the mountain alone, in case Gesader comes slinking back here."

Greylen stiffened. "Ye know about her pet?"

Matt smiled. "Did you never wonder what a leopard cub was doing in Scotland eight hundred years ago?"

Grey narrowed his eyes. "Robbie and I both questioned that fact, and carefully watched the cat as he matured, but we saw no signs that he was anything other than a panther and a good companion for Winter. Why do ye worry about her running into him now?"

Matt shrugged. "He was a bit drunk on catnip the last time Winter saw him, and I want to be there when they meet again."

Grey lifted a brow. "And just where did he get the catnip?"

Matt grinned, gave a slight bow, and started toward the stairs. "From me," he said, stopping a few steps down and looking back. "You might want to keep him out of Megan's bed, before he grows to like it too well."

That said, and not responding to his mother-in-law's gasp, Matt ran down the stairs, opened the front door, and stepped onto the frosty bridge, immediately realizing he was still carrying his boots. With a curse blaming his wife for his inattention, he leaned against the rail to put on his boots while keeping an eye on the path leading up from the barn. He was just tying the last lace when he heard a noise coming not from the barn, but from the road leading up the mountain.

He shrugged into his jacket as he hurried across the bridge, stopping only long enough to reach into the inside pocket and pull out his pen, cursing again when his hand emerged covered in ink. He flicked his wrist and the pen turned into his sword, and Matt started running toward the tote road.

The dark shadow of the massive leopard appeared on the path just as Matt reached the canopy of trees. "Hello, you black bastard. How's your head feeling?"

Kenzie snarled and whipped his tail through the air, then turned and started trotting up the tote road. Matt hesitated, glancing back toward the barn. Surely Winter was riding up the mountain, not hiking.

Kenzie stopped, gave another snarl, then continued up the road until he disappeared into the darkness. Matt slid his sword through his belt and started jogging after him, cursing the fact that his little fairy wife had apparently felt like a stroll this morning instead of a ride. Aye, a good two-hour stroll, straight up.

Matt had been jogging less than five minutes when he heard her, and slowed to a walk as he came up beside Kenzie. He smiled when he realized the woman was actually singing. He tapped Kenzie's shoulder to slow their pace, his smile widening as he made out the words of her song.

"Big old black bear, don't ye come out tonight, come out tonight, come out tonight . . ."

That was when he remembered Talking Tom, and the old hermit's habit of warning the bears he was passing through their territory. Matt followed in silence, he and Kenzie keeping just out of sight, and decided that for as talented a painter as Winter was, she couldn't sing worth a damn.

They hiked for nearly an hour in the forest, the darkness broken only by what light filtered down from the half moon, before Winter suddenly fell silent and stopped. Kenzie moved off the path to the left and crept through the trees, and Matt went right, being careful not to make a sound as he moved closer to see why she'd stopped.

He found her standing in the middle of the rutted tote road, holding her pencil in her hand. Remembering what had happened back at the cave when he'd tried to teach her to light the fire, Matt watched with apprehension. The stench of burnt cloth was still trapped in his nose hairs, and he'd likely never get the smell out of the upholstered seats in his jet.

"Abracadabra!" she suddenly said, waving the pencil in a circle above her head. When nothing happened, she lowered the pencil, and Matt could just make out her scowl. She shook the pencil violently, just like she had in her bedroom, then stopped, all but glared it to death, and snapped her hand in a quick twisting motion. "Become my staff!" she commanded, only to yelp when a few weak sparks sputtered out the sharpened end.

"Curses," she muttered, dropping the pencil and stamping her foot in frustration. "Why won't you work for me!" She threw her head back. *Why can't I control the energy?* she shouted at the sky. "I've accepted my calling, now give me the power!"

Matt shook his head, wondering what in hell made Winter think scolding Providence would help. He smiled then, guessing that being spoiled as a child had her believing the magic was simply hers on demand.

But truth told, Matt was a bit puzzled

himself by his wife's inability to conjure up something as simple as fire. She had the magic all right, right there at her fingertips; he could *feel* the strength of the energy humming around her as it enveloped her in a halo of pristine light.

But the magic appeared to be even more confused than she was, as if Winter were speaking to it in a foreign language. He'd explained to her back at the cave that all she had to do was gently ask for what she wanted, and picture it happening in her mind, but no matter how hard she tried, the energy had only responded in unpredictable bursts of haphazard chaos.

Matt watched Winter pick up the pencil, hold it in front of her face, and heard her let out a frustrated sigh. She bent down and gathered a few leaves and twigs into a pile, stepped back, pointed the pencil at the twigs, and softly whispered, "Please, *please* light."

Unable to watch her continue to struggle in frustration, Matt silently willed the pile of twigs to burst into flames. Winter jumped back with a yelp of surprise, then started dancing from foot to foot, laughing and cackling as she clutched the pencil to her bosom.

"Yes!" she squealed. "I did it!" She

dropped to her knees and held one hand over the warmth of the softly burning fire. "I did it." She turned and quickly pulled together another pile of twigs a few feet from the first one, stood up, pointed her pencil again, and said, "Light!"

Her enthusiasm, coupled with Matt's own soft petition, caused an explosion that blew Winter clean off her feet, and ignited the upper tree limbs. The light from the fireball reflected in her shocked face.

"Curses, curses, curses!" she cried, jumping to her feet and running farther up the tote road, out from under the burning treetops. The sparking embers caught on the wind, and one tree after another started igniting.

Holy hell, the whole mountain was catching fire. Matt stepped back into the shadows of the flaming forest, lifted his arms skyward, and silently commanded the wind to cease, the clouds to gather, and the rains to come in a torrential downpour. Within minutes he was drenched to the skin, as was Winter. She was looking at the smoldering destruction through the rain, her mouth gaping wide enough that Matt feared she might drown.

He lowered his arms and the rain stopped just as suddenly as it had begun. Kenzie came slinking out of the woods, also soaked to his skin, and padded up to Winter. She folded at the knees to sit on the ground, wrapped her arms around the panther, and buried her face in his soggy fur. "I can't control it!" she wailed to her pet. "I'm going to kill us all before I figure out how to save us."

Dammit, she was right. If she didn't get control of the magic by the winter solstice, Kenzie would definitely get his wish to die — right along with the rest of mankind! Why in hell couldn't she work the magic?

His wife's bout of self-pity lasted a good ten minutes before she finally felt the cold seeping into her wet clothes and started shivering. With one last sniffle, which she wiped on her sleeve, she stood up and continued her journey up the mountain. Kenzie fell into step beside her, and Matt moved back onto the path and followed just out of sight, but not out of earshot.

"I know you were drunk the other day, and I forgive you for chasing me," she told her pet.

And there it was again, that unwavering compassion that had drawn Matt across centuries. Kenzie could have really hurt Winter without meaning to, and yet she was just that quickly, just that simply, forgiving him.

She suddenly glanced over her shoulder, and Matt quickly stepped into the shadows. "Where do you suppose that rainstorm came from?" she asked Kenzie, staring up at the treetops. "Do you think Providence is babysitting me?"

Somebody sure as hell had to, Matt decided. But maybe he would leave that task to Pendaär, since the old man was so hell-bent to mentor his heir. That would leave Matt free to help Greylen and Robbie search for whoever had cut the pine.

"Matt and I are married," she continued. "Don't growl," she said with a laugh. "We made it legal in Las Vegas two days ago, and for our wedding night I slept on the couch in his Utah office and he slept on the floor. Wasn't that romantic?"

The panther curled back his lips in a grin, turned and started walking up the mountain again.

The first hint of daybreak was just starting to show as Winter stepped into the clearing at Pendaär's cottage. Matt worked his way around the edge of the clearing while Winter and Kenzie mounted the steps to the porch, but she didn't even get to knock before the door suddenly opened.

"It's about time ye showed up," Pendaär said without preamble. He took a step back and pointed at Kenzie. "Yer black demon can't come in with ye."

Kenzie sat down, looked up at Pendaär, and licked his lips.

"How did ye get soaked?" Pendaär asked, just now noticing that Winter was also drenched and shivering.

"There . . . ah, a quick-moving rainstorm hit when we were walking up. It must have been part of a squall line. It didn't rain here?" she innocently asked.

Pendaär sighed and turned away from the open door as Winter and Kenzie disappeared inside. Matt immediately darted from the trees to the side of the cottage and sat down with his back to the logs under a window. He pulled his sword from his belt and set it on the ground, ran his hand over his wet clothes to change them into his ancient — and *dry* — plaid, then wiggled his finger at the window sash until it opened an inch. He then pulled his knees up to his chest and huddled inside his warm plaid as he settled in to listen.

Winter stepped into the cabin with a sigh of relief, and Gesader immediately padded over and squeezed between the cookstove

406

and the wall to lie down and soak up the heat. Winter walked to the fieldstone hearth, unbuttoned her jacket and slipped it off, and hung it on a peg on the mantel to dry. "I've visited the pine tree," she said as she held her hands toward the warm fire. "It's very weak."

Daar came over to stand beside her. "I wouldn't know," he said, also staring into the fire. "I've lost my ability to sense its energy. In fact, I can't feel anything now, other than my achy old bones."

Winter turned to face him. "I'm sorry, Father," she whispered. "I didn't know that when I hugged the pine tree you would lose your power."

For a moment Daar continued to stare at the fire, then shrugged. "I had to lose it eventually." He turned his head to look at her. "I was pleased when it happened, actually," he said, and Winter realized how old he suddenly looked. "Because it told me ye had accepted yer calling." He clasped his hands at his waist and shifted uneasily. "Do ye understand all that goes with it, lass?"

"I understand," she said, turning to gaze back at the fire. "You forgot to mention the other day, though, that if I have a baby I would have to give up my calling." She looked at him. "Nor did you think to warn me that if I fall in love but don't have children, I will have to watch my mortal husband die right along with everyone else I love."

Daar looked down at the floor. "I knew ye'd figure that out on yer own." He looked up. "But ye accepted yer calling anyway."

"Yes," she said. It seemed he had nothing to say to that as he continued to stare into the fire. Winter took a tiny step away and also looked down at the flames. "And I married Matt Gregor two days ago," she said.

Daar whipped toward her. "Ye what!"

"And I'm pregnant," she added without looking up.

He lurched back with a gasp. "Winter! What have ye done!"

She faced him and crossed her arms under her breasts. "It turns out that Matt is actually Cùram de Gairn," she calmly continued. "And that he came here not with the intention of destroying mankind, but to seduce me into helping him right an old wrong."

"And ye let him!" Daar shouted, his wrinkled face turning a blotchy red. "Did ye know the bastard was Cùram when ye married him?"

"Aye."

"And ye did it anyway!"

"Aye," she calmly returned. "Because I love him."

"Ye can't love him. He's a soulless bastard who will do anything to get what he wants."

"He's far from soulless, Father." She dropped her arms to her sides. "He's actually trying to fix the mess he's made."

"I bet he is," Daar snapped, "by killing the trees." He waved an angry hand at her. "And now he's stolen yer power by getting ye pregnant, so we have no way to fight him."

"I don't want to fight him," she whispered. "I want to help him. He's lost hope, Father. Couldn't you feel it in the air when our pine began to weaken? Didn't you sense the chill wind coming this way? It was when I hugged the pine that I realized it wasn't anger or revenge driving Cùram, but despair. He was willing to let mankind die because he had lost hope."

"*Is* willing!" Daar snapped. "Not was. And he's succeeded, hasn't he, if he married ye and got ye with child." He pointed a crooked finger at her. "Ye let yer heart overrule yer head, girl." He shook his head and turned away. "Love is a curse that's always interfering in our work."

"No," Winter said. "Love is the strongest

emotion of all. It's what will save us, not doom us."

"And that's exactly why women have never been allowed to be *drùidhs*," he shot back with a glare before walking toward the wood cookstove. He spun around to face her again, his complexion red with anger. "Women are weak. Ye spin fairy tales of sweetness and compassion and everyone loving each other. Ye don't have the strength of heart to fight the dark side of human nature, thinking that just by falling in love with a blackguard ye can suddenly turn him into a saint."

"Then why was I born?" she quietly asked. "If women don't have the fortitude to be *drùidhs,* why did you expend so much effort to get my father and mother together so I would be born?"

He frowned, his jaw tensing as he looked down at his hands.

"Because Providence realized having only male *drùidhs* wasn't working," Winter answered for him. "The energy is shifting to include females, because it's our very sweetness and compassion that was lacking. My child isn't going to mean the end of mankind, Father," she softly informed him. "It's going to be our salvation. I know you were brought up in a time when marriages were practical rather than emotional, but whether you can learn to accept it as fact or not, love always was and always will be the most powerful energy in the universe. That's why Providence has gotten itself a female *drùidh,* so I can fix the mess you men have made," she said with a crooked grin. "And just as soon as you teach me to control the energy, that's exactly what I intend to do."

He didn't smile back, but scowled instead. "How do ye know all this?" he growled.

"A little bird told me," she said, laughing when his scowl deepened. "A crow, actually, came to me in a dream and explained that I have the ability to put the continuum back on track." She frowned. "Except he didn't explain *how* I was supposed to do it. He only said that I would figure it out by the winter solstice."

"A crow," Daar said. "In a dream ye had. And on this alone you've risked everything?"

"You still haven't told me why I was born," Winter said instead of answering him.

Daar's face reddened, not with anger but with chagrin. "I was told to make yer birth happen."

"Who told you?"

His face darkened even more, and he dropped his gaze to her feet. "I was told it in a dream," he said, lifting his chin defensively. "I only saw a shadow surrounded by brilliant colors. It told me to get Greylen born and then get him married off to some woman in the twenty-first century." His shoulders slumped and he walked to the table and sat down in a chair, hanging his head as he spoke to the floor. "I did what I was asked, though I never understood why. I was only told that the energy was shifting from the summer solstice to the winter. I was operating blind."

"Not blind," Winter said, going to Daar and kneeling in front of him so he could see her smile. "You knew my parents were ordained to have seven daughters, and that the energy was shifting even while you didn't want to admit it. You didn't like that the upset Cùram had caused centuries earlier had started a chain reaction that only a female could fix." She touched his bearded cheek, then stood and pulled her sketch pencil from her jacket pocket. "I seem to be having a wee bit of trouble with my power, and I need you to teach me how to control it."

He turned to face her. "Control it?" he asked in surprise. "That's not something anyone can teach ye."

He stepped toward her, his face paling. "Where's the staff I made ye?"

She held up the pencil. "It's right here."

Daar rushed over and took the pencil from her, examining it as if it were a bug in his hand. He looked at her. "Ye turned yer pinewood staff into a pencil? Why?"

"I didn't. Matt did. It's easier to carry that way." She smiled crookedly. "Do you really expect me to walk around with a cane, Father? I'm twenty-four years old, and I don't limp." She took the pencil away from him. "This is easier. It fits in my pocket."

"Ye mustn't let Cùram touch your staff!"

"He's been trying to help me control the magic, but I burned all his clothes, his blankets, and his supplies."

Daar eyed her suspiciously. "Maybe he's only pretending to be helpful, but is really sabotaging ye."

"Nay," Winter said. "He needs my help to keep a promise he made over eight hundred years ago. But to do that, I have to be able to summon the energy."

"What promise?" Daar asked, still skeptical.

Winter shook her head. "I can't say without breaking my marriage vows."

Daar harrumphed and turned away from her. "Does yer papa know who ye married?"

"Yes, and so does Robbie."

Daar snapped his gaze to her. "MacBain

knows Gregor is Cùram de Gairn? And he did nothing? Nor did Greylen?"

"Robbie and Papa trust me," she said. "And they realize they must work with Matt now, to find out who cut our pine."

Daar's eyes widened in surprise. "Work with him?" he repeated. He shook his head. "I don't believe it. MacBain would never willingly work with de Gairn any more than I would."

"We all have the same goal, Father," Winter said with a sigh, tucking the pencil in her pants pocket. "And a common cause will force even enemies to cooperate with each other. Which is why you will also help, by teaching me how to control the energy."

He had nothing to say to that, though he did look like she'd just asked him to swallow a sour pickle, which Winter guessed was exactly how he felt.

"Matt is not the threat, Father," she said into the silence. "Whoever cut our pine is the true danger, and if we don't find out who he is and why he's here before he does any more damage, it might be too late for all of us. Please, won't you help me?"

"It became too late for me to help ye when ye married de Gairn," he whispered, seemingly unable to get past that fact. "He's the one who put this whole mess into motion."

"But it's fixable," Winter snapped with waning patience. "I can make everything all right on this winter solstice, but only if I have command of my power. And that's not going to happen without your help." She stepped closer and set her hand on his slumped shoulder. "Ye have to trust the universe to know what it's doing, Father. Passing down your knowledge to me is not playing into Matt's hands, it's fulfilling a promise that was put into motion a thousand years ago."

Daar reached up and scrubbed his face with both hands. He walked over to the door, opened it, and looked out over Pine Lake. "I did feel another entity in the air before I lost my power," he admitted as he stared out at the vista. "I thought it was de Gairn trying to confuse me." He looked over his shoulder at her. "Are ye sure Cùram had nothing to do with the pine being cut?"

"Yes, Father. He's as worried about it as we are."

"Can ye feel this strange energy?" he asked, looking back at the lake. "Still? It's still here?"

"Yes." She frowned at his back. "But instead of being strange, if feels . . . familiar some how." She shook her head when he spun toward her in surprise. "I know it's not Matt's or mine, but it seems to be . . ." She shrugged, tossing her hands up and letting them fall to her sides.

Daar stared at her for what seemed like forever, then suddenly sighed and stepped out onto the porch. "Come, then," he said as he turned toward the stairs. "Show me the problem you're having with yer staff."

Winter ran out onto the porch and down the stairs to where Daar was standing in the middle of the clearing. "Every time I ask for something as simple as a fire to light," she told him, pulling her pencil from her pocket, "everything but the twigs starts bursting into flames."

Daar scurried to the side when she pulled out her pencil, positioning himself slightly behind her. "There," he said, pointing at a large boulder at the far end of the clearing. "Instead of asking for fire, see what happens when ye ask that rock to turn into a pebble."

She pointed the pencil at the boulder, but Daar covered her hand with his. "Simply *picture* it as a pebble, girl. Gently, very gently," he warned, removing his hand.

Winter squinted at the boulder, pointed her pencil, and pictured a tiny round pebble sitting where the boulder stood. When nothing happened, she squinted harder, concentrated even more, and said, "Turn into a pebble!"

The boulder exploded with enough force to shake the ground as a million granite missiles spewed out in different directions. Winter grabbed Father Daar and threw them both to the ground, using her body to shield his.

Strong hands were on her within seconds, even as the tiny pebbles she'd created continued to fall. Winter was picked up, spun around, and hauled against a hard, half-naked chest as an unyielding broad hand covered her head.

She smiled into her husband's chest, even as the last of the pebbles finally finished falling. "Good morning," she said, tilting her head to look up at him.

He lifted a brow. "You don't seem surprised to see me."

Winter lifted her own brow. "Did you hear enough to be satisfied I'm keeping my vows?"

He scowled at her. "I don't doubt you'll keep them. It's Pendaär I don't trust."

"Saints and curses," the old priest muttered, awkwardly climbing to his feet and brushing himself off. He turned, gasped hard enough to nearly knock himself over again, and stepped back. *"Cùram,"* he hissed, his hands balling into fists and his eyes narrowed in hatred.

Matt stepped away from Winter and inclined his head. "Pendaär," he said, his tone civil. "It's a privilege to finally meet the great *drùidh* of Pravad."

"Pravad?" Winter repeated. "Where's that?"

Both men ignored her, what with being so busy eyeing each other — Daar with a fierce scowl and Matt with an even fiercer grin. Winter stepped between them, speaking first to her husband. "You will stop presenting yourself like that," she scolded.

He gave her an innocent look. "Like what?"

She waved at his clothing. "Like an ancient warrior *drùidh.* You do it on purpose, just to push people's buttons."

"My clothes were soaked," he said, still appearing innocent, except for the sparkling gleam in his golden eyes. "You see, there was this sudden rainstorm on the way up, and I needed to change into something dry."

Winter felt her cheeks redden. "Thank you for putting out the fire," she whispered, quickly turning to Daar. "Quit your scowling, Father, and help us figure out why I can't control the energy."

Daar leaned slightly to the left, looking up

at Matt standing behind her without letting go of his scowl. "There's no reason she can't control it, other than maybe she doesn't want to," he said smugly.

"But I do!" Winter insisted, turning to Matt. "I *do* want to control it."

Matt looked over her head at Daar. "Do you suppose it's because she's a woman?"

"Oh, of all the —" Winter stamped her foot. "Being a woman has nothing to do with anything!"

"Aye," Daar said, scratching his beard as Winter spun to face him. He squinted past her to Matt. "That might be it," he said with a nod. "The energy is used to responding to a man's way of thinking. Women think different, ye know." He finally looked at Winter and frowned. "Ye don't think straight, girl. Women think in dizzying circles," he said, waving his hand in the air. "You're always talking yer way around a problem instead of hitting it straight on. Ye need to start thinking like a man if ye want to control the energy."

"It was male thinking that got us into this mess," she growled. "And circling a problem and looking at it from every perspective is what's going to get us back on track."

"Not if you keep blowing up the world one rock and tree at a time," Matt said with a chuckle. He pulled her back against him, wrapping his arms around her as they both faced Daar. "It will only take practice then," he told the once-again scowling priest. "Winter and the energy are going to have to learn each other's language. May I suggest that she work with you while I help MacBain and MacKeage figure out who else is in this game?"

Daar looked like he was having to force down another sour pickle, but he finally nodded curtly, turned, and silently walked back to his cabin, making a wide swing past Gesader, who was hiding under the porch.

Matt spun Winter in his arms to face him and gave her a hearty, passionate kiss on the mouth. "Good morning, wife," he whispered.

She patted his bare chest. "That was very sweet of you."

He smiled. "My kisses are sweet?"

"No. What you just did for Daar."

He reared back. "What did I do?"

She traced one finger through the soft hairs on his chest. "You let him keep his dignity by making him feel needed."

"He is needed," he snapped. "I can't babysit you and hunt the strange energy at the same time."

She kissed his chest, pulled away with a

laugh, and started walking down the mountain. "Sweetness isn't a flaw but a strength," she said, spinning toward him. When she heard him growl, she began walking backward. "And whether you want to admit it or not, I am married to a very *sweet* man."

He suddenly waggled his fingers at her, and Winter stopped with a gasp and looked down at herself in surprise. She fingered the beautiful plaid she was suddenly wearing, which was draped over a lovely white cotton blouse.

The plaid had a base color of deep flannel gray, with wide forest green stripes running in one direction, and narrow yellow and red stripes running in the other. She looked back at Matt, only to find him standing three feet away.

"This — this is the Gregor plaid?"

"Aye," he said, smiling in approval. "It's time you started wearing my colors."

"Papa is going to throw a fit," she whispered, looking down at the way the plaid draped over her shoulders like a shawl and gathered around her waist before falling all the way past her knees, all being held into place by a thick leather belt. She bent slightly and looked down at her legs, finding them covered by tall suede leggings that turned into leather-soled shoes.

She looked up at Matt. "Ah, maybe I should have a jumper and some shirts made out of it instead." She gave him a daring smile. "Thank you. Getting me out of my wet clothes was a very *sweet* thing to do."

That said, Winter turned tail and bolted down the steep mountain path, squealing in delight when Matt caught up with her. Without breaking stride, her husband tossed her over his shoulder and proceeded to carry her down the mountain, and he didn't even snicker when they passed through the burnt remains of her little forest fire.

She was married to a very sweet man, and Winter knew she had more than enough hope for them both.

CHAPTER
TWENTY-THREE

Winter dipped her finger in the bowl of whipped potatoes, tasted her progress so far, and decided she needed to add more butter. She plopped in several more table-spoons' worth and started the beater again, smiling as she listened to her mama and Megan arguing over how to get the lumps out of the gravy.

It was hard for Winter to believe she had been married five whole weeks. She and Matt were living at Gù Brath because not four days into her marriage, Winter had lost her first real fight with her husband. She had been soundly defeated, though Matt's getting her family, Robbie, and even old Tom involved in their little domestic dispute hadn't been fighting fair.

Winter had wanted to move into the cave while they built their home, arguing that it was cozy and warm and had everything she and Matt needed. Her parents and Megan had been appalled to think she would even consider living in a cave all winter, Robbie had flat out told her she was crazy, and Tom had laughed himself silly and immediately taken Matt's side.

Which was why for the last five weeks, Winter had spent her time getting her gallery ready for the fast-approaching Christmas shopping season, and Matt had been putting in twelve-hour days getting a road cut through the forest and having a small cottage built down on the lake below the meadow. Once their permanent home was finished up on the mountain — in about two years, Matt had estimated — the lakeshore cottage could then become their summer retreat. But even while waiting to get a temporary home built, Matt had been adamant about not having his pregnant wife living in a cave. So he had been pushing himself and his construction crew to get their cabin done by Thanksgiving, and trying to help Robbie and her papa hunt down the strange energy still lurking about.

There had been yet another puzzling incident since the pine had been cut, this time involving their precious cave. When Winter and Matt had gone out to see what could be salvaged from her accidental fires — and maybe find some privacy for some *noisy* lovemaking — the cave was gone.

The soaring granite cliff was still towering over the meadow, but the entrance to the cave had disappeared. No matter how hard Matt repeatedly tried using whatever powers or spells he could conjure up, he couldn't make the entrance reopen.

So for the last five weeks Winter had been dividing her time between the gallery, visiting Daar for her lessons on wizardry, and helping her mama collect furnishings for their nearly completed cottage. The gallery was getting busy, her lessons with Daar were proving more frustrating than helpful, and Winter didn't much care if her curtains matched her table linens or not. She just wanted to get moved out of Gù Brath so she could make love to her husband without worrying about her papa breaking down her bedroom door.

Gesader was still lurking about, although he'd been spending more time with Megan than with either Winter or Matt. And though her papa kept putting the panther out every night when they all went to bed, Megan had confided to Winter that Gesader would be up on the garage roof within minutes, and she would let him in her window so he could curl up on the bottom of her bed and keep her feet warm.

Winter still couldn't bring herself to tell Megan that Gesader was really an ancient highland warrior. At first, once she'd realized the implications, Winter had been appalled to think she'd been so cozy and cuddly with her husband's brother for over two years. She had remembered swimming — naked! — in the high mountain pond with her pet, confiding her deepest secrets to him, and even telling him about her terrible dates with men who had thought they were God's gift to women.

Matt had laughed at Winter's outrage and asked if she thought he would have sent the panther here if it truly was his *brother* sharing her bed. When Kenzie was an animal, Matt had explained, he was nothing more than the creature he embodied, albeit an exceptionally intuitive creature. Megan was safe, Matt had assured Winter, at least until the upcoming solstice. Then all bets were off, he'd said with a very male grin. Once Kenzie was back to his old self, he would certainly find his way back into Megan's bed.

As for Megan, her belly had popped out almost overnight, and she'd begun wearing maternity pants and baggy tops. She seemed to have come to terms with her pregnancy and hardly ever cried anymore. In fact, she was finally so mad at Wayne Ferris, Winter feared Megan was thinking of hunting him down and dispatching his black heart to hell herself.

Winter carried the huge bowl of potatoes from the kitchen and put it down on the large dining room table that was set to serve seven for Thanksgiving. Father Daar was already seated — toward the head of the table right beside her papa's place, probably just to aggravate him — and the old priest had his napkin tucked in his collar and was already holding his fork.

"Who's the seventh place for?" he asked, frowning down the empty table.

"Tom," Winter told him, straightening one of the napkins. "He's been here for the last two Thanksgivings, remember?"

"I remember he ate more than he talked."

"Just like someone else I know," she said, rolling her eyes and heading toward the living room, but having to stop when Daar spoke again.

"He's late," the priest said. "It's impolite to make us wait. The food's getting cold."

"We're starting, Father," Winter assured him. "If we wait any longer, Tom will be embarrassed to have held us up."

Daar harrumphed and Winter stepped into the living room to find her papa and husband deep in conversation, sitting facing each other in front of the brightly burning hearth. She smiled with quiet joy. Who would have thought the two men she most loved in the world would end up getting along so well considering their precarious beginning? But whenever Matt wasn't away on company business, he and her papa had been scouring both Bear and TarStone Mountain with Robbie, looking for whoever — or whatever — was interfering in their business of saving mankind.

"Dinner's ready," she said softly.

Both men looked over, smiled, and stood up. "What parts did you cook?" Matt asked, walking up and kissing the tip of her nose. "So I know what to avoid."

"I cooked the turkey and the potatoes and the squash," she said, giving him a smug smile when he groaned. "I waved my pencil over the turkey just before I put it in the oven."

It was her papa who groaned this time, as he stopped on his way to the dining room and glared at Matt. "I thought ye took that damned thing away from her."

Matt grinned. "She's learned enough to keep it hidden from me," he said in his own defense. He looped his arm over Winter's shoulder and guided her back into the dining room just as Megan and Grace showed up carrying more bowls of food.

"The turkey's on the counter," Grace said, sitting down on the left side of her husband's place, opposite Daar. "Would you get it, Grey?"

"Tom's not coming?" Matt asked, holding first Winter's chair and then Megan's as they sat down. But instead of sitting beside Winter, he then walked around the table and sat next to a scowling Father Daar.

"If Tom shows up, we'll feed him," Grace said, placing her napkin on her lap. "But everything was getting overcooked, so we're starting without him. Father," she said when Grey set the enormous turkey on the table and sat down, "would you say grace, please?"

"I blessed the food while it was cooking," Daar said, reaching for the bowl of potatoes. "We can begin eating."

Winter quickly slid the potatoes out of his reach. "Then maybe you could bless *us,*" she suggested.

"All of us?" he asked, darting an uncharitable glance at Matt before glaring back at Winter.

"I hope I don't drop the pumpkin pie when I bring it out," she said, keeping her hand on the bowl of potatoes.

Daar snapped his gaze down to his empty plate, folded his hands together, and said, "We ask ye God, to bless all the *good* people here today, that we might finally get to enjoy yer bounty. Amen. Let's eat."

Apparently eating was more important than worrying about sitting down to dinner with the enemy, and Daar took the casserole, spooned himself a huge helping, and bypassed Grey by handing it directly to Grace, obviously not wanting to interrupt the carving. "I'll take that leg and thigh, Laird, if ye're wanting to get it out of yer way," Daar said, holding his plate toward Grey. "And some of that stuffing."

"So, Matt," Grace said as she passed Winter the casserole, "have you found a way into your cave yet? Or do you think it even still exists?"

"I can feel an energy coming from inside the cliff," Matt told her as he took the cranberry sauce from Megan. "But only sometimes, and usually at night."

"You've been going to the cliff at night?" Winter asked in surprise. "When?"

"I misspoke," he told her. "I mean in the early morning, just before dawn. I often stop by on my way to check the progress on our cottage, just to see if anything's changed at the cliff." He looked over to include Grey.

"If I place my hands on the rock and concentrate, I can make out a vibration coming from inside." He looked to the far wall, and Winter saw him rub his fingers together on his right hand. "Actually, the granite feels unusually warm, and I can hear faint tapping sounds coming from inside." He looked back at Grey and shook his head. "I've tried to place the sound, but I can't."

"So you think something is going on in there?" Megan asked. "That the cave still exists and someone is working inside it?"

Daar stopped stuffing food in his mouth long enough to glare at Matt. "Who else have ye angered over the centuries?" he asked.

Matt looked startled. "No one," he said. "I haven't angered anyone . . . else."

"The vibration you felt," Winter asked, drawing his attention. "Is it the same energy we sensed near the pine?"

"It feels the same," Matt said, though he was shaking his head. "Whoever it is, he's much more powerful than either of us, I'm afraid. He's able to cloak his identity even from me, and he's made the cliff impervious. I tried getting inside from a different direction, but I couldn't get within ten feet of the original cave."

Winter grinned crookedly. "You keep calling the energy a 'he.' Maybe it's a 'she.' Maybe that's why you can't wiggle your way around her power."

"Neither can you."

"Not yet," she said, filling her fork with potato and popping it into her mouth, smiling at Matt's frown as she chewed.

Daar stopped eating long enough to ask Matt another question. "What were ye doing up on TarStone yesterday? Ye made a terrible racket that shook the mountain hard enough to knock my lantern off its peg, and ye caused a landslide that missed my cabin by only a few yards."

Again, Matt looked surprised, then suddenly turned narrowed eyes on Winter. She quickly popped some turkey into her mouth, chewed, then said, "Megan, would you pass me the cranberry sauce, please?"

"Winter?" Matt growled.

At the sound of the doorbell, Winter rose to answer the door. "Hello, Tom. We'd given up on you, I'm afraid, and have already sat down to eat."

"I'm sorry," he said, pulling off his cap and inclining his head in apology. "I lost track of time." He looked toward the dining room. "Is there anything left?"

"There won't be if you don't beat Daar to the dessert," she said with a laugh, slipping her arm through Tom's to escort him into the dining room once he hung up his coat.

"I'm sorry," Tom repeated to the table of people as he walked over to the empty chair beside Matt. "I lost track of time," he told them, a gleam in his eyes as he looked at Winter. "I got involved working on Winter's birthday gift."

"Oh," she said, clasping her hands in delight and looking up the table at her parents. "Tom is carving something special for my birthday. He's keeping it under a sheet in his workshop and won't let me in, but I saw just enough to know it's nearly as large as a small car. Tom, there's really no reason to wait to give me my gift."

Tom chuckled as he began filling his plate with food. "I know it's quite a difficult concept for you to imagine, Winter, but patience can be a useful virtue." He gave her a wink, then scanned his gaze up the table. "Did any of you hear that loud noise on the summit of TarStone yesterday morning? I was hiking into town and I swear I heard thunder, but there wasn't a cloud in the sky." He looked at Matt. "At first I thought it was your jet breaking the sound barrier, but I saw you driving down to your cabin not ten minutes later."

"I heard it," Daar piped up between bites

before anyone could answer. "Something caused a powerful landslide that pretty near cleaned out my cabin."

"It could have been seismic activity," Megan quickly offered with a smile, reaching over and poking Winter's thigh. "We get tremors every now and then, when the land rebounds from the weight of the old glaciers."

"Even a small tremor could trigger a landslide," Grace added, winking at Winter.

Winter just kept eating, deciding that maybe she should start driving to the next county to practice her magic. She had been able to master some things, like masking her own vibrations of energy at least enough to hide her pencil from Matt. And she had finally conquered fire — well, mostly. But learning to think like a man was about as likely as her learning patience.

"I have an announcement," Matt said, drawing everyone's attention. "Our cottage is finished. It cost me a bundle in bonuses, but the crew pounded the last nail and put on the final coat of paint yesterday afternoon. We can move in tomorrow."

"But tomorrow is the first official shopping day of Christmas, and my busiest day of the year," Winter said. "And both Megan and Mama have to help me out in the gallery. We can't move in tomorrow."

"You don't have to lift a finger," Matt said. "I'll move us in."

"And hang the curtains?" Grace asked, giving Matt a skeptical look. "And unpack all the boxes and set up the kitchen and bathroom? We're going to be busy right up until Christmas."

"Don't you wish there really was such a thing as magic?" Tom interjected with a smile. "That we could just wave a magic wand and make everything happen just like that?" he said, snapping his fingers in the air.

Winter could only blink at her friend, and when she looked over and saw the gleam in Matt's eyes, had to cover her mouth with her napkin so she wouldn't burst into laughter.

Yes, if only they had a magic wand . . . or two.

Matt sat on the couch facing the brightly burning fieldstone hearth that dominated the north wall of their cozy three-room cottage, frowning at his wife draped across his lap. "You aren't falling asleep on me, are you?" he asked, giving her a small shake. "This is our first night in our very own home. We should be dancing naked in front of the fire."

"You dance," she said drowsily, snuggling deeper into his embrace. "I'll watch."

"Poor baby. Hard day at work?" He tenderly stroked her thigh. "Were you sick again today?"

"Only queasy, because I didn't have time to throw up," she said with a tired sigh. She looked at him and smiled. "I did finally call Heather, and she said having morning sickness is a good sign that the baby is settling in for a long and happy stay."

"Heather's the doctor, right? Your oldest sister who lives in California?" He laid his hand across her flat stomach when she nodded, his fingertips spanning her waist from hip to hip. "Seven daughters," he said with a chuckle. "Your poor papa." He smiled when she frowned. "You're not going to take after your mama, I hope. I want at least a few sons."

"It's the man who donates the Y chromosome," she told him, her frown deepening as she wiggled around to see him better. "How come you know so much about the twenty-first century, about stuff like physics and business?"

"I've been living here for almost three years now."

"Since Kenzie came? You came here when he did?"

"No, shortly after."

"Did you come to Pine Creek? How come I never saw you?"

"I only came here four times a year, and stayed just the twenty-four hours Kenzie was human. The rest of the time I spent out in the world, learning as much as I could about modern society and technology, gathering wealth and knowledge while waiting for when you were ready."

"Ready? For what?" she asked in surprise.

"Me," he said, leaning down and kissing the tip of her nose. "And actually, you did see me a few times in the last couple of years." He nodded toward the hearth, to the large painting hanging over the mantel. "Even though I was damn good at masking myself, you were still able to sense my energy. I'm right there in *Moon Watchers,* in the top left corner." He frowned when she looked from the painting to him. "I don't like that you made me a fairy, and I've a mind to make you repaint my image."

She lifted her chin. "Artists do not change their vision to suit picky patrons. I sensed a warm, *sweet* spirit that night, and that's what I painted. You don't like it, hang it back in the gallery. I could probably get double what you paid for that painting the way business was today."

Matt pulled her more tightly against his chest. "I am not selling *Moon Watchers.*" He kissed her nose again. "And I am not sweet."

She looked around their perfectly furnished living room, then brought her gaze back to his and lifted her brow. "I would say busting your butt to get us moved in today without using your magic makes you sweet."

"It wasn't sweetness motivating me, it was lust," he said, lifting her shoulders to kiss her full on the mouth this time. "I worked my tail off to get us moved in here, so I can finally make you scream again without worrying about your father charging in on us with his sword."

His wide-eyed little wife giggled and wrapped her arms around his neck. "Papa's been living in this time over thirty-seven years, and he still sleeps with his sword by his bed." She kissed the pulse on Matt's neck, then grinned up at him. "I've noticed you're in the habit of placing your fountain pen on the bedside table. Maybe I should start sleeping with my pencil."

Matt involuntarily shuddered. "Lord, lass, don't do that. You'll burn down our home and we'll have to move back in with your parents."

She ran her fingers through his loose hair, making him shudder again. "It was rather exciting trying to make love without making any noise," she whispered. "Maybe even decadent. I liked doing it in the shower with the water running."

Matt smiled sadly. "Too bad you're so tired. I planned to try out the hot tub on the front porch tonight," he said with a sigh as he leaned his head against the back of the couch.

But he quickly snapped forward with a surprised grunt when his suddenly wide-awake wife squealed in delight and scrambled off his lap. "We have a hot tub?" she cried. "Why didn't I see it when I came home?"

Home. Matt decided he liked the sound of that, especially when Winter said it. "Because you came in through the back door," he explained, leaning against the couch again and lifting one brow. "Get a second wind, did you?"

But he was talking to her back, as Winter ran out the front door. Matt got up with a rather tired sigh of his own. Moving an entire household in one day hadn't been easy, especially considering that he'd only resorted to using his magic toward the end, when it had looked like he wouldn't get done by the time Winter got home. He followed his wife onto the porch that overlooked the lake, and found her already stripped down to her bra and pants.

"Quick, get undressed," she said as she kicked off her shoes, unfastened her pants, shoved them down her legs, and stepped out of them. She stopped in the process of unclipping her bra. "The tub is all warmed up, isn't it?"

"It's warm," Matt said, unbuttoning his own shirt. "Wind up your braid so it won't get wet. The . . . ah, hot tub won't hurt the baby, will it?"

"No," she said, tossing her bra away and sliding her thumbs under the elastic of her panties. "As long as it's not too hot, and I don't stay in too long."

Matt had a little more trouble unfastening his own suddenly tight pants, and had to sit down to unlace his boots — and hopefully get control of his lust before either of them reached the tub. But he only ended up making knots in his laces instead of undoing them, when he spotted his naked wife with her arms raised to twine her hair on top of her head, bathed in the soft light coming through the huge front windows.

She was so stunningly beautiful, so vivaciously alive and filled with such innocent promise, that sometimes Matt found himself wondering if this was nothing more than a dream.

Or maybe it was hell. Maybe Providence was punishing his sins by giving him just a taste of Winter — offering him this one small glimpse of hope — before it all disappeared just as suddenly as the entrance to his cave had. Aye, maybe the energy he felt coming from inside the cliff was really an avenging angel, waiting for just the right time to deliver his deathblow.

If that was the case, then so be it. Matt had placed his future in Winter's delicate hands, and he had four weeks left before he met his fate face on. He would damned well meet it with the courage of a warrior.

But in the meantime, he had every intention of basking in the warmth of Winter's hopefulness, regretting none of his actions that had ultimately brought him to her. She would at least save his brother, Matt knew, and protect their child at all costs — even if it meant destroying him — because her strength of spirit would not allow her to do anything less.

As long as there was life there was hope, she'd told him in the cave the day after he'd claimed her, and at this single moment in time Matt felt more alive than he had in centuries.

"Oh, this is heavenly," Winter breathed, sliding into the warm swirling water up to her neck. "Run inside and turn out the lights so we can see the lake and the stars."

Matt gave up and tore his laces free, finished stripping off his clothes, reached inside and hit the light switch beside the door, and quickly climbed in the tub.

"I'm so glad I was smart enough to marry a sweet man who's enamored with modern technology," she said, floating toward him until she was just barely straddling his thighs. Matt's eyes had adjusted to the starlight enough that he could make out her smile when she asked, "How far are we from Tom's cabin?"

"Almost a mile," he told her, only to suck air through his teeth when her floating breasts bumped his chest.

"And will sound carry almost a mile?"

"It — It depends on the sound," he rasped when she slid her hips forward along his thighs.

"Oh, say a scream, for instance," she whispered, one of her hands dancing over his shoulders and into his hair. "Would a scream carry a mile down the shoreline?"

His shout of surprise sure as hell did, when his anything but compassionate little wife suddenly reached down and wrapped her other hand around his shaft.

She actually laughed. "I've been waiting five weeks to make you shout," she said, guiding him inside her with painstaking slowness. "I can't tell you how many times I was tempted to do this at Gù Brath," she whispered as she nipped his neck just below his ear. "I think I'll see if I can't make *both* of us scream tonight, husband."

Oh, yes, Matt thought when he felt a sudden lurch very near where his heart used to be, capturing his sweet vixen fairy and kissing her deeply. As long as there was life, there truly must be hope.

CHAPTER
TWENTY-FOUR

Winter stood insentient, unable to do more than stare in disbelief at her pine tree. Its bark was shriveled like mummified skin, its remaining branches drooping bonelessly, its needles turned brown and scattered over the pristine blanket of last night's snowfall. Sometime between two days ago and this morning, somebody had dug a large, deep hole at the base of the pine, exposing its roots to the frigid air and ultimately delivering a fatal blow.

Winter had made a point of visiting her pine tree every few days since Gesader had brought her to it nine weeks ago, so she could sit and hug it and share enough of her energy to keep it alive. But this morning, eager to greet the dawn of the winter solstice in the company of her magical white pine, she had arrived at sunrise to find only death and destruction. And since first hearing Matt's heartbreaking story of despair,

Winter finally understood the chilling definition of hopelessness.

She'd lost. Without her tree of life she had no way to save mankind or help Kenzie. On the dawn of her twenty-fifth birthday, her gift to the world was its end, her having failed Providence miserably and completely. If she only could have mastered the magic she would have been able to help the men find and defeat the strange and destructive energy before it had rendered this mortal blow.

So confident she had been. So maddeningly sure of herself and her ability to rebalance the continuum with nothing more than her strength of conviction. Loving Matheson Gregor unconditionally hadn't saved him, but had doomed them all.

Winter finally came out of her stupor, unfastened her snowshoes and kicked them off. She rushed through the foot of new snow — skirting the deep hole — wrapped her arms around her pine's shriveled bark, closed her eyes, and listened for even a whisper of life. She pulled off her cap and threw it to the ground to lay her ear against the trunk . . . and felt nothing. Tears streamed down her cheeks and froze on her jacket as she tightened her embrace and willed her life-energy into the tree . . . and still she felt nothing other than her own pounding heart racing in horror.

"No!" she cried, digging her fingers into the bark and pressing her body closer. "Wake up! Give up your stored energy, Tar-Stone, and nourish my pine!"

When still nothing happened, Winter slid to her knees, turned, and leaned against the lifeless trunk, burying her face in her hands. All was lost, including her magic. She couldn't even feel TarStone's energy; she couldn't feel anything but the dark, colorless void of . . . of nothing.

Winter sobbed uncontrollably, surrendering to self-pity and shame. She had been so busy being happy and hopeful that she had neglected the real threat right under her nose. Thinking love alone would make everything right, she hadn't even bothered to consider the strength of her enemy's determination.

How naive she had been, and how foolish to have so readily dismissed the power of despair. She *knew* that when something had been set into motion, be it a physical object or a train of thought, that it wanted to *stay* in motion. For one thousand years, despair had been hurtling toward mankind's end, gaining momentum to the point that even her own promised destiny hadn't been able to stop it.

She didn't have what it took to be a *drùidh.* She was so blind to the negative energy that made up the dark side of life, she was ineffectual to recognize it, much less defeat it.

Which brought Winter back to her question to Daar. If she didn't have the wisdom to be a *drùidh,* to be powerful and smart enough to vanquish despair, then why had she even been born?

Winter reached in her jacket and pulled out her pencil. She swiped her tears away so she could see and rolled the pencil between her fingers as she thought about what she could do. She flicked her wrist — only to gasp when her pencil suddenly turned into her pinewood staff! She stared at the softly vibrating stick, and her heart thumped with renewed hope as she felt the energy's warmth flow through her body.

All *wasn't* lost. She still possessed the magic!

Matt. She needed to talk to her husband; he would know what to do. Maybe they could combine their strengths and bring her tree back to life.

But Matt had left long before daybreak to finally give Tom the supersonic ride he had been promised. Oh, why had Tom asked to go today of all days!

And Father Daar couldn't help her, since he'd lost his own power. Robbie! Maybe Robbie could help. But then Winter remembered Daar had told her the pine was Robbie's source of power as well. Had his guardian energy died with the tree?

Winter pulled out her cell phone and punched in Robbie's number, and Catherine answered on the fifth ring. "Hello," Winter said. "Is Robbie home?"

"No," Catherine told her. "He's at Gù Brath with your sisters. Happy birthday," she added. "How come you aren't at breakfast with everyone? Finding it hard to get out of bed being a newlywed?"

"I . . . ah, I'm just headed over there now," she told Cat.

"Then I guess I'll see you this afternoon at the big bash." Cat laughed. "I still can't believe all you girls were born on the same day. Everyone made it home for the party, didn't they?"

"Yes, everyone's come home, including husbands and children. I have to get going, Cat, before they eat all the food. Thanks for the birthday wish, and I'll see you this afternoon."

"Bye," Catherine said, hanging up.

Winter pressed the End button, stared at

her phone for several seconds, then dialed Gù Brath. But she quickly pushed End again before it could ring.

She just couldn't bring herself to ruin everyone's day. This might be the last birthday the seven of them spent together, so how could she call home in a panic and pull her papa and Robbie away when they were also helpless to do anything?

Matt was still her best hope. He still had his power, didn't he? Or had he been tapping her pine tree, since it had grown from the root of his own tree? Darn it, she should have been more curious about the source of his energy.

And that was when Winter realized exactly where she'd gone wrong. Since the day she'd sat in the cave with her back to Matt and he'd told her his heartbreaking story, all she had thought about was how *she* could fix the mess he had made. She'd never once stopped to consider that maybe Matt was the one who needed to do the fixing.

How arrogant she'd been about loving Matt unconditionally. How obsessed she'd become with making everything right, to the point that she'd forgotten about Matt's very real need to be part of the solution.

Darn it, where was that crow when she needed him! Why couldn't he have explained all this to her in her dream, instead of giving her just enough information to make her think she could right another man's wrong all by herself? She wasn't the means to the end, she was only half of the answer! She couldn't *make* Matt find hope; she could only encourage him to look deep within himself to find it again.

Winter hugged her pinewood staff to her bosom, closed her eyes, and willed her husband to come back at *twice* the speed of sound. Darn it, she needed him right now; he should darn well sense her desperation. That's what being married was all about. They were a team, and it was going to take the both of them to fix this mess.

She wasn't giving up. She refused to lose hope. She had her staff and she had Matt, and they had their baby's future to protect. And if they blew the top off Bear Mountain getting at that accursed energy inside, then by God, that's exactly what she and Matt would do — together!

Winter stood beside her old Suburban at the Pine Creek airport and held her hand over her racing heart, undecided if it was still pounding from dread or from her record-breaking snowshoe run down the mountain to where she'd parked her truck.

But she could finally feel herself calming down as she worked the genes she'd inherited from her mama and weighed the possibilities and probabilities of various courses of action she and Matt could take.

She did have a few good points to consider. For one thing, her staff was still powerful. And Matt's staff was too, she hoped. Second, the sun was still shining, the earth was still spinning, and the apocalypse hadn't suddenly arrived with the death of her pine, which only proved her theory that as long as there was life, there was hope. Winter lowered her hand from her heart to her belly as she came to her third and most positive point: the future was growing inside her, and Winter knew Matt would help her move heaven and earth to protect their child.

The odds were in their favor, Winter decided, and just as soon as her husband got back they would head up to the cliff on Bear Mountain. And there Winter would call on the genes she'd inherited from her papa, and combine her warrior's heart with Matt's to vanquish once and for all the energy bent on destroying them.

Winter shaded her eyes to see the sleek jet setting up for a landing, and snorted at the irony of it all. It appeared that it mattered naught if Providence was hoping to bring feminine thinking to the forefront; it was still going to take a fierce battle to win the war.

She watched the jet set down on the tarmac, its engine reversing with deafening power to slow it down, and Winter decided she didn't dare discount the negatives. There was still that unknown energy that appeared determined to punish her husband for a thousand-year-old mistake. Not that Matt hadn't already been punished enough by having to live with the knowledge that Kenzie had suffered for centuries because of him. And then there was Winter's worry that nine weeks of marriage wasn't quite long enough for Matt to realize that he *did* love her just as much as she loved him.

But the optimism she'd inherited from both of her parents, Winter decided as the jet taxied back down the narrow runway, still put the odds in her and Matt's favor. Two people of like minds, with their two hearts beating as one, had the strength of a legion of warriors.

The jet came to a halt by the tiny hangar and the engine whined down to a stop. Winter started running toward the jet just as the side door opened and a set of stairs dropped onto the tarmac. Matt emerged first and ran toward her, catching Winter in his arms long before she reached the jet.

"What is it?" he asked, holding her against him. "What's wrong?"

"My pine is dead," she said, looking up at him. "Somebody dug a hole down to its roots and killed it."

He took hold of her shoulders and held her facing him, his golden eyes dark with concern. "You're sure it's dead? You couldn't feel anything? Not even a spark of life?"

She shook her head. "I couldn't even feel TarStone's energy. It's all gone. Except for my staff," she said, reaching into her pocket and pulling out her pencil. "It still has power."

He frowned. "It shouldn't. Not if your tree is dead." His hands on her shoulders tightened. "You said the hole was dug down to the roots?" His frown deepened. "Then he must have been after the tap root, and that means at least part of your tree is still alive."

"Woo-wee, that was one hell of a ride," Tom said, walking up to them.

Matt turned and slid his arm around Winter, anchoring her to his side. "I'm glad you enjoyed it," he told Tom as he gave the old hermit a tight smile. "But next time we go up, I'm wearing a G-force suit. Within five minutes of taking the controls, you pretty near had us turned inside out."

Tom chuckled in delight. "Aw," he scoffed, waving Matt's concern away, "that was just a little maneuver I learned from my grandfather years ago."

Winter eyed him curiously. "You have a grandfather?"

"Don't we all?" Tom said with a laugh. "Oh, by the way, happy birthday."

"That's right," Winter said. "You're supposed to tell me your life story today." She stepped away from her husband, slipped her arm through Tom's, and started leading him toward Matt's truck parked beside the hangar. "So, Mr. no-last-name Tom, who are you?"

"It's not your official birthday yet," Tom said with another laugh, lifting his free arm to pull back his sleeve. "You told me you were born at the exact time of the winter solstice, and that doesn't occur for another six hours and . . . and twenty-three minutes," he said, squinting at his watch. "Which means," he added, covering her hand with his, "twenty-five years ago from right now, you weren't even born yet."

Winter rolled her eyes and started them walking again. "You're doing it on purpose, making me wait just because you know it drives me crazy. So does that mean I don't get my gift when we take you home this morning?" She pouted up at him when they stopped beside Matt's truck. "You're not really going to make me wait until the party this afternoon, are you?"

Tom ran his hand down her hair, pushing it back over her shoulder. "You'll get your gift in exactly six hours and twenty-two minutes."

Matt chuckled seeing Winter's frown as he opened the back passenger door and took hold of her arm. "We'll come back and get your Suburban later," he told her, helping her climb in and handing her the seat belt before softly closing the door.

He opened the front passenger door. "Thank God there's not a steering wheel on this side," he said as Tom climbed in the front seat. "Or you'd be trying to pull another triple loop."

"Did you really do loops in Matt's jet?" Winter asked when Matt closed the door and walked around the front of the truck, which now had an eight-foot snowplow attached.

"Just one triple," Tom said with a chuckle. "But I quit when your husband started to turn green."

"So you used to fly jets, did you?"

"Six hours and twenty-one minutes, Miss Impatience."

Winter fell silent once Matt got in and started the truck, letting her husband carry the conversation with Tom as they headed toward Bear Mountain. Tom had arrived at their cottage in the wee hours before dawn, having snowshoed the mile down the shoreline to meet Matt for their jet ride.

Winter had waited until they'd left before she'd thrown back the covers and gotten dressed to head out to greet the sunrise with her pine. Her poor tree, she thought sadly as she looked out the side window. For all of its towering size, it hadn't even been three years old when someone — or something — had come along and lopped off its top, then finished it off by digging up its roots.

The closer to home they got, the more impatient Winter became to get up to that cliff, and the madder she got when she thought about her murdered tree. But it seemed to take forever to navigate the road down to their cottage. Matt hadn't wanted to build a new road along the shore, and had carefully engineered this spur off the old road so it didn't intrude on the meadow or Bear Brook. The results were a very narrow and winding path that followed the contour of the rugged land, and the foot of new snow that Matt had only minimally plowed on his way out this morning added even more precious minutes to the arduous journey.

They reached home around ten in the morning, and Tom used up another twenty minutes telling Matt what a beautiful job he'd done on the cottage as they stood outside looking at the log and stone structure. It was ten-thirty before Tom finally strapped on his snowshoes to head down the shore toward his own cabin.

"If you come back by one o'clock," Matt called after him, "you can ride to Gù Brath with us."

Tom stopped and looked back. "No need. I'll get there on my own. But thanks."

Winter waited beside Matt as they both watched Tom disappear into the dense woods, then turned and grabbed Matt's sleeve and started dragging him back toward his truck. "Come on, let's get going."

"Where?" he asked, pulling them to a stop.

"To the meadow. We are getting inside that cliff today if we have to blow the entire mountain to hell."

He lifted a brow. "When did you decide violence was the answer? I thought you were convinced love and compassion and hope was enough to keep the world spinning."

"I decided it when someone tortured and murdered our tree of life. And he's in that cliff with our tap root, and we're damn well going to blow him to hell if we have to, to get it back."

Matt lifted a brow at her cussing. "So it's *our* tree now, and the energy in the cliff is a *him?*" he said calmly. He took hold of her shoulders and shook his head. "We wait, Winter. We go to Gù Brath this afternoon and attend your birthday party, and then we'll go to the cliff tonight."

"But why wait?"

"Because of Kenzie," he softly reminded her. "He'll become himself on the solstice in another few hours, and you still have enough power to make him stay that way this time. And I want it done before we try to penetrate the cliff because I don't know what we'll find inside. But even if it all goes to hell in a handbasket, my brother will at least have the dignity of dying human."

Winter stared up at her husband, then suddenly threw herself against his chest and wrapped her arms around him in a fierce hug. "Oh, Matt, I'm sorry," she whispered past the lump in her throat. "I wasn't thinking. Of course we'll help Kenzie first." She leaned away and blinked through her tears to smile at him. "Is . . . is he as handsome as you are?"

Matt kissed the tip of her nose and pulled her tightly against him again, holding her head over his strong warrior's heart. "Do you remember the look on Megan's face when I walked into your gallery that first day?" he asked, and Winter nodded against him. "Well, she'll probably faint the first time she sees Kenzie." He kissed the top of her head. "But Fiona was really the one with the good looks in our family. She took after our mother."

He used her hair to gently lift her face to his and kissed her. "This evening after the party, we'll bring Pendaär, Robbie, and your papa with us, and we'll go to the cliff together and see if our combined strengths can't open it up." He smiled tightly. "And if we still can't budge the rock, I'll let you and your lethal pencil raise your own havoc."

Winter leaned into him. "So what do we do until this afternoon?" she whispered. "I'll go crazy just sitting around here waiting and worrying."

He brushed his fingers through her hair. "I suppose we could build a fire in the hearth and play Monopoly."

"Naw," she whispered, shaking her head. "I don't care much for losing to you again."

"We could soak in the hot tub until we

wrinkle," he offered next. "That might relax you enough to actually enjoy your party. And you can go over everyone's names for me — uncles and aunts included — and who they're married to, what they have for kids, and what each of their husbands does for a living." She looked up and he smiled. "I'm never going to keep everyone straight. Gù Brath must be near bursting with people just from your sisters and their families. Do you have this party every year before Christmas?"

"Yes," she said, stroking his ribs as she stood in his loose embrace. "And every summer solstice we do it again with mama's six brothers, their wives, and children and grandchildren." She reached up and started toying with one of the buttons on his shirt. "But I don't feel like reciting my family tree right now."

"Then what do you feel like doing?"

She flattened her hand on his chest, right over his heart. "Do you love me, Matt?"

"Aye," he whispered. "More than life itself, lass."

Winter couldn't hide her surprise, or her frown. "Since when?"

"Since you took my hand and led me through the woods that night, to listen to TarStone breathing."

Since then? He'd loved her from the very beginning? "We'd just met," she snapped. "And you hustled me down the mountain before I even had a chance to catch my breath." She smacked his chest. "I asked you in the cave if you loved me, and you said you couldn't ever love anyone."

He captured her hand and held it over his heart. "I didn't realize that I loved you then. Not until later."

"When, later?"

"When you stood in a seedy little chapel in Vegas and pledged yourself to not only Matheson Gregor, but to Cùram de Gairn."

"That was nine weeks ago." She couldn't smack him again because he was still holding her hand, so she dug her fingers into his chest. "And you didn't once think to tell me you loved me since then?" she growled. "What, it just slipped your mind?"

Matt bent down and slid one hand under her knees and swept her into his arms with a body-shaking laugh. "I was waiting for you to ask me again," he said as he mounted the porch stairs. He stopped and used his hand under her knees to open the front door, then straightened and shrugged, shaking her again. "Have pity, lass. It's a hard concept for a man to wrap his mind around."

461

"Love isn't a weakness, you know."

"I know," he said, striding through the living room and into the bedroom. "But then, neither is patience," he added, holding her over the bed. He smiled rather mischievously and suddenly let her go. But he followed Winter's short fall to the mattress, softly landing beside her and throwing one leg over hers as his hand went to the zipper on her jacket. "So, have you decided what you feel like doing for the next couple of hours?"

CHAPTER
TWENTY-FIVE

By two-thirty that afternoon, Gù Brath could have been a case study in social chaos. Winter realized a newfound respect for the men who had been brave enough to marry MacKeage women. Oh, she didn't admire them for surviving the scrutiny of both Greylen MacKeage and Robbie MacBain, nor even for winning over Grace Mac-Keage's heart. Winter was instead impressed by the fact that the husbands possessed the courage to not only come here every winter solstice, but to actually enjoy themselves.

But more than being a study in chaos, the MacKeage birthday party was also a discourse on filling up the most space with the most bodies, and on catering efficiency. No matter how huge Gù Brath was, there wasn't a corner not taken up by a gaggle of children, their new toys or pets, and vigilant adults. And the food! A White House state dinner couldn't be more elaborate. Winter still didn't know how her mama managed to make it all come together each year, all within a few days before Christmas.

Not twenty minutes after arriving though, Winter was in the kitchen trying to wipe ketchup off Matt's shirt, which Sarah's youngest son had dropped there, when Heather burst through the door from the hall. "And where were you this morning?" she asked, shifting Elizabeth's three-year-old son to her other hip. Heather finally noticed Matt, did a double take, then brought incredulous eyes back to Winter. "Never mind," she whispered, leaning closer, her face glowing with delight. "I remember being a newlywed." She turned to Matt and held out her free hand. "You must be Matt Gregor. I'm Heather, Winter's oldest sister from California."

"Unky Matt!" Joel said, hurling himself from Heather's arms toward Matt. Matt had met Elizabeth and her two kids weeks ago, since they lived right in Pine Creek. And even though Joel had only seen Matt maybe three or four times, the toddler had taken to him immediately and kept insisting on riding on Matt's shoulders.

Winter sighed at the realization Joel's hands were sticky with some sort of candy and had added a blue stain next to the ketchup on her husband's shirt. Matt caught the three-year-old missile and swung him up onto his shoulders with a laugh.

"So," Heather said, linking her arm through Winter's as she smiled at Matt. "I see you've discovered the MacKeage curse the same way all our unsuspecting husbands did."

"The MacKeage curse?" Matt asked, carefully removing Joel's sticky fists from his hair and holding them safely in his hands.

Heather laughed when Winter reached over and pinched her in warning. Not that it did any good.

"It seems all us girls got pregnant the first time we made love to our husbands. Or should I say our soon-to-be husbands," Heather said with another laugh when Matt shot his gaze to Winter.

Winter felt herself blush all the way to her toes. "That's why Camry is scared to death of dating," she said, canting her chin defensively.

Matt looked back at Heather and lifted a brow. "And none of you ladies thought to warn your soon-to-be husbands of this . . . ah, curse?"

"We didn't put two and two together until after Chelsea got married," Heather explained with a shake of her head. "No matter what birth control we tried, it didn't seem to work." She looked at Winter and smiled sadly. "It doesn't look good for Megan, though. I don't think Wayne Ferris is man enough to step up to the altar."

"She doesn't need the bastard," Matt growled before Winter could respond. "The right guy will come along one of these days, and Ferris won't even be a memory."

"Bastard," Joel repeated, bouncing on Matt's shoulders.

"Aw, hell," Matt muttered.

"Aw, hell," Joel squealed.

"Oh-oh, come on, tyke," Heather said with a laugh, reaching for the toddler. "I better get you back to the flock." She stopped at the kitchen door with Joel in her arms and looked at Matt. "Has Camry found you? She works for NASA and she's just dying to talk jet engines with you."

"I'll find her," Winter said, not stopping to think exactly what she was getting her husband into.

They did indeed find Camry, and the NASA scientist had Matt backed into a corner for the next hour discussing propulsion theories. Winter left her poor husband to his fate with a cheery smile and spent her time reminiscing with her sisters, a few of which she hadn't seen for a full year.

Matt ended up being the main topic of conversation, no matter how hard Winter tried to move onto something else. Who was he, where did he come from, had he really commissioned her to pick the spot for their home, was he truly richer than God, how had she dared to run off and get married without telling Papa . . . and on and on it went until her mama finally came to Winter's rescue and said it was time to cut their birthday cake.

The cake was a monstrous, three-tier masterpiece of pink and yellow confection that sat in the middle of the dining room table as the centerpiece of the banquet, or rather, what was left of the banquet. The entire house was decorated for Christmas, except that the dining room had an eclectic assortment of birthday balloons and streamers crowded in with the holiday cheer.

For practical reasons, birthday gifts had stopped coming to each of the girls when they turned six, simply because of the chaos it created. Being together was gift enough, Grace MacKeage had declared, and besides, she should be receiving the gifts since she was the one who'd birthed them. So the table in the corner contained only eight gifts, one from each of the daughters to their mama, and one from their papa to his wife.

Grace rang a bell and everyone — aunts, uncles, cousins, sons-in-law, grandchildren — ceased whatever they were doing and gravitated toward the dining room, spilling out into the living room and foyer and even up the stairs.

"We have two new additions to our immediate family," Grace began once the crowd had quieted down. "Most of you know that Chelsea had another son in May whom she named Clayton, and Winter married Matt Gregor two months ago." She waited for the cheering to die down, then continued. "For our extended family, Michael and Catherine had Angus MacBain four months ago, and Morgan's son, Duncan, just had a baby girl on Thanksgiving Day."

The cheering resumed, and Grace had to raise her hands to quiet everyone again. "Now you know that we —"

The door knocker sounded loudly, and Grace fell silent with a frown. "Who's not here?" she asked.

Nobody said anything as they all looked around and mentally took count, which would take the rest of the afternoon, Winter figured. Somebody opened the front door, and Winter stretched to see who was almost two hours late for the infamous MacKeage birthday party, but she couldn't see past the turned heads all looking toward the door.

The low murmur started in the foyer, moving toward the dining room as the crowd parted, or rather as everyone scurried back and looked down at the floor.

It wasn't until the people in the dining room parted and a large black crow flapped onto the table that Winter understood the look of amazed confusion on everyone's faces. The crow, carrying a small red silk bag in its mouth, boldly walked up the table past the platters of food and didn't stop until it was standing right in front of Winter.

Matt set his hands on her shoulders. "A friend of yours?" he whispered in her ear, and Winter could hear the amusement in his voice.

But she only kept staring at the crow, who had cocked his head and was staring back at her, the little red bag dangling from its beak.

"I think he wants to give you a birthday present," Matt said, using his hands on her shoulders to nudge her forward. "Go ahead, take the bag."

It was one thing to dream about being visited by a wise old bird, and even finding a feather in her bed the next morning, but it was a bit disconcerting to be seeing him in all his feathered flesh in front of dozens of witnesses. When she still didn't move, Matt reached past her and set his hand under the crow's head. The crow opened his thick black beak and simply dropped the gift into Matt's hand.

Matt held the bag by its drawstrings and dangled it in front of her. Aware the dining room was quiet enough to hear a mouse sneeze, Winter rubbed her damp palms on her pants, finally forced her gaze from the crow to the bag, reached out and took it from her husband.

But instead of opening it, Winter looked back at the crow that was still standing staring at her, his dark round eyes shining with what looked like amused anticipation.

"Open it, lass," Matt softly commanded, placing his hands reassuringly on her shoulders again.

"Y-you open it," she whispered, not moving.

"It's not my birthday."

Winter frowned at the bag.

"Oh, for the love of God," Daar snapped from across the table. "Open it so we can see what the bird brought ye."

Winter still didn't move.

"You told me the crow in your dream brought you good news," Matt whispered into her hair. "So what has you worried, lass?"

Winter tilted her head back to look up at him. "What if it's my tap root?" she whispered, well aware of the small but substantial weight in her hand. "What if the crow is really the strange energy who killed my tree, and he had only been trying to give me a false sense of hope in my dream? I — I haven't heard from him for nine weeks."

"If he's that energy, then this is your chance to confront him," Matt told her, turning her around to face him, likely so she'd quit staring at the crow. He reached for the bag she held between them. "I'll open it, then," he offered, pulling on the silk to loosen the drawstrings.

He opened the bag, held it up to look inside, and frowned. "It's a statue," he said, pulling out a tiny figurine.

Winter gasped and took it from him. "Tom!" she cried, holding up the granite carving of a bear whose body was wrapped around the figure of a woman made from wood. Winter spun back toward the table. "T-Tom?" she whispered, stepping toward the crow.

"There's a note with the statue," Matt said, holding a piece of rolled birch bark in front of her to see.

"Well, what's it say?" Daar asked, glaring over Winter's head at Matt. "Don't keep us all in suspense. It's a crow, for God's sake, and he wants ye to read what the gift is about."

Winter looked from the silent bird to the statue in her hand as she heard Matt unrolling the scroll behind her. The statue was an amazing work of art, intricately blending stone and wood together. The sleeping granite bear was only about five inches long and three inches wide, and it all but surrounded the wooden female figure lying inside its tender, protective embrace.

"It — It seems to be a wedding invitation," Matt said into the silence, his voice thick with . . . Winter couldn't decide if Matt was overcome with emotion or angry. He cleared his throat and began reading. "To all present who believe in the power of love, you are invited to the high meadow on Bear Mountain this afternoon at the time of the winter solstice, to witness the union of Winter Sutter MacKeage and Matheson Macalpin Gregor."

Winter looked across the table when Daar gasped.

"You're from the Clan of the Mist," Daar whispered, his face as pale as new snow. "Yer great-great-grandfather was Mathe

Macalpin, Bear of Gairn."

"Aye," Matt said thickly over Winter's head, and she could feel the tension radiating from him.

She turned around. "What's wrong with being from the Clan of the Mist?" she asked Matt.

"Nothing," Daar said, causing her to turn back toward him. "It's Mathe Macalpin that means something, girl. Legend says Mathe was the original *drùidh,* sent by Providence to straighten out the mess mankind had made of the world by that point." He nodded toward the man standing behind her and shook his head. "Ye married Macalpin's great-great-grandson, but Matt's grandfather wasn't the *drùidh* who threw away his calling. It was yer grandmother, wasn't it, boy?" he asked, lifting his gaze to Matt. "Joan Macalpin." Daar looked back at Winter. "Providence *did* try to find a softer energy several millennia ago, but Joan wanted none of it. So Providence is trying again with you."

"But what does Matt's heritage have to do with anything?"

"Maybe ye should ask him," Daar suggested, nodding at the silent crow still perched on the table.

Winter tightened her fist around her statue

and looked down at the bird. The crow spread its wings, lifted its beak, and let out a loud *caw* that echoed though Gù Brath. It rose from the table to glide past Winter, and she spun around to watch it land on Matt's shoulder, where it looked down at the scroll in his hand.

"There — ah, there's more," Matt said, staring at her with unmistakably worried eyes before he looked back at the note and began reading again. "The ceremony will be presided over by Father Thomas Gregor Smythe."

Matt looked at Winter when she gasped. "T-Tom's a priest?" she whispered. "And — And a Gregor?" She lifted her gaze to the crow, then back to Matt. "He's related to you? But how?"

Apparently forgetting he had a crow sitting on his shoulder, Matt shrugged. The startled bird gave a disgruntled *caw* and rose into flight, swooped over the stunned crowd, and disappeared through the open front door, leaving only silence in its wake.

Winter looked down at the statue in her hand. "I don't understand what's going on," she said, looking up at Matt. "Who is Thomas Gregor Smythe? And why were we just invited to our own wedding?"

"Because yer first wedding wasn't witnessed by yer loved ones," Daar said with a curt nod and smug smile. "I told ye that wasn't right."

"We have less than an hour before the solstice," Greylen MacKeage added, and Winter looked up to find her papa smiling. "We need to get going before you miss your wedding, don't you think?"

Winter looked around at the stunned faces of her extensive family, noting that those who had married into the MacKeages appeared confused. Although Winter knew all the husbands were somewhat aware of their wives' rather strange heritage, this was likely the first time they were witnessing the magic firsthand. "I . . . ah, I don't think the children should come with us," she suggested, turning to look at her husband. "Because we're not sure what we're going to find," she said, reminding him of his earlier worry back at their cottage.

Matt nodded and looked at Grey and Robbie. "She's right," he added. "It would be best if the children stay here. And anyone else who can't make it through deep snow to the meadow."

That left just her sisters and husbands, her parents, uncles and aunts, and a few grown cousins, Winter figured. Well so be it. Whatever they were about to encounter at the cliff, they would stand united.

Utter chaos once again ruled as parents explained to their offspring that they were leaving for a while, but that they'd be back soon to continue the party. Children cried, those staying behind tried to soothe them, and everyone else went in search of their coats and boots.

Matt took Winter by the shoulders and turned her toward him. "He's lived here for almost three years. What do you know about Tom?"

"Absolutely nothing," she said, clutching the statue between them. "Only that he showed up one April morning, moved into your cabin, and that his carvings are beautiful works of art." She shrugged. "I don't even know how he supports himself. He always gives the money from his carvings to people in town who need a little financial help."

"He was obviously a pilot," Matt said, "considering how he handled that jet this morning." He shook his head. "I don't know any Thomas Gregor Smythe."

"D-do you think it's safe for everyone to go to the meadow?" Winter asked. "What if it's a trap?"

"To trap what, lass? A bunch of women and a few men, most of them old? For what purpose?" He smiled and smoothed her hair back from her face. "You've trusted Tom this long, maybe you should trust him now. You've never felt anything dark or foreboding when you were with him, have you?"

"No," Winter said softly, looking down and fingering the head of the bear statue. "I always felt . . . I felt peaceful when I was with Tom." She looked up. "Didn't he make you want to just crawl up on his lap and tell him all your secrets?"

Matt gave her a lopsided grin. "No, I can't say Tom ever had that effect on me," he drawled. He took the statue from her and studied it. "Is this us?" he asked, holding it up for her to see. "In our cave, that first night I came to you?"

"No, the second night," Winter told him, taking back the statue. "Once there were no secrets between us, and you came back and kept my nightmares away, holding me safe and secure so I could have a dream that promised hope for our future."

Matt had just cupped her face and was leaning down to kiss her when he suddenly stilled with the strangest expression. He slowly broke into a smile that made his eyes gleam with golden warmth, and he kissed her tenderly on the mouth. "Are you ready to hear me repeat my vows of trust and loyalty to you, Winter?" he whispered, pulling mere inches away from her lips.

"Yes, I am."

He kissed her again, then straightened with a laugh. "Then come on, Mrs. Gregor," he said, taking her hand. "It's time to go meet our future."

CHAPTER TWENTY-SIX

The new road leading down beside the meadow could have been in Boston during rush hour, it became so clogged with vehicles. Then, getting everyone across Bear Brook without anyone drowning was a feat worthy of an engineer. Robbie ended up having to carry Daar through the deep snow, as the old priest had refused to stay at Gù Brath and miss all the excitement. There were less than five minutes remaining to the solstice by the time everyone was standing at the base of the cliff, though they could have been in church they were so quiet. Even the late-December weather was cooperating; the low-hanging sun was shining a weak but brilliant red, not a whisper of wind was blowing, and the air felt like Indian summer in October.

Tom suddenly appeared, walking up from the meadow and silently moving to stand at the base of the cliff in front of everyone. At least Winter was pretty sure it was Tom. The man had Tom's expressive eyes and features, but he was cleaned up quite nicely and dressed in a ceremonial robe and headdress like nothing Winter had ever seen before. The long robe was modern if not futuristic looking, while still possessing ancient Celtic detail. Across the front of his . . . cassock, for lack of a better word, was a large depiction of a tree of life embroidered in what looked like spun gold threads. The tree wasn't any species Winter recognized, but looked to be a combination of both a majestic oak and a mighty eastern white pine.

Tom raised his hands and cleared his throat, though it wasn't really necessary since everyone was curiously silent. "I wish to thank you all for coming here today, to witness Winter and Matt pledging themselves to each other," Tom said, his soft voice carrying over the crowd.

Winter opened her mouth, but quickly closed it again when Matt squeezed her hand.

"Laird Greylen and Grace," Tom said, inclining his head toward them. "You've given the world a remarkable group of girls, and I wish to personally thank you for that." His eyes twinkled. "I am also thankful you didn't stop at only six daughters, as I am especially endeared to your seventh."

This time when Winter tried to speak up, Matt wrapped his arm around her and squeezed.

"And Pendaär," Tom addressed next, looking at the frail priest standing beside Robbie. "You served your calling well and can finally find peace in the knowledge that you are the very reason we're here today. Enjoy your retirement, old man, and bask in the sun on your mountain for a good long while yet."

"MacBain," Tom said with a chuckle when Robbie groaned at the prospect of Daar's longevity. "I wish to thank you for taking such special care with my grandmother these last twenty-five years, by being both Winter's guardian and friend."

It was a good thing Matt had his arm around her, so he could catch Winter when her knees suddenly buckled, just as a collective gasp rose through the crowd.

"Yeah," Tom said, walking up to Matt and Winter. He reached out and touched Winter's jacket, just over her belly, and smiled. "That's my mama you've got growing in there."

"But —"

Tom cocked his head. "Did you never

consider that if your husband and Robbie and Pendaär can so readily travel back and forth in time, that someone from the future might not also do the same one day?"

"But . . . you . . . you're our grandson? But you're old!" she blurted, only to wince and shake her head. "I mean, I can't picture having a grandson older than I am. It . . . it's —"

"It's magic," Tom whispered, his twinkling eyes lifting to Matt. "In about forty years you're going to take me on my *first* supersonic ride, and get me hooked on flying at the age of eight." He moved his gaze to include Winter. "I'm not your daughter's first child, you see. I'm her third. I have an older sister and brother, and a younger brother as well."

"Are they . . . are they *drùidhs?*" Winter whispered. "Any of them? A-are you?"

Tom smiled. "We all have our special gifts," was all he said. "Which you will discover . . . in time."

"But —"

He touched his finger to her chin. "Patience, Grams. What's the point of getting out of bed in the morning if you already know what's going to happen? The real magic is living each day as it comes, the joy

482

being the anticipation of what's around the corner."

He nodded toward Matt but continued looking at Winter. "Take your husband, for instance. He had no way of knowing if what he put into motion all those centuries ago would get the results he wanted or not. Hell, he couldn't even predict *your* response to him, but that didn't stop him from trying."

He looked at Matt. "If you had known you'd be standing here today, deeply in love with your wife, would you have proceeded with your desperately conceived plan?"

"At the time, being who I was and how I felt about the world in general?" Matt asked even-toned. He shook his head. "No. I would have done anything to avoid engaging my heart."

Tom nodded and looked back at Winter. "And that is why I'm not answering one question about what happens from this moment on, no matter how hard you work your considerable charm."

"But you just told me I'm having a daughter," Winter pointed out with a smug smile.

Tom smiled even more smugly. "For your firstborn," he said with a shrug. "After that, well, don't you just wonder how many there'll be, and what they'll be?"

He laughed at her glare, but it was Daar

who spoke next. "Are ye getting on with marrying them or not?" he asked. "Ye have two minutes to the solstice, and Winter can't be pregnant and not married proper. It's blasphemous."

"It's ancient thinking, Father," Winter said, turning her glare on Daar. "And we are married. We got married in Las Vegas." Winter suddenly snapped her gaze to Tom, squinting up at his laughing eyes. "You! You're the Mad Hatter who married us," she yelped, pointing at him, only to narrow her eyes again. "Our witnesses. Who were they?"

"My brothers and sister."

"Our grandchildren?" Winter squeaked, clutching her jacket over her chest. "Th-they witnessed our marriage?"

Tom broke into laughter and shook his head. "You looked like you expected them to steal all your money and clothes," he said with a lingering chuckle.

Winter spun toward her also-amused husband. "Will you please quit laughing. This is not funny. I still don't know if we're *drùidhs* or not."

"Do you want to be a *drùidh?*" Tom calmly asked.

Winter spun back to face him. "We both have to be wizards. There's still . . . stuff we have to do."

"Ah, I see," Tom said, turning and walking to the cliff. He stopped beside the solid wall of granite, turned back and waved them forward. "Then come be *drùidhs.* Open the entrance to the cave and see where your power truly lies."

Winter looked up at Matt in uncertainty, but Matt was staring at Tom. Her husband suddenly took her hand and led her to the cliff. "How do we open it?" he asked, holding Winter against his side as they faced the cliff.

"Just ask it to open," Tom said with a negligent wave of his hand. "Gently," he added, giving Winter a wink.

Matt reached into his jacket pocket and pulled out his fountain pen, and Winter quickly pulled out her sketch pencil.

Tom covered Matt's hand with his own. "You don't need it," he said, turning his wrist to see his watch. "As of two minutes ago, your sword lost its ability to conduct energy."

"No!" Winter cried, clutching her pencil. "Not yet. We need just a few more hours."

"Ask the cave to appear," Tom said calmly.

Matt reached out and placed his and Winter's hands on the rough cliff, and Winter immediately felt the tingling warmth of a powerful energy pulsing through the granite. She pictured the old entrance to the cave, how it twisted to keep out the weather, and how the interior had felt warm and safe and welcoming.

Several gasps came from behind them, and Winter opened her eyes to find herself standing in front of a taller, wider entrance to an even larger cave. The interior walls glowed with several softly swirling colors this time, and the cave appeared to be four or five times its original size. It was also spotless, not one sign of the singed supplies they'd left behind.

And sitting directly in the center of the cathedral-like room was a larger-than-life-sized granite bear curled around a sleeping woman made of wood that was an exact replica of the tiny figurine the crow had carried to Gù Brath. Without even stopping to think, Winter walked right up to the statue and touched it, only to have her mind's eye become washed in blinding light.

"She's made of pinewood," Matt said from beside Winter, taking hold of her hand so she wouldn't touch it again.

"H-how did he do that?" she whispered. "How did he get the woman so snug inside the bear's embrace? I don't see any seams in the granite, but he couldn't possibly have fit the woman in there without cutting the rock."

"It's one of my gifts," Tom said from the other side of the statue. He looked at Matt. "You recognize the white pine."

"You're the one who cut the top off."

Tom inclined his head.

"And the root. You stole the tap root last night. Why?"

Tom walked around to stand beside them and pointed at the woman nestled inside the bear. "Do you see that faint image of her heart?" he asked. "Right under the bear's paw? See how he's protecting both the woman and their shared heart? The heart is made from your original tap root, Cùram, from your oak tree. And the woman is carved from the top of Winter's pine."

Tom then touched the tree of life emblem on his chest before he pointed up at the ceiling. "You'll find a new species of tree growing on the top of the cliff, and by the time I'm born, it will have scattered its seed to the protected valleys of Bear Mountain."

"But why?" Winter asked.

"Because Providence *hopes* you'll both succeed. But just as you finally realized this morning when you were sitting with your dead pine, Winter, it takes a combination of strengths to do that. So a new tree of life has been created from your two trees, as a reminder to all of us."

Winter blinked at the strange-looking tree on Tom's chest. She looked up at her husband to find his expression unreadable, and then glanced back toward the entrance to see what Pendaär and the others thought of all this. "The entrance is gone!"

"Just temporarily," Tom assured her. "We only need witnesses for your wedding, not for the decision you have to make now."

"And that would be?" Matt asked, stiffening.

Winter slid her hand into his and also looked at Tom.

"You appear to think you still must choose which you want more, maintaining your marriage and having babies, or remaining *drùidhs* so you can keep your promise to Kenzie," Tom said to both of them, but directing his words to Matt.

"No!" Winter cried, stepping between her husband and Tom. "That's not fair to make him choose between me and his brother. It's too cruel."

"Then you choose for him," Tom suggested.

"No!" Matt growled, pulling Winter back beside him.

"Then maybe I'll choose," Tom offered

with a chuckle, "since I seem to have a vested interest here."

"We each get to choose our own destiny!" Winter cried. She narrowed her eyes and pointed at Tom. "If you're here, then that means we obviously chose marriage over being *drùidhs.*"

"Not necessarily, as that is but one of the risks we take when we indulge in time travel." Tom waved his hand to encompass the cave. "This could all be nothing more than a dream. You could wake up and I would simply not exist. It is only the acts of the present that determine the future." Tom smiled warmly at her. "So which would you choose, Winter?" he asked softly. "Your future with your husband and children or your calling to help Matt keep his promise to Kenzie?"

"I choose both!" she snapped, balling her hands into fists.

Tom nodded, then looked at Matt and grinned. "Why doesn't that surprise me? And you, if you had to choose, which would it be, Cùram de Gairn, your marriage, or your calling?"

Matt said nothing.

Winter couldn't decide if she should smack Tom or her silent husband. "That is not the way this is going to work," she hissed at Tom as she turned to face Matt. "Think, Matt. As long as there is life, there is *always* hope. So dig deep and remember how you felt when you ran away from home and went after your dream of becoming a warrior. You thought you had found what you'd been searching for, but when it wasn't all you hoped it would be, you picked up and went back home. And when that didn't turn out very well, you picked up again and went looking for Kenzie."

"And what happened then?" Tom asked. "When you found your brother, only he was dying?"

"I got angry," Matt said.

"Yes," Winter agreed, clutching his hand. "And lost hope."

Matt looked at her, his eyes dark with pain. "I didn't lose it then, lass. I lost it when Kenzie asked me to end his life."

"Then how did you get this far?" Tom asked. "If you had no hope for the future, how come you came after Winter?"

Matt looked at Tom, seemingly startled. "I took a gamble she could help me. Mac-Keage's daughter was my best chance to keep my promise to Kenzie."

Tom smiled and looked at Winter. "There really is no such thing as hopelessness, you know. Hope is an integral part of our collective energy, and it can never be lost because it's not . . . it isn't of this material world. It's only human perception that becomes blind to hope's existence." He smiled at Matt. "Winter can't keep a promise you made, and you can't keep it yourself as long as you remain blind to any part of the energy that makes us all who we are. If you want to hold onto your powers so you can help Kenzie, and if you want to hold onto Winter, then just open yourself to the full spectrum and realize that you *can* have both."

"He can?" Winter asked in surprise. She snorted and shook her head. "I was just being sarcastic."

"You were being your spoiled rotten self," Tom said with a laugh, looking back at Matt. "Anything is possible as long as you remain open to *all* the energy. Winter figured she'd choose being a *drùidh,* and *then* she planned to damn well figure out how to save Kenzie," he said, smiling when she gasped at his insight. "That's not blind faith, Matt, that's wide-eyed faith. Not only must you trust the universe, but you must also trust yourself."

Winter squeezed her husband's hand again, but Matt continued staring at Tom.

Tom smiled. "The choice is still yours to

make, Matt. But it's not really between Winter and your calling, is it? It's between you and yourself." He looked over at the statue, then back at Matt. "We have entered a new millennium with this winter's solstice, so what's *your* hope for the next thousand years? That maybe like Winter here, you believe you can have it all? Can you see your calling as a blending of each color of the spectrum, including hope, just like that couple in the statue? Open your inner eyes wide, Matheson Gregor, and the future will be whatever you make it."

Matt stood stiff and silent for what seemed like *forever* to Winter, and she was just about to really smack him when he suddenly took her hand and led her over to the statue. Together they reached out and placed their hands on the bear's paw covering the woman's heart; time stopped, the cave filled with a *full* spectrum of swirling colors, and the sound of a single beating heart echoed throughout the chamber and strongly resonated through every cell in Winter's body.

She squinted past the blinding light and saw the bear and woman's shared heart gently pulsing in time with hers and Matt's. And then Winter would swear she saw the smiling pinewood woman wiggle deeper into the bear's embrace with a sigh of contentment.

"So," Tom said, rubbing his hands together. "Are we having a wedding or not? Everyone must be freezing out there."

"What about Kenzie?" Winter asked, turning away from the statue but still holding Matt's hand.

"He's likely standing at the back of the crowd," Tom said, smiling at her surprise. "It's twenty minutes past the solstice. You don't think he'd miss his brother's wedding, do you?"

"But we have to make him stay a man," Winter said.

"He will," Tom assured her, walking over to where the cave entrance should be.

"How?" Matt asked.

"United, you both possess the power to grant Kenzie's wish," Tom assured them, turning and inclining his head. "But please, allow me the honor as my wedding present to you both." His bright blue eyes twinkled. "And maybe also as a little something for my great-aunt Megan, I'm thinking."

Winter still couldn't comprehend that she was talking to her seventy-something grandson on her twenty-fifth birthday.

"Ah, if I might make a suggestion?" Tom said, waving his hand at the cave. "Have you ever considered making this cliff part of your new home? You could incorporate a lovely log and stone structure into this cliff, so that the cave becomes . . . oh, I don't know," he said with a shrug. "Your bedroom, maybe?"

"Why don't you tell us?" Winter asked, smiling smugly. "Surely you ran through the halls of our as-yet-to-be-built house as a kid."

"And I explored every inch of Bear Mountain," Tom said with a laugh. "And sailed Pine Lake and slept in the lakeshore cottage you're staying in now." His eyes twinkled again. "Do me a favor and don't fix up the old camp on the point, okay? I kind of like it just the way it is."

Winter clutched Matt's hand. "Y-you're leaving us tonight, aren't you? You're going back. I — I mean *ahead* to your time."

Tom nodded and smiled sadly. "I must. I've served my purpose here. You two need to realize your own future now."

"But when will we see you again?" Winter asked.

Tom canted his head. "Oh, in about thirty-one years, give or take a few months. We'll have lots of fun together, Grams," he told her, then looked at Matt. "And you, Gramps, will have to persuade my mama to let you teach me to fly."

Matt smiled back, and Winter's heart warmed at how he suddenly looked so relaxed. "Being forewarned, I could just avoid that problem by teaching *her* to fly first," Matt drawled.

"What in hell is going on in there!" they heard Daar shout through the granite. "We're freezing our whiskers off out here!"

Tom stepped up to the wall but turned toward them. "If you will, please?" he asked. He waved his hand when Matt reached for his pen. "You don't need anything but your strength of conviction to summon your powers from now on," he told them, looking over to include Winter and giving her a wink. "Gentle convictions," he added. He looked back at Matt as he reached into his cassock pocket. "Oh, I almost forgot, this is for you," he said, handing Matt a tiny piece of jewelry. "When you dug up Mathe Macalpin's sword, you missed Fiona's locket. She had buried it there the day you left, hoping you'd eventually come back to claim your destiny."

"But she was only a child then," Matt whispered, reaching for the locket with a trembling hand, then holding it in his palm as he stared down at it. He looked back up at Tom. "She was what . . . twelve?"

"She was a guardian," Tom told him. "And she's been watching over you for all this time."

"But how? I never saw her again after I ran away from home. I would have at least sensed Fiona if she were near."

"Do you not remember a large golden hawk perched nearby through the long day and night you lay dying in that field?" Tom asked softly. He smiled. "And she was with you countless other times, you'll realize, once you think about it. When you didn't want to go on but something made you anyway, know that it was Fiona who pulled you up by the bootstraps. And she's been there for Kenzie for all these centuries. No matter what animal your brother became, Fiona mothered him each time."

Winter looked at the locket in Matt's hand and watched him close his fist over it and raise it to his lips. She squeezed his hand, using her free hand to brush away her tears of overwhelming joy.

"Winter!" Daar hollered again as they heard him pound his cane on the granite wall. "It's dark and cold out here! Let us in!"

Matt quickly tucked the locket in his pocket, squared his shoulders with a fortifying sigh, and gave a negligent flick of his wrist toward the wall. The entrance suddenly appeared again, along with several cold-looking faces glaring at them.

"Come in. Come in," Tom said, waving them forward. "I think you'll find it much warmer in here. Step closer, the walls won't bite. Father Daar, come stand beside me. I'm sure Winter wants to have your blessing as well."

"And Matt. He wants your blessing, too, Father," Winter said as she wiped away the last of her tears, even while having to tug on Matt's hand to cut him off in midsnort.

But then Winter went utterly still when she spotted the tall, long-haired stranger dressed in the Gregor plaid when he stepped inside the cave at the back of the crowd. "Kenzie," she whispered, squeezing Matt's hand.

But Matt had already spotted his brother. "Come, Kenzie," he said, waving him forward. "Everyone, this is my brother, Kenzie Gregor." He slapped Kenzie on the back — rather hard — and laughed. "He's standing up as my best man."

"And Megan will stand up for me," Winter said, searching for her sister. She finally saw Megan leaning against one of the walls, her eyes wide with awe, her mouth hanging open as she stared at Kenzie. "Heather, help

Megan over here. It seems her wits have frozen from standing outside so long."

And finally, twenty-five minutes after the solstice, in her future cave-bedroom, Winter repeated her vows to Matheson Gregor for the third time. And the moment he took her in his strong, protective arms and kissed her with all the passion and hope of a promising future, Winter felt Tom's mother stir inside her for the very first time.

LETTER FROM LAKEWATCH

Dear Readers,

I have found that sometimes Mother Nature simply refuses to be ignored, and that she's not above screaming in our ears when she wants our attention. I was reminded of this early last fall, when I was writing my fifth Highlander book. A murder of crows (yes, that's what they're really called), nine to be exact, started screaming at me from the trees on my front lawn. One particular fellow (that I named Talking Tom) seemed to think it was his duty to sit outside my bedroom window and wake me up at 4:00 A.M., and he would *caw,* quite loudly and nonstop, until I got up, got dressed, and headed across the yard to my writing studio.

It may have taken me the better part of three weeks, but I eventually realized that my crows wanted to be in my book. Or else the noisy buggers had been told I was a pushover, and they merely wanted free food.

Now I don't know many people who feed crows, but I can tell you that once you've started, you had better not stop with the handouts. Every morning that fall and through the winter, I would get up at the crack of dawn, get dressed in multiple layers, and head outside to arrange dinner scraps and little piles of dry cat food on the ground as I made my way to work.

This seemed to appease my black-feathered friends, and actually proved entertaining. But that entertainment often came at the expense of my husband, who was enlisted to snowblow a circular path through the deepening drifts in the middle of our front lawn so I could continue to spread food scraps. When people asked Robbie why he was snowblowing his lawn, he would only mutter something about it being cheaper than a divorce.

I got so crazy in fact, that I began devising elaborate menus. I begged for scraps from neighbors, I brought home doggy bags from restaurants, and I even purchased canned dog food, knowing my pets needed plenty of protein in sub-zero weather.

Crows do not like canned dog food, I found out. They wouldn't touch it. Heck, they took one sniff, looked toward the house, and started scolding. And they don't like shrimp or carrots or overcooked broccoli. But they do like home cooking (smart birds). Beef stew was a winner, spaghetti and meatballs got scoffed up, and their favorite food turned out to be steak (Robbie and I ate the steak; they got to pick the bones).

Despite my generosity, sometime in early December, my nine crows disappeared — right when I was shoulder-deep in my book. Suddenly, I was at a loss. I slept through the sunrises, and I awoke uncertain and directionless, unable to write. The noisy inspirations for my book — especially for one of my main characters, Talking Tom — had abandoned me.

But one week later, quite literally out of the clear blue sky, three of my crows flew in off the frozen lake and landed in a tree overlooking their old feeding spot. The potbellied squirrels had eaten everything I'd put out, and my crows made such a ruckus that I rushed out to give them the leftover stew we were supposed to have for dinner that night.

My crows were back! My book was saved! I immediately headed to my studio and started writing again. And now that you have read *Only With a Highlander,* and met Talking Tom, know that he truly does live

— not only in my imagination, but in my dooryard.

So what is Mother Nature trying to tell us when she demands our attention? For me, she's saying listen to the universe, for that is where inspiration dwells. Sometimes I'll hear only a whisper, or merely sense an unspoken urge, and sometimes I'll be blasted with a deafening cacophony that demands I examine my direction and purpose.

Do you ever stop and listen? What do *you* hear?

Until later . . . keep reading!

Janet

ABOUT THE AUTHOR

Janet Chapman is a native of rural central Maine, where she lives in a cozy log cabin on a lake with her husband and two sons. Three cats and a stray young bull moose keep them company. The winner of the Pearl Award for Best New Paranormal Author and a two-time finalist for the Romance Writers of America's RITA award, she is the author of four other enchanting time-travel romances set in modern-day Maine — *Charming the Highlander, Loving the Highlander, Wedding the Highlander,* and *Tempting the Highlander* — and the novels *The Seductive Impostor* and *The Dangerous Protector.* Visit her website at www.janet chapman.com.

The employees of Thorndike Press hope you have enjoyed this Large Print book. All our Thorndike and Wheeler Large Print titles are designed for easy reading, and all our books are made to last. Other Thorndike Press Large Print books are available at your library, through selected bookstores, or directly from us.

For information about titles, please call:

(800) 223-1244

or visit our Web site at:

www.gale.com/thorndike
www.gale.com/wheeler

To share your comments, please write:

Publisher
Thorndike Press
295 Kennedy Memorial Drive
Waterville, ME 04901